Praise for
To Shape the Dark

The year has barely begun and I can already name *To Shape The Dark* as one of my favorite books.

> — Pat Cadigan, author of *Synners*,
> winner of the Hugo, Clarke, Locus, and World Fantasy awards

A great anthology with sophisticated and vivid settings, characters whose dilemmas feel meaningful and true, and real science. Highly recommended.

> — Kate Elliott, author of the *Spiritwalker* Trilogy,
> the *Crossroads* and *Crown of Stars* series, and the *Novels of the Jaran*

One of my favorite anthologies of 2013 was the acclaimed *The Other Half of the Sky*, edited by Athena Andreadis. Athena is back with fifteen new stories featuring striking women characters who are engaged citizens of the future. All the familiar science fiction marvels are here, aliens and AIs, faster-than-light spaceships and mind-blowing inventions, but they are framed so as to reveal new wonders. *To Shape the Dark* is destined to be one of the most talked about books of 2016; don't wait to join the conversation!

> — James Patrick Kelly, author of "Think Like a Dinosaur,"
> winner of the Hugo, Nebula, and Locus awards

The delight of *To Shape the Dark* is simply that it is science fiction, just as we all fell in love with it, but with a slight shift: this time, the women step forward. The scientist-protagonists of these stories follow their vocations for many reasons, as different from each other as each human is from the next, and the authors give these women individual voices and lives and discoveries. There are travels through wonders, alien races, and experiments with new ways of being—as well as family, love, and even the inevitable but necessary struggle with bureaucracy! Science is adventure, and there is adventure here, and it is for all of us.

— Rosemary Kirstein, author of the *Steerswoman* series,
multiple Locus award nominee

By turns inventive, moving, wondrous, and provocative, *To Shape the Dark* upends tiresome genre tropes to offer fresh portraits of women scientists as heroes engaged in the most epic journey of them all: discovery.

— Ken Liu, author of *The Grace of Kings*,
winner of the Hugo, Nebula, and World Fantasy awards

A terrifically eclectic collection of stories about women scientists interrogating their worlds and themselves, delivering neat jolts of sense of wonder straight from science fiction's mutant heart.

— Paul McAuley, author of the *Quiet War* series,
winner of the Clarke, Dick, and Campbell awards

This is a beautiful, invigorating anthology. These are among the newest and freshest voices in SF, and they have much to say.

— Alastair Reynolds, author of the *Revelation Space* series,
winner of the BSFA award

This is a marvelous collection of entertaining and incisive short stories, very often describing women wielding science like a scalpel to carve a better world out of this one. Great brain-engaging fun.

— Kim Stanley Robinson, author of the *Mars* trilogy
and *Galileo's Dream*, winner of the Hugo, Nebula,
Locus, World Fantasy, and Campbell awards

Athena Andreadis has again put together a challenging, entertaining, and visionary anthology that includes some of the finest writers of science fiction. Highly recommended.

— Pamela Sargent, author of *The Shore of Women* and *Earthseed*,
editor of *Women of Wonder*

To
Shape
the Dark

edited by Athena Andreadis

Candlemark & Gleam

For information, address
Candlemark & Gleam LLC,
38 Rice Street #2, Cambridge, MA 02140
eloi@candlemarkandgleam.com

Library of Congress Cataloging-in-Publication Data
In Progress

ISBN: 978-1-936460-67-0
eISBN: 978-1-936460-68-7

Cover art and design by Eleni Tsami

Book design and composition by Kate Sullivan
Typefaces: Pyke's Peak and Calisto MT

www.candlemarkandgleam.com

To Kay Holt,
and to those who stood with me when it counted.

"When do we set sail, so I can take the helm?"

— *Hellenic folksong from the Dhodhekánisa archipelago*

Contents

Astrogators Never Sleep...................1
Athena Andreadis

Carnivores of Can't-Go-Home.....9
Constance Cooper

Chlorophyll Is Thicker Than Water....35
M. Fenn

Sensorium......................... 65
Jacqueline Koyanagi

From the Depths.......................... 79
Kristin Landon

Fieldwork.............................109
Shariann Lewitt

Of Wind and Fire.......................137
Vandana Singh

Crossing the Midday Gate..........167
Aliette de Bodard

Firstborn, Lastborn 189
Melissa Scott

Building for Shah Jehan........... 203
Anil Menon

The Age of Discovery 221
C. W. Johnson

Recursive Ice.................................243
Terry Boren

Ward 7.. 271
Susan Lanigan

Two Become One........................ 289
Kiini Ibura Salaam

The Pegasus Project 321
Jack McDevitt

The Seventh Gamer.................... 339
Gwyneth Jones

About the Contributors 371

Astrogators Never Sleep

Athena Andreadis

"From the stars we came,
and to the stars we must return.
And though science will build the starships,
it's science fiction that will make us want to board them."

— from "The Double Helix:
Why Science Needs Science Fiction"

The first book I clearly remember reading is the unexpurgated *20,000 Leagues under the Sea*. Had I been superstitious, I would have taken it for an omen. For me, a major allure of the book was that Captain Nemo was a swashbuckler in a lab coat, a profile I imagined myself fulfilling one day. I envisioned scientists as paladin sorcerers—pathfinders consumed by the flame of the quest, removing obstacles to uncover hidden kernels and weave disparate observations into coherent patterns that make sense of the world.

When I did become a scientist with a lab of my own, I found out that the vocation was more complex than my starry-eyed young self had conjured. For good and ill, science and scientists are embedded in society, the ivory tower cliché notwithstanding. Yet the part of the vision that remained intact, even in the most pedestrian or fraught circumstances, was the overwhelming sense of epiphany when tumblers clicked in my brain and I knew, with bone-deep certainty, that disparate pieces of a puzzle suddenly fit—a book in a library, a tile on a starship. Paradigm-shifting science comes from leaps of informed intuition (though that never removes the requirement for the painstaking, constant re-testing of premises and conclusions). In many respects, scientists are close kin to artists.

With this mindset, it's no surprise that one literary genre I fell into and never stopped reading was science fiction (SF). And just as science beguiled me while frustrating me, so did SF. Science-based wonder is the core of the genre. Yet its writers mostly cast science as either triumphalism or hubris and exalted the lone (and almost invariably male) genius, neglecting such crucial attributes as cooperative labor and pride in craft. Additionally, contemporary science fiction has grown increasingly distrustful of the urge to comprehend the universe, deeming dystopias and apocalypses edgier than the engineer's can-do problem-solving attitude of the Golden, and even Silver, Age.

There are real-world reasons for this shift. Today's humanity is keenly aware of the blowbacks from our technological prowess, some of them looming as existential risks for our species and our planet. Many parts of the world are undergoing a resurgence of fundamentalisms with their inherent hostility to science. More narrowly, SF remains almost exclusively US-centered. That nation's loss of undisputed global dominance and its stampede toward toxic ultra-conservatism made it insular and solidified its traditional disdain for expertise—science in particular, as can be seen by the obstruction of research in stem cells and climate change, and the "controversies" over including contraception in healthcare and teaching evolution in schools. Even as this fallout deranges their culture, Americans cling to their iPods, SUVs, and X-boxes and still expect instant cures for everything from obesity to hurricanes, seeing scientists as the Morlocks who must cater to their Eloi. These views are mirrored in SF, always a reflection of its time and place; in turn, this means that the genre also mirrors prevailing views of women.

Women have been scientists ever since humans became knowledge explorers, despite cultural handicaps that persist to this day. I won't list these (too obvious) nor will I bore you with the litany of the names of women whose scientific break-throughs were either ignored or usurped. On the side of SF, ask a reader to name a woman scientist and the likeliest reply will be Asimov's Susan Calvin. Granted, she's a genius of the loner misfit type; but Asimov dwelt on her lack of standard feminine attributes—and explicitly made frustrated mother-hood the major force that drove her to engage in AI research. Sci-fi films and TV series are even worse: the way they portray basic scientific concepts and social precepts has regressed to primitivism since the eighties. Compare the treatment of Dr. Carol Marcus in *The Wrath of Khan* versus *Descent into Dark-ness* and you get the gist.

So here I was, holding these tangled threads: a research scientist (on brain dys/function yet—a prime anxiety nexus); a politicized world citizen aware of the larger contexts and double edges of my own work and of all scientific undertak-ings; a zero-generation immigrant to whom cultural faultlines are visible; an unrepentant feminist and book devourer who detests the standard SF portrayal of scientists in general and women scientists in particular.

Since my first editorial venture, *The Other Half of the Sky*, had met with resounding accolades I knew at least one path out of my difficulties: I decided to launch an anthology focus-ing on women scientists who pursue science not-as-usual. The invitations flew out, and my fellow-wrights and crewmates answered the call. I decided to call this starship *To Shape the Dark*—because, after all, that's what scientists do.

What were my parameters? As with *The Other Half of the Sky* and all my reading in or out of genre, I wanted swash-buckling with layers, ambiguities, dilemmas; nuanced charac-ters, echoing histories, original worlds and societies. In par-ticular, I asked for women scientists, mathematicians or en-gineers who are not subject to the snooze-inducing conflict of work versus family and who are aware of the limitations and consequences of their vocation; and for cultures where science is a holistic endeavor as necessary as art—or air.

Many argue that science and scientists are hard to portray excitingly in SF but both aficionados and detractors of "hard" SF confuse accuracy with verisimilitude. Of course, nothing dates a story faster than dwelling on tech details (the infamous "As you know, Bob," passages) but the real problem is parochial imagination and endless repetition of recipes. Top-notch SF routinely conducts gedanken experiments that contravene reality: FTL travel, stable wormholes, habitable exoplanets very different from Earth, anthropomorphic aliens, mind uploading, telepathy and telekinesis, to name only a few. What matters is the larger context—the lucid dreaming and where it takes the reader's mind. So I didn't specify scientific accuracy for the stories. That said, some respect for basic scientific concepts is crucial to avoid Avatar-type handwavium. You won't find cracks in black hole horizons or instant organism-scale transmutations in this anthology.

The stories in this volume have at their centers women passionately pursuing their science. When I sent out the call, I asked that we don't end up eyebrow-deep in the most shopworn scientific occupations in SF: computer science and psychology. To my immense gratification and without any prompting from me, each story protagonist has a different vocation and their disciplines span the spectrum from quarks to galaxies: quantum physics, molecular virology, protein chemistry, neurobiology, tissue engineering, alchemical surgery, plant engineering, botany, ecology, cultural anthropology, materials science, geology, Newtonian mechanics, planetary physics, hyperspatial mathematics.

It's equally gratifying that most of the protagonists are not in their first or even second youth and many are acknowledged authorities, founders of intellectual dynasties, paradigm-shifters, inveterate hell-raisers, respected eccentrics—and, unlike Cassandra, they're heeded whether they're mentors or apprentices. These incarnations have been routinely available to older men and have the added perk of creating positive feedback power loops, but have been rarely vouchsafed to women in either literature or real life. And I was ecstatic to see Eleni

Tsami's stunning cover reflect the average age of the story protagonists.

Yet while fused to their work, these women are also enmeshed in their kinships and societies, defying the too-common SF stereotype of scientists as socially inept or excused from familial and civic obligations because of their brilliance. They're (grand)mothers and (grand)daughters, but also sisters, cousins and aunts, lovers and partners, friends and comrades. Some are singletons; others are parts of dyads, extended families, group marriages. The aliens are equally fascinating: the Europan viroids of "Fieldwork"; the spacefaring amphibians of "The Pegasus Project"; the cephalopods of "Sensorium" and cetaceans of "From the Depths", both bioengineering adepts; the giant symbiotic plants and insects of "Carnivores of Can't-Go-Home"; and the depth-specific ecosystems of "Of Wind and Fire."

The societies extend from city-states ("Sensorium") to galactic empires ("Crossing the Midday Gate") and every other configuration between; the spacetimes range from an alternate ancient Egypt ("Two Become One") to parallel Earth near-presents ("Chlorophyll is Thicker than Water", "Building for Shah Jehan", "The Age of Discovery", "Ward 7", "The Seventh Gamer"), to futures where humans roam the solar system and beyond ("Carnivores of Can't-Go-Home", "From the Depths", "Fieldwork", "Recursive Ice", "The Pegasus Project") to eras so distant that Earth has been all but forgotten ("Crossing the Midday Gate", "Firstborn, Lastborn") to universes where Earth may have never existed ("Sensorium", "Of Wind and Fire").

Many of the scenarios unfolding in this gathering are vastly improved, absorbing versions of pop films, TV series and games: *Jurassic Park* ("Carnivores of Can't-Go-Home"), *The Little Shop of Horrors* ("Chlorophyll is Thicker than Water"), *Star Trek*'s famous episode "The Devil in the Dark" ("Sensorium"), *The Abyss* ("From the Depths"), *The Martian* ("Fieldwork"), *Avatar* ("Of Wind and Fire"), *Moon* ("Recursive Ice"), *The Fly* ("Ward 7"), *Dr. Frankenstein* ("Two Become

One"), *Prometheus* ("The Pegasus Project"), immersive RPGs and Second Life ("The Seventh Gamer"). I spent happy hours contemplating whom I'd cast in these films.

Then there are the echoes from myths, songs and stories that ever haunt us: the proto-engineer of "Of Wind and Fire" is a fusion of Daedalus and Galileo; the revenge-bound pair of "Firstborn, Lastborn" could be descendants of Atreus— or Arianhod; the battered but unbowed hero of "Crossing the Midday Gate" combines aspects of Lilith and Pandora; and the self-possessed pivot of "Carnivores of Can't-Go-Home" could pass for a far-flung embodiment of Spider Grandmother. The two formidable women in "Chlorophyll is Thicker than Water" are thoroughly revamped versions of Baba Yaga and the three entangled women in "Two Become One" and in "Fieldwork" are takes on The Triple Goddess, while the daydreamer in "The Age of Discovery" is a novel incarnation of Zefram Cochrane. "From the Depths" recalls the epic journeys of the Polynesians on their catamarans; "Building for Shah Jehan" brings to mind Shelley's "Ozymandias"; and "Ward 7" could be a near-future retelling of Sarah's travails.

Contemporary SF appears to deem portrayal of science passé except in cautionary tales. Don't misunderstand me: scientists are as fallible as all other human beings, with egos and mortgages that need feeding, and the politics of science and its applications are fraught. It's also true that riches and fame figure in scientists' equations, as well as the desire to do something for the greater good. Science is a truly collective enterprise that can inspire immense loyalties (and deadly enmities). However, the deepest, most fundamental reason that makes people willing to become scientists, to put in endless amounts of energy and time into the effort, is the license to dream, the hope of making a novel connection, no matter how small—of experiencing those moments of epiphany that make it all worthwhile.

The wish to experience moments of extraordinary comprehension is not confined to intellectual elites, but is recognized as a universal human prerogative—and not that high in the hierarchy of needs, either. When the textile workers rose up in protest and organized the historic strike of 1912 in Lawrence, Massachusetts, they demanded "bread and roses." They recognized that the right to dream was as vital as having food and shelter.

If science disappears altogether from SF or survives only as the gimmick that allows "magic" plot outcomes, SF will lose its greatest and unique asset: acting as midwife and mentor to future scientists. This is no mere intellectual exercise for geeks. To give one example, work on the worldships so denigrated by today's determinedly earthbound SF might also help us devise solutions to the inexorable bottleneck of finite resources.

The stories in *To Shape the Dark* shimmer with the sense of wonder from scientific epiphanies; but beneath the dream-nets of spider silk glints the honed steel of discipline and hard labor that makes such discoveries possible—and the underdrone of the possible unintended consequences of each discovery. The protagonists make their choices fully aware of the thorny issues swirling around the products of their lab benches.

Scientists are humanity's astrogators: they never go into the suspended animation cocoons but stay at the starship observation posts, watching the great galaxy wheels slowly turn while they attend to the hydroponics. *To Shape the Dark* is part of that vigil.

"Warm and rest are yokes for us.
We chose thorns, shoals and starlight."

— from "Mid-Journey"

Carnivores of Can't-Go-Home

Constance Cooper

After all our weeks of travel, those final few miles in a wagon drawn by ox beetle seemed the longest of all. The wagon reeked of peat, and the ox beetle periodically dug its claws into the mud and surged forward to free up the wheels. McMurrin, our dour driver, actually managed a chuckle as his insect's motions flung me and Gwen back and forth. Gwen kept her pet project, a custom high-eye, cradled protectively in her arms.

Every moment I knew that we were getting closer and closer to haunted, hated Can't-Go-Home Bog, right on the southern fringe of settlement, where no other botanist had ever set foot.

The anticipation was almost more than I could stand.

The wagon's high sides blocked any view except for the feathery tops of the tufttrees and the crescents of the Big and Little Sisters peeking between patches of cloud. Finally I precariously stood up and saw that fields and pastures had given way to lush, head-high vegetation. I took a last try at questioning our driver.

"Mr. McMurrin, does your village use any medicinal plants from this area?"

"No, ma'am. Can't trust what grows in the bog, or the animals neither. There's bugcatchers big enough to have you for dinner, and the treetops are full of dragonfly nests. And o'course, you have to look out for hummers."

"Hummers?"

"Hummingbirds, you know? Nectar eaters. Not dangerous, but they'll steal your food if you don't take care."

Since we were about as likely to encounter a real, Mother Earth hummingbird as we were a dragon or a dinosaur, I assumed he was talking about some native insect I'd never seen.

"And o'course there's the ghost," McMurrin said darkly. "Some ten years back, Old Man Meeker's wife died, and he came out here to drown himself. Folks see his spirit drifting through the bog on moonlit nights, calling her name. 'Moonrose! Moooooonrose!' Aye, you two best take your pictures and get out as soon as you can."

By then I was resigned to being considered a photographer. No one in the village had ever heard of a botanical survey.

Can't-Go-Home was a dismal scattering of cottages populated mainly with Banished-Impenitent refugees from the Rearrangement decades ago. The previous night most of the village had gathered in the square for some grim sort of observance that involved burning the despoilers of Mother Earth in effigy. From the window of our rented room, Gwen and I had squinted at the words painted on the flaming burlap torsos. Were they the names of corporations, or individuals? Maybe this far from the data fount no one remembered anymore.

Our driver clacked his pole against the ox beetle's carapace, bringing the wagon to a halt. Ahead lay a pit of rich-looking mud that stepped down in tiers. Dark slices lay drying in rows nearby.

"Nothing good comes out of the bog," McMurrin pronounced as we climbed down and donned our packs. "'Cept for peat." He eyed Gwen's fresh face and my grey hair, and shook his head gloomily. "You folks don't know what you're getting into."

A shadow flicked over us, and Gwen yelped as an iridescent spear grazed her head. There came the chaff of a shot, and the dragonfly dropped to the ground. I reset the spring on my salt pistol, holstered the weapon, and glided over to re-trieve my student's cap from the insect's claws.

McMurrin was gaping.

"This isn't my first expedition," I told him calmly. "I think we'll manage. Though, Gwen? I did tell you that cap was not wise."

Gwen's cap was a peculiar knitted thing with multiple pockets, bright green with a black center stripe. I gathered that it had been made by Someone Special back home. It was un-clear whether they'd intended it to look so much like a beetle.

We left McMurrin loading the dragonfly carcass into his wagon.

Following the advice of Mr. Stirling, one of the more solid-seeming citizens from our Can't-Go-Home welcoming committee, I chose the trail furthest from the road. We en-tered a canyon of greenery higher than our heads.

My legs are tough enough from a lifetime of hiking, but I set a slow pace, soaking in the details around me. Sunlight glowed through stripes and spots in the broad leaves, and in-sects and small crustaceans scuttled among the roots. The ground was slippery, and before long both Gwen and I had taken falls in the mud.

"How soon should I launch the high-eye?" Gwen asked, reaching back to pat the machine strapped to her pack.

"Let's get farther from the road."

According to our contact in New Glasgow, one reason Can't-Go-Home Bog was still unmapped was the low surviv-al rate of aerial cameras. Microsized ones were preyed upon by raptorial insects, who mistook them for food. Larger ones were shot down by local citizens, who sold them for parts. And high-altitude cameras never showed much except a blur of tufttrees.

We had heard rumors of carnivorous plants in Can't-Go-Home Bog, but we weren't sure if they were any truer than McMurrin's ghost stories. It didn't take us long to find out.

Just off the path we spotted a shoulder-high patch of fleshy green whips covered with vivid red hairs, which were tipped with clear droplets. One whip was hugging a shiny black beetle the size of a soup bowl.

Naturally I'd researched what the data fount had to offer on Mother Earth bog environments, as had Gwen. This plant resembled a Drosera, a Mother Earth sundew, but sized to snare the insects of our world. There was intriguing evidence of kleptoparasitism—broken hairs where some large animal had ripped away the sundew's catch.

As Gwen photographed the giant carnivore with her pocket comm, I sketched it and took measurements and notes. I was trying to collect a sample of the mucilage on the trigger hairs when a whiplike leaf folded around my sleeve.

"Oh, hell. Gwen? You're not photographing this, are you?"

"Nnno."

Probably she was *filming*. I suspected that video would be pure treasure among Gwen's fellow students.

The sundew's adhesive had bonded to the shirt, except where the fabric was already smeared with mud. "Too bad you didn't fall down more," Gwen said cheerfully. "Then it wouldn't have stuck at all."

I ended up slicing off the sleeve with my pruners. I decided to call the plant a sleeve-eater until I could think up a more dignified Latin name.

Soon after, we found a parallel to the Mother Earth pitcher plant: a tall mass of leaves curled into cone shapes. It was an elegant design: prey lured by the nectar under the protruding lid would slip on the waxy sides of the pitcher and drown in the pocket of water below.

For each species Gwen performed a camera walkaround with her high-eye so it could build a model. "I'm going to try a test search now," she finally announced.

The high-eye, Donny (Gwen had created a plausible acronym, but admitted that the name had come first) was painted yellow and black like an eagle wasp to signal its inedibility. It had four sturdy rotors and excellent image recognition software. But Gwen was proudest of the voice recognition that let her quickly program it in the field. She murmured to it tenderly for some minutes, then crooned "Go fly!" and watched the machine whir off.

I fully expected that we would never see Donny again, but that evening the high-eye homed in on Gwen as she knelt by our campstove. It had correctly recognized, photographed, and mapped four of our new species, as well as three other plants with similar structures.

Gwen proudly switched the high-eye to sentry mode. She was in high spirits as she used her chopsticks to tweeze a clump of noodles out of the cookpot. "Just think," she said gleefully, "while we're eating supper, all around us in the dark bog, plants are slooowly digesting their helpless prey." (My student has a taste for the macabre.)

"Actually, that's less creepy than the ceremony last night in the village."

Gwen shivered theatrically. "Don't remind me. I was brought up Banished myself—but Chastened, not Impenitent. We didn't blame other people for the Removal, we blamed ourselves. We'd hold a tree planting or something and sing songs asking for forgiveness."

"Do you still lean that way?"

She shrugged. "I'm more Experimentalist these days."

"Ah, another Lab Crab." Like most of my students.

"Yeah. I mean, look at what the AOE did. Transporting two whole nations of people? Copying all of humanity's public data? You don't get that advanced unless you've got a lot of curiosity."

(I still find it amazing that folk of all different leanings ever agreed on a common way to refer to whatever force removed us from Mother Earth. That early politician who pompously referred to an "agency of extraction" probably never expected the populace to find it so humorous, or to come up with so many creative variations. But it's a great boon to have an abbreviation that could mean anything from "An Omnipotent Entity" to "Astonishing Overwhelming Event" to "Alien Overlord Enemies.")

"Wouldn't the AOE have to be benevolent, too?" I asked Gwen. "What about the Hundred Years' Supply?"

"Aha, you must lean Beholden." Gwen nibbled on one of the precious mochi sweets her father had made for her to take on the trip. "Nah, that's the experiment—to see how far we'd get with all our knowledge before the food and supplies ran out. Think what might've happened if we hadn't had such good leaders. How many more people would've died in the Confusion, or the Allotment Conflicts? What if the data fount hadn't stayed public, or if the Clean Slaters had managed to destroy it? Things could have played out so many different ways."

"The Simulationists think they have."

"I don't lean *that* far. I think we're flesh and blood, and we really are on a whole new planet."

I gazed out over the red-lit clearing. *No,* I thought, *we're the ones who are new.*

In peat bogs on Mother Earth, people had found human bodies that turned out to be thousands of years old. What was it like, to have that sort of history? Here on Daughter Earth we know for certain we'll never find anything like that.

But it was no use feeling nostalgic for a planet I'd never seen. Brusquely I reminded myself that Mother Earth was all but unlivable by the time of the Removal. Only a few extremists cherished any hope of return.

"Intruder," Donny announced.

Immediately my salt pistol was pointed at the dark shape at the edge of our camp.

"Don't shoot," shrilled a young male voice. "I—I saw your light, and your stove, and I thought, maybe you could cook this?" The boy held up a plump soldier mantis.

Soon Dunk, as he named himself, was squatting on our groundcloth and using his grubby fingernails to peel the last noodles from the pot. He wore grey, mud-stained clothes woven from the nubbly local silk, and his flimsy reed sandals were nothing I would have trusted in the bog. He looked far too young to be on his own.

"Should I be calling your parents?" I asked him bluntly.

The boy snorted. "Mum knows perfectly well where I am. She's given up taking me back to town. Knows I'll be back here soon enough."

"Dr. T.," Gwen interrupted, thrusting the mantis rather too close to my face. "What do you think those marks are?" The mantis's thorax and its large "saluting" claw were mottled with lighter patches.

"That's just where I ripped it off of the glue plant," Dunk told her. "It's fine to eat. I do it all the time."

I raised my eyebrows. "You steal food from carnivorous plants?"

"Wouldn't call it *stealing*—"

"Don't worry, I'm happy to hear it," I told him as I set the mantis to roast. "I'd love to ask you some questions. We're doing a survey of local plants."

Dunk looked alarmed. "You won't hurt them, will you? Mum always says someday she'll come tear them out by the roots."

"We often take specimens to propagate, but we'd never take them all. Is there some plant in particular you're thinking of?"

Gwen and I listened as a picture emerged of disaffected Can't-Go-Home youth foraging through the bog for a species they called the honey barrel, whose nectar had intoxicant properties. Some youngsters evidently binged for days at a time, sustaining themselves on scavenged prey.

I was beginning to understand why the villagers reviled the bog. Hadn't some of them told me it stole children away? I'd thought they were being superstitious.

"Dunk, could you guide us to some of these plants? We can pay eight pounds an hour."

He was staring at my feet.

"You could buy yourself some good slughide boots," I suggested.

"I guess I could. None of my friends have 'em." He gave a sudden, brilliant smile. "It's a deal."

Not much later he was curled up on the edge of our groundcloth, looking even younger in his sleep.

Night was full of clicks and whistles and the high-pitched barking of bog puppies. Donny's proximity alarm buzzed briefly a few times, but on the whole I slept soundly, and so did Gwen.

Dunk did not.

"He didn't take any money." Gwen blinked in the morning light. "He could have bought a lot more food with that."

"Or with what we were going to pay him," I agreed sadly. "But then he'd have to go into town. Maybe he doesn't want to leave his nectar source for that long." I unbuttoned the flaps on my backpack to see if any travel bars or dried seaweed might have been left behind.

Even the half-eaten soldier mantis was missing.

"I need to reprogram the sentry mode," Gwen fretted. "Donny was looking for animals entering the perimeter. Not leaving."

I sighed. "Mr. McMurrin warned me. I should have watched out for the hummers."

"We can collect meat from the bog plants," I said as I marched down the trail with my lightened pack. "And water's easy." I flicked a leaf, sending raindrops flying.

"I just wish he'd left us the stove. Raw bug's so goopy."

Up ahead three glossy red pitcher plants protruded from the ground. They were too small to be the honey barrels Dunk had described, but they might provide food.

The nectar had been licked away from all the pitchers. I looked into the biggest pit trap, and tried too late to shield the view from Gwen. Bobbing in the foul-looking liquid was one of her treasured mochi sweets.

Gwen's pale complexion turned pink. "Dunk," she hissed. "He steals from us, but when it comes to plants, he *pays*?" Her good temper didn't return until she had programmed Donny to look for the largest pitcher plant it could find. She all but kissed the high-eye on the nose before telling it "Go fly!"

The specimen that Donny found towered over us. Its pitchers were pale orange and dark green, mottled with translucent spots to confuse trapped insects looking for an exit. From Dunk's description this had to be a honey barrel, though it was a hell of a name for such a majestic plant. I would have to ponder carefully to find a name it deserved.

The honey barrel was a frequent hummer destination, judging by the way the trail led right to it—not to mention the ladder leaning against its largest pitcher.

The ladder was made of the interlocked fighting arms of "ladder lice." These lay scattered everywhere in this region—the chitin was too thick for most predators to risk their mandibles on. I'd never seen louse ladders until Can't-Go-Home, where every stilt-house had one at its front door. Maybe no other community was willing to put up with the lingering odor.

Someone had gouged out the nectar glands on the underside of the pitcher's lid. It was far more destructive than what we'd seen with the "sweets jar" plants earlier in the day, but still I tucked sample bags into my belt pockets before I set foot on the shiny brown bottom rung.

A few steps later I called down, "Gwen, could you pass me my gloves?"

"Good idea! That nectar might have contact effects."

I'd been more concerned about cutting my hands on the ladder, whose smooth surface had been deeply abraded. I put out one gloved hand to steady the leaf-lid.

What sort of prey would this enormous species attract? I bent over the lip of the opening, peering into the green-lit well of liquid some ten feet below. From the lumps I could see, the plant had been absurdly successful. Was that a skull beetle?

I recoiled in shock—and lost my balance. I grabbed for the pit trap's side, but the glossy surface provided no handholds at all. I pitched forward and fell headfirst into the reeking digestive well.

I raised my head out of the liquid, eyes burning as if from seawater. My hat had come off, and my hair was plastered to my face. My arms bumped the husks of partly digested insects. My legs knocked against the harder angles of what I very much hoped were the rungs of a previous ladder.

Small insects scurried over me—commensal organisms, no doubt, which would normally help the pitcher plant break down its prey. Their excreta probably provided valuable nutrients, though at the moment I was having trouble appreciating that phenomenon.

I fumbled at my belt for the sheath of my hori-hori, the long digging knife I used for excavating specimens. "Stand back!" I called to Gwen.

The blade was c-shaped in cross-section, so I couldn't simply slash my way out. Still, eight inches of razor-sharp steel, serrated on one side, pierced the wall that many flailing insect claws had not. I heard a yip from outside as liquid sprayed out of the cavity—Gwen had evidently not stood far enough back.

I stabbed the wall in a zigzag line, and when I'd carved out a big enough oval I emerged in a gush of digestive juices. Gwen had been recording my exit with her pocket comm, but she froze when she saw my face.

"Keep filming," I gritted. "We may need to show the police." I hopped down from the opening to let Gwen see in.

Half-dissolved insect and crustacean shells lay in a black mound like wet cinders. Mixed in were remains that could only be human: the long white shapes of bones.

Sheriff Taggart was a sturdy-looking man whose thinning

hair was a startling moon-orange. I'd talked with him briefly at the mayor's welcome reception in Can't-Go-Home, in between Ms. Wilbridge's painful poetry recitation and Mr. Stirling's impromptu guitar performance.

"Thanks for calling," he told us gruffly. "Surprised your comm could reach the tower, this far out."

"Donny here flew up to relay the transmission," Gwen explained, petting the high-eye on its rounded top.

"Good thing. We mostly just get hummers out this way, and if one of them showed up in town talking about bones, who'd have believed him? My neighbor's kid sees rainbows and elephants, from what I hear."

Of course, the police hadn't believed me either until I'd sent them some rather gruesome photos.

"Poor kid," Taggart said, looking down at the canvas where his junior officer had just added a frighteningly clean skull to the collection of bones. "Miracle no one's drowned before, with these devils growing everywhere."

"So you think it was an accident?"

The sheriff gave me a strange look. "Well, ma'am, I think we can rule out murder. We're in a peat bog, for God's sake. No one's going to haul a body up a ladder and dump it somewhere it might be found when they could just sink it in a patch of bog."

"I fell into the plant myself, and the liquid wasn't that deep. There's no way I could have drowned."

"You weren't nectared up." Taggart looked away. "Could have been suicide, I guess, but I'd rather say drowning if I have the choice."

"AOE," the other officer swore from over by the mutilated pitcher. She had been cutting the edge down in a spiral as she removed the contents, and by now was encircled by a ragged ribbon of plant tissue. She extracted a metal object from the pile of insect husks. It was a steel digging blade similar to my own.

The sheriff inspected it. "Not the usual kind of knife for a kid."

"It's a hori-hori," I told him. "Gardeners use them."

"Ah. Should help identify him, then."

I frowned. "Except it might not have belonged to this person. We've seen evidence that the, uh, hummers sometimes put small tokens into the pitchers. As a sort of gift."

Taggart's face twisted as if he'd just found a maggot in his snail steak.

The junior officer returned. "That's it, sir. Should I put up string around the site?"

"Don't bother. We've got photos. Pretty clear what happened. Time to head back to town and find out whose kids are missing." The sheriff gave me a nod. "Thanks to you, we can tell Duncan's mum he's all right. Going to be a nightmare for the other families, though."

"And us," the junior officer said gloomily. "The bog'll fill up with parents hunting for their kids, and getting hurt and lost."

"Maybe our high-eye could help," I offered. "Gwen—is its pattern recognition good enough to find the other kids?"

"Of course!" she said reflexively.

"That would be a big help, ma'am." The sheriff eyed my matted hair and slime-crusted clothing. "But you don't have to stay out here. We can give you a lift back to town in the electric."

"We'll stay, and continue our survey," I said firmly.

I lean Beholden. I believe the AOE did the Two Nations a great service when they transplanted us to an unspoiled planet—a favor we'll have to repay someday by rescuing another species. I'm grateful that the data fount let us regain much of our technology within centuries, and I think we've been right to focus on communications.

But anyone who studies biology is aware of what we've lost—all the domestic animals, crops, and medicinal plants humans had bred or discovered over millennia. In just two days in this bog, Gwen and I had already cataloged dozens of plants with food or medical or industrial potential. Next to that thrill, washing my hair didn't hold much attraction.

"Well, you two be careful," the sheriff warned. "Always thought these damn things could kill, but now we know for sure." He shoved the sliced-apart pitcher with his boot. "Wish I could do them all this way. I tell you, Professor, if bogs could burn, I'd light this one up myself."

I watched the police squelch away down the trail. Did all the villagers share Taggart's views? Around me the crowding bulbs and vases and candelabra of the pitcher plants suddenly seemed as fragile as red and green blown glass.

Within the hour we were receiving images and video snippets of what Donny thought might be humans. Unfortunately, it turned out that many varieties of standing pitcher plant resembled a human silhouette—especially if one imagined a tall, thin human wearing a sinister hooded cloak.

"Donny's doing his best," Gwen said defensively. "I guess I didn't give him enough human images to train on. Just what I had on my pocket comm."

"What on earth *do* you have on your comm?"

"Photos of some friends. And, uh. A few of Ichiro Weybridge."

"The film actor? From *Death on Demon Mountain?*"

"I like him."

"Maybe you should write and tell him he looks like a carnivorous plant from the edge of civilization. That would get his attention. He might even write you back."

"Do you really think so?"

"No."

It was not until late afternoon that Donny sent a genuine result.

"See, that's definitely two teenagers," Gwen said triumphantly, pointing to the display on her comm. "We should notify the sheriff." She paused. "Although—I'm thinking we shouldn't send him this video."

"No," I agreed hastily. "Er, could you stop the video, please? And now delete. Thank you. Obviously they didn't see Donny."

"Well, they were distracted."

"Quite. I wish we knew their names, so we could tell their parents they're all right."

"We know where they are now—we can go ask them," Gwen pointed out.

"All right. But for heaven's sake, let's make lots of noise while we're approaching."

The long summer evening was darkening and the noises of the bog had ratcheted up enough to cover the sound of footsteps or even conversation by the time Gwen and I found the group of hummers. Five of them were gathered around a peat fire, squatting on their heels in the local fashion. Two were young women who looked like sisters. There was also a hefty, adult-sized young man, a more spindly teenager, and a little boy.

Two of the hummers held sticks around which were curled rolled-up armadillo bugs, their plates crisping in the flames. Except for the alien-chem-lab shapes of the surrounding bog plants, the scene resembled any number of my childhood camping trips, right down to the burnt-shell smell of roasted crustacean.

The hummers gawked at us as we stepped into the firelight, and the large young man aimed his stick as if it were a spiderhunting spear. They all looked ready to bolt.

"Have you heard the news?" Gwen burst out.

I silently blessed my student as she began to tell about our horrific discovery earlier that day. Perhaps it was Gwen's youth that made them more comfortable—or perhaps the fact that she gave the account in the most lurid, spellbinding fashion possible—but soon none of the hummers showed signs of going anywhere.

"And no one knows whose bones they were, that lay there in the darkness of the pit," Gwen concluded, in ominous tones that might have owed something to Ichiro Weybridge.

The hummers applauded.

"It's not a *story*," I objected. "It happened this morning. Look, I still have gunk in my hair."

The boy shook his head. "No one could really drown in a

honey barrel."

"Even if they were under the influence?"

"Of *nectar?* It doesn't make you *unconscious,*" the younger sister sniffed.

"You don't seem very worried!" Gwen said hotly. "It could have been one of your friends in there!"

The lean older sister shook her head. Her blond hair was cropped as short as doggerpillar fur. "Takes a week for a honey barrel to eat something big. I've seen everyone in the last couple days, even the loners like Dunk and Robbie."

"Whoever it was, they *did* take some nectar," I insisted. "The lid of the plant was all cut up."

Shocked expressions spread around the circle. "That's against the code," the younger sister said indignantly.

"You have a code?"

"Protect the plants," the large-shouldered young man said earnestly. "And give whenever you take."

"So you always put something in the pitchers, when you take their nectar?" I set my pocket comm to record. I've gotten good at doing that surreptitiously.

"Aye, or you're just a parasite."

"They like poop," the youngest member of the group volunteered.

"Of course they do," I said matter-of-factly. "So, how do you harvest the nectar?"

"We just lick it off."

"Before the poop, though," said the little boy helpfully. "Otherwise—the smell."

"Getting back to the body," I said. "The sheriff told us no one was missing from town."

"Must have been a stranger, then." The hummers gazed at us.

Suddenly I was aware of how foreign we must seem in our blue cottonspun coveralls. Although I spoke fluent British, and Gwen was a native speaker, both of us had grown up near the data fount, where universities flourished and the Two Nations had mixed for centuries. Whether we spoke British or Nihongo, we both had a distinct Central accent.

More than that, we were adults—like the hummers' bitter parents.

In the darkness around the fire, the bulbs of pitcher plants stood like vials of poison, and the zizz of dragonflies and don't-touch-mes sliced through the air.

Even if the honey barrel's victim hadn't been a hummer, might hummers still have placed the body there? Maybe they'd consider a corpse an extra-nice gift. I pictured a gang of nectar-addled adolescents, stumbling across a dead vagabond and bestowing the meat upon a honey barrel in some sort of improvised bogland ritual. It would be only slightly more bizarre than some of their parents' ceremonies.

Could they have produced the corpse themselves by murdering a stranger, or even one of their own, with one of those long knives they all wore at their belts? Like the knife the largest of them was taking out now....

The young man carved a chunk of bug meat and offered it to me. "Want some 'poly?"

"What?"

"Holy-moly-poly. Don't you know them? I thought they lived everywhere."

It smelled delectable.

"We call them armadillo bugs, where I grew up," I said, flustered. I was being fanciful. None of these teenagers would kill someone, just to thank a plant.

Still, Gwen and I camped some distance away that night.

"I can't trust hearsay from hummers," Sheriff Taggart's weary voice came over my pocket comm the next morning. "You saw five. That still leaves seven kids not accounted for."

I tilted my head back, watching the early sunlight gleam off Donny's yellow paint as the high-eye hovered level with the treetops. The hummers had melted away during the night, leaving only a patch of ashes and a small pitcher plant filled with dinner scraps.

"I want you two back in town," the sheriff said. "Those photos you sent, of the bones inside the plant? Sorry to say, they found their way out of the police station. Now half of Can't-Go-Home's heading up to the bog to clear out the killer plants. And it's going around that you two are collecting seeds to breed more of them—so I'd rather have you where I can keep an eye on you."

I remembered the faces of the townsfolk, jeering as the effigies burned. "From what you're saying, it sounds more dangerous for us in town." I glanced at Gwen, who nodded. "But thank you for the suggestion."

"It wasn't a suggestion, ma'am. I'm sending our police car for you if I can spare it, or I'll ask someone who owns a private vehicle. Please make your way back to the peat mine. And keep that high-eye close by you, so you can contact me if you run into trouble." He clicked off.

I grimaced. Private vehicle? That would mean Mr. Stirling or Ms. Hanks. Being pulled away from our work would be bad enough without enduring hours in a car with Mr. Stirling's perfumed hair oil. As for the longwinded Ms. Hanks, I had faked a coughing fit to escape her at the reception.

Donny drifted down from the treetops and grounded itself next to Gwen, who began to polish it lovingly with a square of cloth.

"Poor Donny, no more adventures for you. But at least you made us a map, didn't you? Yes, you did!"

"Really? It mapped the whole bog?"

"Only parts. I'll show you." Gwen fiddled with the display.

"That's a real shame. I hope we don't get lost on our way back to the peat mine."

Gwen and I exchanged glances, and continued to sift through the data.

"Look at that area," I said. "See how it's fenced in by plants, with standing water all around? I'm guessing that's the best-preserved area in the entire bog. Not even hummers would go there."

"You're right," Gwen breathed. "It's almost totally inaccessible."

Waist-deep in muddy water, I forced my way between the stems of what we'd been calling palisade plants. I popped out into a clear area, sloshed up an incline and stood, clothes drooling onto a carpet of moss. Gwen bounced up behind me.

Ahead, stands of red-and-green tubes rose from the shallows. Arcs of mottled leaves jutted from the ground like the ears of a submerged giant. The ground was a quilt of leaves and bulbs and flowers.

After an hour of survey activities, I grew uneasy. "This place is too beautiful," I complained. "Notice how the parts that are good for walking just happen to lead to scenic vistas? And there's so much variety, even more so than in the rest of the bog. It feels like we're walking through a botanical garden."

"Those hummers didn't look like the gardening type." Gwen obviously thought I was crazy—up until we found the hut.

It was a mud-and-wicker building set on stilts and thatched with bundles of tree fluff. Its ladder was painstakingly constructed of wood, not louse arms, and decorated with dried flowers. Nearby was a row of vigorous-looking pitcher plants that seemed to serve as a latrine (though not recently, I noted.) On the other side of the hut was a path bordered by carefully tended flowers. Each blossom consisted of two large white petals and two small orange ones, like the Big and Little Sisters in the sky.

"Gwen," I said, "remember that ghost story about Old Man Meeker? His wife was called…"

"…Moonrose," Gwen said softly, staring at the flowers. "Whoa. You're thinking—"

"Maybe Mr. Meeker didn't drown himself after all."

The hut's door hung open, and after a moment we climbed the ladder. The single room was obsessively orderly, from the drinking water stored in plant-husk containers to the woven fiber hammock. Not much food storage was in evidence, and I wondered if whoever lived here gathered food fresh every day. Perhaps the space inside the palisade was one enormous kitchen garden. Here in the bog, the right mix of plants could supply both vegetables and meat.

On the rough table lay an oversized book, made of hand-pressed paper bound with slug leather. It lay open to an illustration of a flower done in colored ink, with copious notes in precise British lettering. The drawing was marred by a splash of green from an overturned bowl which lay crusted to the table with dried ink.

I paged through the book. It was full of sketches, plant and animal observations, and maps of different areas of the bog, along with the occasional poem. I showed Gwen the writing on the front page that said, "In memory of my wife Moon-rose." More journals were stacked on a shelf.

"Forget Dunk," Gwen exclaimed. "This is the person we need to talk to!"

I cleared my throat. "I hate to say it, but if none of the hummers are missing, and everyone in town is accounted for—"

"Oh, no."

"It would explain the hori-hori that the police found in the pitcher. He *was* a gardener. Maybe he wore one on his belt."

"That's awful. I bet he was really old and frail, and he got injured when he fell in."

I exited the hut and stood gazing at the moonroses. "The rungs on that honey barrel's ladder were scratched," I said. "Like someone climbed it wearing hobnailed boots. But the hummers we saw didn't have boots. From what Dunk said, none of them do."

"So Mr. Meeker wore boots."

"Then why weren't there any hobnails in the pitcher cavity? I think someone killed Meeker, and dumped his body in that pitcher."

"Why would anyone kill him? He'd been here for ten years."

"Some old feud, maybe?"

Gwen gave an angry sigh. "Why do people have to be so complicated? Why can't we just kill for food like animals? Or even like plants!" She waved her arm at the nearby pitchers. "Look at them. They don't care what they catch, so long as it's protein."

"Maybe," I said slowly, "the murderer didn't care who got killed, either—so long as there was a body to be found."

"What? It's pure luck it got found at all. All the nectar was scraped off that pitcher, you could see that from the ground. The hummers had no reason to climb it."

"What if *we* were meant to find it? No botanist could resist studying that monster. And we make much better witnesses than hummers. Respectable adults, who aren't afraid to call the authorities. We even have cameras, so everyone can see just how dangerous the honey barrels are." I grimaced. "They chose a spot not far from the peat mine, right on the path that was recommended to us—that's got to be it. Poor old Meeker was just easy to catch. He wasn't the real target. Someone wants the villagers to hate pitcher plants."

"Are you saying—"

I nodded grimly. "The honey barrel was framed."

A lanky middle-aged man stepped out from behind the hut. He was dressed in well-made town clothes, except for his hobnailed boots. He would have been clapping his hands, except that he was holding a pistol. As it was, his left hand was making an unimpressive patting sound against the skin of his right wrist.

I placed a hand on Gwen's shoulder, hoping she wouldn't do anything rash.

"Mr. Stirling." I gave a small gracious bow. "Thanks again for your directions. They led us to an interesting find."

"I'd say so." His craggy face formed a smile. "Your photos of those bones have been making quite a stir. That's why the sheriff asked me to collect you."

His thin hand gestured with the gun, an unfamiliar type which possibly held something deadlier than salt. "Please, put your comms away, both of you! We all know they can't reach the town from here. I *will* take that salt pistol of yours, though, Professor. And I see your student has one too. Just toss them into the water over there. Thank you."

He shook his head. "This is so unfortunate. I was looking forward to being a hero, bringing the foreign visitors back safe. I was planning on drinking toasts to you both. The experts who exposed the threat! But that was before I came back here to clean up, and heard you talking." He glanced regretfully at his pistol.

My hand darted the few inches to Donny's power switch and flipped it on. By the time Stirling looked back up, my hand was back on Gwen's shoulder.

"I'd like to understand," I told him quietly, "why you want the honey barrels destroyed." (I so needed to come up with a better name for that plant.)

I was guessing he had a nectar-addicted child, but he surprised me.

"It's not them in particular—it's this whole bog. The regional council is so concerned about the flora and fauna and the ecological balance—" he gave this in a bitter singsong— "it's made them blind to what's underneath."

"Are you talking about the peat?"

"Pff! Much more valuable than that. Lignite deposits, large ones."

"Lignite?" Gwen burst out in dismay. "That's brown coal, isn't it? Why would you want that? It's one of the dirtiest fuels there is."

"Mr. Stirling," I said carefully, "the council is right—a big mining operation would ruin this bog. And there's so much biological wealth here, more than a mine could ever produce. As soon as Gwen and I make our report, your town will be booming."

Stirling's face darkened. "This is *not* about money!" he shouted.

We froze.

"I already know we could spend our lives fussing over weeds and bugs, and probably make a fat profit on it. But there are more important goals. That lignite could power Can't-Go-Home for decades. We could build workshops, bring back technology we haven't had since Mother Earth."

He drew a breath, calming himself. "It's frustrating getting anything done here with such a large Banished community. Anything useful our ancestors did always seems to count as a sin. But thanks to you two, we'll make progress tonight."

"Tonight?" I ventured.

"There's a council meeting, and this time I know they'll accept my land-use proposal. Those council members are conservative, but they're not fools. No one wants to be the one fighting to protect a bunch of plants that just killed and ate a child."

"That plant didn't kill anyone. It was you!" Gwen accused. "And it wasn't a child, was it? It was poor Mr. Meeker."

Stirling blinked. "I was hardly going to use one of my daughter's schoolmates, was I? Couldn't look her in the eye if I did. But no one will miss old Meeker. No one noticed him much when he was alive, and no one will remember him now. Even if they do identify his body, it'll be too late. Tonight's vote will be over and done."

He looked resolute. "And soon they'll be finding two more bodies—or maybe just the bones. People will see it's dangerous studying those bloodthirsty plants. I do apologize, Professor—but scientists take risks, don't they, trying to learn new things?"

"You're right," I said levelly. "We take risks to find things out. And to share what we find." I shifted my hand farther up Gwen's backpack, where I'd been quietly unbuckling a strap. "Thanks for this conversation, Mr. Stirling—I'm sure the sheriff will want to hear my recording. Donny, go fly up."

"A of E!" Stirling cursed as the black-and-yellow machine lifted over our heads. The dark mouth of his pistol rose to follow it.

Gwen and I sprinted toward the wall of palisade plants.

As I ran, I fumbled the send command into my comm.

I heard the whipcrack of Stirling's gun. That was no air or spring pistol. Chemical propellant, stabbing steel into the bog—maybe even lead. An import from one of those regions where the Accords were poorly kept.

I flicked a glance upward. The high-eye was at the bottom level of tufttree branches. It would not have enough altitude to contact the village tower until it reached the top of the canopy.

Ahead of me Gwen dove between the upturned trumpets of the palisade plants. Stirling's pistol cracked again. After the fourth report Donny came twirling down like a helicopter seed, its indicator light still winking red for 'Attempting To Send.'

Stirling appeared around a bend in the path. Before he could aim his pistol at me, I hurled the comm in my hand as hard as I could. The small weight bashed into his nose, and bounced off into the muddy water.

While Stirling yelped and pawed at his face, I burrowed into the palisade thicket. Gwen, the idiot, had waited for me on the other side.

"He took Donny down before it could transmit," I reported breathlessly. "He's still coming after us. He would have shot me if I hadn't clipped him with my comm."

"How bad is he hurt?"

"I got him in the nose, but it won't slow him down much—" I saw the look on Gwen's face. "Oh. Not much damage, just the rotors."

"Did you hear Stirling swearing?" Gwen said as we hurried away. "He said 'A of E.' Not 'AOE,' like most people."

"I caught that too. I'm guessing it's short for 'Annexers of Earth.'"

"He's an Evicted?" Gwen's eyes went wide. She'd probably never encountered that leaning except in sensational films.

"It would explain why he's not worried about pollution. Why bother preserving your planet, if all that matters is making weapons and getting back to Mother Earth as soon as you can? And punishing the thieves who stole it? That's how

Evicted think."

"He can't let us tell what we know. He's going to kill us, isn't he?"

"That will depend," I told her, "on how well he knows the bog."

Hot on our trail, Stirling pushed through a screen of foliage with a victorious yell—and plowed face-first into a wall of sundews.

The jewel-beaded tendrils reacted, twining around his arms and torso. He cried out and jerked back, but the sticky liquid at the tips of the hairs had already bonded to the fabric of his shirt—and the skin of his gun hand. He kicked desperately at the plants, triggering more tentacles. One wrapped itself around his forehead, tilting down low over one eye like the brim of a festival hat. He stared as we swam our way out of the sundews, our mud-plastered skin and clothing pulling loose with tiny popping sounds.

Gwen grinned. "Dr. T.? I think that sleeve-eater might lead to a good industrial adhesive."

"There may also be surgical applications," I said judiciously. "It seems to bond well to human skin. Although it may work better as a concentrate—as is, I don't see it holding for longer than a few days. Plenty of time for us to walk back to town, though." I met Stirling's glare. "If you're polite, Mr. Stirling, we'll tell the sheriff about you right away."

"Enjoy your pet plants while you can, Professor," Stirling said stiffly. He would have lowered his eyebrows if the sundew had allowed it. "This whole bog'll be gone soon enough. You can accuse me all you want, but your recording's lost in the mud. No one's going to believe two foreigners over a respected local businessman."

"This just shows," Gwen said diffidently, "why it's wise to take multiple samples." She dipped her hand into her pocket and showed us her own comm. "I was recording too."

Stirling's eyes widened. "I don't care," he rasped out. "You're too late to affect the vote tonight, and others will carry on the work." His voice deepened with emotion. "Can't-Go-Home will become a center of industry, a beacon for believers. Someday they'll change its name to Can-Go-Home. Because we *can* go home, if we work hard enough. If we make sacrifices, and use this world to fuel our dreams. We *will* go home, to the true Earth, and when we get there, we will free her."

I looked at his impassioned face—the sweat-soaked temples, the streak of blood under one nostril. I remembered him on the mayor's patio at the reception, impeccably dressed. Someone had pointed out how lovely the moons were that evening, and he had picked up a nearby guitar and played, with great intensity, a classical piece about Mother Earth's single moon.

Many people regarded the Removal as an intellectual puzzle. Did the AOE pick two island cultures on purpose? What groups of nations might now exist on other planets? What could we deduce from the foods the AOE left us, or the design of the shelters?

At the opposite end of the spectrum, there were people whose feelings overwhelmed them.

What would it be like to believe, as Stirling did, that Mother Earth was captive and suffering? It was our birthplace, source of all our oldest, most treasured songs and art and stories and cinema. There was no one who hadn't seen the beauty of Mother Earth, preserved for us in the data fount. Every child wondered what chocolate had tasted like, or how fresh grass had felt underfoot, or what it had been like to see animals with facial expressions we could understand.

As a biologist I probably spent more time than most musing about all the species we used to know. I felt a deep connection to that planet I had never seen. But unlike Stirling, I'd never felt compelled to imagine a terrible fate for Mother Earth, or cast myself as its savior.

Daughter Earth was my home—mine to explore and appreciate and understand.

"You're quite the motivational speaker," I told Stirling. "But you're wrong about the vote."

I turned to my student. "Gwen, may I have your comm, please? And also—if you don't mind terribly—your cap."

I set the comm to transmit the recording, along with a brief explanation, and buttoned it neatly into a pocket of the vivid green cap. I found a tufttree stick, and raised the cap high.

My arms had only just begun to tremble when a blur of blue swooped down and snatched the cap in its claws. The dragonfly climbed upward, darting through the gaps in the branches, all the way up to its nest atop the tallest tree.

I shaded my eyes. "That's plenty high enough to transmit. The sheriff should be here within hours."

I looked back at Stirling, still stuck fast.

He'd used me and Gwen to take pictures of Meeker's bones. Would he have tried it, if he'd understood everything survey botanists do? The sketching and mapping and collection. The noting of minute details. The complex observation of how organisms fit together.

"The council won't appreciate how you tried to make fools of them, Mr. Stirling," I told him. "I'm certain they'll make this bog a protected zone. Especially when they see all the specimens and data that Mr. Meeker collected over the years. It's really a monumental achievement."

It came to me then. The perfect name for that enormous, towering, corpse-devouring pitcher plant: *Monumentum Meekeri.* Meeker's Monument.

Chlorophyll Is Thicker Than Water

M. Fenn

Afternoon, Dr. Yamamoto."

The old woman looked up from the flower seed display she had been studying while waiting. "Afternoon, Billy. How's your mother?"

"Good! She told me to thank your partner for the lotion, if I saw you. Her hands are much better."

"I'll tell Hina you said so. And how's *your* skin doing?"

The boy blushed. "Fine."

She smiled kindly. "Good. I'll tell her that, too. Did my order come in?"

"Yes, ma'am! I was just going to call you. Hang on."

The gangly boy—his spotty complexion noticeably improved since her last visit—hustled into the back room of the ag store. Susan Yamamoto clucked her tongue at an African grey parrot glowering on the other side of the room. He squawked in return but remained on his perch.

"Grumpy old thing."

She trundled her round frame closer to a display of wind chimes. *Hina would like one of these new copper ones,* she thought, brushing her calloused hand against the metal pipes. A ceramic frog mounted on the top remained stoic as the chimes tinkled.

Billy returned, his arms wrapped around several boxes

of varying sizes. "Here you go, ma'am. Are these for your research?"

Susan brought the chimes to the counter and pulled a wallet out of the back pocket of her faded jeans. "Yes, indeed. The search for intelligent life goes on."

Billy gave her an unsure smile as he took her credit card and rang up her purchase. "I was trying to explain your work to my friend, Adrian, but I couldn't keep it straight."

Susan chuckled. "It is a tad complicated. Basically, Hina and I are trying to figure out how plants think and if we can speed the process."

Billy nodded. "I get that part, I think. But why?"

"You know how climate change is only getting worse?"

"Right."

"Well, if we can speed up how a plant thinks somehow, it's possible it could protect itself from the invasive aspects of climate change. Plants can't get up and walk to cooler climes, but perhaps, with quicker 'thought processes,' they could develop new defenses to new bugs moving north in time to protect themselves. Make sense?"

"Of course!" Billy rolled his eyes. "It always does when you say it. But it sounds like a bunch of bafflegab when I try."

"That's all right, dear. You know me—I don't mind holding forth."

They both laughed and he returned her card and the charge slip for her signature. "Is the garden tour still on for Saturday?"

"Of course. Will we see you there?"

He smiled more confidently this time. "Wouldn't miss it."

Billy loaded the boxes into the two cloth bags Susan placed on the counter and carried them out to her car. The parrot ruffled his feathers and squawked at the empty room.

With the exception of the parrot, who didn't like anyone, everyone in Whitman's Feed & Grain/Garden Supply loved

Susan Yamamoto. Most people in North Bennington who knew her felt the same. The Plant Wizard, they called her. From liberating a Christmas cactus from the clutches of rot to landscape suggestions for the many micro-climates that existed in southwestern Vermont, she was the expert.

She and her wife had retired from the college of agriculture and life sciences up in Burlington—Susan, a professor of plant biology; Hina Okada, of biochemistry—buying ten acres of rocky hills and a beaten-down cottage on the outskirts of town for next to nothing in the early aughts. Over the ensuing twenty-five years, they'd transformed the place, turning the small, decrepit farmhouse into the model of an English cottage, only better suited to the vagaries of Vermont's weather. The warming of the climate over the years provided a helpful assist.

Most of the land remained wooded, only now bearing well-marked trails. The couple turned most of the unforested land over to flowers, shrubbery, and fruit and nut trees. A large vegetable garden took up one corner of the property, leaving only one gently sloping patch where they allowed a small lawn to exist. Neither of them cared for mowing.

Local townsfolk, along with past students and out-of-town visitors, flocked to see the rejuvenated landscape at the annual tour the pair hosted. Susan's voice had weakened as she aged—she had just turned eighty-nine—causing her narration to grow more succinct in recent years. However, if someone brought up a topic closer to her heart than others, she would expound as she used to, even if she was whispering by the time she finished.

Fifty years had passed since the two women had moved to Vermont, long-time companions and, more recently, legal spouses. It was a long journey—in many ways—from where they first met: a camp in Arkansas where their families were shipped at the start of the war with Japan. Hina left the camp angry and already jaded at a young age; Susan began searching for some positive meaning in life. They gravitated to each other and teaching.

Susan's previous attempt at marriage—meant to appease her traditionalist Japanese-born grandparents—ended quickly when her husband discovered she wouldn't be quitting her job to become the wife of his house, and children would have to wait. Her grandparents blamed the marriage's failure on their granddaughter's troublemaking friend—"that Hina!"—and removed her from their wills.

"How much money do war refugees have, anyway?" Susan asked her mother.

"Not much. It's the statement that's important. But you wouldn't know anything about that."

Susan inherited her sarcasm from her mother. Her father gave her his love and knowledge of plants. After the war ended he found work teaching botany at a community college in southern Illinois, where many of his students were on the GI Bill, a privilege they earned while his family sat out the war behind barbed wire fences. His daughter followed in his footsteps, teaching a new generation, many of whom found themselves drafted into another Asian war.

"I'm home," Susan called, opening the side door into the kitchen. She set her bags on a square butcher block table in the corner and crossed the small, bright room to the refrigerator, looking for a drink. With a bottle of root beer in hand, she turned to see her mate standing in the inner doorway that led to the dining room and the rest of the house.

"Hello, love." Susan set the bottle on the counter as the taller, thinner woman joined her.

While Susan was happy with her white hair cut short, Hina Okada's hair—a shade more silver than white—fell past her shoulders, today tied back in a ponytail. Her skin was darker than her partner's, a golden ochre to Susan's light amber.

"Did you get everything we needed?"

"I think so. And you, did you get everything for the tour tomorrow?"

Hina smirked. "You didn't notice how full the fridge is?"

Susan's expression turned sheepish. "I only noticed you got more soda. I'm sorry. But I got you this." She pulled the wind chimes from one of the bags.

Hina laughed and kissed her. "Thank you. They're beautiful. Here, let's take these bags to the greenhouse and set up the next experiment. Dinner's in the crockpot."

The two women unpacked the bags on an old, cluttered work table in the greenhouse. The building was long and narrow, its glass ceiling soaring above, welcoming the sky. The glass flowed down the side-walls, anchored into stone. The wall opposite the door was stone, too, serving as a heat sink. A large fan was mounted at the top. The close air smelled of earth and living greenery.

Tables of potted plants filled one side of the building. Plants rooted in raised beds of earth filled the other, along with a freestanding supply cabinet in the back corner and, in front of it, a paper-strewn desk and the table, now filled with clear plastic bags and jars. A paper label on each container held the fertilizer company's logo and a detailed ingredient list; nothing out of the ordinary, these lists. Given both women's experience and interest—as well as their desire to raise a beautiful, healthy collection of plants—the variety of combinations wasn't unusual.

Hina opened the cabinet and pulled out a tray of glass vials, each holding a few cc's of a more unusual green liquid; the green was different in each vial, ranging from a pale pastel to a virulent shade so bright it nearly glowed. Susan brought a few potted plants to the work table.

"Why are you smiling?" she asked as Hina filled several syringes, one from each vial.

"We're having such good luck with our experiments after all these years. Here and in the community. It bodes well."

"I hope you're right." Susan reached for a clipboard on

the desk. "Shall we begin?"

She took notes as Hina filled a syringe and injected the contents of one vial into one of the plants, the liquid vanishing under the epidermis of the plant's main stem. Hina did the same to the other plants on the table and then to two more growing in one of the raised beds. Afterward, she threw a handful of fertilizer on each.

"I'm guessing this'll be the quickest to respond," Susan pointed her pen at the plant Hina was working with just then, thick-stemmed and covered in dark green, bristly leaves.

"That's an easy guess. It's the most potent combination."

"Only because that fellow reacted the best to the stimuli in the last trial."

Hina chuckled. "I feel as if I should give it a treat, it behaved so well."

"They're all learning so quickly."

One of the plants on the table stretched, reaching into the air. Its leaves, long and thin, twisted like the fingers on a bellydancer's hand, seeming to sample the air.

"Hina, look." The two watched as the plant oriented itself toward them. Susan touched her wife's shoulder. "Move closer to it. See what happens."

Hina gave her ponytail a tug and did so. The plant's reaction was immediate. All its leaves reached for the woman, the tallest ones touching her face.

"Amazing!" she said, petting the plant.

"It must be the CO_2 you're giving off. Let's see."

Susan hurried to the cabinet and pulled out an air monitor. The device gave a reading of the various elements in the air, well within normal limits where she was standing. As she approached her partner and the plants on the work table, the numbers shot up.

"My goodness! This plant is releasing much more oxygen than usual."

Hina laughed. "Must be because it's mainlining the CO_2 I'm exhaling. I can feel it." She stepped back, leaving the plant's leaves to flail. "Here, see for yourself."

Susan took her place, stepping close to the enhanced plant. The leaves held still momentarily, assessing the change, but soon began to caress Susan's face almost as urgently as they had Hina's.

"How will we know when the other factors of the experiment are working...or not working?"

Susan squeezed her wife's shoulder, holding her close with one arm. "It might be a more subjective test. Recognition of us as friends, or even family...how will we know?"

"I already know. Can't you tell from its behavior?"

"It's breathing our exhalations, love. It can't do anything more. We haven't introduced the next step."

Hina crossed her arms and smirked. "Speak for yourself."

Susan tightened her grip on her wife's shoulder. Slowly, she turned her oldest friend to face her, now holding both of her shoulders. "What do you mean?"

Hina laughed. "Susan, you look scared to death. It's what we've been planning, isn't it? You've been so frustrated with the slowness of the dermal applications. I just jumped a little sooner than expected. I couldn't wait!"

"Are you...how do you feel? When did you do this?"

"Day before yesterday. And I feel okay. No differences I can measure easily." She turned back to the plant and stroked its leaves. "However, I can tell this plant senses family in me. I feel the connection, myself."

Susan looked from the plant to Hina and back. "If what you're sensing is true, our plans might work."

"They have no ears, and yet they hear. No eyes, and yet they can see. No brains, and yet—well, can they think? Can you think without a brain?" A slight smile wrinkled Susan's old face. "I might mention a politician or two, but that's a trite and easy target, isn't it?"

She walked further down the path weaving through the gardens, this year's tour in full swing. Billy had asked about her research again and she couldn't help but lecture a little. She stopped near a pair of flowering butterfly bushes. Their namesakes fluttered amidst the white and purple blooms.

"Consciousness comes in many ways to many creatures. Even this far into the twenty-first century, we're still tearing down Descartes' insistence that humans are the only animal that can think or feel emotion. It makes the research of plant intelligence all the more difficult.

"Tompkins and Bird's old *Secret Life of Plants* didn't help either," she continued. "So unscientific, most of that book. And those of us conducting research to see what plants actually experience? We were lumped together with the New Age fluffy-wuffy types." Some of the group clustered around her chuckled, encouraged by her indulgent smile.

"Can plants think?" a little girl asked, her fingers twisting her own cornrows.

"Like we can, you mean?"

The girl nodded.

"No. At least, not that anyone's confirmed. But they can learn. Their roots can discern friend or foe, family or enemy, in the soil. We can condition them to stimuli in such a way that they modify their behavior. They can communicate with each other and call for aid from other species through the chemicals they exude."

"What do you mean by family and enemies?" Billy asked.

"Well, you understand plant families, correct? Species related to each other will work together for survival and send out chemical signals warning against enemies.

"Those can be destructive insects, bacteria, or viruses. Other plants, too, can pose threats. Given time, plants can protect themselves from a variety of environmental dangers." She glanced at each member of her rapt audience.

"What about those enemy plants, professor? Can you make everyone get along?"

Susan smiled at her former student, a bald, middle-aged man she remembered as an average but eager student. "You raise a good point, Evan. If all plants sense kinship with each other, will that prevent even more destruction? Or would more aggressive plants—kudzu, for example—only take advantage of their new 'quick thinking' to expand their territories? It's an interesting puzzle." She fell silent as they passed the greenhouse sitting behind the house.

"What's in there?" The little girl pointed at the building, a fist still firmly wound in her cornrows.

"Quite a few things, dear, but nothing so interesting as lemonade and cookies, I wager." Susan pointed behind the girl and she turned to see tables laden with all sorts of goodies.

"For us?" she squeaked.

"Yes, indeed." Susan opened her arms. "Please, everyone, enjoy yourselves."

What's the fuss? It's not like I have to kill anyone.

Kim Ménard sped south on Route 7 in a small late-model rental car. Her conversation with the executives in Toronto had left her puzzled.

Standard corporate espionage, they had told her, and not even as elaborate as that could be. Break into a rural greenhouse—most likely unguarded—and steal a plant or two. For extra credit, find a memory device holding the documentation on said greenery. At most, there would be two old women to deal with. Really old. Like in their eighties or something.

I can do this kind of job in my sleep.

So, why were the suits so nervous? Her bosses had warned her to be careful—at the same time, reminding her that the folks writing the big checks would deny any knowledge of her activities if she were caught. They didn't even know her name.

Blah blah blah. Standard corporate ass-covering.

She slipped a mint into her mouth as she exited the highway into the rolling hills of Vermont. The GPS system led her through miles of tree-lined country roads, past farms and antique shops, gated driveways and tiny villages. Turning down a narrow lane, she let the car roll to a quiet stop a short distance from her target. Midsummer, the trees were a lush green fading to grey in the late twilight, not the flaming red and orange these forests were known for.

Still pretty, though. The leaf peepers are missing out only coming here in the middle of October. Not that the state lacked for summer tourists; traffic on the highway had been proof of that.

Ménard got out of the car and sniffed the air. It didn't smell like the city she was used to; she hoped she wouldn't start sneezing before the job was through. A bag hanging off her muscular shoulder held locksmith tools, gloves, a couple of flash drives, an old camera—on the list for an upgrade when this job paid off—gallon-sized freezer bags to hold any plants small enough to fit, and a few garbage bags for anything bigger. She patted the inner pocket of her light jacket where a semiautomatic pistol with a silencer rested.

It didn't hurt to be prepared. The Girl Scout motto, right?

After the tour group left and Hina finished her last cigarette of the day, the two women retired inside, Susan to read and Hina to talk with her plants. She spoke with them all every night before bed, petting their leaves and sniffing any blooms. "Tending to the children," she called it.

The interior of the retired professors' cottage was more lush than the outside. Plants from a myriad of ecosystems flourished—large-leafed elephant ears and birds of paradise, succulents of all sizes, from tiny jelly bean plants up to large flowering cacti. Several aloe plants grew on a kitchen window sill, ready for cutting, their juices to be smeared on a wound or a burn. Herbs, too, for cooking or for the ointments and lotions Hina made.

They had furnished the place with antiques found in thrift stores and backroad junk shops. Glass-fronted cases overflowed with books. The walls of the short hallway running from the living room to their bedroom were covered in photographs of their life together, beginning with their youthful meeting in Arkansas—two photographs, two families, puzzled, frightened, worried. Except for Hina: her young face showed only defiance.

It remained Susan's favorite image of her.

"Will you be long, love?" she asked from her easy chair. "I'm falling asleep over my book."

Hina found the worst part of aging to be the lack of sleep. Sleep had once been a great ocean trip she looked forward to every day. Eight or nine hours of peace and dreams, dreams she remembered and recorded in dozens of journals. Now, sleep was more like a multi-stop ferry ride. Two hours under, with one hour staring at the ceiling, a pattern that repeated until she was bored or morning came. She took naps to make up for her missing night voyages. They cured the sleep deprivation, but never brought back the journey she missed.

Two hours after drifting off, she woke.

Right on schedule.

She listened to the night noises—her bedmate's soft breath, crickets in the yard, owls calling to each other in the wood—hoping they would soothe her back to sleep. Instead, her brain turned to the work in the greenhouse. If she wasn't going to fall asleep anytime soon, maybe she could putter around out there for a while.

Oh, all right.

Getting out of bed, she slipped a pair of low boots onto her bare feet and a long denim coat over her pajamas and went outside.

The out-of-town Girl Scout rifled through the papers on the desk, looking for any references to the plants on the tables or in the dirt.

At least everything's labeled. But so much paper!

Ménard's bosses had told her these women were most likely old-fashioned in their record-keeping—the biochemist, Okada, had even written an essay once on her preference for handwritten research notes—but the idea still startled her. Nobody lived like this anymore. No one she knew, anyway. The world had moved on.

She waved the flashlight on her phone over the desk and yanked open drawers, looking for anything capable of holding more data than a plain sheet of paper.

Nothing. Was she going to have to search the house?

She sighed and refocused, reading the pages quickly but with more deliberation now, looking for clues as to which plants to take—the ones that could think.

She had refrained from rolling her eyes when her employers explained what she was to look for. She didn't bother restraining herself now—it was all so absurd—although conducting this search in a dark greenhouse on a dead-end road in the middle of nowhere didn't make her any less wary. Odd sounds kept distracting her.

A breeze in the fan.

Mice in the leaves.

Bats on the roof.

She pushed the distractions away and was rewarded, discovering a clipped-together sheaf of papers describing in some detail the latest research these old women were on about. Each plant was labeled and grouped according to the tests they were conducting: hearing, communicating—

"Problem solving, too? Seriously?" She looked up from the papers, squinting at the cramped space. Had it been this crowded near the desk when she first sat down?

"Don't be stupid," she told herself, leaving the desk to hunt for the plants listed in the notes. She stumbled on her first step and shone the flashlight at her feet. A vine stretched from the soil across the floor, twining around a table leg. She stepped over it, turning her attention to the potted plants. The first two listed on the page were the first two she looked at. Each one went into a freezer bag and into her pack.

The next plant on the list, though, wasn't to be found on the tables. She frowned, casting the flashlight's beam into the miniature jungle on the other side of the central path. But these plants wore labels, too, she discovered, little pieces of white paper here and there caught in the light. White strands like spaghetti in the dirt reflected the light, too.

"Roots?"

Another mouse scurried behind her, or so it sounded. She spun around but saw nothing but vines on the floor. *Were there this many before?*

Shaking her head, she got back to work. The next plant she sought stood three back in the second row. She pulled a trowel and a trash bag from her bag. *Three plants and these notes should give the techies plenty to work with.*

The last plant she wanted stood a couple of feet tall, its stems thick and covered in bristly leaves. Not nettle sharp, but they didn't look comfortable to take hold of, even in the dim light. She paused to slip on a pair of leather gloves.

Grabbing the plant, she held it away from her and dug around it, loosening the soil.

"Ow!" A loose branch brushed her arm, scratching the skin. "Damn it! This better not be some kind of poison ivy."

The leaves didn't match her memory of poison ivy. They were shaggy and dull, not flat and shiny. "Something's not right." She sat back on her haunches, looking at her arm as it flushed red, the pain growing. She inhaled. No trouble there, no allergic reaction. She held still for a few more breaths. The pain in her arm wasn't getting any worse but it wasn't going away either.

"Okay, let's get this one out and call it good." Ignoring her discomfort, she loosened more of the dirt, but when she grabbed the main stem again to pull out the plant, pain grabbed her—

What the hell?

Startled, she looked down. A dozen strands of the spaghetti-like roots flowed over one of her boots, rooted in the dirt on both sides, but they weren't causing the pain. A vine twined low around her ankle, tightening as it worked its way around, was the culprit. She grabbed at it and the roots, trying to tear them away. The roots broke easily, but the thick vine only tightened further as she struggled against it.

Hina took her time reaching the greenhouse. She'd already broken one hip a few years ago, learning the hard way her body was only growing more fragile as she aged. She stopped part way down the path, puzzled to see a faint light in the out-building. It shifted around but not in the dancing way a firefly might. And then someone inside sneezed.

She rubbed her face, wondering who might be visiting, un-invited. She chuckled, thinking it could be the curious little girl from the garden tour, but that made no sense. Her parents would have put her to bed hours ago. She walked on, only to pause at the door, wondering if she should wake her wife. Her braver self took over, opening the door a bit. The light was steady now but fainter.

"Who's there?" she asked. Taking a hair tie from around her wrist, she bound her hair back as she peered through the doorframe.

A fragile voice replied, "Help?"

Hina frowned and opened the door wider, taking a short-handled shovel from a rack nearby. "Who's there?" she de-manded again, entering the building.

"I'm...I'm stuck."

Hina's frown deepened as she walked further into the greenhouse, noticing the empty gaps on the tables and finally the disheveled desk. She turned toward the light source, see-ing the crouched figure in the dirt, and raised the shovel in defense. "Who the hell are you?"

A pale face returned her sharp look. "I'm...you don't know me."

"No? Stand up so I can get a better look at you."

The stranger brushed the hair out of her eyes. "I can't."

Hina tilted her head to one side. "Why not?"

The woman sighed. "The plants are holding me."

"Oh, for heaven's sake. That's ridiculous." She paused, considering her words, her eyes widening a little. "Wait a moment."

She hurried back to the door and switched on the overhead lights. The intruder, a short, muscular blonde in her early thirties, blinked in the sudden brightness. Hina returned, shovel still in hand. "Now, let's see what we're dealing with." She studied the scene in front of her. "Well, look at you."

The first vine was now wrapped snugly around the interloper's calf and knee, the leading tendril exploring her thigh. A second runner had grabbed her other bent leg, holding it tight to the earth. More root strands were weaving across it, tying the leg to the soil.

Hina laughed. "You're a modern-day Gulliver."

The woman strained against her bindings. "Your plants are attacking me."

"I know!"

The young woman flinched at the elder's enthusiasm. "I think I'm having an allergic reaction, too. Will they kill me?"

Hina ignored the question and rushed to her desk. "Fascinating." She cast the plants' captive a disparaging glance. "You've got my papers all out of order, you know."

"What the hell is wrong with you?"

Hina leaned the shovel against the desk and folded her arms. "Young lady, you broke into my greenhouse and attempted to steal my work. I suggest you show a little humility."

The stranger sighed, forcing her anger down. "Will you let me go?"

"Of course." Hina paused. "Although it may not be up to me. You don't realize what a breakthrough this is, I see. Why would you? Do you know what you were trying to steal?"

"Something about thinking plants?"

Hina's excitement grew. "Yes! Plants thinking—not on our level—but on our time scale. Quick enough to do this. Sense an intruder and react in time to prevent or limit any damage it—you—might cause. Isn't it wonderful?"

"Well—"

"Ah, perhaps not so much for you."

"Not exactly, no." She tried to pull the vine away from her thigh. Her fingers got a good hold on it, enough to flex the thing and try to bend it back the other way, but they slipped and the vine tightened its grip, extending its reach, squeezing tighter. "Damn it!" She glared at the old woman. "Is this what your research is for—attack plants?"

Hina chuckled. "Not at all. That aspect is just a useful surprise. Science works that way now and then."

"Are you going to help me or not?"

Hina looked up from her notes, refocusing on the living creatures in front of her. "Yes. Certainly. This is a delicate matter, though. And I need assistance." She stood, a mischievous smile on her lips. "I'm not as young as I used to be."

Hina left her alone, the vines and roots continuing their work. The trapped woman tore at the roots fairly easily, shredding them enough that she could move her foot, but the vine held firm. One more twist pulled her leg out from under her, dropping her to both knees.

She kept struggling, frightened by the pins and needles running up and down her legs. She thought she was making some headway, forcing it to let go a little bit, when the silver-haired woman returned. She wasn't alone.

"Young lady, are you still here?"

She groaned. "Yes."

"What did I tell you, Susan?" A cigarette dangled from her lips.

The newcomer, Susan, shorter, rounder, and dressed in a heavy, paisley bathrobe, bent down and stuck her face into the younger woman's. "Who are you?"

"Kim Ménard," she replied, her tone defeated.

"Who sent you here?"

The bound woman said nothing more.

"Huh. They must pay you well, to keep quiet in a situation like this." Susan stepped back, touching Hina's arm.

"She has a gun."

Her mate moved closer to see, then reached for the weapon inside Ménard's jacket. Ménard tried to hit her, reaching back to swing her arm. Her forward movement stopped with a jerk and she looked up: another vine had twisted around her wrist.

"Damn it!"

Hina laughed. "Did you see that? What did I tell you? Our work is proving itself."

"To protect—"

"To protect us! The skin treatments are working better than we thought."

"Do you think—?"

"We should try an injection on her. I suffered no ill effects. If it works again—"

"Hina!" Susan hissed. "You can't be serious." She gave the young woman a quick glance and pulled her partner aside, both of them stumbling over the vines on the floor.

Hina tried to laugh. "Be careful, dear. Neither of us needs another visit to the doctor."

Susan replied in a sharp whisper. "We should call the sheriff."

Hina's expression darkened as she tapped ash from her cigarette. "And throw away this opportunity? If this works, it's further evidence we're on the right path." She rubbed her fingers together. "And we would have an avenue into her employers."

"We don't even know who they are."

"If the serum works, she'll tell us."

"If she knows. A lot of layers could lie between her and the corporation that wants our research."

Hina's gaze flicked to Ménard and she scratched her nose. "Plants know how to dig through layers."

Susan shook her head. "I don't like this. So many things could go wrong."

"And so many things could go right! Also, consider this. If this one's arrested, someone else will be sent to succeed where she failed. We may not be so lucky next time."

Susan squinted at her mate and rubbed her cheeks. "Where

would we keep her while the serum's working?"

Hina tried to hide her small grin. When Susan's arguments turned to questions, getting her way was near at hand. "The study?"

"In the house with us? Too dangerous!"

"Only the first day or so—I'm sure of it. Forty-eight hours in, she won't be antagonistic at all."

"But what if it doesn't work?"

"Then we'll call the sheriff."

"And face kidnapping and assault charges."

"Susan, it's going to work!"

"What are you talking about?" Ménard asked.

"Nothing to worry yourself over." Hina stubbed her cigarette out in a copper ashtray on the desk and searched the pocket of her denim jacket, retrieving a ring of keys. She unlocked the supply cabinet and pulled out a small vial from the middle shelf. The vial's contents glowed green.

Ménard's eyes widened as the old woman stuck a syringe into the container. She struggled against the vines. "What the hell is that?"

Hina didn't answer her question directly. "We have a proposition for you. If you agree to it, you'll contribute something much more positive to the world than the business that sent you. If we're successful, you'll understand immediately what we're trying to accomplish. We'll be kin. If everyone is kin, this planet may finally have peace."

Ménard frowned at the two women. Her bosses hadn't told her they were crazy. "And if I don't agree?"

"We call the authorities," Susan said.

"And hope the vine around your leg doesn't reach your throat before they arrive."

"You wouldn't let it—"

"You don't know me, young lady. Don't push it."

Susan hugged herself and Ménard swallowed. "Okay," She replied slowly. "What am I agreeing to, exactly?"

Hina held up the syringe. "This serum will alter your biochemistry in such a way that it senses kinships with anyone sharing the same chemical signature. As it is in the plant world, kinship encourages cooperation. Can you imagine how different the world would be without humans fighting over everything?"

"You think you're going to create world peace?"

Susan interjected. "If humans don't learn to cooperate, climate change will kill us all."

"Aren't we working on that?"

Susan's lips twitched in a cynical smile. "We're watching Florida sink before our eyes and most of the Pacific islands are already gone. We could work harder."

Ménard pulled against the vines to no avail. "I don't want to be one of your pod people."

"It's not like that," Hina said. "We're not fascists. Your free will remains intact, but you'll be able to see relationships and alternatives you didn't see before."

One vine had reached Ménard's groin and was weaving around her hips like a sluggish boa constrictor.

"You'll let me go if I take your shot?"

"Yes! Well, shortly thereafter. The serum takes full effect in a couple days."

"A couple days?" Panic clenched her chest. "You're going to hold me until then?"

"Until we're sure the serum is working, yes." Susan gave Hina a worried look. "But we have a nice room for you. And we're both good cooks."

I'll break out before you can cook one meal, crazy lady.

"The shot won't hurt me?" She plucked at the vine now working its way around her stomach.

"Not at all. I've already given myself the same injection. I'm fine."

"How is this connected to the attack plants? Will I become another of your watchdogs?"

Susan chuckled. "Two different sera at work, Ms. Ménard. We gave this plant both. You'll only get one."

"The kinship one."

"That's right."

Ménard fell silent, weighing her options. *They were probably lying; they're definitely nuts.* But it was the only sure way to get loose. The vine wasn't stopping. "Will you call off your vines?"

"Heh. Not before the injection. You'll pardon our caution."

Ménard sighed. "All right. Let's do this."

Susan rolled up the sleeve on her free arm and wiped an alcohol swab on the freckled skin. "Make a fist, please."

Ménard did so and Hina stabbed the needle into a vein in the crook of her elbow, the plunger shooting green liquid into the bluish-red showing through the skin. She stepped back, the syringe between her fingers. Ménard's eyes squeezed shut and her body tensed, waiting. All was quiet, except for the bats on the roof and the mice in the leaves.

"What am I supposed to feel?"

"Nothing yet. Now's let's see if we can get you loose."

"If?"

Susan patted her shoulder. "We've never done this before."

"Oh, great."

Hina crouched beside her, petting the vine with her tapered fingers. She murmured, too, in a singsong way, sweet-talking the plant into letting go. The shaggy leaves brushed her face and she smiled.

"Be careful," Ménard said. "Those leaves gave me quite a rash."

"Of course, they did. You were a stranger."

What am I now?

After a minute or so, Ménard felt the vine's grip lessen. Bit by bit, it retreated. She sucked in her breath as blood flowed back through her leg, waking the numbness.

"Damn it!" She hopped up, shaking her legs and arm, dancing in place.

Susan couldn't help but laugh. "You'll need to walk around a bit to get all the feeling back." She bent to help Hina regain her feet.

"Before we lock you up," she said.

Ménard stopped dancing.

Susan and Hina helped each other back to the house while keeping a close watch on their guest. Hina made an obvious show of handling Ménard's gun. They led her down the hall, past the photographs, to a small room next to theirs. More overflowing bookcases lined the walls, along with a bureau and a daybed on one end and a desk at the other. Pots of dark green plants sat on both the desk and the bureau.

Susan squeezed by them to remove two slim handhelds from the desk. Ménard snorted in frustration.

"You *do* have digital devices. I was told—"

Hina looked at the tablets in Susan's hand and then at her. "Your employers think we're Luddites?"

Susan chuckled. "Because we're old, I expect."

"I wonder what else they got wrong," Hina mused as she handed the gun to Susan. "Don't let her get close to you, love."

She gave Ménard a knowing smile before she headed down the hall. "You'll have to tell us about the folks you work for sometime."

"Yeah, sure."

"I hope this room will be comfortable." Susan said, eying Ménard warily from the doorway. "I'm sorry all we have is the daybed."

"I guess I'll have to make do." She studied the room, glaring at the plants. "Am I safe from those?"

Susan glanced at the greenery on the bureau and smiled. "Oh yes. They're part of our control group. Perfectly safe."

Ménard grunted quietly and edged closer to the old woman.

"Susan," Hina called from outside. "Lock her in and come help me, will you?"

"Yes, dear." She backed into the hall and Ménard noticed the lockset for the first time.

"Electronic? Were you expecting me?"

"Don't be silly. All the doors in the house have keyless locksets. Thank goodness for modern technology."

She shut the door with a tight click, leaving Ménard to stew in her own frustration. The tools she needed to pick that lock were in her bag. On the other side of the door. That left the window above the desk. Would it be keyless, too?

She rushed to check and smiled to discover an old-fashioned latch. But as her hand touched the window, her view went black with a dull, wooden thud. Ménard stumbled back, cursing as a drill outside whined, screwing the covering in place.

The morning dawned early, although to Kim Ménard, in her dark cell, it remained deep night. For the most part. A tear in the plywood covering the one window let in a slim slice of pale sunlight, but she slept on, unnoticing. Nothing troubled her till her bladder's urgent need pressed her to consciousness.

"Where am I?" she muttered. She couldn't tell; opening her eyes made no difference. Dark was dark. She wasn't even sure the thin line of glimmering light was real, until she watched it further deepen from a pale blue-white to a golden yellow.

Vermont. The old women.

Trapped.

It all came back now. She rolled onto her back, diffusing some of the tension on her lower belly. Her brain kept spinning, however, furious at what she had allowed to happen the night before. Things would have to change for the better this morning, somehow.

Someone knocked on the door and she sat up, tense, squinting in the dark. "Yes? Who is it?"

"Breakfast," a voice answered. "Stay away from the door." A flood of light fell into the room as the door clicked open. Ménard covered her eyes, waiting for them to adjust to the change. "Now, stay on the bed."

She could smell food: eggs, melted butter on toast, fruit of some sort. "Are you hungry?" The voice drew closer and her stomach grumbled in answer.

"I really have to pee."

"Hm, all right," the voice answered. "Just a minute." Ménard looked up to see that it was Susan, the one who had showed up later the night before. She set the tray of food down on the desk and returned to the doorway. "Now, come with me."

Ménard rose from the daybed, finger-combing her blonde hair and studying Susan's small, round frame. She approached, slowly at first, and then in a rush, pushing Susan aside and breaking for the hall. She made it only a few feet.

"Nice try." The other woman, Hina, was also in the hall, pointing her own gun at her, no sign of hesitance, her arms strong as she held it in both hands. Ménard stopped, a frustrated sigh her only response.

"Are you all right, love?"

Susan leaned against the door-frame, brushing herself off. "I'm fine. Good thing I'd already set the food down."

"I'm sure. Now, you—" Hina returned her attention to their houseguest. "We're going to have to restrain you, aren't we?"

Ménard wrinkled her nose in disgust and raised her hands to her waist. "Wait. I—"

"You'll be good? No, I don't think we should take that chance. Do you, Susan?"

Susan joined her, squeezing her arm. "If we're not going to let her go, it seems the only way to be safe."

"We've already given her the shot. We can't let her go yet."

"I know, but...she's dangerous, Hina. We shouldn't have done this."

"She's dangerous now. That will change."

"I hope you're right."

Hina nodded. "I am. You'll see. But we need to keep her from doing this again. Would you get the cable ties from the toolbox while I keep our guest company?"

Ménard rubbed her nose, her shoulders slumping. "Will you let me pee, please?"

"Of course." Hina waved the gun toward a door partway down the hall.

"How are you feeling?"

Susan had returned with her lunch: an egg salad sandwich and a root beer, Hina hovering behind her, still armed. Ménard sat huddled on the bed, one arm bound to a rail of the headboard with a thick plastic cable tie.

"Fine," she grumbled. It seemed that way, at least. At most she felt a little warm: maybe a light fever or perhaps the embarrassment of her predicament. Even if she managed to get out of this in any respectable fashion, she would never live down getting into it in the first place.

"I'm glad to hear it. Hina tells me the transition will be painless."

Ménard glanced at the other woman looming over Susan's shoulder as she took a bite of the sandwich. She said nothing.

Susan turned to Hina and motioned her away. "Let me try to talk to her," she whispered. Hina frowned but retreated so their prisoner couldn't see her. Susan remained in the doorway, studying her.

"Do you need to use the bathroom again?"

Ménard shook her head. Susan scratched her nose, sorting through the questions she wanted to ask.

"What got you into this line of work?"

Ménard bit into her sandwich again. "The money's good."

"Ah."

"And it's exciting." She smiled ruefully. "Although I'm usually better at it than this."

Susan chuckled, crossing her arms. "Don't feel bad. You ran into something completely unexpected. If you had packed pruning shears in that bag of yours, things might have gone differently."

"The way those plants moved? I don't know."

"That was amazing, wasn't it?"

Ménard sipped her drink. "It surprised you?"

"It did. Hina and I have been working in this field for sixty years. It's only now that we're seeing breakthroughs." She smiled. "And they're coming fast. It's quite gratifying."

Ménard swallowed the last bite of her sandwich. "What are your plans for me?"

"Plans?" Susan chewed on her lower lip. "Nothing very definitive, as we said last night. I am sorry for the position you've put yourself in. I hope you'll soon understand why we've done what we've done."

Ménard rubbed her bound wrist and said nothing.

The afternoon crept by. Even though Ménard's kidnappers left the light on and the smaller one brought her magazines to pass the time, she spent most of it staring at the ceiling, cursing herself and trying to think of any way out.

I can do this kind of job in my sleep, huh? What a joke.

She sat up in a rage, throwing the magazines on the floor, glaring at the plants on the bureau again. "And what about you guys? When are you going to start talking to me and telling me all about my long-lost relatives? Jesus, what a mess!"

She stood and dragged the bed closer to the door. Focused and still, she waited.

Susan returned a few hours later with her guest's dinner, stewed chicken and dumplings and iced tea. She opened the door to find Ménard and the daybed a few inches away.

"Oh, my goodness."

Ménard told herself to get going, grab the woman before the other one could do anything about it and force them to let her go. But something held her back. She could really hurt this woman. Was she certain she wanted to?

"Everything all right?" Hina asked from the hall. Susan raised a questioning eyebrow at Ménard, who shook her head, trying to clear it.

"Yeah, fine." She pushed the bed to give Susan room to enter and sat down, scratching her head and wondering what had just happened.

Susan handed her the tray. "Are you sure you're all right?"

"I think so." She sampled the stew. "Solitary confinement doesn't suit me, I guess."

"It shouldn't be much longer." Susan stood in the doorway, waiting for any new sudden moves. "Any other developments?"

"My rash is clearing up."

"That's a good sign."

"Does it mean I'm being absorbed into your plant collective?"

"It doesn't work like that, like we said. You'll still be you."

"I'll still know my family and friends?"

"Of course. You'll also find that your family has grown larger."

Ménard pondered that as she slurped her stew.

"You have a close family?"

"Kind of. My job keeps me away a lot."

"Where are they—you—from?"

"Québec, near Sherbrooke. Dad's a teacher, Mom's a programmer." She gave a short laugh. "They wanted me to work in something steady like advertising or insurance. Not for me."

Susan smiled. "My family wanted a more traditional life for me, too."

"Did they accept your choices?" Ménard twisted the napkin in her hand, surprised at how important the answer was to her.

Susan shook her head. "No, not really. My father, at least, understood my love of plants. Other things…were too alien to him…to them. It frightened them to be that different."

Ménard nodded. "My folks are frightened of a lot of things. Our family's been settled in our little town since the Brits founded it. No one's left besides a couple of cousins…and me."

"The Brits?"

"Yeah, British loyalists who came north after your revolution."

My revolution? Susan looked at her with some amusement, before returning to the main thread of the conversation. "Do your parents know what you do for a living?"

Ménard gave her a wry smile. "They know it's not advertising or insurance." Her expression dimmed. "They worry about me."

"Of course, they do. All good parents worry, even if—especially if—they don't understand what their child is up to."

"Will this serum make it easier to understand each other?"

"We hope so."

Susan joined Hina at their breakfast table and sipped the fresh, black coffee in front of her. Phoebes and robins twittered outside. "She wouldn't talk to me this morning."

Hina took a bite of mushroom omelet. "Do you think she's ill?"

"Maybe. She was still in bed and kept her back to me. I left her food on the desk."

"Hm. We should check on her after breakfast. She might be having a bad reaction, or it could be a trick."

"I don't know. The last couple times we've talked, she seemed to be loosening up."

"All part of her plan, perhaps. I don't like how she was waiting for you last night."

"Okay, love. You go in, but I'll be standing right here with the gun if she tries anything."

"All right." Susan took a breath and opened the door. The lights were out.

"Kim, dear, how are you feeling?"

"Susan?"

"Yes. May I turn on the light?"

"Sure." The bedclothes shifted as Kim sat up, squinting as

the light came on.

"Well?" Hina asked from the doorway. "How are you? You had us worried."

Kim looked at Susan and Hina, her eyes wide. "I'm fine, I think. But it's almost too big to comprehend." She swallowed. "The air tastes...green."

Kim Ménard left the greenhouse with two plants—ones that hadn't done well in the researchers' trials—one slim memory disc with only the vaguest information and a small sample box. Nestled in a corner of her bag, it contained vials of serum. The plants and one set of vials she would give to her employers, successfully completing her mission. The other set she would use herself, on her employers and, when she discovered them, the people who had actually hired her. This was her new mission.

"The scientists will inoculate their plants, you will inoculate the scientists," Hina explained. "More serum will be created, more inoculations. We've already begun with our small village, through Hina's lotions and ointments—a slower process—but your company and its connections offer a much larger, potentially paradigm-shifting opportunity. Whether integrated into the food supply, the cosmetic industry, or a vaccine program, your work will help us reach so many more people. And the irony that a group antagonistic and grasping of our work becomes our closest friend isn't lost on us."

"Whatever I can do to help," Kim had replied.

Alone in the car, she wondered how she had changed.

Other than a sore body and a scratchy arm, all she felt was contentment and a sense of purpose, a feeling she was doing more than a job, more than she had ever felt stealing corporate secrets. The plan of peace, Susan called it.

She wondered what her parents would think.

The grey parrot stretched his wings and hopped onto a higher perch, disturbed by the breeze when Susan opened the shop door. It squawked as she approached.

"What say we be friends, eh?" Susan pulled a small green nugget—freshly baked that morning—out of her pocket; holding it by the tips of her calloused fingers, she offered it to the grey parrot. "Want a treat?"

The bird tilted its head and studied the offering with a suspicious greyish-yellow eye.

"Go on, give it a try." He hopped to a lower perch and reached for the treat, taking it gently in its beak. "That's a good—" The parrot abruptly spread its wings and squawked at her, dropping the nugget on the floor. Startled, the old woman stepped back.

Billy came out from the back. "Hello, Dr. Yamamoto. Is Tony bothering you?"

"No, Billy. He just didn't like the present I made for him. Silly bird." She turned toward the counter. "May I place an order?"

"Sure thing." He opened a drawer and retrieved an order pad. "How's the research coming?"

She smiled. "Very well. A little bit of progress every day."

Sensorium

Jacqueline Koyanagi

Yora spends her first night in cultural realignment training thinking about the isolation of a life lived between stars.

The Tagli came to Ila, her planet, ten years ago, having crossed unthinkably vast distances in slow increments, bodies and vacuum separated by a mere skin's breadth of material. Full generations had passed with no knowledge of ground and sky. And then they came, a bombardment of unfamiliar life on Yora's planet, their twisting ships suspended over fourteen cities like itinerant gods.

Yora's thirdmate, Fen, had been among the first to see them. She was dressed in pristine red to observe an open trial, a bag of her secondmate's steamed perri dumplings in hand to last the day. The way Fen told it, the skies parted for the curved bellies of those strange vessels; they seemed to shiver from their rippling light. For some time she believed she was looking at some rare meteorological phenomenon before her brain caught up with her eyes.

Each time Fen repeats this story to her hadir, she recalls the astringent orange smell of the man who stood next to her in the thickening crowd, the exact cream-and-gold color of the clouds wreathing the vessels, the vibration of trains beneath her feet. She always adds that only later did she realize she had forgotten the weight of the dumplings in her hand,

and left them to be trampled on the ground. Their second-mate, Relo, now makes the dumplings every year on the anniversary of the Tagli arrival while Fen tells the same story, ending it by wondering where the orange-scented man is, and whether he noticed her.

Today, the ships remain over those fourteen cities on Ila, with their calcareous filaments gnarling down to the surface like great roots, blooming pale biotic settlements that change with the needs of the colonists. Yora has never seen inside the ships or the colony on the outskirts of Hinn, her city-state. As a child, she ran close to the border with two of her friends, heart pounding faster the closer they drew to the white wall demarcating Tagli holdings. Eventually, they beat the chalky surfaces with their fingers and ran away. Bravery came easily in tapping and shouting when their neighbors had no sense of hearing.

The colonists may lack auditory sensory organs, but without chromatophores, it is the people of Ila who lack voices, and with barely any ability to detect polarized light, they can see very little compared to the Tagli. And of course, the oxygen needs of the Tagli are different—higher—than that of the Ilan population, necessitating some amount of artificial atmosphere in the settlements. Neither these divergent physical needs nor strained communications lent themselves to close interaction, but Yora craved it.

As she grew older, the games stopped but Yora's desire to know the colonists remained. She studied mathematics and engineering beneath the border's yawning bonelike edifices, watching them illuminate from within. Filigree patterns chased each other across coralline ogees, signifying some alien message. Every Tagli home, from ship to settlement, was born of their bodies. How many pieces of flesh had contributed to their environments? How must it feel to give of yourself and see it grow into a colony? Questions thrummed in the background of Yora's mind while she worked through her studies.

Even well into the middle of her life, she talks through her problems in the shadow of those glittering arches, though only now does she receive a reply.

The city's Renewal Initiative has conscripted cyberneticists and psycholinguists from Hinn and several of its principalities, many of them selected by the Tagli. A growing insurgency in one of Hinn's southern territories—where Tagli colonists had grown their settlement directly into the heart of the town—meant that Hinn could no longer afford a separatist approach. Working with the Tagli to quell unrest will require intimate cooperation.

Yora is among the chosen, an initial group of ten whittled down from a larger pool of candidates plucked out of academies and research centers across Hinn. People whose skills and interests appealed to the Tagli.

The faces of her two mates darken in the failing daylight. They cannot pass beyond the temporary opening in the border, the yawning tunnel that will lead her to the Tagli and close behind her.

"How do we know we understand what they're saying?" Relo says. He doesn't look at Yora while he folds and refolds the jacket he brought for her. "How do we know they aren't dangerous in there? We don't really know how they think. We don't even know if we *can*—"

"We don't," Yora says, and takes the jacket from him. She will not be able to bring it all the way inside with her, but he doesn't need to know that. "But this is how we'll change that."

"It doesn't have to be you," he says.

Fen takes his hand, then takes Yora's with her other. "Yes, it does."

Yora joins the circle by linking her free arm with Relo, and the three touch foreheads. "Thank you for trusting me in this."

Cultural realignment will last four months, during which Yora will bond with one Tagli colonist and implement the diplomacy solution the Initiative asks for. Her body and mind will make room for the Tagli just as her Tagli partner's body and mind will make room for Ilan ways.

Realignment will occur along a timeline carefully scheduled to minimize the psychological fallout of each participant while maximizing interpersonal attachment. Hinnali participants would be given more time to adapt to a changing physiology than the Tagli. A generous gesture.

For the duration of their bonding, Yora was told, the Tagli-Hinnali pair will exist together in a unit: two small, Tagli-grown rooms connected by a sphincter in the wall that would only sometimes close to offer solitude.

Yora hears the door open but finishes pinning her hair up while waiting for the roomlight to flicker across the walls. Responding to the sound alone would be rude. Two beats pass, and then she sees the roomlight.

Before she looks, already a mossy, damp scent curls around her. She stands up from the Hinnali-style padded bed, turns, and forces herself to make a greeting gesture before she looks directly at the Tagli. Again, no speech.

She breathes and centers herself. Then, she lets herself see.

Everyone studied Tagli captures and stills in their childhood mandatory sensitivity courses. Yora had memorized them. Even so, her expectations cower before the wonder she feels.

One horizontal pupil draws in her gaze immediately; with eyes set on opposite sides of the head and proportionately massive, she cannot see the other from where she stands. Tagli were known to have a double-layered retina at the back of the eye, and three visual pigments much like Yora's species. From here, it looks like a slick of dark water pooling in a well of amber skin. The way it looks at her strips her down.

The Tagli's long forelimbs, midlimbs with dual digits, glimmering skin with hidden polarized depths of meaning—these are all well-known physiological attributes, the sight of which now hooks onto her mind and surges into an adrenaline rush. A sheen of pale light haloes nerim forelimbs and pulses with nerim movements.

Human-made biomechanical attachments hide this Tagli's spiracles, aiding neris in breathing the same air as Yora. Already part of her mind goes to work designing something more efficient to replace the overhuge augs complicating the Tagli's breathing, but she stops herself to wonder why this biologically-driven species has not yet adapted to Ilan oxygen levels.

Her Tagli partner moves through the entrance with those precision four-beat steps and touches either side with nerim midlimb digits. Yora does not flinch backward, even as the scent of her partner deepens from faint moss to decaying vegetation, a slippery, pungent smell that coats her throat. Acrid notes drift up beneath it and she realizes it's her own sweat.

Fractal patterns spiral outward from the Tagli's digits along the walls, a complex creeping vine of communication. Yora's neurolinguistic aug tells her this translates roughly into a warm welcome, but all the nuance and mathematical beauty dissolve at the borders of her understanding. This tragic loss of meaning is what Yora intends to rectify.

Nerim skin ripples with color in curling forms across the elaborate hindfrill. Several of nerim mid-body tentacles reach forward and flick deliberately, and a fresh scent like wet stone breaks through the otherwise cloying air. Again Yora's aug translates as best it can: *There is an overarching sense of positive regard and concern for your well-being or comfort.*

She is reminded of Relo. *We don't really know how they think.*

Yora motions gratitude in response. Less eloquent than a pre-verbal toddler by comparison, she lacks two out of the three critical layers of Tagli language. The only remaining avenue—gesturing—is woefully incomplete with only two limbs for speech, and far less flexible ones at that. The attachés say the Tagli are patient, so Yora does her best to stay optimistic. As much as Ilan people wonder over these chromatophoric light displays and conscious chemical emissions, the Tagli supposedly feel a sort of taboo fascination with the sound-based languages of Ila.

As instructed, they take each other in without further comment, habituate themselves to the presence of the other.

Yora had been assigned to this Tagli just as neri had been assigned to Yora. The colonists had felt her child-self pounding at the wall, seen the curiosity in her adult body of work, tasted her eagerness in the air around her. They had watched her as she had watched them. She is part of a small, silent population of the observed: those whose lives were on a path of convergence with the Tagli, whether they craved it or not.

The roomlight dims. Reddish blush glows across nerim forefrill.

Neural ports arrive with information. The Hinn designation for the Tagli's name is Sel. Hinnali ports typically list gender, title, and hadir status and rank, but this is altogether different. Tagli have reproductive roles but no gender, much like the Jan to the south of Hinn. Linguists say the Tagli similarly have a social classification that reflects something the Hinn do not have a concept for, although the linguists can't seem to offer a straightforward explanation of what that concept might be. Something to do with the alignment of chromatophores on the skin and how one is inclined to express certain concepts, like tone or personality.

Both participants are instructed at length not to fixate on the other's unrelatable social constructs despite any impulse they might have to do so.

Yora's neural port informs her that Sel's reproductive type is what the Hinn are calling "nurse," which involves injecting nerim chemical signature into a fertilized egg in the early stages of gestation, preparing the way for parental bonding. Being privy to this information makes Yora an intimate of Sel by default; the reproductive role of Tagli individuals is considered part of the private sphere of social interaction. This makes Yora akin to a mate for Sel.

With a space in her own hadir for a fourthmate, Yora tries to imagine Sel filling that space. Sel will not bear Hinnali children. No one in her hadir will, if Sel is to take the fourthmate spot, regardless of whether neri will actually function as such. What will a hadir without the potential for Ilan children look like? Yora tries to shape her thoughts around these possibilities, but her mind fatigues at its cultural edges.

She hopes her decision to accept this diplomatic role was the right one to make as firstmate. She believes it will bring them prosperity and social currency, even more than Hinnali children would, but she can't know that for certain.

Sel has no professional title to the Tagli, but the Hinn use the term genist to describe what neri does. Where Yora develops cybernetic enhancements to human bodies, Sel programs sloughed flesh and bone to biogen the latticework and overlays that grow their structures and medical treatments alike. The blood of both their vocations is electrical impulse, a straightforward enough common ground. Sel helped develop some of the initial Tagli programming for the Renewal Initiative by synthesizing the flesh of both Tagli and human, whereas Yora's team has taken the psycholinguistic research of others and applied it toward a cybernetic solution to communication.

Sel's hindfrill shivers in anticipation-questioning, nerim body leaning forward until their two chests are uncomfortably close. Anxiety pulses up Yora's back at the sheer size of Sel's body moving in front of her, but again she breathes through the adrenaline rush. It abates, allowing her to gesture an approximate sense of appreciation and honor without shaking.

At least, that's what her people say these gestures mean. Tagli emotional axes may have no accurate parallels to *appreciation* or *honor* or anything else she might want to communicate. Linguists tell her the gestures signify Tagli concepts moreso than Hinnali, and that her understanding of the movements is a translation rather than the other way around. Either way, she has little choice but to trust that Sel understands.

What she means to say is, "Thank you for receiving me, it's an honor."

Sel lowers all hindlegs and forelegs, dropping nerim height slightly, while pale warm colors shiver between the two great eyes. Faint chalky notes tinge the air.

The aug translates for Yora again. *There is an intent to be soothing, combined with an intent to create [unknown].* She can't guess what the missing concept might be.

Agreement, Yora gestures, deciding diplomacy is more important than her own comprehension. *Yes, thank you.*

Their first joint project will introduce chromatophoric biogens into Yora's skin, opening at least one additional avenue for communication. In the meantime, she will gesture until her hands grow sore if necessary.

Colors drip from the walls, onto the floor, onto Sel, where it contours nerim body as neri shapes it into meaning. There are separate threads of understanding when color emerges from within versus imbuing from without; Sel demonstrates the latter for Yora. Specks of light shimmer across the floor in parabolic dances, slithering up onto Sel's forelimbs. They pulse there along nerim skin, enhanced by a heady scent emanating from Sel.

Yora catches hints of what neri is saying. Something about happiness?

An illustration piece used to teach Tagli young how to paint narrative, Yora's aug tells her. *It describes three basic combinations of emotion and how to integrate them into your meaning.*

Using the genpalette given her, Yora attempts to replicate at least part of the message back to Sel as an indication of understanding, woven with traces of her current emotional state. Each time she traces the rough forms for base emotional categories, her experience turns inside her: frustration...anger... despair. She is chasing herself, and the patterns she creates on the genpalette are a meaningless mess. Too much thought interferes with the painting. Decanting intuition from will—a critical jump in Tagli narrative—eludes her.

Sorrow-care washes through Sel's colors as nerim tentacles stiffen and the roomlight flickers; Yora knows neri simplifies all expressions for her benefit. Yora attempts to gesture in apology and explain her frustrations. She is not living up to her own expectations. Very little of this is expressed to Sel through her clumsy, defeat-laden flailings, but she tries.

Speech lodges hard against the back of Yora's throat when gesturing fails her. She wants to give into the impulse to shout pointlessly at Sel, to make noise in the dense quiet of their small space. Life in realignment is a synesthetic fever dream that she can do nothing to escape, and her mind is a frustrated foam of trapped ideas. She is supposed to be bonding to this person and there is so little she can do to communicate, although the Initiative's attachés assured her that Sel will pick up on her body's communications even when she can't consciously convey them.

Colors resolve into an image on the wall to Yora's right: her own smiling face staring back at her. Sel flutters nerim hindfrill.

On day eight, Yora stops fighting the urge to speak. What would otherwise be a grave insult to Sel is tolerated like a child's tantrum. An extinguishing period, they call it. Words hemorrhage from her mouth as if she is running through the full gamut of spoken language until the last of them falls out. Yora herself expected this, felt it coming at the first stirrings of impatience with Sel, although she is inwardly flustered at her predictability.

Sel watches with keen eyes.

By day twelve, Yora's upgrades begin. Skin subtly puckers around her fresh augs; she taps the itch away. Chromatophoric dermis. A crude predecessor to the sleek, more integrated version they already dream up together. Along with the upgraded neural augs she designed with Sel and her new, Tagli-modified scent chemistry, she is prepared for this next phase of bonding. The urge to speak vocally no longer suppurates inside her; her hemorrhage long dried up. Words will now come only when needed.

She doesn't mind that she is expected to undergo more preliminary changes than Sel. It was the Tagli who adjusted to the air and dust of Hinn, who had no ears with which to perceive spoken language, whose values cleaved to their silent existence.

It was the Tagli who grew their new home near an unfamiliar star.

She looks at the back of her right arm and focuses her attention on the desire to express optimism. Shades of pink and gold undulate across her skin. She waits for Sel.

For two days, they learn. They are students at each other's feet and hindlimbs, studying what it is to be Sel, to be Yora. They are opening themselves to what it will mean to become more than they are. Yora tells of her hadir, of the responsibilities of being selected as a firstmate by the reproductive council, of her secondmate's skilled hands and keen diagnostic eye, of her thirdmate's social prowess and smooth voice. Yora describes her fascination with the flesh-grown Tagli settlement, and of the possibilities of the body that led her to cybernetics many years ago. She speaks her existence to Sel, speaks of what it means to be Ilan, to be Hinnali, to be Yora.

While she is no thirdmate—with their sculpted words and their ability to moodshift a room—she is earnest in the telling, and she hopes Fen would be proud.

In turn, Sel explains the Tagli passage across emptiness. *Given the projected lifespan of our star, we had more history behind us than future ahead.*

Sel's narrative blooms behind neris in fractal loops and ogees. Color shimmers across nerim head and forelimbs, midlimbs gesturing subtly. By now, Yora would have understood perhaps half of the oversimplified message without aid, but her augs translate the remainder. She flashes intrigue-compassion across her own colors, knowing her upgraded chemistry will verify these emotions when Sel tastes them in the air.

Sel sways briefly in appreciation. *We are scattered now, but we are alive. Some will die at our original home, by design. Someone must have this experience. Most left and will live elsewhere, like us. We are different Tagli now. Us, and those who traveled elsewhere. Us, and those who stayed behind. New Tagli.*

When Yora asks, Sel says neri has no idea whether the other ships made homes anywhere. Mild agitation flashes across Sel's belly as neri explains: when these first groups parted ways many generations ago, they saw the last of each other. Ila is the first planet Sel's ship encountered capable of sustaining complex life, although they had identified other targets that would take more generations to reach.

While the estimates for habitable planets are astronomically huge, so are the distances between them, Sel says. *There is a strong chance the others have found nothing yet.*

Do your people miss it? she asks Sel. *Your planet. Do you miss each other?*

We narrate it, neri says, although the literal translation of whorl and color is something more akin to, *visualization of time in many threads with grave emphasis,* which in turn her augs translate to "narrate."

We are many thirdmates, Sel says. Neri flutters nerim hindfrill to accentuate the colors that flash across nerim skin in a flurry of pleasure over the novel use of the Hinnali thirdmate concept. *We moodshift and talk to continue existing.*

Yora is not certain about this last translation, but she understands that Sel is likening Tagli narrative to the role of Hinnali thirdmates. The comparison is not entirely accurate. Still, Yora uses her implants to express pleasure, the Tagli equivalent of a smile.

Will you teach me your sounds when your ears are mine? neri asks.

I won't need to, Yora says.

At the end of the third month, Yora and Sel teach each other the encoding schemes of their respective species' brains, painting connectome portraits like Sel's narratives. For three days, Sel maps Yora, and for three days after, Yora maps Sel, their sensory probability distributions decoded and integrated into a new scheme. All of that which is each of them. Their minds must stretch to make room for each other, and their neural maps must expand to make room for new bodies, to be alive in two places, to share flesh.

Integration weeks follow. Yora becomes bifurcated between two spaces, and has nightmares about her skin. Layers of flesh sloughing off in great sheets, coating the floors and walls until there is more of her *there* than *here*. Flashes of light and fire burn away her body while mouths grow in dark patches beneath her feet. Her mind reaches out, finds Sel, wraps itself around and within nerim psychescape. Phantoms of unknown perception suffuse her mind. She wants to call out—no, Sel wants to call out, to use nerim new vocal cords, to live inside the sound of nerim new voice, in joy and in fear. Waves of terror roll over both of them in their dreams.

They each push and tug against their own minds, against conjured, flickering images of grass and sand and coral spires and artificial environments on generational ships. Unfamiliar sounds and polarized light assault their shared consciousness. More memories: Fen, who dreams of citrus and tells stories to her hadir; Relo, who can read Yora's body; Sel's distant memory of a parental limb broken off and consumed postnatally; nerim forelimbs carefully teasing through the delicate fronds of another's hindfrill. They are human, they are Tagli; their lives and memories are now communal property between them.

Fen is the first human to see them, bag of steamed dumplings in hand to welcome her firstmate out of realignment and carry her home to Relo. The way she will tell it to the hadir, Yora and Sel emerge from debriefing huddled near to each other, neither protective nor affectionate, but a closeness of instinct, like curling into oneself during sleep.

Each time Fen repeats this story to her mates, she recalls the startling but soft baldness of Yora's scalp, Sel's enormous hindlimbs and forelimbs stepping in such perfect time with Yora's rhythms, both pairs of eyes simultaneously moving to meet hers, the woodsy-sweet smell of their combined presence. Sel, who is her firstmate, whom her firstmate is, greets Fen with a shiver of tentacle and chromatophore.

We don't really know how they think.

"This is Sel," Yora says, as Sel's hindfrill stretches in presentation, speaking the same words in vivid color and motion, announcing Yora as Yora announces neris.

Sel laughs through Yora's mouth, and together their colors flush in a cascade of light.

From the Depths

Kristin Landon

Rinna!"

Rinna Heinonen turned, one hand on the hatchway that would let her out of the family quarters, and suppressed a groan. Her fifteen-year-old daughter stood across the small common room from her—in her iso suit, fluorescent orange, its hood and mask dangling around her shoulders.

Rinna sighed. "Just where do you think you're going?" Sealed in, Petra would be ready to leave *Hokule'a* with a minimal chance of contaminating the air and sea with her human DNA and microflora.

Petra's long mass of tight braids was tied back in a ponytail, and she carried her backpack. She smiled tentatively at her mother. "I thought you might need a hand today."

"No," Rinna said firmly.

"The Captain's going to allow your flight. I know it."

"I don't. Your father says the storm is too large." Rinna looked beyond Petra to where Isaam was polishing their breakfast plates clean in the tiny galley. He grimaced and shook his head slightly. *Your turn.*

"Rinna," Petra said, so warmly that Rinna almost heard *Ama* behind the name. "I want to come along. Please."

"Why the sudden interest in ecology?" Rinna asked, an edge in her voice. At fifteen, almost an adult, Petra still had not settled on a life path. *Neither one of you had any choice,* she'd said once to her parents. *I do. I'm going to use it.*

Petra frowned. "But I can help you." She stood very

straight. "You'll be bagging a lot of samples. I can carry them for you, free you up to make your notes."

"It's too dangerous," Rinna said firmly. "The storm's getting closer. Anyway, the Captain doesn't allow passengers on research flights."

Petra's chin went up. "If you were my work mentor, I wouldn't be a passenger."

"But I'm not," Rinna said. "You've been very clear about that, Petra—you don't want to apprentice with your father or with me. So the Captain's order applies."

Petra looked away. "And you'll do as she says."

"Yes," Rinna said. "She's the Captain, Petra. This far from home, we can't all just—"

"Ta'aroa *is* home," Petra said flatly. "When are you going to understand? This isn't some mission. We're settlers. All of us."

Rinna sighed. As if a world without land could ever be a real home for human beings.... Petra was right in one thing. They could never return to Earth. Though Earth hardly mattered to Petra, born in space. "This *is* a mission, for all of us. We're explorers. Earth is waiting for what we can teach them."

Petra's gaze was challenging. "Earth is dying. We need to start figuring out how to live here. Maybe on one of those big floating weed mats you're so interested in. That's why I need to see one." She met her mother's look. "Please."

Rinna glanced impatiently at the chrono in the bulkhead over the reading corner. Dawn in just a few minutes. "No, Petra. This discussion is over."

Petra's face went still. Then she pushed past Rinna through the hatch and let it slam behind her.

Isaam dried his hands and came over to Rinna, touched her hand. "Don't mind her, love," he said. "You go. Talk to the Captain. Get your flyer. I'll get Ayodele up and off to school."

"That's Petra's job!"

"I'm not thinking she'll be back soon," Isaam said. "I can be a little late to my shift."

Rinna wrung her hands. "Why can't she just—"

"Because so much of her is *you*," he said, the hint of a

smile on his lean, dark face. "Go to work, Rinna. Discover new things. Make your dull old weatherman proud."

As usual, Rinna took the long, winding stairwell rather than the lift, up through the pylon from the subsurface living quarters to the research and navigation superstructure with its huge open landing deck. At the top, she undogged the light but rigid hatch, swung it aside, and stepped out onto the maindeck of the exploration vessel *Hokule'a*. She blinked in the dazzle of light, leaned into the stiff, cool westerly wind as it met her.

She loved this wild air, damp with the scent of Ta'aroa—the world that was an ocean, the ocean that was a world.... In their quarters below, they might as well still be on the transport that brought them here—long years of limitation and enclosure, of lessons and training and preparation. Then the yearlong wait on the orbital station while the transport was modified into pieces of *Hokule'a,* landed, and finally assembled. She remembered, with a pang, her old teacher Nattana's words on the last day of her life. *You and your children will breathe free air.* Her beloved mentor, who did not survive the harsh acceleration of landing. As they both had known she would not.

Nattana would have known what to say to Petra, how to guide her toward a focus in life....

Rinna moved to the tough, close mesh of the outer rail, considering her arguments for the Captain at their meeting in an hour. The sky shimmered above, immense, pale as pearl with the light before dawn. She looked toward the fading dark in the west. And for the first time she saw the storm—a mass of clouds just over the horizon. *But not here yet.* She turned east. Across the wide deck, a high fishbone pattern of cirrus clouds caught the raw-gold light of the morning sun, still below the horizon. Far overhead, a vee formation of the flying creatures everyone called skrees arrowed west toward the storm, seeking their daytime fishing grounds. To the northeast, in flyer range at last, lay what must be their nesting ground—a vast floating mat of tough, ribbony sea grass that must also support plenty of other organisms. Dozens of kilometers across, and dense enough to have a surface people could walk on.

Rinna was determined to walk on it today—to collect samples for the ecology team before the storm scoured the mat's surface. Fed by fifteen hours of sunlight every day, it might well harbor a richness of life even the infinite depths could not match. She would point this out to the Captain. Until now they had studied only storm-torn fragments of smaller mats, never an intact web of commensal plants and animals.

Even a home-year after landing on Ta'aroa, the thought still burned in her. An entire world to explore. A universe of life to study, begin to categorize, try to understand. *I've got to get over there.* She gripped the mesh tightly. *I will.* She turned from the rail and headed forward along the platform toward the command pylon and the navigation tower.

She kept her balance easily now, despite *Hokule'a*'s slow rise and fall on the great swells that marched endlessly around the planet. One ocean, landless, averaging almost two hundred kilometers in depth. With the storm coming, the sails had been spooled in at sunset last night. She could not hear the engines far below, but she knew they were at work, maneuvering over long hours to keep them near enough to the mat but out of its path. *Near enough for my flight.*

Her grip-soled boots scuffed over the gritty deck surface as she strode past the tied-down fliers and equipment sheds, past the green-painted football pitch, toward the bow and the tall nav tower. Near its top was her first goal, the weather station. She nodded at the platform crew as they moved around on deck, checking tiedowns, verifying that everything had made it through the night and would be secure against the coming storm. Rinna paused to tug the edge of a cover into place. Things did wash away sometimes—none of them replaceable. Earth was too far. Their first data, sent last year, would take almost sixteen home-years to arrive there. *And what's the use of it? Earth is dying.*

Which did not change what must be done, what they must

all do. Rinna stepped through the tower's main hatch. Inside, ranks of storage lockers loomed in dimness, sealed against waves that might wash over the deck. She bypassed the lift, which was in the hands of a maintenance crew, and hurried up the open metal stairs. Like everyone else on *Hokule'a* who was not an elder, she had only vague memories of Earth—grey skies, thick wet heat, the white-painted bunkroom in the children's home. She had been just five when she was tested and selected for this mission—one of three thousand especially curious, intelligent, cooperative children from all over Earth, destined for the first of the six interstellar transports that would voyage here over a span of years. Rinna had grown up in space, learning her profession from the elders who voyaged with them all and taught them. At forty-one, this was the only world she had ever truly seen.

The only world my daughters will ever see.

She climbed past the bridge, the backup control room for the engines, and the sensor room, and finally reached the weather pod. Only flight control for the drones and flyers was higher.

Alexei—the chief elder for meteorology—was crewing the weather pod as usual, finishing the solitary night shift he preferred. He looked up and nodded at her, a smile creasing his lean old face. As her husband's teacher and now mentor, he was family. She smiled at him and moved, as she always did, to the angular bank of windows that currently looked east and north. The golden light of the sky filled the room now, dimming the weather readouts and satellite screens, its reflection a pale glow on the silver-grey surface of the ocean. She caught her breath as a sunspark flashed, vanished, flashed again on the horizon. Then, startlingly abrupt as always, an arc of sun popped up. The windows dimmed, and Rinna turned away to begin the day's work.

She looked first at the main satellite screen, tabbing in the data overlays. The storm was definitely gaining strength, and the mark indicating *Hokule'a*'s position was near the center of its projected path. "That doesn't look good."

Alexei glanced down at his board and shrugged. "You may have time for a short flight, if the Captain allows. But the winds will be picking up all day. After the storm would be more prudent."

"When there might not be anything left to sample," Rinna said. She straightened. "She *has* to listen. She has to let me go."

"Patience, daughter," Alexei said, and grinned.

She sighed. "Always." She took out her pad and swiped onto it the storm data, the projected track of the mat, and the sharpest sat image she could call up. "Oh. Isaam will be a little late. He has to take Ayo to school."

Alexei must have heard the edge in her voice. "And how *is* Petra?"

Rinna gave him a rueful smile. "Just the usual push and pull. Isaam will give you the summary."

His grin broadened. "I seem to recall some push and pull from *you* at fifteen..."

She tilted her nose in the air and left him there, intent on her meeting with the Captain. Intent on getting that flyer—no matter what.

Rinna shifted her grip on the slick, heavy package of specimen bags and shoved them into the cargo compartment of the flyer with a satisfied grunt. In the end the Captain had shaken her grey head and said, "There is commitment and there is foolishness, Rinna." But she had permitted Rinna a flyer. The other five members of the surface ecology team had agreed days ago that Rinna would make the flight; she weighed the least, so she could bring back the largest payload of specimens. Specimens collected in situ, sorted and tagged by human hands, not something randomly scooped up by a hovering drone.... Context! How could you begin to grasp a whole ecology if you didn't have that?

She leaned into the piloting compartment to check the emergency pack. When she straightened again in the increasingly gusty wind, Petra stood facing her in the shadow of the flyer. Still in her iso suit, covered by her long red slicker. "I told you you'd get it," she said. "So—"

"So?"

"So, let me come with you," Petra said. "You won't see the Captain again until we're back. You can just tell her there wasn't time to ask permission."

"It's out of the question," Rinna said flatly. "Go. Please. Get to your maintenance shift."

Petra was silent for a moment. "It's your choice, then, Rinna," she said, and was gone.

Rinna balanced at the top of a yielding pile of crimson vegetation and looked east across the tangled, uneven surface of the mat toward the sun, now halfway up the sky. Its light brought out the rough, hillocky surface in sharp relief. Pockets of the sea grass were rotting into a kind of mulch, she had already learned, and new life was taking root in them—green plants. *Seeded from where? Skree droppings?* And those hand-sized arthropods burrowing in beside the new growth—with a new body plan entirely. Nattana would have been beside herself.... The wind rattled the stiff plastic of Rinna's hood. *Better keep moving.* She glanced over her shoulder. The flyer was startlingly far away, a white speck against the dark sea. She saw no sign of *Hokule'a*. Above, thin streamers of cloud clawed northeastward toward the sun.

She hesitated, suddenly dizzy, realizing that she stood up here with *nothing* between herself and the horizon on any side. Exposed to anything, with no shelter nearer than the distant flyer.

At that moment her datapad blipped a warning that she was almost at the maximum permitted distance from the flyer for this mission. She glanced at her mission timer, shook herself, and made her way carefully down from the high point, looking back along her route. A string of filled sample bags, fluorescent yellow-green, stretched out behind her, marking her walk out from the flyer. She'd have to turn around soon, start collecting them and moving toward the flyer again. But just a little farther.... An endless vista of tangled red weed stretched away on all sides in the watery, weakening sunlight, pools of trapped rainwater glimmering here and there. Hiding what?

She knew what lived in some of them now. Small larval forms of *something*, swimming in nest schools, darting aside as her shadow fell across them. Meaning they had predators—skrees, most likely. Tiny insect/crustacean-like creatures clung to the weeds at the water's edge. Though she could smell nothing through her mask, her datapad's instruments registered the heavy organic stink of all of this—a mass of life, and of old death, warming in the sunshine. Meters thick above the surface, maybe more below. What kept it together? What made it float so high? This structure hadn't aggregated in a season, or a year.

She climbed a small ridge and stopped. Beyond, a ravine stretched across her path. A deep, blue-shadowed slash at least fifty meters across, receding toward the horizon on both sides. End of the road, obviously, but—

No. She turned, got a good grip with her gloved hands on the weed at the edge, and started down. There might be open water down there. A chance to collect from a layer closer to the sea, a new niche. *Can't pass that up.*

She climbed down carefully, her nearly empty backpack hindering her a little as it caught on tough stubs and tendrils of weed. As she descended, the light faded. Cold rose around her, and the sense of being cut off from the world. From home.

She knew from briefings that the floor of the ravine might be unstable, too thin to support her. Ten meters short of it she switched on the headlamp on her hood and looked around. And her head jerked in surprise, making shadows jump.

At the bottom of the ravine was a big, circular hole, three or four meters across. A perfect circle, sharp as if it had been cut, and filled with darkness. She felt certain that it reached down to the water surface meters below. What kind of life form would create such a thing?

Something that wants access to the surface of the mat.

Something big.

She was already recording, sound and visual, had been since she left the flyer. But now she crouched frozen, wanting to make spoken notes, but afraid to make a sound. What if something lurked at the bottom of that hole? Waiting for prey to come near? Her team had known since landing that larger creatures swam the abyssal deeps—but that one might come to the surface, crawl out onto a mat, didn't seem possible. What would it be seeking that it couldn't find in the sea?

She took a careful step, then another. The ravine floor felt solid. But the throat of the hole looked odd. Not a tangle of matted weeds like everything else. It was smooth. Tight and regular. Not a slash through the weeds, but—something *made*. She stooped and shone a light on it, careful not to let the beam drift into the depths of the hole.

And stiffened. *It's braided.* Braided plant fibers, tightly woven into a lining that would preserve the shape of the hole.

Woven by something with hands.

Without another thought she leaned over the hole and snipped off a patch of the braided material at the upper edge. Hands unsteady with haste, she bagged it, then tapped the tab that would record her exact position.

Then listened. Nothing moved. She heard only the distant lapping of water, meters below in the dark.

Her datapad's voice spoke in her ear. "Time to turn back. Time to turn back. Recall has sounded."

That can't be right. I should have at least thirty more minutes here. Rinna looked down into the darkness of the hole, then up at the racing clouds in dismay. The storm must be coming in faster than expected. If she didn't head back immediately, she'd have to abandon the samples she'd bagged up on the way out.

She scrambled back up the wall of the ravine, her eyes on the sky. Absurdly afraid of what she might see if she looked behind her. *Like a scared child,* she told herself angrily. But a small part of her felt glad that her only task now was to collect the sample bags, get back to the flyer, escape to safety.

Escape whatever had...*built* that hole.

Rinna raced the storm home low above the dark swells, through spray wind-torn from their crests. She kept her palms flat on the control screen, ready to take over if the flyer's autosystems failed under stress. Clouds massed ahead of her, kilometers high. The little flyer knew its way, but it lurched oddly in sudden updrafts, lighter than she had expected. So it was nowhere near its functional limit even in this wind. She grimaced in frustration. *I could have collected twice as much.* Damn the Captain and her cast-iron margins for error.

Her heart did give a thump of relief as *Hokule'a*'s towers loomed out of the mist and she saw the flashing red lights of the landing target ahead and below. With a last wild lurch, the flyer settled to the deck. Rinna pushed out of the piloting compartment into horizontal rain and helped the flight crew tie the flyer down. It shuddered under their hands as they worked. Spray was sheeting across the open deck by now, so, flouting safety regulations, she rode the lift with the flyer and the flight crew down to the platform sublevel. As the hatch rumbled shut overhead, Rinna pushed a rolling cart to the flyer's cargo hatch and began offloading her boxes of precious sample bags. The flight crew chief glared at her. "That was too close. We could have lost that flyer! ...And you."

"I obeyed recall," she said. "And I got what I went for." She grimaced, thinking of her final sample. "And more."

He snorted. "The Captain lets you science people go too far. Soft on all of you."

Rinna loaded the last samples into the cart and closed the lid. "We're why you're all here."

He looked sour. "Oh, we know that." He glanced past her. "Here comes your team."

She looked up. All five of them had come up, with Julien in the lead, his narrow face urgent with questions. As he helped her trundle the cart down the long passageway to the lab-pylon lift, she gave them all a fast summary of what she'd seen, and what she'd sampled. She saved the most significant for last, as they rode the lift down to the ecology deck, and she got the reaction she expected. Julien snorted. "Trick of the light. It was dark down there. You were spooked."

Rinna bristled. "Get a good look at the sample I collected there, before you say that again." She took out her datapad, intending to show him the relevant images, but saw the red text of an urgent message. From Isaam. Four words: *Tell me you're safe.*

She tapped out *Safe*, and sent it. For more than that, he would have to wait.

Three hours later, Rinna leaned against her workbench, staring down at the swatch of braided material. Sanjiv had snipped away some fibers for analysis, and it had been imaged in every possible way. When the techs were finished, Rinna had taken it back to her station to think about it some more, away from her colleagues' flood of speculation and perplexity.

Chilled and humidified to match the conditions where she'd found it, the sample rested in a clear box, set at the center of her bench. A question demanding an answer she might not find for a long time. *Or ever.* The sensors she'd set up on the mat surface had mostly failed when the storm hit; the few that were left reported scouring wind hurling gouts of water and flecks of torn vegetation. She might never find that particular spot again. The sensor she'd left down in the gully had been one of the first to go dark.

The rest of the eco team would probably work all night—sorting, classifying, recording what she'd brought back—but she could not. Deep exhaustion tugged at her, urging her toward home and sleep. Dinner first—then rest. Safe with Isaam and the girls. She sketched a wave at Julien and left.

As she stepped through the hatch at home, Isaam looked up with a smile, but kept stirring a pot on the burner in the small corner cooking area. The warm scent of vat-fish chowder filled the compartment. Ayo ran to Rinna from the reading corner, clutching Susu, her battered stuffed sloth. "Ama! Did you have a good day?"

"Yes, pip. A very good day." Rinna picked her up and carried her to Isaam, kissed him. "And you?"

He winced. "Now that you're safe, I can say it was all right…. They thinned leeks in hydroponics today, I put some of those in."

"Smells good." Rinna set the little girl down. "Will Petra be home for dinner?"

Isaam shrugged with one shoulder. "I messaged her. No answer, as usual. But she didn't mention any other plans last night."

"I'll locate her." Rinna touched her datapad. "Oh. She's in her room."

Isaam frowned. "That's odd. She didn't come out when I got back with Ayo."

"Maybe she's asleep." Rinna walked down the narrow passage leading from the living space to the sleeping quarters, a tiny bunk space for each girl and a slightly larger compartment she shared with Isaam.

Petra was not in her bunk, or Ayo's, or her parents'; she wasn't in the toilet or the shower. Rinna went back to Petra's space, touched the light on, and took a closer look. One set of her clothes hung on its peg, the other had been left heaped on the narrow bunk. Surely wherever she was, she wasn't still in her iso suit? Reflexively Rinna picked up Petra's shirt and shook it out to hang it on its hook on the wall.

A small, dark object thumped onto Petra's bedcover. Rinna stared at it, then picked it up with an unsteady hand.

Petra's locator.

She knows better than this! Petra should never have taken this off. It was one of the safety essentials drilled into all of them since early childhood. In case—the cold thought took her—*in case we're swept overboard.*

Clutching the device, she hurried back down the passage. Isaam looked up and frowned. "Rinna? What's wrong?"

She held out Petra's locator, and saw his frown change to a look of fright. He snatched it from her. "What did she do?" His voice was urgent. "Why would she leave this here?"

"I don't know," Rinna said, and took a shaking breath, hating the thought that was beginning to form in her mind. "She showed up at the flyer this morning. As I was leaving. She was still in her iso suit. She—she asked to come along again."

"And you said no, again." Isaam looked grim.

"Of course." She looked away from his eyes. "I said no, and she left. I finished loading and got into the piloting compartment and—" Her voice failed.

"Was anyone helping you load?"

"No, they were all out securing the deck."

"She wouldn't," Isaam said. "She *wouldn't* stow away in the cargo compartment." He was looking at her as if hoping for reassurance she couldn't give.

"If she did—" Rinna closed her eyes. "They recalled me thirty minutes early."

Isaam took a breath and drew himself up. "I'll call this in. Request a search of the vessel." He brushed her cheek with the back of a finger. "She wouldn't do this, love. She's impulsive, but she's not a fool. She's off with Mila or Josip, playing some prank—"

But Rinna stood frozen, staring down at the deck. Remembering the scream of the wind. The sheets of foam and water. The blue-black clouds racing in from the west.

And she knew.

My daughter is out there. In the dark.
Alone in the storm.

Rinna kept to the bridge all night, silently harboring her last, fragile thread of hope. All night, with the Captain at the helm, *Hokule'a* drove hard, chasing the mat. They knew it lay somewhere ahead, driven off course across the current by the storm; but the satellites couldn't image it through the clouds, and all of the sensors Rinna had placed were dead. Air Control told her that drone flights would be futile, even when the light returned—the winds would still be too high, the spray too thick. They were all trying so hard not to give her unreasonable hope.

As if she had any hope that would survive tomorrow.

At 29:30, almost midnight, she sat stiffly, dry-eyed, in a dim corner of the bridge, consciously keeping her body still, though her tense muscles ached. Everyone left her alone. Ayo had been taken in by a neighbor. Isaam, of course, was up in the weather room with Alexei, gauging the winds and currents, providing the constant stream of updated data that sped their progress—as much as anything could. *Hokule'a* was nothing like the graceful, double-hulled Polynesian voyaging canoe she had been named for; she was a huge, awkward, more-than-half-submersible vessel that had been designed as a research base. A floating village, not a ship. The wind outraced her easily. And the smaller, faster boats she could launch in calm weather couldn't face the storm.

The one time Rinna had gone up to the weather room, Isaam had sent her away at once. "Go below, love," he had said raggedly. "Get some sleep. Let us do our work."

But Rinna knew she could not face their silent, empty quarters. She'd returned to the bridge, where at least she felt a sense of progress. That something was being done. The Captain's wife, her round, kind face distressed, had brought her chamomile tea, now cold in the mug between her hands. Rinna shivered, remembering the cold striking up from the dark water, down in the shadows by the hole in the mat— She broke off the thought, again.

She dozed now and then, in a chair at an empty work station, but real sleep evaded her. Toward dawn, she stood up stiffly and looked around the bridge, and one of the navtechs gave her an artificial smile. The Captain had retired for some rest, he told her, and the storm was passing, but the situation had not changed. "The mat isn't in sight yet," he said. The smile faded to honesty. "At least—"

She faced him. "Tell me."

"We've caught up with some fragments. Nothing more yet. I'm sorry."

And that may be all that's left. Grief and fear surged again. "Thank you," she said in a tight whisper, and left the bridge.

This time, when she appeared in the hatchway of the weather room, Isaam got up slowly and came out to her. "Rinna."

"Fragments," she said, a little wildly. "They said, fragments. But that doesn't mean it's gone." She took a breath. "If we wait until—" she said. Then, "When the light is better, we might—"

"I can't think beyond this moment." Isaam's voice broke, and he took both her hands in his. "You must see, you must know, how little chance there is that we will ever find any sign of her."

She closed her eyes. He went on, his voice unsteady, "Go in and sit. I'll get us something to eat."

Alexei looked up from his workstation as she entered, his eyes shadowed. His silence added to her fear. She knew it was not the old man's way to speak when there was nothing good to say. There *could* be nothing good. Her heart thumped slowly, like the ship's bell announcing a death. Her teacher's. Her daughter's. Her own.

She moved to the broad window, periodically cleared of rain and flying spray by wipers. In the growing light, in the blue gloom after the storm, she saw only foam, and spray, and racing clouds.

Only the empty ocean. Only the empty sky.

By early afternoon, they began to encounter larger fragments of the mat, dark tatters sliding up and down the swells.

Rinna left Isaam to his work, left the nav crew to theirs. She went down to the deck, walked forward from the tower's base to the peak of the bow rail, and stood gripping it, staring at the sea. The horizon was lost in grey mist. Far below, the leading hull plunged into the slow swells, then rose heavily, shedding rivers of foam. Spray soaked her, she was cold, she wasn't cold. It didn't matter. Nausea didn't matter.

Because she knew what she needed, now that real hope was gone. *The work.* Pick up one piece, assess it, place it where it belonged in the puzzle. Pick up the next. If she could do nothing else, if she was good for *nothing* else, she could do that. As she had dealt with her loss and confusion as a little child, after the floods that drowned her parents and so many others—when she'd found that it silenced the cry of pain in her mind to pick up her reading screen and seek, learn, understand something new. That always mattered. That way was always open to her. Whatever controlled her life did not control this.

And she might find something today. Something new. That would be—something that this day could give her, to balance against what it was about to take away.

The weaving. She would start there.

She took the central lift below, far below, to the deep research pod above *Hokule'a*'s immense deadweight keel. She found an empty work room on the observation deck there, a hundred meters below the surface. Even down here near the ship's center of gravity, she felt the slow surge as *Hokule'a* rose and fell on the swells; but it was less, and the dim light through the small ports was diffuse, steady, stilling her nausea.

She called up her files from the eco lab and began methodically working through the scans and images of the fragment from yesterday. A tight, regular weave, glossy purplish red—the color of the sea grass it must have been made from. Her fingertips remembered its cold, slick surface. She rotated the image floating above her work pad, watching it shift in the light. Comment stars floated around it, shifting as it did. Touching one would take her to someone else's notes.

One was flashing, requesting her attention specifically. Jingfei's color. *The structural physiologist?* She tabbed it, and her data panel flooded with text. Rinna scanned it, frowned, and called Jingfei.

The old biologist's seamed, gentle face appeared in place of the image of the weave. "Rinna. How are you, child?"

She shook her head impatiently. "Your notes on the weaving. Those fibers. You say they're artificial?"

Jingfei sighed, but accepted the deflection. "In a way. My analysis says they are extremely unlikely to be an evolved form. Those fibers were not manufactured artificially. They were grown. But the plant that they came from was probably engineered."

Rinna tilted her head. "They look just like the grass that's all over the mat."

"They *are* the grass," Jingfei said. "The *grass* is engineered."

"How? Who?" Rinna stared at her in puzzlement. "We haven't found any sign of that level of civilization. No power generation. Nothing."

Jingfei nodded slowly. "Nothing. Except the fact that the fibers exist."

Rinna chewed at a knuckle, then said, "We've never found anything else like this."

"But we've found it now," Jingfei said. "As Nattana would remind you, it's a very big ocean, Rinna." She looked owlishly out at her. "You should rest, you know, my dear."

"Work is better," Rinna said flatly, and broke the connection.

A few hours later, Isaam's voice startled her. "Rinna? Are you all right?"

She turned and saw him standing tensely in the dim space, his back to the doorway, his dark face in shadow.

"I'm working," she said. Then took a breath. "Like you."

"Ayo asked for you."

"This isn't a good time for—"

"She's here," he said gently. And there she was, looking out from behind her father's legs. Still clutching Susu. Her eyes wide in her small brown face. "She's been with me since midday. But she needs you, too."

Rinna rested her hands on her work pad, and struggled for words. How could she tell him that if she stopped working now, she would lose her hold on everything? Everything that was left to her?

Then she let go of the work pad and knelt on the cold metal deck. "Ayo, love. Come to Ama." She got the words out before her voice broke. She buried her face in the girl's silky neck, breathing in her simple cleanness. Remembering. Long years ago, Petra. The same. Not the same.

"Don't cry, Ama," Ayo said. "Baba doesn't cry."

Rinna looked at Isaam over the child's head, and saw the raw pain in his eyes. His face twisted, and he turned away and left them there. *Back to work.* Like her. She glanced at the wall chrono. She'd worked through half of the afternoon. Half to go....

"Ama," Ayo said, "Baba said give you this." She held out a greasy cloth packet that smelled of fish. "Are you hungry?"

No, baby girl. Never again. But she took it, nibbled the edge of a fish cake. "That's good, Ayo. Thank you." She stood up. "Ayo—Ama has to work. Can you play with Susu over by the heater? Can you be good and quiet while Ama works?"

"I can be good and quiet," Ayo said in a very small voice.

An hour later Rinna leaned back and rubbed the back of her neck. She had re-examined a third of her data, maybe, in half a day, reading all the team's findings. No more anomalies, so far.

And no one but Isaam and Ayo had come near. Meaning there was no news of Petra. No news, good or bad. There was that, at least. She looked over toward the corner, where Ayo had been sorting shapes on a datapad.

Then jumped to her feet. Ayo was nowhere in sight. This was a safe deck, only data stations and the deep observation bubble forward. But there were always hazards. She scanned the room. "Ayo!" she called. "Ayo! Come out!"

No answer.

She climbed the few steps to the main deck level, looked both ways. Silence, only the slow surge beneath her feet. Called again. "Ayo! Answer me!"

The answer, when it came, was soft. "Hush, Ama." From the end, there. From the observation bubble. Rinna saw the faint purplish-greenish glow in the hatchway, the remnant of daylight that could penetrate a hundred meters of water. "Ama!" Ayo's voice was a strained whisper. "Ama, come and see!"

She ran.

And saw Ayo standing across the room, Susu slumped at her feet. Ayo was gazing up at the broad expanse of the observation window.

At shapes, floating there. Shapes with eyes, looking in at the girl. *Big* shapes. Not fish. Something...different—

In three steps she reached Ayo, snatched her up. When she looked back at the window, it was empty, cloudy green dimness fading to dark below, to faint brightness above.

"Ama," Ayo said reproachfully, "you *scared* them." She twisted away to peer into the gloom. "Let's wait. I want them to meet you, too."

Rinna wanted to run, climb to the surface, take Ayo safely up to the light. But—

But this is important.

But I have to see for myself.

She touched her datapad and called Julien. "You need to check the cameras outside the deep observation pod. Check sonar."

"We're on it," his voice said. "Lots of movement near every pod, more every minute. It's like they're trying to look in. They're coming a lot closer down where you are. What did you see?"

"There were some big organisms near the window, keeping pace with us, but they—Wait. See that?"

Shapes far out in the murk, moving closer again, angling in parallel to the ship's slow course. Now her eyes could sort them out. Dark, sinuous bodies, powerful tails. Strong pectoral fins.

And...*hands.*

"Hands," she breathed. It couldn't be. It didn't fit any of the body plans they'd found so far. But there they were, one on each side of the huge flattened heads. She didn't move. Ayo clutched at her neck and squeaked in excitement.

"I'm coming down there," Julien said.

"No. They're skittish. I already frightened them off once. Wait and watch. Follow the inside and outside cams."

Closer, closer. They had broad froglike faces, wide-set yellow eyes—not blank, but unreadable—and they were fixed on the window. The creatures were huge, six or seven meters long. Their bodies gleamed darkly. The hands—*swirled.* They looked like slightly stiffened clusters of tentacles. The stiffening meant they could probably be used to grasp and manipulate in a complex way. Was there intelligence behind those eyes? She shrank back, clutching Ayo.

Who laughed. "See, Ama? They're nice. Put me down." On her feet again, she approached the window, and the nearest of the creatures nosed closer.

"Rinna," Julien's voice said. "It's those same animals everywhere. Swimming with us. All around the ship."

"Are they coming close to any other viewports?"

"Not yet," he said. "They seem to be clustering at your depth. Stay where you are. We're getting—Hold on."

Ayo was waving at the creatures. The nearest sank a little lower and raised one of its "hands." It unfurled slowly, a graceful but alien gesture. *Waving back?* Rinna caught her breath just as Julien's voice returned. "Rinna. There's a big life form coming up from below." She heard the tension in his voice. "*Really* big. It must be one of those leviathans we've seen on sonar. Captain's ordered all stop, she's worried about the screws."

"Right," Rinna said distractedly. Ayo stood right in front of the glass now. Rinna's hands itched to pull her back, but she was in no more danger there than in Rinna's arms. Ayo raised her hand and pressed it to the glass.

The creature on the other side—pressed its own hand to the glass. Huge, delicate, alien. Pale with pressure. The "fingers" writhed a little.

"Are you seeing this?" Rinna asked in a shaking voice.

"We all are," Julien said.

Ayo laughed again and moved a couple of meters along the glass—and the creature moved with her. "They like me," she said.

Now there were two of them watching Ayo. Three of them. More. The outside monitors were picking up clicks, whistles. Animal sounds? Or language? One or two stayed focused on Ayo, but another moved toward Rinna. With the engines shut down, the momentum was beginning to come off *Hokule'a*; more and more of them were closing in. "Where's the big creature?" *Leviathan*. Vast, shadowy—until now seen only on blurred images from deep probes.

"It's hovering about a hundred meters farther down. It's almost as big as the research pod, Rinna."

"Then we'd better hope it's friendly."

There was a stir in the swarm of creatures outside, and one of them—an especially large one—swam closer to the window. One of its clusters of tentacles seemed damaged, stubby. Then Rinna looked closer. *It's holding something.* Curious, she raised her hand and flattened it against the glass in the gesture of greeting that had worked for Ayo.

Smoothly, the creature—the being—rotated, bringing the clumped tentacles near to her. They unfolded in a long, smooth motion, leaving only one gripping the thing inside. The thing it had brought to *Hokule'a*.

Rinna stifled a cry, recognizing it. *Petra's datapad.*

Rinna stood tensely, facing the sub bay chief, a short,

heavyset woman. "We're locked down," Charlotte said again. "We're secured by the Captain's order. I can't give you a sub. I won't open the bay door, not with those things out there. Not without a direct order." Her voice sounded high and buzzing in the helium/oxygen atmosphere of the high-pressure bay.

Isaam set his hand on Rinna's shoulder and said to Charlotte, "Can you at least set the matter before the Captain?"

"The Captain is aware," a dry voice said from the comm panel, and they turned and saw her on its screen—spare, silver-haired, in her usual plain black worksuit.

"I sent you the recording, Captain," Rinna said. "What one of them is carrying. You must see what it—might mean."

The Captain glanced at Isaam, then studied Rinna. "You think there is a possibility that your daughter is alive? That this is not some kind of trick, or trap? Or the random act of an animal?"

"If Petra is dead," Isaam said, "why would they bring her datapad to *Hokule'a*?"

"And if she is alive," Rinna said fiercely, "will we do nothing?" She fought to keep from twisting her hands, from crying out in pure frustration.

The Captain rubbed the back of her neck wearily, was silent a moment, then sighed. "One sub. A volunteer pilot. And you, Rinna."

"Thank you," Rinna said on a thread of breath. The Captain nodded at her, once, and cut the comm. Rinna leaned into Isaam's shoulder as Charlotte turned away and went with obvious reluctance to a control panel by the sub bay.

It took twenty minutes to warm up one of the little research subs. Rinna, standing tense in the circle of Isaam's arm, felt the fizzing tension in him as well. In the dimness outside a cloud of the creatures lingered, hovering gracefully, perhaps curious about the frantic activity they must see through the ports of the sub bay.

Charlotte looked past Rinna toward the airlock. "Ah. Here's our volunteer."

Rinna turned. A young man had just come through the

pressure lock and was touching his palm to the log board. A very young man, not much older than Petra, his long red hair knotted at the back of his neck, his face marked with curling tattoos. *Will*. That was his name. She had seen him, now and again, at the edge of the crowd of Petra's friends.

Will nodded soberly at Rinna and Isaam as he passed, boarded the chosen sub as it floated in the launching pool, then lowered himself through its upper hatch. A few moments later its jets churned to life. Rinna checked the seals on her iso suit again. With a wordless squeeze of her hand, Isaam released her. In her last look back at him she saw how haggard he had become over the past day. But he smiled at her as she climbed down into the sub.

The hatch closed, the clamps released, and the sub dropped slowly from the surface toward the wide hatch, which had just opened for their launch. "No running lights," Rinna said as they passed through. "They may not like them. Hover here for a moment, all right?"

"Got it," Will said. He seemed subdued. Worried about Petra, maybe. Or about piloting a little research sub out among a school of creatures almost its size, with instincts—*or intentions?*—no one could fathom.

Then something big thumped against the rear of the sub, making it lurch. And again. Will looked up at her, rattled, just as the comm spoke. "*They're attacking the sub*," Charlotte's voice said. "*Will, I'm recalling you. If you breach—*"

Rinna slapped off the comm key. "Get us moving. I'll let them see me." Rinna worked her way forward through the cramped space into the observation bubble at the bow. And there was the one carrying Petra's datapad. The largest of the group. It swam closer. Its wide-set eyes swiveled forward and fixed on her. Unreadable still—but not animal eyes. The chittering sounds were louder now.

She pressed her hand against the curve of heavy clear polymer, and the largest creature studied her a moment longer. Another thump at the stern, and it curved smoothly away. The smaller creatures took up formation around it and followed, setting a northward course.

Setting a *course*. "Follow them," Rinna said. "They know where Petra is."

"You can't be sure of that."

"If they don't know," Rinna said tiredly, "no one does. And that means Petra is dead."

He flinched, then let out a sharp breath. Touched the board. The sub surged forward, following.

Rinna sensed the bulk of *Hokule'a*'s deep hull dwindling behind them. She felt in her bones the abyss that yawned below them, more than a hundred kilometers of deepening cold and absolute blackness. And mounting pressure that would crush their bodies to nothing, if they died out here.

The creatures led them onward, surrounding the sub closely enough that Rinna felt the turbulence through the hull as she knelt on the deck. Will shook his head again but kept silent. Nothing touched the sub. They traveled a gradually ascending course toward the surface and north. The light slowly intensified as they rose, from the purplish-green glow at depth to dark green, then blue-green. On the surface above Rinna saw drifting shadows that increased in size as they went. Pieces of the mat, larger and closer together. Maybe there was some of it left after all.... She set her hands firmly on her knees, and kept herself still.

There was no point in letting herself imagine something that might not happen. But hope burned again inside her, making her whole body tingle, bringing her near tears. She kept her attention on the sea outside. The cloud of creatures around them grew as they climbed. A miniature version of the others, a juvenile probably, darted in close to her, hovered an instant, then flicked away. Testing its courage? She must look frightening enough—a dry, bony, angular *thing* in a bubble of deadly air.

Eventually they were near enough to the surface that the deep wave surge rolled the sub a little. Darkness loomed ahead, rays of shadow spreading beneath it. But they didn't surface. They were going to pass *under* the edge of the mat.

That can't be right! But ahead their guides swam steadily onward, into the shadows.

"Sorry, Rinna," Will said. "I need lights now." He looked
pale, but his voice was steady.

"Fine," she said. "Low as you can though, please."

In the weak glow she saw a broad upside-down field of
purplish-brown seaweed, stretching out of sight on all sides
above them. Saw a huge, bulging net, woven from sea grass,
that contained a dense school of silvery fishlike creatures.
They swirled and scattered when the light touched them. The
being they were following, and its attendants, swam steadily
onward. In the distance now she saw a rim of some pale, iridescent substance, smoothly curving, hanging below the level
of the seaweed. As they approached she realized how large
it was. "What the freck is that?" Will said, puzzled. "It looks...
kind of pearly."

As they drew closer Rinna saw the roughness above
the rim. "It looks like a shell," she said in a tight voice.
"But—huge...."

Now they were dipping under the pale rim, and at once
the sub's lights glittered back at them from a water surface
immediately above. The being with the datapad stopped, rose
toward the surface. Darkness above, though it was still day. So
they had not reached the surface of the ocean. This was an air
pocket. Which might mean— "Take us up, Will," Rinna said
tensely. In a moment she would know.

They broke surface and floated. From the upper ports she
saw a domed ceiling of iridescent white, the sub's lights glittering and rebounding from it. The space was broad and high,
the "roof" above ten or fifteen meters away. She tugged up her
hood and crawled toward the ladder. "Wait," Will snapped.
"Just getting the data—" Then he let out a sharp sigh of relief.
"It's air out there. Breathable."

So Petra might still be alive. "I'm going up," Rinna said.
She pulled up the hood of her iso suit, sealed her mask into
place, moved to the ladder. "Pop the hatch, Will. Now." She
heard it click and, feeling shaky, she climbed the few rungs

to the top, pushed it open.

Dark rippling water all around, and a domed roof with shining walls. Near the walls all around, a narrow cushion of mat material floated. And there to the left, not twenty meters away, a small orange-clad figure rose slowly to its feet. "Here," it said in a weak voice. "I'm here."

Rules be damned. *She needs to see* me. Rinna pulled back her hood, dropped the mask to dangle at her collar. Tried to speak and couldn't.

"Ama!" Petra shouted, and started to cry.

The instant the sub bumped against the mat where Petra waited, she swarmed aboard and flung her arms around Rinna's shoulders. As the sub rocked beneath them, Rinna hugged her briefly, then pushed her away and scrambled out onto the tiny upper deck. "Get below. Now." But as Petra stepped into the hatch, the creature with her datapad broke the surface. Its tentacles uncurled from the pad and it raised it toward Petra.

"No," Petra croaked. She pushed both hands forward in a gesture of giving. "Keep it." She looked at her mother with a ghost of a smile. "It'll never work again anyway."

"Get below," Rinna said again, sharply, and followed her down. As soon as the hatch was dogged, she turned to Will. "Take us home," she said. "Fast."

Will was staring at Petra as if he'd never seen her before. He shook himself and said, "Right."

As they got under way, Rinna settled to the deck beside Petra, who was draining a bottle of water from the sub's little stock of supplies. Rinna felt battered to numbness by relief, terror, rage. But she would show none of it until Petra was safe aboard *Hokule'a*. Until they all were safe.

Petra gulped down another bottle of water, then demanded food. Between bites of an emergency ration bar, the words spilled out of her. Her shock when Rinna's flyer lifted off without her. The looming storm, the driving spray that drove her down into one of the deep gullies on the surface. "It was dark," Petra said, her voice shaking. "Completely dark. And the worst thing was when—"

Rinna took her hand. "What, love?"

Petra took a breath and shook her head. "Something *grabbed* me. Started pulling me. I couldn't see it but it had my ankles. It was strong, Ama, and I was so afraid, I couldn't keep a hold on anything. It dragged me down through a hole in the mat."

"I saw one of those," Rinna said.

Petra nodded. "We slid all the way down to the water, and I thought that *thing* was going to d-drown me—" She broke off again.

"It's all right," Rinna said, stroking her hand. The mindless soothing she had once given the child Petra. Beyond, she saw Will sitting stiffly at the conn, his head half turned to listen.

Petra closed her eyes and went on. "I took a breath and it pulled me under…and before I ran out of air we surfaced in that place where you found me. I climbed out fast and it didn't follow me. It was so dark until you came, only a little light coming up from below. So quiet." She looked up at Rinna, her face still streaked with tears. "How did you find me?"

"Those—beings that were following us—they led us to you," Rinna said.

Petra shook her head. "I think they're people, Ama. Not 'beings'."

"Maybe." Rinna wanted to shake her. Shout at her. *Do you know how stupid that was? How afraid we were?* She sat still.

"Rinna," Will's voice was tight. "Turbulence coming. Hang on."

"Turbulence from what?" They were alone in the sea, as far as she could see; their escort of creatures had suddenly vanished.

"It's rising. The leviathan. Just to port. *Really* close."

Rinna felt the sub buck on the lifting surge from below, saw Will's hands tight on the controls. Petra scrambled forward into the observation bubble, and Rinna followed, slowly.

A wall of mottled, scarred flesh rose beside them. And then a vast eye, half the length of the sub. It did not move or focus on them, but suddenly the sub was filled with sound, a rumbling bass moan that shook Rinna's blood and bones. Then silence. The eye passed upward as the creature continued to rise. She lost her view of it as Will changed course, forcing the sub directly away from the surge of the thing's passage. Rinna moved to a rear-facing port.

They were regaining their escort of smaller creatures as the leviathan hovered, much closer to the surface, behind them. Then, slowly, its vast mouth opened. For a moment Rinna was sure it would engulf them, in among those ridges of bone and flesh, to be filtered and swallowed into darkness unending.... But the leviathan was receding now, letting them go. Rinna unclenched her sweating hands and took a breath.

She wanted to see it better, wanted to record it, but the light was fading. *There will be other chances.* Somehow she knew that. Something was taking shape in her mind now—the beginning of a theory. Nattana would shake her head. Nattana didn't approve of theories, not when there were so few data. But—

"Petra," she said quietly, wonderingly. "I think you've found us a new world."

After the confusion of their return to the crowded sub bay, after they'd passed through into surface pressure—and after Isaam firmly took them all home and closed the hatch in the faces of their neighbors and friends, promising time to hear about it all tomorrow, *Petra needs rest*—

After the girls had fallen asleep together in Petra's bunk, curled close in the warmth, in the weak golden light Petra insisted on leaving on. *No dark tonight, Ama*—

In the big reading chair, Rinna leaned against Isaam's warm shoulder. Absorbing peace. Breathing in hope, as life-giving as air. She told him of what she'd seen, and what she thought of it; and he nodded, listening. He was a man who could stand in a new world and assess it fearlessly, with clear eyes; it was what she had loved about him first, long ago on the journey here, when they were both younger than Petra. It was how he had looked into Petra's face, the night she was born. How he looked into hers, now. He did not laugh when she tentatively showed him the notes she had made on her datapad during the long return to *Hokule'a*. Told him her thoughts.

The mats...are farms.

Factories.

Technology without *power. Shaped by genetics, by breeding, maybe by engineering.*

...These are people.

"We thought this would be our home," Rinna said quietly, holding the datapad against her chest. "But it seems that we're guests."

"Invaders," Isaam said, half-seriously.

Rinna remembered the leviathan, and the immense power of its voice. A greeting. Or a warning. "We had better not be," she said. Her hands tightened on the datapad, which held the beginning of the report she would prepare for her team and, ultimately, for Earth.

We had better not be invaders, here in our only refuge. This delicate floating shell, one of only a few that would ever voyage here. A bubble of home, life, work, family. Down the passage, their daughters slept on, deep under the surface. A bubble of warmth. Adrift in a bubble of water around a warm orange star. Swimming itself in a swirl of motes in golden light, turning and turning in the warmth. A dance that almost made words.

Someday, she would learn to understand them.

She picked up the datapad and bent to her work.

Fieldwork

Shariann Lewitt

Grandma, do you think Ada Lovelace baked cookies?" We were in her kitchen and the scent of the cookies in the oven had nearly overwhelmed my childhood sensibilities.

"I don't think so, sweetie," Grandma Fritzie replied. "She was English."

"Oh. Mama doesn't bake either."

Grandma Fritzie shook her head. "There wasn't any good food when she was young."

"Did her Mama bake?"

"Maybe. But not after they left Earth. They only had packaged food on Europa, and no ovens or hot cookies or anything good. That's why your Mama is so tiny. We're going to make sure you get plenty of good things to eat so you grow up big and strong."

Grandma Fritzie sneered when she said "packaged food." She was the head of the Mayor's Council on Children and Family Health, and I lived with her while Mama was in the hospital.

My mother won the Fields Medal when I was eight. That might not have presaged another breakdown if the press had reported it as "Irene Taylor, Russian-born American mathematician working in algebra" etc. etc. But of course they did not. Some reporter even asked me, "So what was it like, being Kolninskaya's granddaughter? You never knew your grandmother, of course...."

To which I replied that I knew my grandmother very well,

that she lived all of three subway stops away in Brooklyn just like me and would tell me not to open the door to strangers. Then I slammed the door in the reporters' faces. I went to live with Grandma Fritzie and Grandpa George three days later when Mama went to the hospital.

The press couldn't just leave her alone. She'd been a hero, done something amazing and brave when she'd only been a bit older than me, and now she'd only been the fourth woman to win a Fields Medal, and the media had to be horrible to her.

Even when I was eight I knew she wasn't like other people's mothers, was fragile in some way I didn't understand, and I swore that I wasn't going to be like her. I was going to be like Daddy and Grandma Fritzie and Grandpa George.

And maybe even, though I wouldn't admit it, like Tatyana Kolninskaya, the famous grandmother I had never met. The one who had died and who my mother never talked about. Because at least Kolninskaya had gone out and explored, left her room, left our planet even. Unlike Mama, who never wanted to leave our brownstone in Park Slope except to go to her office, and even then didn't like to take the subway. *Too many people*, she said, which confused me. I thought she'd feel better with lots of people around. But, as Grandma Fritzie said, I was a sensible child and my mother's neuroses were not comprehensible to me then. I don't understand them now, either, but at least I understand where they came from and I'm pretty impressed that she's managed to function at all. Let alone become one of the leading mathematicians of her generation. Besides, everyone knows that mathematicians are a bit strange, even those who grew up on Earth with loving parents and all the fresh food they could ingest.

None of the Europa survivors returned to anything close to normal. Most accepted implants to mitigate the worst of their nightmares, but Mama was afraid that it would interfere with the part of her brain that saw into math the way she does. So she uses drugs to lessen the bouts of PTSD that even the Minos Station orphans who took the implants suffer to a lesser extent.

Now that I've been there, now that I've seen the ice and what remains of Minos Base, and flown that journey and have some idea of what she went through, finally, now I can forgive her. For her fears and her craziness but also for the way she disappeared into her work for so much of my life.

There is only forever the ice. It expands to the dull greenish horizon flat and greyish green, as if it teases at being alive. Only of course it is not. Underneath is the sea, pulsing and alive. Maybe alive.

But the sea never fascinated my mother the way it did everyone else. She only cared for the ice.

The ice spoke to her. She loved the cores she pulled from it. Here a dusting of dark material that possibly came from an asteroid strike, and on another layer a slight change in color that indicated a change in chemical composition. She couldn't wait to get it back to the lab and see what had happened in that place, back then.

She loved the ice and it killed her. It killed all of them, and then we were trapped and there was the horror of the return I dare not remember. Therapy and meds forever keep me almost safe for moments, but then I drift and I can't quite understand with the clarity I have when I forego the chemical equilibrium. So I try to keep away from memories of the ice. Aunt Olga in Moscow has never been kind about it, but she is not the one who wakes up screaming from dreams about the long trip home, the pressure of navigation and celestial mechanics on the shoulders of a thirteen-year-old because almost all the grownups had died.

I read my mother's memoir on the way out. She had given it to me, me alone, not my brother or my father. And even though I had known that she was Tatyana Kolninskaya's daughter, that she had lived for more than two years on Europa and that it had formed her and destroyed her together, I had never really thought of her as a young girl living in that environment. I had only wanted to see her as a mother, as my mother. I didn't want to have to recognize her as a person apart from my need for her.

But then, I had asked far more of her and I knew it. And I was curious to know what Minos Base, and the great Tatyana Kolninskaya, had been like.

Tatyana Kolninskaya did foundational work on the preconditions for life on other planets, which had been a fundamental question for science. Kolninskaya, like many others, believed Europa the most likely body to host that life. Warm seas lurked under that ice, seas and oceans both, heated by friction.

According to the reports they sent back, they had discovered at least virus-like fragments of DNA. Not quite full animals, which was disappointing, but viruses could survive even hard vacuum. Had they come from asteroids or comets? Or were they the result of some previous contamination?

But the samples never made it back and until our mission, no one had been able to corroborate the finding. We were going to sample and survey and see if they had made a mistake. We knew there was a possibility of contamination from their trip, or even possibly earlier robotic vehicles, but our PI had worked out a program to compare the DNA so that we'd be able to tell if some virus had hitched a ride and flourished here. Or confirm, finally, whether there was, in fact, life in the oceans beneath the ice.

I was always sure she loved the ice more than she loved me, but she was so happy at Minos. She sang with me in the evening when she got in. All us kids got a skewed education. Surrounded by scientists and engineers in a narrow range of specialties, we did learn a fair bit about planetary geology and evolutionary biology, a smattering of useful mathematics, and how to play the clarinet. We all spoke the four mission languages (Russian, English, Mandarin, and Spanish) and, while we had no inkling of human history we had a firm grasp of the politics of getting grants (which I later realized mapped onto all human history with painful accuracy.)

Mama was acknowledged a genius at funding as well as math. Not only for herself, but for her grad students and half the department. "I learned from my mother. It is the only talent we shared."

Somehow, I doubted that.

Apart from the sciences, our education had been—idiosyncratic. We studied the poetry of Neruda, Li Bai, Li Qingzhao, Luo Binwang, and Jorge Luis Borges formally. Otherwise literature was left to whatever random selections we made from the central computer library, which included the complete work of Isaac Asimov, Alice Munro and Tolstoy. The full works of Nabokov and Henry Miller were also there but barred to those under sixteen, but little of F. Scott Fitzgerald, George Bernard Shaw, or Federico Garcia Lorca had been included. Nor were any French or German language writers represented. I didn't realize that people who were not from the Mission language groups ever wrote anything of note, though I am grateful for escaping Moby Dick.

Theater and music formed most of our evening entertainment. Carlos' mother was a magical guitarist and my father played the violin, so sometimes we had impromptu concerts in the dining hall. We learned to play the clarinet because that was the only instrument available that the adults would let us children touch. Their own were too precious for beginners. Sometimes we would perform plays by Shakespeare, Chekhov, and Gilbert and Sullivan. I got into a nasty hair pulling fight with Wang YeFei when I was cast as Helena to her Hermia in A Midsummer Night's Dream. Well, we were supposed to fight in that scene after all, but the adults stopped the production and both of us were not permitted to perform for three months. Which was especially painful for the audience of Pirates of Penzance since YeFei had the best voice of us all.

We were celebrities of a sort, the Minos children, the Minos survivors. I was thirteen when I was placed in an elite Planetary Educational Foundation Center under yet another grant for the children of explorers with the rest.

There we learned that our greatest deficiency was table manners. We had none. My mother's sister's family in Moscow, who took me in for those first holidays after our return, was aghast at my inability to behave like a civilized person. They did not make any allowance for the trauma, and when I started screaming the morning we woke to an ice-covered world, they returned me posthaste to the Center. I was never invited to return, and I have never seen them again, not even when I have visited Moscow as an adult.

The other Minos orphans had had much the same experiences, except Martin who had gone to LA where there was no ice. But he shrieked and dove under the dining table whenever jets flew by or *trucks rumbled on the street, and so his family reacted just like all the rest. So the nine of us, who had lived together on the ice, bonded even more firmly. There were too many strangers. The food tasted wrong. We wore little clothing, and that all disposable. And the place was dangerous in all the wrong ways.*

We could breathe the air and walk out without a suit. We wouldn't freeze or asphyxiate or die in explosive decompression (which made up many of our scary childhood stories,) but we dared not speak to people we didn't know.

At least all the children had made it home. One of the two grownups who had survived and returned with us, flown the ship that I had navigated, never left a supervised facility again.

"Mom's doing serious math," my big brother Sergei said when I got home to make the announcement.

Bad news. That meant she was off her meds. Which meant *do not tell her anything important and most of all do not ever mention Europa.* Just the word once set her off in a fit where she threw dishes out the window of our Park Slope brownstone. They hit the sidewalk when Mrs. Coombs was walking Tyrus and she told the entire neighborhood that Irene Taylor was off her head. Again.

I was only ten at the time and still in school in the neighborhood and the other kids looked at me like I was some kind of freak show. As usual, I went to live with my grandma when mom went crazy.

I have a perfectly good grandmother who is nothing like Tatyana Kolninskaya. Grandma Fritzie bakes the best chocolate chip cookies ever, is five foot ten with skin the color of milk chocolate and laugh lines around her mouth. She's a family physician, now head of the Mayor's staff specializing in children's services, and she works with domestic abuse victims on Thursday nights. Grandpa George is a dentist. He disapproves of cookies on principle and always tried to get us to eat apples instead. I don't need to tell you how well that went.

Tatyana Kolninskaya was a name in a textbook until I became advanced enough that I read her original work. And yeah, it was that brilliant. Really that brilliant. Of all the Minos team, she was the one who made the conceptual leaps about the possibilities for Europa.

But I never felt any particular connection with her. I knew the history and I couldn't avoid my mother's neuroses, but Kolninskaya had been dead for decades before I was born. No one looking at coffee-with-an-extra-cream-skinned and nappy-haired me would ever guess I was half blond Russian. And I kind of like to keep it that way.

I'm just plain Anna Taylor and if anyone makes the connection to my Dad, well, okay. Dad insisted that they give me Kolninskaya as a middle name but I don't acknowledge it. No K on my degrees anywhere. No one has made any big deal that Paul Taylor, the jazz pianist, is married to Irina Maslova, who is the daughter of Tatyana Kolninskaya. Mom has gone by Irene Taylor ever since they married when she was a grad student, and all her degrees and publications and awards are under that sanitized, Anglicized name. As if changing her name could erase the Irina who had lived through Minos Station and navigated that ship back to Earth when she was just a kid.

Grandma Fritzie did not want me to go. "Honey, you'll be gone how long? It'll be years, and dark, and it's dangerous. I remember when Minos Station was lost in the ice. And think of the malnutrition. That's why your mother is so tiny. They didn't have any decent food out there on Europa. All those Minos children grew up undersized. What if you get pregnant and you have some tiny undernourished baby?"

I shrugged. "Mama isn't the only person in the world under five-ten." Grandma Fritzie and I are the shortest people in the family, excepting Mama, who is barely five-two. "And I'm not getting pregnant. After Minos, children aren't allowed on exploratory expeditions anymore. Besides, I'm not even dating anyone.

"We're not staying. We're just doing a prelim survey to confirm the findings from Minos, and it's a job and I'll get a ton of papers out of it. We just need a few samples to bring back. They didn't bring anything back, you know, so no one could verify their results."

"You're not dating anyone?" Grandpa George said. "What happened to that nice boy we met at Thanksgiving?"

"He didn't want kids. Besides, this is an amazing opportunity for me, especially right out of grad school. No matter what we find, there's so much to discover that there are going to be a zillion journal articles and I've got to publish my ass off to get myself a nice academic—"

"Language, young lady."

"Sorry, Grandma."

"But she can't tell Mom," Sergei interrupted. "Mom's doing serious math." Which is why we were all huddled in Grandma and Grandpa's huge living room in Grand Army Plaza instead of Park Slope, even with Sergei visiting from Paris with his French wife and their new French baby.

"Honey, I don't know how she'd tell your mother even if Irene were taking her meds and then some," Grandma Fritzie said. "I'm not even sure that I approve."

"I certainly don't, that's for sure. I don't approve of any grandchild of mine leaving this planet," Grandpa George said. "Bad enough you have to study something as dangerous as volcanoes. I don't see why you couldn't study something safe like computers and stay right here on Earth. Humans belong on Earth, not traipsing around the solar system getting themselves killed or starved or abandoned on ice."

I sighed. They knew perfectly well that I had to do fieldwork. I love fieldwork. That's why I fell in love with geology, actually. How could I explain it? Everyone else except Mom was into things to do with people. Even Sergei, the bad boy, went off to Paris and became a chef. Though maybe after my announcement I'd be the bad one and Sergei, with his new daughter and new restaurant, would have joined the ranks of respectability.

Only Mom really understood that things that have nothing to do with people could be just—fascinating. All by themselves.

I did not become a geologist because of my famous grandmother. I became a geologist because when I was ten we went to Hawaii and I saw a volcano erupt. It was all very proper, in a helicopter over Volcano National Park, but I had never seen anything ever so thrilling or so beautiful.

I became obsessed by volcanoes. I read about them, watched them, studied them constantly. When other tween girls had pictures of teen dream movie stars or boy bands up in their rooms, I had pictures of exploding mountains and lava floes. I became a volcanologist.

Then the Europa project appeared. I fell in love with the possibilities. And I understood Tatyana Kolninskaya, understood what had driven her off Earth and onto the ice.

The project manager had been one of her graduate students, but hadn't qualified for the Europa mission because he had a heart condition. He hadn't realized that I was her granddaughter and I've kept it that way. Just Anna Taylor from Brooklyn, you know. Forget that K. Doesn't stand for anything. But he quivered with excitement when he talked about the waters of Europa, about the seas trapped in the ice, separate from the oceans beneath them, and the friction that kept them warm. With explosive plumes very much like volcanoes—one of which had killed most of the Minos team.

There may be volcanoes beneath Europa. They wanted a volcanologist who could study the ice plumes and the tides, and also possibly locate volcanic vents.

I'd done my dissertation on underwater vents on Ganymede, Europa, and Enceladus. Volcanoes presage life. Life needs heat, and heat can come from the planet's core or star, or tidal friction as with Europa, or any combination. But unique life forms have evolved around oceanic volcanic vents on Earth. If it happened on Earth it could happen elsewhere.

I was hooked, and I was hired. My dissertation had been grounded in the observations we had from flybys and robot landers, but the Minos material had more depth. How could I pass up the opportunity to go there myself?

"I want to go. I need the publications and this could make

my career. It's not my fault my mother is crazy."

"No, it's not your fault. But we don't have to like it just the same," Grandpa George said, and Grandma Fritzie nodded in agreement.

Sergei ignored me, but then he was in the kitchen preparing something intricate. I set the table, which at least gave me something to do. The starched linen cloth was so old it was wearing thin in places, the fine china with the gold scroll pattern along the edges that Grandma Fritzie had gotten from her grandma and the heavy silver that had come from Grandpa George's family connected me with my own history. The serving spoon engraved with the elaborate B for "Browne" came from Ruth Browne, who had been Grandpa's great-grandmother's in Syracuse. She had been a nurse and had been a little girl during school desegregation. I'd grown up on the stories of Great-great-grandmother Browne being bussed to a white school district and how grown women had screamed nasty words at her and thrown eggs. But that hadn't bothered her so much as the kids in her class wouldn't ever pick her for the dodgeball team. And she was always in the last reading group, every single year, although she tested at a ninth-grade reading level in fourth grade.

I hoped she would have been proud of me, and I felt her courage as I laid the heavy serving spoon on the table. I loved my family. I loved my work. I never wanted to hurt anyone, ever. But no matter what, I was going.

I wondered, for the first time, whether Tatyana Kolninskaya had faced resistance as well, whether my Great-Aunt Olga and their parents had been afraid and tried to talk her out of it. Mama had said that Aunt Olga had been elegant and stern and disapproving. But Tatyana was taking along a child, my mother. I, at least, was going alone.

Ice. So many many colors of ice. And so abnormally flat, as well. Europa is the flattest body in the solar system. I was standing on a great body of water. More water was frozen right here on the surface of Europa than existed in all the oceans of Earth.

And I was here. Standing. On. Europa.

Like my mother and my grandmother before me. They too, had seen the colors of Jupiter with its rings above the horizon and the endless smooth ice. As I looked at the gas giant above it didn't seem so strange, suddenly, the ice and the stranger in the sky. I felt as if my mother were with me, as if I saw it through her eyes as well as my own. And Tatyana Kolninskaya was there too, watching. Silliness, I knew, but this was a place they had known and now I had come, the third generation.

We had set down ninety minutes previously and gone through a meticulous systems check before we suited up and started hauling equipment from the outer hatches. We would use the lander as our indoor base—we'd already been sleeping there and had our few personal items comfortably stowed.

More importantly, it had an efficiently designed lab that we could access from outside, including an airlock with a built-in laser spectrometer, scanning microscopes, sequencers and all requisite instruments so that we could run the basics without contamination. But we had to haul the larger equipment out to the sites, drill out cores, and survey in situ.

The lander had been designed so that we had to lift and carry as little as possible. After five months in zero G, even with all the mandatory exercise, we were weak. I was not looking forward to dragging all that apparatus anywhere, even if it was just to the power sledge.

I only weighed a hair over twenty-one pounds on Europa. After five months in space, it felt like a ton. Our equipment, fortunately, only weighed about six hundred pounds on Europa, and there were six of us to haul it out and secure it to the sledge. Back home it would have been a joke.

We'd trained for the physical challenges of the mission. We'd worn the bulky suits in saline tanks and practiced securing the power pack ties to the sledge frames and getting the drill tripods set up, but nothing could simulate what happens to the body after five months of zero-G. We all worked out on the trip out here and geologists are a pretty fit crowd to start with. Even I, the city kid, was an avid camper and thought nothing beat a white water canoe trip or an afternoon of snowshoeing for a great time. When we ran the drills back home I never broke a sweat. Now I was breathing hard just getting the panels detached.

By the time we set up and returned to the lander I felt like I'd been run over by a tanker. The only reason I peeled out of that cumbersome, overstuffed suit was that I thought maybe I would hurt less without the constant pressure of the tubing across my aching shoulders and the steel rings restricting my movements. My teammates looked every bit as exhausted as I felt. None of us were good for one more step, not even Richard, the hydrologist post-doc who had been an alternate on the US men's Olympic speed skating team once upon a time.

"Anyone want dinner?" Ilsa Grieg, our chief organizational martinet (whose official position was aeronautical engineer and not Boss of Everyone) asked, but I was too tired to eat. All I wanted was to fall asleep, and I barely made it to my bag before I did.

The first week went by in a blur of agony and exhaustion punctuated by awful food. Grandma Fritzie was right, there was nothing good to eat out here. Not that I noticed; I was too tired to pay attention to anything except the fact that my shoulders felt like they were tearing apart and my legs were constantly sore. And we all stank. The recirculated air in the lander smelled of unwashed bodies. We showered for a timed five minutes in lukewarm water on a three-day rotation and used dry shampoo on our hair. Whoever had masterminded supplies had probably thought scientists wear white lab coats and sit at benches all day. But drilling ice cores at minus one hundred sixty Celsius while wearing a suit is not exactly sitting in front of a screen eating Doritos and wearing a tee shirt. No, we knew the real reason was because water is heavy and hard to haul, and drinking takes precedence over bathing. But still, yuck.

My mother had grown up here? I could barely imagine surviving more than our three weeks of data collection. My grandmother and mother had lived here for twenty-seven months, and would have stayed much longer. I could not imagine how someone could be a child here, how to play and run in suits, how to get away from the grownups in the cramped quarters of Minos Base. And yet my mother had written about it in her memoir as if it had been normal. I suppose for her it had.

In that thin atmosphere and low gravity, we could almost fly and our games always involved long jumps and chases. We were not heavily supervised as the adults went about their work, so we learned to take care of the suits ourselves.

The day of the accident Victor and Madison had lab time, and so were in charge of watching us. We kids had a kind of pact with Victor and Madison. They were two of the younger expedition members and not parents themselves, so they didn't have the same fears for us as the other adults. Like all children, we wanted independence and to be away from the eyes of grownups. Victor and Madison were both willing to be very lenient so long a we gave them the quiet they desired to concentrate on their work.

In the second week things began to change. We broke into three teams of four, and I had lab time as well as fieldwork. For several shifts a week I did stare at a screen as the sensors processed samples we'd retrieved. My body had adjusted to the hard work and the minor gravity and I was no longer so utterly spent. I could pay attention to the ice formations and the view of Jupiter overhead.

Ice.

I am a volcanologist, but first I am a geologist and the ice on Europa holds such promise, teases with such secrets. Under all that ice burns a hot core, heated by constant friction of the tide as it is pulled by Jupiter. Some astronomers have conjectured that Jupiter is a proto-star, a dwarf that, had it developed fully, would have been a binary for our Sun. Instead it remained a gaseous smudge above us, duller than the surface of this moon. Though to be fair, Europa has the highest albedo in the system.

And deep in its heart, at the bottom of those liquid oceans

under the ice are volcanoes. Very probably in those oceans is some form of primitive life as well, though the narrow band of atmosphere would not support much on the surface.

We drilled. We took measurements. We compared them with the Minos readings and found that they agreed. The only uncertainty was—had we brought it ourselves?

The partial DNA we found in what we thought was a virus matched a set of readings that Minos Base had recorded and sent back. It was rare and it seemed to be distributed far more densely in the area close to where Minos had been located.

"So is it spontaneous, or did it come with the first mission?" Michael Liang asked over what passed for our seventeenth dinner on site. Michael, being the top evolutionary biologist and one of the mission PIs, was in charge of the gooey stuff. Like looking for life.

"I don't know how Minos could have contaminated the environment," Ilsa Grieg answered. "They kept strict protocols on containment of all biological material, including waste from meals...."

"If you call that swill biological," I muttered.

"As I said, they kept strict protocols," Grieg was not about to be interrupted by a mere post-doc.

"They were killed in an ice plume. That means dead bodies," I interrupted again, the image so much more clear in my mind now that I knew the ice. The flat, brilliant surface reflected a billion shades of white and red rust trapped in the upper layers. Sometimes the rust lay on top, as if a comet had dusted the surface with cinnamon, and we'd run spectroscopy on every sample we could lay gloves on and I could tell them half the specific comets that had left deposits. Had the bodies truly been captured by the Jovian gravitational field, or had they been ripped apart and some pieces pulled back to the surface of Europa?

"Those bodies were encased in suits," Grieg said. "They should not have been breeched, even in an ice plume."

"Suits can be breeched," Liang said. "And those bodies were thrown out of Europa's gravity by the plume. But it's possible that some—debris—from the accident came back down. All the surfaces of the lander and our equipment were blasted with radiation, but it's still possible some virus survived. Contamination has always been a consideration. Back in the old days, they deliberately crashed a probe into Jupiter rather than take the chance it would crash here and contaminate any possible life on Europa. But that was before we started getting more robust readings and had to come in and take samples...and the samples pass the protocol that compares them to known sequences."

"And our sterile precautions are much improved," Grieg had to get in her point. "We are far more advanced about such things now. Between the radiation sterilization and the other precautions we should no longer be a danger. The tests show that even dropped into a full volcano the suits remain intact."

"And I am Marie of Romania," I muttered under my breath. Richard shook his head at me.

"So what have you found?" Richard changed the subject.

Liang smiled. "We've confirmed the virus. The rest is—speculative. But promising. Very promising. Tests so far appear to confirm that this is not contamination."

"So we did it. We found extraterrestrial life. Proof that life exists on places other than Earth. It's here, around us, in this ocean," Richard said like a prayer in the stillness of the tiny lander common space.

We didn't jump up and down, congratulate each other, yell, break out champagne. We didn't have champagne. And this was bigger than a boisterous celebration, this was momentous, this was awe.

Had Minos hung on this moment too? Had my grandmother known this indrawn breath of the last of the old knowledge before the new universe broke around us? We are not and never have been alone. We had confirmed life on Europa.

"Viruses can survive almost anything," Liang said as if this were a perfectly normal conversation. "Anna, we need to find that volcanic vent you proved in the mathematical models, we need to find real warmth to see if there are native animals here and make sure they are not contaminated by the earlier mission. We have to go on the assumption that we can screen for contaminated material. We've only got four days left and a lot of work to do."

So we turned things over to Team Two. Since Europa keeps the same face toward Jupiter, we had light to work and had split into groups to maximize the time. Also to minimize the use of resources, like sleeping bags and heaters. I was in Team One and should be going off shift, but I was too excited to sleep, so I went back to my charts, looking for seismic activity to see if I could identify any possible volcanic activity in our survey region. Not that I hadn't run the data before, but this time I tightened the grid and used the ice plume indicators. I was not convinced that the ice plumes had anything to do with subsurface volcanic activity. Richard and I had spent the first week here, when we weren't drilling or sleeping, looking for ice plumes and what created them. I considered this a safety issue as well as scientifically interesting. My grandmother had died because they had been taken unaware. But the more I looked the more I was convinced that the plumes were the result of interaction between the weak magnetic field of Europa and the strong one of Jupiter which creates some very strange phenomena.

In any event, I started a much finer search from the vibration receptors we had placed at the collection sites. The next morning, over something that the supplies had labeled coffee but resembled that dearly missed beverage only in color and some degree of bitter kick, I showed Michael and Richard what I'd done. "If we can set up a deep heat sensor here, maybe in a few hours even we can have some idea whether it would be worth drilling." I indicated a spot deep in a crevasse. I'd specifically looked at crevasse areas to minimize the drilling—hard, heavy work with sixty-five klicks of ice to go through before you hit liquid water. And the heat vent would be far below that.

"You didn't sleep all night, did you?" Liang looked at me like my advisor used to when I'd made a particularly stupid mistake.

I shrugged. "It was interesting. I couldn't sleep."

He grunted. Richard crossed his eyes at me. "Hit the bag. We'll probably go place the sensor, but you're not doing anything until you get some sleep."

He was right. I was seriously sleep deprived and not making the best decisions, which meant I argued that I had to go with them to position the sensors. He wasn't a geologist and Richard was a hydrologist who didn't know squat about volcanic vents, and I ended up spilling imitation coffee all over my pants, which didn't make my case any stronger. But I'm stubborn, and when I'm tired I'm worse, and Liang was a decent PI so he figured it was easier to give in than to fight. We were only placing a sensor. Besides, who would go with him? Liang? Or Grieg, who wasn't a geologist either? Richard couldn't go alone.

This was not heavy work, but rules were than no one went out on the surface alone. No one, never, not for any reason. I'd never thought about the rule because all my previous forays had been drilling, or placing sensor arrays, which took as many able bodies in the field as we could muster. This, though? This weighed less than one pound under Europa gravity and I knew exactly where it went, and I was cranky from being up my whole sleep cycle. We took the scooter, since the site was nearly ninety klicks off. I tried to set the coordinates for the area but my hands were clumsy from exhaustion and too much caffeine. I'd say I could do the sequence in my sleep, but I was just about doing that and it wasn't working. Finally Richard took the navigator from me and keyed the sequence while I suited up.

The scooter had barely room for two adults and a sample kit. The sensor rode on top of the sample case and the rope ladder secured below as we skimmed over the slick surface. *Like flying*, my mother had said, and she was right. At this velocity, if I just added a light hop I would be sailing overhead—almost like paragliding but without the sail since Europa's atmosphere wouldn't support us. But velocity and muscle would still make for quite a ride.

And then we were at the crevasse. We unloaded the rope ladder and secured it to the edge and started down. I hoped it would be long enough. We'd used it to explore several of the crevasses before, though it hadn't reached close to bottom on some others and we'd lowered equipment deep into them and waited to get readings back from deep inside. What made those deep grooves that laced the surface of Europa? That was Richard's question and he could talk about the crevasses endlessly. Richard strapped the sensor on his back after a brief argument (I insisted that it was my equipment, he insisted that I was too tired. I tried to take it but my hands were jittery and I lost the argument right there.)

Climbing into the depths is like climbing back into time. Or it would be on Earth, where we know that ice has formed in layers. On Europa? Kolninskaya's main theory stated that it is not, that all the ice formed at once. Certainly it appears that way, without the striation that one sees on Earth. Cloudy white-grey with hints of blue and reddish brown, lots of reddish brown that always made me think of cinnamon sprinkled over and swirled through.

We didn't know what made the crevasses on the surface. Before Kolninskaya, geologists debated whether they had been caused by liquid ocean responding to tidal forces, or earthquakes, or even volcanic activity. Kolninskaya settled that one—the readings had made it clear that the lines followed the moving magnetic field of the moon. The rust is iron and the salt water beneath the surface responds as Europa moves in and out of Jupiter's powerful magnetic field. Ice shifts and cracks appear.

Richard had studied the patterns of the surface crazing, hoping to identify older and younger stress lines and trace the action across the surface. Only now I saw the red as blood frozen from—debris. Or perhaps the red of a rag of suit.

Climbing down is always harder than climbing up. I didn't like looking down into what looks like forever, even when I weighed less than thirty pounds. The thin polymer struts that make up the rungs of the ladder didn't look like they could support the massive boots, though of course they did quite well even under full Earth gravity. But on Earth I only wore hiking boots to set sensors. On Earth I could feel the rope with my hands, I could feel the breeze, I could smell the air and enjoy the warmth of the sunlight.

The joy and wonder of an alien environment is balanced by the hard truth that you can't get out of it. There is no warmth, nowhere to run, none of the comforts of home. I still felt awe every time my sterile glove touched Europa ice, but I knew that when it came time to leave, I would be more than ready to go. Twenty-seven months? How had they remained sane?

"You coming?"

I shook myself from my reverie and continued down. We only had a kilometer of ladder. Who knew how deep the crevasse went? But I was fortunate this time and we had let out only three quarters of the ladder before we hit the bottom.

Richard stepped carefully, aware that the ice was not even. He used a probe before taking any step to judge the solidity and texture beneath. Minos teams had gone down into several crevasses, but we had done only sensor readings for the survey. From the previous mission we knew the bottoms of these cracks did not follow the pattern above, but that the ice itself could be broken and even soft. In a few areas Minos Team had found sections that appeared to be near the consistency of slush on the surface. That had been the most exciting finding of all, surface water, proving the existence of at least one of the lakes earlier scientists had theorized. But with the destruction of Minos Base and the emergency evacuation, no samples had returned for us to study. One of our first mission objectives had been to head to those coordinates and pick up samples of the slush, both to analyze in our own lab and to take home for others to study.

I followed in Richard's footsteps since he had the probe. We only needed to go a few steps to find a good stable platform to anchor the sensor. Even working with the thick gloves, between the two of us it was easy going. Though the temperature plummeted this deep, we were not blinded by the surface albedo. And then we started the long climb back.

We were perhaps two thirds of the way up—far enough at least that I could see the brilliant light of the surface—when the shriek of the alarm tore through me. "Suit breach, suit breach," it cycled through in the mechanical voice.

My suit had torn and might be leaking, but the only possibility was to keep climbing. The suits have multiple redundancies built in for every system. A mere outer breach would not endanger me, certainly not until we were able to reach the scooter. There would be supplies there to patch it up until we got back to the lander.

"Alarm noted," I told the system to shut off the racket.

"You get that?" Richard asked once my ears stopped ringing.

"Yeah."

"It'll hold. Keep climbing."

Climb. Just climb. Hand, hand, boot, boot. Look up, never down. Redundant systems. The suit is not depressurizing. There is plenty of air. I'm fine. Richard is fine. We'll get back to base. Just climb.

My mind shut down so that I saw only the next rung and then the next. I refused to think about anything else, though the ghost of Kolninskaya crept through. I could hear her in my mind. *Yes, child, one at a time. Slowly. The suit will hold. You will go home. I will not let you die.*

The fear froze like the ice around me. Cold, unfeeling, I felt distant from my body, and it seemed as if something helped me up.

And then I was over the top and Richard had his thick glove down to offer me a hand up. I stood on the brilliant white ice crusted with cinnamon rust.

My suit had a snag near the left elbow. There was duct tape on the scooter. Dear old duct tape, good for everything, everywhere. Even on Europa. Richard tore off large swathes of it and ran it around the outer layer of my suit. "You're good to go," he said.

When we got back to the lander and peeled out of the

suits, I took mine into the common space and started to pick off the silver grey tape.

"I wouldn't look," Richard said.

I had to look. The tape stuck fast and it took more work than I anticipated to tease the stuff off, but I was trained to be patient. Anyone who has had to use a paintbrush to dust down layers of sediment knows that slow and steady eventually gets you there.

At minus two hundred thirty Celsius, ice is magnificently solid. Shorn apart, it is crystal sharp, like obsidian. The suit held well enough, though, with the duct tape. Which only proved that duct tape is the one of the great forces of the universe.

Which also proved that the suit was not impregnable.

Not that it mattered in terms of contamination, I reminded myself. The third layer had closed. Nothing had gotten in or out. As for the Minos Team's deaths, eyewitness accounts and sensor recordings agreed that the bodies in the ice plume were jetted away from the surface and Europa's weak gravitational field. They had plummeted toward Jupiter and had most likely burned on entry to the gas giant's atmosphere.

I wondered again if my mother had seen them. The witnesses who testified later were the two adults who had been observing the party. The children—well, Victor and Madison hadn't paid too much attention to them that day. My mother said that those two had generally tried to shirk any teaching responsibilities. She didn't mind—when they did give lessons they were neither interesting nor rigorous. She preferred lessons with the more senior team members, who often forgot these were not even university students. Mama had managed to convince Professor Chiang to teach her naïve set theory before she had started high school.

We felt it blow more powerfully than we had ever felt anything blast since we'd left Earth. The ground shook us all so we tumbled; no one could stand through the violence of the tremor. But only Carlos looked up. The rest of us started to run as soon as we felt the first shock...I don't remember how I got back to Minos Base. One of the older kids, I guess, probably Martin, got us back. We hadn't wandered so far.

The base remained untouched. Victor and Madison looked at the sky and held each other, sobbing. Then they said we had to leave. Now.

We asked where our parents were, and Madison said carefully that they had all been killed in an ice plume. That we had to get back to Earth immediately. That we had to prioritize and pack, food and water, suits and tanks first, then records and samples, whatever we could salvage.

Victor sank to his knees, wrapped his arms around himself and started to rock back and forth. He said nothing intelligible for months. I understood much later that they would have heard our parents die.

We hauled what we could to the transport, food packs and water. Our parents had been strong people, large and powerful, but we were all small for our ages. Stunted by the lack of food, by the lack of gravity to work our muscles, we tired easily and had trouble getting even the barest necessities stowed away. Paul Song, the smallest of us, though not the youngest, downloaded the records, or as many as he could get over.

The ground shook at times and reminded us that we were not on solid ice, that we could be blasted out to Jupiter or churned into ice. We went too fast in our fear, we ran as fast as we could, as we dared. We wanted to finish and be gone from this place that had become a nightmare.

I am not so sure we even cared so much about remaining alive, but getting away was something to fix our minds on rather than the fear. Better to go through checklists, to calculate escape velocity and fuel reserves than think about the body of my mother hurled toward Jupiter, cremated in its atmosphere.

I took navigation; even before we left Earth my talent for mathematics had been clear. Aunt Olga had offered to keep me home so I could attend the best math schools in the country, maybe the world. How many times on Europa did I wish I were back on Earth instead of far away? I had wondered constantly why my mother had insisted on dragging me off when I could have remained in Moscow and won school prizes and worn dresses and shoes and not a vacuum suit whenever I left the enclosure. Where people would have praised me and paid attention the way they always had and said what a prodigy I was instead of having only this pack of unevenly educated kids as friends. Didn't she know my life was horrible?

And then she was dead. Gone forever. I did not mourn so much at first, but later, later....

I had to navigate. Madison stepped in as pilot and she was barely qualified. Her training was in evolutionary biology and she'd only completed the required safety training for any crewmember. All she knew were the basics of how to fly. Victor, who had been one of Mama's graduate students, was no better trained, and less help. Paul took care of the onboard computer systems and little YeFei turned out to be quite good at mechanics. Every hour I worried about asteroids, gravitation and fuel requirement and how to get home. I had constant nightmares of getting the reentry angle wrong and burning us all alive. To this day I wake up in panic thinking that I am burning, burning, dying inside the Rosalyn Yalow.

The only way I could remain sane was to focus on the math. Trajectories, geometries moving through space, distant, abstract equations that had nothing to do with life or death, that comforted me in their stillness, were my safety. They whispered to me and I could see into them, see the next movement and the one after as if it were a thing done. So I moved into that space in my mind, where only the equations existed. Nothing threatened me there. Nothing hurt and no one died. Here in the equations only truth existed, and the deeper I went into the truth the more clearly I could see it. Why would I ever want to leave that place for the real world of hurt and fear and lies?

We were so very close to Earth by then and I believed Earth would be my salvation. I was wrong. Earth is full of nightmares. Only in the world of mathematics am I safe.

I read my mother's private memoir during the months we flew out, and I was surprised by how deeply I felt for her. I was amazed at her courage. What had appeared as fragility all my life attested to a kind of nerve beyond anything I had ever imagined. She never spoke of her time on Europa or her mother's death. Only when I told her I was going, in the dining room of my grandparents' apartment, she surprised us all.

Dad brought Mama in. As always, she was the only blond porcelain-skinned person in the room, and she was a good four inches shorter than anyone else at the gathering (Sergei's French wife being the next smallest and fairest member of the family.) She looked delicate, her wide blue eyes haunted, still so thin that one might think that she had never seen a decent dinner since her return to Earth. We gathered around the same table where we had every Thanksgiving and Christmas dinner and birthday and graduation party in my life. Sergei served some fancy concoction and Grandpa George stood up. "I believe we are here because our brand new Dr. Anna has an announcement."

I stood up to general applause, though they'd called me "doctor" to death a month earlier at my graduation.

"I've got an amazing opportunity for my post-doc," I started, not daring to look at my parents. "I'm one of the geologists for Michael Liang's expedition and we'll be leaving in eighteen months." I took a deep breath. "For Europa."

Dead silence. Then I glanced under my lashes to see my mother smiling slightly. She nodded. "Yes, I always knew you'd go," she said as everyone else held their breath. "You are just like her, you know. My mother. Tatyana Kolninskaya. You are her very image."

Which I found very hard to believe since Kolninskaya had been all the colors of ice, white skin and pale blue eyes and platinum hair.

"And now," she said with a quiver to her voice, "let us enjoy this wonderful meal Sergei has made. It will be a long time before I have my children together again."

She even tried to smile. Was this the mother I had known as a child? I was in awe of her courage.

I was right about the vent. We drilled and took samples and this time it was Liang who didn't sleep. We had to make our re-entry window, but he wanted to make every minute count. On our twentieth dinner he announced that he had confirmed an actual cell sample from the vent area. True extraterrestrial life.

"I'll still have to run more screens for contamination," he said when he made the announcement. "But the first pass looks like no match to anything of Earth origin."

I spent the week before we left for Europa in Brooklyn. The day before I had to leave, Mama took me for a walk around the Japanese garden in the Brooklyn Botanical Gardens. We wandered around the reflecting pond with the azaleas and cherry trees and drifting willows, all as serene as my mother appeared. We sat for a while on one of the benches in silence, just appreciating the scene.

Then she pressed a chip into my hand. "My memoir," she said. "Of Europa. I've never shown anyone, not even your father. But you are so much like my mother, and you're going there."

But as she pressed it into my hand, she did not let go of my palm and we sat together, her tiny bird fingers strong, grasping my much larger hand.

"What do you mean that I'm like your mother?" I had to ask. The whole idea confused me. I thought of myself as much more like Grandma Fritzie and perhaps Dad.

She smiled softly. "You need so deeply to know things. You are so passionate. You are strong and single minded. But also, you love. That is the gift you gave me. I wondered why my mother took me to Europa, why she did not leave me in Moscow with Aunt Olga."

"Aunt Olga is a twit," I couldn't help but respond.

Mama laughed. "Agreed. But more, I realized, I realized for myself when you children were born, and the more I knew you, that she took me because she wanted me with her. We believed it was safe then, after the Lunar colony established protocols for children living in space communities. She enjoyed my company. She told me what she did in the day, what interested her, why she loved the ice. I think she was sad because I did not love it, too."

"So it's okay."

She smiled. "We're surrounded by these cherry trees. You know what the Japanese say about the cherry blossoms and their beauty. I think that is true of all life, of all of us. Come back to me, my Anna. You are so like my mother, so unafraid, so sure about your great adventure. Come back."

Growing up, I thought Mama was weak and afraid of everything. This woman before me was something different, some person I had never seen before. I held her very hard against my chest and if I cried on her shoulder, no one saw.

Our return trip was fairly uneventful. I started writing up the papers that I would submit on my return and Richard and I started talking about more than just geology. Okay, yeah, I'd noticed when we first started working together that he was cute. But after nearly two years we had both begun to admit that we were—interested. We had another year to go on the post-doc, and then there was job hunting and the two-body problem, and it's not exactly like there are a million jobs screaming out there for geologists and planetary scientists. But both of us decided not to think about it until after we finished our post-docs. After all, a thousand other things could go wrong in the meantime. He might not want children. He might not want to settle on the East Coast. He might leave his dirty socks in the living room or not like basketball. Or he could be a Lakers fan.

Mom and Dad had come down to Houston to spend some

time with me while I did the de-comp and re-established my wobbly Earth legs. I knew it was a big deal for Mom especially, but she was smiling, normal, even when everybody in the flight center tried not to stare at her too much (though one of the interns did ask for her autograph on one of her books, which she granted graciously, and even let him snap a selfie with her and said book.) Though most of the time it was both my parents with me and Richard, Mom and I did ditch the guys to get our nails done, and so that Mom could talk to me alone. But she didn't want to talk about Richard, or even about Europa.

"You remind me so much of her that sometimes it frightens me. Did you read what I gave you?"

I nodded.

She bit her lip and the two little lines between her blue eyes stood out hard. "I don't know, Annushka, if you can tell me, but you are like her. What do you think? Why do you think she took me with her to that place? Why didn't she leave me safe in Moscow?"

"Mom, mama," I took my one dry hand and touched the back of her arm. "She took you because she couldn't bear to be away from you. Don't you see it? And when you say I'm like her, I'm like you. I'm just like you. But maybe not as brave."

"But I am not brave and I hate the ice," she said.

"Mama, you're the bravest person I know. But look at this."

I showed her my first article from the Europa mission right there in Geology. With me as first author. Anna Kolninskaya Taylor. "And I've been offered a more senior position on the Enceladus team as well."

Mama blinked and swallowed hard. "You will go out again?"

I smiled. "No, Mom, it's a robot mission." I sighed with frustration. "Maybe if this turns up enough to warrant it." I shrugged. "Funding. You know."

And Mama laughed. Not a little giggle or sad smile, but a full out laugh. "Oh, yes, Anna, you have a lot to learn. Not

only about your volcanoes, but the process of getting grants. I
will help you. I am very good at this, you know."

Of Wind and Fire

Vandana Singh

I have been falling for most of my life. I see my village in
dreamtime: an enormous basket, a woven contraption of
virrum leaves and sailtrees, vines and balloonworts, that
drifts and floats on the wind. On the wind are borne the fruits
from the abyss, the winged lahua seeds that always float upward, and the trailing green vines of the delicious amala—
windborne wonders that give us sustenance. But the village is
always falling. Slowly, because of the sails and balloonworts,
but falling nevertheless. We hang on the webbing, the children and babies tethered, shrieking in joy—and we tell stories
about what might lie below.

The world is the Mountain, which we also call Lohagiri.
The Mountain is the largest thing we know, and its sheer,
rocky cliffs, punctuated by ledges, caves and outcrops, descend as far as the eye can see. In the crannies and on sheltered ledges grow the virrum trees and the forests of kohnaar
and simal, and in many places there are waterfalls, rivulets,
and deep, rocky pools where the greenspun is harvested. From
atop the Mountain we see only the sun and sky above us, and
the clouds below. We are born into air so thin we must breathe
with the help of greenspun, which tints our skins until we
slough it off in late childhood. Far below us, at the boundary
of our vision, the air slowly thickens into clouds and shadows.
When the clouds break up, there are more clouds below them,
and sometimes there are misty glimpses of green swathes and
brown streaks. Some say these are illusions wrought by the
mist—others claim these are the nether realms of the Moun-

tain: the City Antimm, where the gods sleep.

Nearer at hand, though rarely, we might see the dark shadows of the other villages below us, or above, blotting out the sun. Then the windworkers must employ the long speaking tubes, making our presence known with raucous bellows, so that the village above may adjust its rate of fall, or steer away so as to not crash into us. I have heard that there have been wars between villages in times past, but in my time there has been only the peace of falling. Until—but more of that in time.

My name is Vayusha, which is one of the names of the wind. I am telling this story from a place at the end of the world. I am telling it for a reason that must wait until the beginning falls toward the end, the natural order of things. So let it be.

I was born in a ledgetown called Kassi. My mother had stopped there to leave her people (of the village Ashe) and to birth me. She told me how she stood on the platform and watched Ashe falling through the dusk, into the endless abyss; she called goodbye to the people she had known all her life, standing with her child in her arms, the way I would one day hold my own child, feeling her full weight, the beating of the small heart next to her own. I don't remember much about Kassi except for the flitter-monkeys that clambered up and down the cliff walls, making faces at us. I have a vague memory of the darkness of the tunnels, the flaring lights, the shudderings of the Mountain, the rockfalls. We lived in Kassi for two cycles, my mother told me, until she felt ready to leave again. When a village came falling out of the sky like a giant, veined leaf, we left with it.

To go among strangers is not easy. The village that took my mother in—Naupura—spoke a different dialect; the shelters were harvested from virrum leaves instead of windfroth and their people took many lovers. But the Naupuri had a joyfulness to them that slowly filled the void in my mother's heart. Their young men were adepts at capturing the winged

lahua pods, and at hunting skyfish. The women ground lahua meal and roasted skyfish, and threw nets out to capture
floating windborne greens. Some were firekeepers whose red-
rimmed eyes and raucous shouts scared me; others joined the
men at windworking, the most difficult task of all.

I remember as a child being tethered to one of the sailtree
trunks in the center of the village, watching the windworkers'
silhouettes through the filigree of leaves and vines. They stood
on beams, pulling hard on the ropes then easing, pulling and
easing with the rhythm of the wind, working the enormous
sailtree leaves. Thick, woody lianas formed the framework of
the village—the thinner, more pliant ones were webbed across
these. The thinnest tendrils were woven into a fine mesh that
formed walls and pathways, so that the inside of the village
was a maze of tunnels and rooms. From the mesh sprout-
ed the tubular yellow flowers that would fatten into gourds,
and beanpods flashed green and silver among the exuberant
cascades of red avla fruit. The village was alive—within the
tangle of vegetation snapwings nested, and furry little luka-
chhupis made their little warrens, and skyfish laid eggs in the
canopies. When dark fell, the tiny, iridescent chikwikas would
sound their shrill zithers.

So we children were made whole, knit like the tapestry of
life itself by the beings around us.

My mother, being a priestess, knew how to read and in-
scribe the godsongs as well as sing them, and she taught me
as well. I still remember how painstakingly I would write
the symbol for the start of the invocation, a curved downstroke followed by an upstroke, like the two wings of a lahua
seed—the shape of a yearning before it becomes sound, like
two arms stretched toward a lover. In the morning the priests
would sing the gods awake, and my mother's voice would
weave in and out with their music, like the words in her book
of dried heart-leaves, a thread I could follow through the wilderness. I remember the sounds of lodestones tossed into the
air, how they whirled of their own accord, turning and aligning, and their clattering beat.

We children had a fright, once, when we were falling through an area we named Rain Forever. There was a water-fall coming out of the cliff-face, and the white, frothing water sent up an enormous fan of spray, soaking us. We children ran to help the water catchers collect the gift, shouting over the noise of it. Then, one of the babies got his tether loose in the wet, and it slipped off his ankle. And there he was, floating above us in the updraft, and then floating away on it toward the edge of the village. But when I shouted I couldn't even hear myself above the roar of the waterfall. There was spray in my eyes and wet limbs around me, and the lianas bursting into leaf, and my whole body not moving, numb with shock. But then a windworker swung out on a long liana, and caught him just as he was slipping away.

If we didn't have the ledgetowns we would not know about anything but our own village. There we hear the gossip and stories from other villages that have gone before, and exchange ground-grown foods for virrum-woven cloths and lahua meal. We sit around fires late into the night, mouthing unfamiliar syllables, telling histories, learning new ones. The village hangs from the support beams that jut out from the cliff, ghostly in starlight with its mesh of lianas, its folded sailtree wings, its feathery sails, its bulbous balloons that glow when the sun fades. There is nothing stranger than lying by the warm embers of a fire, feeling one's full weight in every breath, every moment, listening to a story, and seeing one's village sway gently like a giant basket in the night.

On the last day the ceremonial census is sung by the ledgetown chiefs, and if they are too many ledgetowners in number, some of them are invited to leave with us. If there are too few, they will allow a villager or two—if they are willing—to join them. More often the ledgetowners are more numerous than their living space allows, and it is therefore common for an old auntie or a young couple who wish to have children to join us. The partings are always sad, filled with wails and weeping. "All journeys are one way," the old people say as they wipe their tears. "As time runs, so does our path in space.

There is no going back."

When I came of age, I took many lovers, but among my people the life-oath is sworn between siblings, whether related by blood or dreamblood. The deepest bonds come from the dreamtime, beyond the merely physical. Such was my bond with Chaha-the-lame, my life-brother. Under his kindly eye I grew up to be a windworker. I loved my work—manipulating the wings and balloons is dangerous and requires strength and skill. As the village falls, we must control its speed, steer it away from the sheer cliff walls or jutting rock-faces, and, when a ledgetown is in sight, we must steer carefully around the docking arms and send the long ropes flying toward the grapples, so that at last we hang suspended, the balloons aglow, the great wings drooping, the whole village swaying, children shouting. When it's time to fall again, we get the fires going, the pipes belching, and the sails open as the balloons fill up. As the wheels of the supports turn, we pull on the ropes, shouting in time with the stretch of the arm, the flexing of the leg, and I feel with my whole body the village shiver, strain to be free, to fall.

Now that I was a windworker, it was my little daughter, Agniya, who, tethered and wrapped in her sleep cocoon, watched me as I clambered overhead among the sailtree wings, working the ropes, my muscles tensing and relaxing in time as I sang under my breath. *Mukkum, it is your breath that moves us. Breathe slow and deep, slow and deep.* But it was another god who gave me visions about sailtree wings and balloonworts, a god whose enemy Mukkum had once been. Chumbak. He entered my dreams and I saw forbidden visions, villages that sailed up instead of down. My daughter chuckled to see me up so high against the bright leaves and sunlight, singing to her and to the gods, and I felt the shock of love and fear like a deep wound inside me. I thought of the little boy we had almost lost. *Keep her safe*, I told Mukkum, but it was Chumbak who showed me how.

There is a game I played with the children using the floatbladders of windborne greens. As we let them go, they floated upward, and children would jump up to try to catch them. At night we played with small balloonworts for their light; inevitably they would get tangled up in the green mesh of lianas overhead, where they'd glow like dim stars. It occurred to me that here was a way to keep the children safe, so I made a device for Agniya and the other little ones when they had to be left to themselves. It was a stretch of tough bluehide shaped into an ombrel, supported by a pliable frame of thin wood. I added clusters of balloonwort bulbs and float-bladders for buoyancy. Whenever I was away from Agniya, working the winds, I would wrap her in her sleep-cocoon, attach the little ombrel, and place around the collar a necklace of munchbeads in case she woke hungry. Some people scoffed at me but others wanted me to make the devices for the other children, which I gladly did. Then some of the windworkers thought it would be a good thing for us to wear during a storm, so I built some larger, adjustable ones that could fold down in a high wind. Building, I felt Chumbak guide my hand, aligning me to the secret patterns of things, so that I learned, in time, what designs were better than others.

My curiosity led me to experimenting with falling objects and float-bladders. I saw that heavy and light objects that were dropped at the same time from a modest height hit the floor at the same instant. But when they were dropped off the ledge into the abyss, it seemed to me that the heavier object might outrace the lighter one. Objects fell differently in a falling village compared to a ledgetown. A stone flung horizontally fell in an arc—the harder the throw, the longer the arc. I was fascinated by these observations, and wondered if these were hints to hidden truths that the gods had left in the world.

Such mysteries were of little concern to other people, and their contemplation was seen as unholy by some, so I spoke of them rarely, and only with Chaha. Sometimes I felt alone, as those with secrets do, but there were many comforts to be had in that life. In the slow-falling, there were quiet days filled with stories and the aroma of roasting sweet tubers, and the teaching and learning of songs and histories. Then there were the storm-days, when the wind roared and the village swung about in its airy clutches, ropes and supports creaking, threatening to tear apart, while we windworkers donned our ombrels and worked the ropes. As we fell through the abyss and the air got thicker, the summer storms got worse too—rain lashed our faces as we maneuvered the sails, and lightning sent arms of fire toward our frail craft. In that terror of losing everything, I would feel a peculiar exhilaration, a madness in which we yelled and cursed at the gods to rouse them to wakefulness.

We made three circles around the Mountain as we fell. The Western side of the mountain was inhospitable, the sheer rock face smooth and mostly devoid of caves and ledges. After three circumlocutions we kept to the Southeastern side, where the sunlight washed us, grew our gardens, and helped keep the balloonworts filled with buoyant gases.

When my mother was old she wished to be left at a ledgetown to die. It was a large, prosperous place, one of the few that made villages. Five of their people, one more than the census required, left with us, so my mother was able to stay behind. I tried to persuade her to change her mind, but she was adamant. "I was born with the other ear," she said, "and so I must listen to that music as well as the music of the world. I've fallen all my life, and now I want to be still. I'll never see the City that lies at the end of the journey, but I'll meet you, my Vayusha, my child, in dreamtime."

She kissed me and my baby. After the ceremonious farewells, exhausted with weeping, I went away with my village, leaving her falling upward, waving to us from the railing.

If it weren't for our morning prayers, the gods would sleep all the time. Sleeping, they dream of the place they left behind, to which they can never return except in dreamtime. The oldest stories tell how the gods were pushed off from their world on a giant virrum leaf, and how they fell through the starry night until they fell upon the Mountain. They lived atop it for a while and made many children, our ancestors, who soon filled up all the flat places, the caves, the nooks and crannies of the world. In time the world got so crowded that the gods decided to leave. They built a great floating village, but before leaving they taught their children the many arts of village-making, because they knew the Mountain can only hold so many. And away they went, falling once more.

"But how will we know that you've reached your destination?" their children asked from the various ledgetowns, as the god-village fell.

"You won't!" shouted the gods. "But you'll know it in dreamtime, and you'll know it when it is your turn to fall. We have been falling a long time. We're tired and we want to get to the foot of the mountain, so we can sleep. We will leave you the flitters, the lodestones, plenty of skyfish, and on our rising breath we will send up for you lahua seeds and floating plants and fruits so you can live well."

So that is how it was. Some stories say that the gods built a great city, Antimm, for their children at the foot of the mountain before they fell asleep. Other stories say that soon after the gods left, fighting broke out among the children, and a long, dark age came to the Mountain. The gods saw this from dreamtime and were angered, and built instead a graveyard of bones and monsters. Perhaps both are true.

For the villagers, the greatest of the gods is Mukkum, who left us the virrum leaves and the sailtrees. Of all the gods he sleeps most deeply, because he likes to wander through dreamtime listening for the old music that he lost when he was banished. His breath makes the wind of the world, the rising updrafts, and the angry winds of the storms. His work in the world is to help the fearful let go—his is the hand that pushes a baby clapwing off the ledge for the first time, and his the hand that lets go of the holding ropes when a village must fall. But it is also his hand that guides the windworkers. We fall toward the dream-place, to the center of all things, and the thin air we breathe is his breath. But because he loves his sleep we must wake him every morning with horns and singing, and musical incantations to rival what he hears in the dreaming.

There are, of course, many other gods, and mostly we let them sleep. Gods aren't always good for us. Some of them, when fully awake, can kill you or drive you crazy. So much of a priest's time is spent simply making sure some gods stay asleep.

My secret favorite god is the two-form Chumbak, who gives us trickery, madness, and the creative fire, and manifests in the world through the lodestone. Once he/she came across Mukkum sleeping. Unable to resist, Chumbak took a long feather and tickled the huge nostrils of the sleeping god. The resulting sneeze was so violent that the Mountain shook to its foundations, and Chumbak was flung up in the forbidden direction, laughing all the way.

Now the gods had said that all order in the world depended on the right flow of things—so time flows from past to present, a human's life from childhood to old age, and so on. So most things must go down, and only a few can go up. What Chumbak did threatened the structure of the world, so the gods woke up and decided to stop him/her once and for all. They came to their children in dreamtime and told the humans what they must do. So the humans, villagers and ledgetowners alike, took up their bows and slings, and shot arrows and rocks at Chumbak as he/she rose up. Pierced and bloodied, Chumbak fell down to Antimm, and was smashed on impact. The lodestones are what's left of Chumbak's body.

But Chumbak still lives in dreamtime. Not even the gods know where in dreamtime he/she lies. We can only reach that place if Chumbak calls us in our dreaming. Because I have had forbidden visions, I know they come from Chumbak.

There are people who dream of the abyss below. Some dreams are of an endless swath of land where giant worms with lodestone-studded heads burrow tunnels through thick forests. Others are of Antimm—stone villages permanently tethered to a ground from which there's no more falling, where people wander through the pathways sipping on fruits of the gods. This is where there are no more goodbyes, no tomorrows. Or so the legends and the dreamers say.

Calamity came to us with a night storm, fiercer and more violent than any we had known. We battled it for many hours until the clouds, thunder and rain gave way to paling stars and a swift sunrise. We found ourselves falling lopsidedly toward a ledgetown, fighting hard to keep one of the sails from flapping away. Looking down through the supports, I saw the children's shelter still secure in the center of the village, although there was plant debris, smashed wood and bits of rope everywhere. Then a beam broke and hit me, and I knew no more.

Windworkers suffer injuries and even death fairly often. My people were afraid they had lost me at first, but the ledgetown had a good healer, and I am hard-headed. Hours or days later I stirred in my bed and saw a lamp swinging above me. Its light hurt my eyes.

Livu, one of my lovers, was sitting by my bed, wiping tears from her cheeks. I saw the relief in her face, as I called her name, and then people surrounded me, and I was fed some kind of pungent broth.

I sat up suddenly, remembering, anxious.

"Agniya? The children? The storm?" To my consternation, Livu started to wail. Fear stabbed my heart.

"What happened, Livu? Tell me!"

So they told me. Livu had seen to the children at the start of the storm, and made sure they were all safe. But during the storm the lashings that held the children's sleep-cocoons had come loose. While docking, the entire village had tilted dangerously, thanks to the missing sailtree wing, which had ripped off after all. They saved the other children in time, but Agniya was already gone, hurtling over the edge of the village in her little sleep-cocoon.

My heart thudded so violently, I could hardly hear myself speak. "When did this happen?"

It had been three eightdays. So many days! I thought of

Agniya in her sleep cocoon, with the float-device attached under her arms. I thought: *we don't know how far we fall, or if we fall forever.* I thought of my observation that when falling from a great height, a heavier object might catch up with a lighter one.

I began to run, leaving the others shouting behind me. I slid down the chute into the suspended village, where repairs were already begun. People came up to me with commiserations on their lips but I brushed them aside. I found my windworker's storm-suit, and my own ombrel.

My life-brother Chaha came up to me then, and saw the decision in my eyes. He set his hammer down and began to stuff things in a pack: food, dried munchbeads, medicinal herbs. My breath was coming in great sobs, my hands shaking so hard I could not secure the ombrel. He pushed a munchbead into my mouth and bade me drink from a gourd, while he lashed everything together. When the pack was secured he tied a grappling rope around my waist. I was aware of people around me saying "What are you doing?" "Are you crazy, Chaha, sending her to her death?" and "Must we lose her too?" and much weeping and sobbing, but a calm had descended upon me. My hands stopped shaking. It was late afternoon already, and there was no time for prolonged goodbyes. I would never see them again. I hugged Chaha swiftly, told him to kiss everyone from me. Then I heaved myself over the edge of the village, feet down, and started to fall.

In that moment I threw away all my old life and loves.

Faster and faster I fell, until the wind's roar filled my ears, and it occurred to me that I had to slow down, else my pack and ombrel would be ripped from me. So I opened the ombrel enough that my descent slowed. Now that I had acted, I could think. Could I catch up with Agniya despite her considerable head start? I thought back to my experiments with falling objects, and felt angry with my ignorance. I didn't even know how far there was to fall. Yet I had no regrets. If there was even a slight chance my child was alive, it was worth it—I thought of how I had weaned her a half-cycle ago, the green patina fading from her skin as she learned to breathe with her own strong little lungs, and her small, clear voice lisping the godsongs. Tears pooled around my eyes, and the wind took them away. The sun began to set, and I found that my hands were cold. I tucked them into my windsuit and hoped and prayed that Agniya's sleep cocoon, made of the same thick blueskin, was just as warm.

What would have taken a cycle, two cycles for the village to fall through, I fell in a day, two days, three days, twenty-four days. Days became nights, and nights turned again to days, and there was no sign of Agniya. The first few days I didn't sleep at all. After that, exhaustion made me doze off, and when I woke I was terrified I'd missed her. But there was nothing above me except for the ever changing sky, and below me the cloud layer came closer and closer.

The cliff face was pockmarked with caves. I passed by a ledgetown where a woman was washing something at the edge of the cliff—I remember staring straight into her eyes for a moment, and her shout of fear. Another time I thought I saw a village below me, but it was further around the mountain and would not have been in Agniya's path. I fell through the odd cloud or two, and emerged sheened with moisture, licking my lips. Sometimes a waterfall threw spray into my path, for which I was grateful—my child could live on munch-beads for several days, but she needed water. Would she know to open her mouth and drink from the spray? Once, weeping, I stopped in a cliff forest and filled my empty water bottle at a small stream, and harvested some wild fruit. Time had become my enemy.

Night and day became a blur. I had moments of despair at the thought that my little Agniya could not possibly survive a fall this great—then, all I wished for was the oblivion of death. I would reason myself into a semblance of calm, telling myself that however slim her chances, I had to do whatever was needed to find her. I alternately cursed the gods and sang to them to wake their compassion.

At last I saw that the rock wall was becoming smoother, bereft of the caves and crevices that would allow a ledgetown to settle there. It occurred to me that I hadn't seen a ledgetown for a long time. The plants and animals were different too—enormous blue-veined leaves jutted from the cliff-face like open mouths, collecting pools of moisture, and unfamiliar, leathery-winged creatures like giant clapwings flapped alongside the ubiquitous skyfish. Mossy curtains fell from the outcrops like veils, where brightly colored insects spread orange wings in the sunshine. The windborne plants became more plentiful—I had no lack of food, and sometimes, I had to whack clusters of snapwort and lahua pods away from me as they floated, trailing delicate green tendrils. Hope rose in me that my child, weaned now from her mother's milk, would know to grab these moisture-filled fruits of the air, and I thanked Mukkum, whose breath gives us these gifts.

I was fast approaching the thick cloud layer below. In the moment before the mist enveloped me, I saw something. There were holes and fissures in the cliff-face, too small to support a ledgetown, but I thought I saw long ropes hanging from them, going down the cliff-side. These were supported by horizontal cables so that they formed a mesh much like a ladder. Swarming up and down these were people. Dressed in green and grey clothing, they looked like cliff-crawlers out in the unfamiliar sunlight, but one of them waved a brown arm, calling to another. Was I hallucinating, after endless days and nights of falling?

Then the grey mist rose up around me.

I was in the cloud layer. I felt moisture on my dry lips, and drank of it gratefully. But it was harder to see here, and the clouds thicker than any I had known. I must be vigilant. So I prepared to adjust my device to slow down a little.

Then I found myself slowing without effort, and suddenly I was still, suspended, caught in a white mist with invisible, sticky ropes. I thrashed about in terror, and the links of the net, or whatever it was, stretched and broke. I fought my way down though the net, beating at it with my knife. The mist was so thick that I couldn't see my hand stretched in front of me, and there was a bitterness on my lips—some kind of sap oozed from the cut mesh. I thought I saw long, pale arms at the edge of my vision, just beyond my slashing knife. Hacking away in a fury (how could a small child survive this terrible place?), yet mindful that Agniya might still be here, trapped, I suddenly fell through into clear air. It was only a couple of person-heights down to a slick, rocky plain—I braced for the fall.

I rose to my feet and I saw that the plain stretched in all directions—its horizontal extent astonished me. I had never seen anything like it. Where was the Mountain? White lumps of clouds rolled about on the plain, obscuring my view, and there was the mist forest above my head. I had not felt my full weight for so long, my breathing was labored, my muscles weak. I looked around me fearfully, daring to hope that the net that had slowed my fall had also saved my child.

In the next moment my hope receded. Something came out of the mist above me, a creature at first sight like a cliff-crawler, but so thin and delicate as to be nearly transparent. It hovered above me, inspecting a break in the webbing, looking around as though for its prey. Its six silver limbs were each tipped with a lethal looking claw. It made a hissing sound suggestive of annoyance, and disappeared upward again.

I collapsed the ombrel, and, still clutching my knife, began to stagger around the plain, trying to find the face of the Mountain. Agniya would have fallen here, that much was certain, although whether she could have survived the predatory creatures above me was a possibility I couldn't bear to consider. I noted the rough, rocky surface below my feet, and the tussocks of unfamiliar plants that grew in the crevices. There was no sign of my child or her craft, or any human habitation, let alone the fabled city of Antimm. I had lost count of how long I had been falling—perhaps it had been lifetimes. Perhaps she had lived, grown old, and died. I passed a hand across my eyes, and felt my sanity slipping. I sank to my feet and wept.

Moments later, I looked up and saw an old man sitting on a rock on his haunches, staring at me. I was so startled, I leaped to my feet, almost falling over from weakness, knife drawn. At which he waved impatiently at me. "You need some rest," he said in an odd dialect. "You have the mad look about you. Been falling off the mountain too?"

That word, that one word, "too" gave me a wild hope. I said, trembling, getting to my feet "Is she alive, then? Is she with you, my daughter?"

"Come with me," he said.

He led me through tattered veils of moisture to a cave between two rocky spurs. A lamp dispelled some of the grey light that suffused the place, and in the radiance an old woman was bent over a child sitting on a seat of rock, spooning something into the little mouth. It was such an ordinary, familiar domestic scene, and so unexpected after all my fears, that I swayed for a moment. But yes, it was Agniya's little face turned toward me, and the heart-wrenching, familiar smile illuminating her face, and the face crumpling, and the cry, *Mama!* I knelt beside her, holding her to my chest while sobs wracked my body. I had weaned her over a half-cycle ago, and yet, as her face pressed against my shoulder, my milk came in, painful and sudden, soaking my inner clothing. I didn't care— I thanked all the gods I knew by name, and kissed the soft cheek, and told her I was all right, that I was crying with gladness, so that her smile peered out through her tears.

The old couple made me welcome. They fed me stew, and the woman, Mina, gave me some clothes to wear and a pallet to sleep on. A terrible weariness was taking hold of me; I couldn't think except for this: that sleep or not, I must have Agniya with me. Nothing would separate us now. I strapped us together and we slept.

She had been caught in the net, they told me, and the old man—Siru—had found her and cut her free before the monsters he called arachnae got to her. How had he managed to find her? Well, he foraged there often for trapped skyfish and other creatures. She was awake, and calling out, and thrashing her little arms to free herself. Hearing this, I wept again. But she was here, safe, and I was with her. I thanked them both a hundred times—Mina, the old lady, had got quite attached to my Agniya and invited me to stay with them. This was the last, best stop on the Mountain, they told me. There was no Antimm, not even a town like a ledgetown. There was no place to go.

I was full of questions. Where were all the people from all the villages that had fallen here since the gods left? How could the old couple live here alone? As my senses came flooding back I remembered the people I'd seen on the cliff-face just before I fell into the mist. Who were they?

"As to those people, they are the Moosar people, cave-dwellers," Siru said. "You'll see some of them soon enough. But they are wild folk, not like the ledgetowners, or the people of the villages. They won't do us harm but—best to keep our distance."

"But where are the people from all the villages?" I asked. "How do they...what happens to them in the mist forest? Where are they?"

I learned that Siru and Mina were from a village that had fallen to this place many years ago, when they were both young. The cave people had rescued them from the arachnae, and the village had stayed on the plain for a while. Then it had left.

I was confused. Wasn't this the last place in the world? Where else was there to go?

Siru said he would show me when I was better. I hadn't realized how my journey had exhausted me—I had lost weight, lost the strength of my muscles. Mina took tender care of me in the next few days, as she evidently had of Agniya, whose cheeks were filling out. I was filled with so much gratitude, it came out in tears. I slept a lot, occasionally interrupted by voices raised in argument or query, speaking a strange dialect, and Siru's calm, deep, soothing monotone. I saw soot-rimmed eyes in faces framed by colored tassels, staring at me. These were the Moosar people, come to see the stranger, bringing fungi and peculiar-smelling meats from the heart of the caves.

Then, when I was strong enough, Siru took me on a short journey over the flatland. The light was wan and grey, and the mist forest above us made me feel trapped. I had an urge to run out and away from the mountain, where there were patches of sunlight between the clouds, and clear air beyond.

We walked past unfamiliar plants with red and blue leaves, and balloonwort growths larger than any I'd seen. Windborne plants, familiar and strange, floated around us. In places there was sunlight between the cloud masses, and I could breathe easier. I saw before me short trees, gnarled and bent, their branches bending to attach to the ground around the central trunk. Beyond them, abruptly, the world ended.

Siru clutched my arm, stopping me. "These are Mukkum's Fingers, these trees. They are edge-dwellers. Hold one of the trunks, and look down."

So I did, and I saw that the plain I was on was an overhang, below which was another great, airy distance obscured by clouds. But I could see between the clouds swathes of green and brown. Somewhere down there, the Mountain continued.

"So this is just a very wide ledge," I said to him as we walked back, indicating the plain with a sweep of my arm. I didn't know whether to be disappointed or not. I would make a home here, with these people. There need be no more falling, ever again. In years to come, I could help my village as it fell through the mist forest, and see my people again.

But now that my immediate fear for my daughter was gone, I had to admit to a kind of disappointment. I had hoped to find Antimm, to discover the meaning of the old stories, to find the sleeping gods. Siru told me that he wasn't sure there were any more ledgetowns down below, at least not for a great distance. The docking arms of a ledgetown are lit at night with balloonworts and other glowing plants, and sometimes these can be seen from above. Siru had never seen any such lights.

The days passed in that grey place, and I longed for sunlight, and for Agniya to run about freely without fear that she would fall off the edge of the plain. I missed my village, especially my life-brother Chaha. When would they make landfall on this plain? I tried to estimate how long they might take, but it was difficult. Due to the lifting tendency of the balloon-worts, and the sailtree mechanisms, villages fall very slowly. More than anything I was afraid that the village would be caught in the mist forest, but Siru assured me that the Moosar would see the village before that, and sound a warning with loud horns. This was reassuring: there was no reason for me to be so impatient. I must wait here for my village; we would fall together into the abyss.

But there were some pleasures here too. As my strength returned, so did my curiosity and my desire to explore. The great, moist plain was broken by ridges of rock and clumps of vegetation—thickets of giant balloonworts, mazes formed by the woody tangles of twistrees, secret gardens of blue palm-flowers and caves of moss enclosing deep pools in which fan-like creatures swam. It was in its way a wondrous place that I would have liked better with more sun and sky.

I was curious, too, about the Moosar, and wanted to see how they lived—a wish that horrified Mina when I spoke it aloud ("They are not like us *civilized* people," she said, although she was ingratiating enough in their presence), but she needn't have worried. The Moosar were an aloof lot, not meeting my gaze even when they brought us fungal delicacies from the Mountain. Only one man—Tharam—did not glance away from me, returning my gaze with a curious, but not unfriendly intensity. The women were shy, and the children like mountain moles, climbing everywhere and calling in shrill voices. The children were so used to crawling about in their stone tunnels that they could crawl faster than they could walk.

One evening, watching bats swoop about after insects during sunfall, the old desire possessed me again, to explore the secret patterns of the world. So for the pleasure of my heart, I resumed my experiments on falling objects. Agniya and I would drop stones from boulders, or throw them off the highest points that were safe for her to scramble to, and I would

time their fall with my pulse. We would collect sprigs of balloonwort and let them go, and I would estimate how long they
took to rise to the height of a rocky outcrop. I would weigh
these sprigs down with small rocks and see how the weight affected their motion. When we harvested windborne plants, we
would first experiment to see which ones would rise faster, before we caught them again in our stick-nets, giggling, to wash
them for a stew or eat them raw.

My studies gave me ideas for redesigning my ombrel, although it wasn't really necessary. But it gave me something
to do, and in any case I wanted to experiment with the new
materials that were available here—no virrum leaves, no blueskin, but there was batwing hide and a kind of twine from
a cave fungus that was stronger than any vine I'd ever used.
I got my chance when Siru told me of the wet season that
was almost upon us—I could hardly believe it could get more
dank and humid than it was at present—so I offered to make
an awning for the cave, and some parasols. On this pretext
I stretched batwing-hide and sewed it with the twine over a
frame of stiff wood slivers. We rigged the awning with great
ceremony over the cave entrance, and we had parasols for
each of us. I even made one for Tharam, who seemed quite
taken with it and me.

Days passed in this manner. Then the rains came, and fell
apparently without end. The damp got worse, and the two
openings in the outer cliff walls that served as latrines filled
with water and became unusable. The cave people retreated
to their warm, dry holes. The awning helped keep the water
from entering the cave, but the damp, and the constant *drip-
drip* of the rain, were unbearable. We built up a fire to dry the
cave, and huddled miserably around it. Then Mina fell sick.

She lay in a fever, muttering, while Siru took a parasol and
splashed through the water-logged plain to harvest some fever-
fern. I brewed thin teas and broths, and fed them to Mina,

and laid wet rags on her forehead to ease the fever. She began to babble in a delirium—she was shivering with cold. I piled blankets around her, but still she was cold. "Do you have any more covers?" I asked her. She opened her eyes unseeingly and said, very clearly, "Boxes...cave at the back," and fell into unconsciousness.

Agniya was asleep in my bed. I went to the back of the cave, using a sprig of balloonwort for a light. Here were piles of boxes, sacking containing odds and ends, every little thing saved against its possible future use. How would I find the blankets among the debris? I pulled open lids, undid sacks, but found only oddments—pots and pans with broken handles, some faded clothing, lovingly folded. The cave walls were covered with a thick, mossy growth. As I bent to see how to open the boxes that were placed there, I saw that the moss on the wall hung loose, like a curtain. I pushed it aside, and there lay a narrow, rocky passageway.

It led to a larger, drier cave that was hung with bunches of dried, pungent shrubs. The air here was still, and would have been stale, but for the aroma of the shrubs. Beneath them, in great piles, were bales of cloth, parts of wheels, rows and rows of earthen jars such as those used in villages to store oils. I walked in my circle of inadequate light, touching and feeling soft fabric, some of it rotted. I saw parts of pulleys and ropes such as a windworker might use. I saw piles of colored stones that would once have formed necklaces. I thought: *these must be traded goods, and the remains of the villages that did not survive the fall.* I thought: *this is a storehouse, that's all, there must be a good reason why they didn't mention it before.* Then I saw a long banner thrown carelessly over a wheel—it had the name of a village inscribed on it, and I recognized both the hand that had inscribed it, and the name. My mother's old village, the one she had left behind—Ashe.

It was destroyed by the fall, my mind said, *and the old couple scavenged it, that's all*—but another part of my mind saw a different truth. It saw the village coming down, getting trapped in the mist forest, and the cave people, and Siru, swarming into the village, not to rescue, but to loot and plunder, to kill. And in fact, as I walked deeper into the cave, I found a priest's singing stick—one, then a whole pile of them. Priests are never separated from their singing sticks, even in death. I could explain one, perhaps two, as part of the debris from a village that had been destroyed by the fall, but so many? When I found a pile of teeth with jewels set into some of them, I was certain.

Then a cold fear came over me, and I crept carefully back into the outer cave, and saw Mina still unconscious, and my child asleep. I stood over the old woman, my mind whirling with conflicting thoughts, and the bitter taste of betrayal was in my mouth. They had saved my child's life and given me shelter; they likely did not mean us any harm, in fact they had grown fond of us. Could it be true that they were thieves and murderers? That there was a reason why the Moosar had not, after all this time, invited me into their homes? By now I knew they were not "wild folk," as Siru had first described them—they looked as human as any of us, and while their language and customs were different, that was also true of the ledgetowns I had known. What set them apart, truly, was their reticence, their odd hostility toward the stranger. I imagined their rocky dwellings filled with the same sort of loot, perhaps put to use instead of being stored up to rot. I thought of the trust with which the villages had fallen to this place through time, and I felt the bile rise in my throat.

Mina stirred in her sleep, moaned. I heard Siru splash through the water—he came in with a dripping bundle of herbs and held them out to me, opening his mouth to speak. He saw my face and stopped.

I drew my knife. His eyes grew wide.

"The cave at the back," I said in a low voice, shaking. "Filled with loot and plunder. What happened to the people? My mother's village.... What did you do to them?"

"Nothing, I've done nothing! It wasn't us!" he protested. His face seemed to crumple; he held out his hands. "It wasn't us that did it," he said again, pleading. "See, the Moosar let us live when we first fell here, because we promised...we promised we would help them find the things they wanted. In the village, the village that had been ours, after the killing. We were younger then, and we could help them. But we didn't kill anyone. There was a terrible battle, up there in the mist forest. The ones that were left—the arachnae got them. We... we've never killed anyone!" He shuddered. Tears made moist tracks on his withered cheeks. The old woman and the child slept on.

"Please try to understand. Not many villages come. Once in a great while. And there is fighting, but we have nothing to do with that. We help keep the things—the things from the villages clean and dry for when the Moosar need them. They let us live. We pleaded with them to let us keep you and the child. They...they like you. And Tharam, he—"

"And when my village falls? Should I stand by and watch my people being murdered, like you and Mina did?"

He raised a hand in protest. "I have been thinking," he said, still speaking low. "If you marry into the Moosar clan you can save your people. Convince them to trade instead of fighting. That man Tharam, he likes you, he has power—"

Mina stirred, groaned. My hand tightened on my knife. A great and sorrowing anger took possession of me, but I must think before acting. Siru and Mina were old and foolish, and killing them would only pit me against the numbers and might of the Moosar. I swallowed my rage, lowered the knife, and frowned, as though considering what Siru had said.

"I will think on this," I said shortly.

He wiped his eyes, nodded. "Vayusha, you're just like a daughter to us," he said. "Your coming here has given us life and hope, where we had none."

My rage burned in my chest all the rest of that terrible season. Trapped with this pathetic old couple, I began to see their kindness as a desperate attempt to absolve themselves of their guilt. When Mina caressed my daughter's hair, I wanted to push the old woman away. I shuddered to think of what they might have witnessed and ultimately accepted. Yet there was truth to what Siru had said—they loved Agniya, and cared for us both. They wanted us to forgive them, to stay. I thought of my mother, and the childhood I had left on the Mountain, up there in the forbidden direction, and the violent death she (and I) had escaped. I thought of her clanspeople, killed by deceit and betrayal. I imagined my village, Naupura, descending into the mist forest some time from now, and heard their death cries, and saw their blood stain the whiteness. There was no question of our staying here anymore, yet where could we go? And how could I warn my people?

In the dank, restless days that followed, all of the forbidden visions that I'd seen in dreamtime, all my longings for my village and my people, coalesced into a single moment of insight. I would build a village for Agniya and me, a tiny one, a hamlet that would ride the abyss in the forbidden direction—*up*, not down.

A proper village is the work of several skilled people and takes a half-cycle or more to build. What I had in mind was a small replica of one, enough to hold a little garden for Agniya and myself, for life and sustenance. I had experimented enough with the great balloonworts that I could imagine constructing a tiny, buoyant hamlet without the sailtrees. If I could find my village before it fell into the mist forest—if Agniya and I could be once more with our dear ones, to warn them first, and then to fall with them together, steering away from the ambush—if I could only do this! The sobering thought that my device might not work came to me, and I resolved that I must have at least one other way to warn my people. I would make messages, winged messages that I would send upward in tens, no, hundreds!

When the rains had receded and the thin sunlight once more bathed the great, soggy plain, I went on long foraging trips, during which I collected materials, and wrote my messages, scratching painstakingly on thin, strong bark with the tip of a fleshy grey leaf that oozed red. I had discovered by chance that the color wouldn't come off easily; my clothes were stained with it—now that knowledge served me well. I rolled the pieces of bark into tight rolls, wrapped moisture-proof sheets of leathervane around them, and tied them with twine. I poked them deep into the tangles of the most succulent, delicious windborne fruits and greens I could catch, which Agniya and I then decorated with balloonwort sprigs. This made them more visible, but also told an observer that these floating islands were contrived. We must have made over a hundred of these, which took much time and patience.

By then I had learned that the mist forest had its seasons—that in the drier cold period following the rains, the arachnae went into holes in the rock and slept, and the mist forest retreated toward the mountain. I had already begun work on the hamlet—I could not afford to wait too long to complete it.

My hands were swift and steady as I made, in secret, the guide ropes and the weaves, gathering dirt in clumps for roots of balloonworts. I had found a hideaway in a small clearing within a maze of twistrees, which kept us from the gaze of the curious. Agniya came with me—all I did, I portrayed to her as play, so she would not, in her innocence, give away what we were doing. Chumbak guided my fingers, so I could anticipate the right angle for my batwing steerplate, or the best distribution of balloonwort bulbs for balance. There were patterns in the world, Chumbak reassured me, and if I aligned my craft along these, it would align, in turn, with my desire. At the cave, Tharam's visits were becoming more frequent, his glances more ardent. But the desire that filled me, obsessed me, was for home, for my dear life-brother Chaha, for the arms of my lovers, for the richness that had woven me, and would weave my daughter into being.

Now the cold, clear days came upon us. The cloud layer thinned, and grew luminous with the sunlight above it, and we could see the mesh of the arachnae from below like crisscrossing shadows, melting and vanishing. Small gaps opened up in the mist forest, then large holes that revealed the turquoise sky. The sight filled me with an impatient joy.

The day came. It was a pale, wintry dawn—the retreat of the cloud forest had left large swathes of sky above us. It was colder than I had ever experienced here. Everything was ready—the hamlet I had so painstakingly constructed was concealed by moss carpets I had torn up from the forest floor. Agniya did not know we were leaving. She came with me trustingly, having planted a kiss on Mina's withered cheek, expecting to return at sunfall as usual. We went toward the forest as though foraging. I tore off the moss cover, tethered her within the green cup that was to be our home, and fastened her ombrel. "We are going to play a game," I told her.

The anchor ropes strained. The bias of the hamlet was toward the sky—the balloonwort bulbs saw to that. The moment I cut the anchor ropes—after a lurch that nearly knocked me sideways, we rose.

As we went up into the sky Agniya and I released the messages I had so carefully constructed. Some of the windborne missives kept pace with us; others rose higher and faster, until they were dots in the sky above. Tears filled my eyes as I imagined my people fishing for greens, coming upon my messages. *Mukkum, keep them safe*, I breathed.

We were rising rapidly above what remained of the cloud layer. I had a strange feeling of disorientation, of wrongness— as though we were going back in time. It was very quiet, except for the creak of the lianas, and Agniya's excited questions. Then suddenly we heard a cry from down below, a shrill tear-at-the-heart scream of anguish. I saw below me the small figure of Siru, looking up at us. So did Agniya, and it was at this moment that she realized we were going away. Her eyes filled with tears; she began to wail. I found myself unreasonably angry at my beloved child—an anger swiftly replaced by fear. Around us sounded a great baying of horns that seemed to come from every direction.

The Moosar were at the cave-mouths in the side of the Mountain. Some had their lips to long horns of brown hide, while others clambered up and down the ladders. What were they doing? What could they do to us without the mist forest to conceal their weapons, without the arachnae? Then I saw, and was afraid.

Archers crouched on little ledges against the cliff. The arrows sang toward us in a volley—I pulled my child down into the deep shelter of the cup that formed my little hamlet. The village swung and shuddered, but continued to rise. I saw arrows embedded in the weave of lianas—in three places the batwing hide was pierced. Up we went, and nearly listed over from the next volley of arrows. I saw to my horror that the tips of the arrows were smoking—there was a smell of burning. I knew now how the Moosar captured the great villages—through arrows of fire that would set alight the combustible gases in the balloonwort bulbs. The burning village would be caught in the mist forest if it happened to fall in the summer or spring, but even in winter the Moosar had a fair chance against the steering skill of the weatherworkers. I did not have any sailtrees to help me steer. We were held still for a moment, then we began to fall, slowly but with an inevitability that was terrifying. Agniya's wails were caught in her throat, for smoke now filled our small cabin, and the rage and fear that overwhelmed me was stopped suddenly by the sound of her coughing. My spirit rose above my anger, to a calm, still place, and Chumbak whispered in my ear: *stop the fire*, and then: *use the fire!*

I pulled a burning arrow from the wreck and crawled up a thick balloonwort stem. Through slitted eyes I saw the people on the cliffside set burning cloths around the next set of arrows. I grasped the arrow I held, although my skin scorched with the heat of it, and plunged it into the side of the bulb that faced the cliff.

Immediately there was a great whoosh of flame, and the hamlet tilted again, dangerously. I hurled myself down and away from the burning bulbs, and grabbed my knife, shouting encouragement to Agniya. The burning gases from the balloonwort bulb, being ejected in the direction of the Mountain, had pushed us in the opposite direction from the cliff face, and we were moving at great speed, swaying and tumbling so I could not tell if we were rising or falling. Agniya's scream filled my ears—the world was smoke and fire, and loops of green twining coming apart from the weave; I pulled desperately at the tether connecting me to Agniya—at last I held her to me with one arm, slashing at the burning wort-stems with my knife in the other. With a fan-shaped piece of batskin I beat out what I could see of the flames; a green liana stem had split lengthwise and the abundant sap helped put out the embers.

I hardly had time to worry about crash-landing on the plain below before I noticed the silence. The shouts of the Moosar, the hissing of the flames, all that was gone. The hamlet was listing badly, swooping downward unevenly but slowly. Agniya's eyes were wide with terror, beyond tears or sobs. I saw that we were still some distance from the plain below, and that we were farther from the mountain, so that the abyss lay not far. My steering mechanism was mostly gone—a modest contraption of batwing sails that now hung loose—so I looked to the pile of burnt debris that lay before me. If I got rid of it quickly enough perhaps I could lighten the load sufficiently that we would rise again, for three of the balloonwort clusters were still standing, unscathed. I flung armfuls of the debris as hard as I could toward the mountain; we lurched away in the direction of the abyss. Alas! Although we cleared the edge of the great, humid plain, we continued to fall.

Over the next few hours, I repaired and patched our craft with sore and sooty fingers, although the hamlet was only half its original size now. We slept under the broken canopy that night, my voice hoarse from smoke and stories, my little Agniya asleep in my arms. Her hair still smelled of smoke.

In the light of morning I saw that we had fallen some distance below the overhang of the plain. And—astonishment!—there was nothing at all below it—only air and light. The world, the Mountain, Lohagiri, just stopped as though something had cut it with a knife. Peering from the edge of the plain with Siru, I had seen the same emptiness, but that is what I had expected to see from an overhang. Here I saw that the Mountain was not moored to the land below, but afloat—over a vast and shadowed plain greater in extent than anything I could imagine. Below the vertiginous expanse of air, between ragged trails of clouds, was the same brown and green land that I had mistaken for the foot of the Mountain.

And I saw the shadow of Lohagiri, an irregular dark patch on the clouds below, as though the Mountain itself was a great village, a god suspended over the abyss. I remembered an obscure story I'd heard in a ledgetown once: when the other gods turned Chumbak into stone, one of them severed the god's head and threw it into the sky. Looking up where the Mountain ended, I saw three great, smooth, round holes on the underside, like giant mouths or nostrils, and as I watched, a pale, white exhalation issued from them. Tiny crawling lines began from the holes and led toward the edge of the overhang, which was lined by numerous smaller holes with raised collars. These, too, exhaled the white breath. I saw that the lines between the holes were alive with movement, like retinues of insects or people.

Later, as twilight fell, we saw far below us, between the ragged edges of clouds, a luminous sign etched or placed on the land below—a curved downstroke followed by an upstroke, like the two wings of a lahua seed.

I knew then that there was no end to the wonders of the world.

We float slowly down between the clouds. I believe the distance to the plain below is less than what I've already traveled. We are going faster than the villages can, and there are plenty of windborne plants for our sustenance. The hamlet is patched well enough, and our ombrels give us some measure of security. Sometimes we are both sad—Agniya remembering Mina's warm embrace, and myself missing my village, my brother, my lovers, hoping fervently that my warnings reached them.

We are made by the world. What is born is just a seed, and the world we inhabit is a living tapestry, formed by the seed and all that surrounds it, just as a needle and the vine together make the weave. I was formed by my village, and helped form it in turn. What will form my child? I worry about this, for even though we are together we are appallingly alone in this great sky. But some days ago Agniya found a yellow gourd-flower blooming among the lianas, and two days later a troop of unfamiliar flying creatures we call shimmer-wings took up residence in the canopy. Perhaps our hamlet will become many-voiced after all. And there is also exhilaration in this journey, and a thousand questions. Who or what will we find below us? If the villages were all plundered by the Moosar, who is making the band of light below us that gets brighter as we fall? Did a village or two escape the looting?

I think now that the Mountain, Lohagiri, is held above the land the way one lodestone can sometimes be made to float above another. I know that the world is larger than my imaginings, and that the more I discover about it, the more wonders it will reveal. My mother comes to me in the dreamtime, as she promised; so does Chumbak, relating secrets about flotation that I barely remember when I wake. Do the gods really sleep in the green and brown land below? Just as my experiments with falling objects hint at patterns that underlie the world like a hidden language, it seems to me that the old stories are also full of intimations and hidden meanings. Will we find Antimm, or build it? We fall toward the answers, toward home.

Crossing the Midday Gate

Aliette de Bodard

D an Linh had walked out of the Purple Forbidden City not expecting to return to it—thankful that the Empress had seen fit to spare her life; that she wasn't walking to her execution for threefold treason. Twenty years later—after the nightmares had faded, after she was finally used to the diminished, eventless life on the Sixty-First Planet—she did come back, to find it unchanged: the Midday Gate towering over the moat; the sleek ballet of spaceships between the pagodas and the orbitals; the ambient sound of zithers and declaimed poetry slowly replacing the bustle of the city at their backs.

It was as if no time had passed. She paused under the wide arch of the gate, catching her breath; and remembered the smell of apricot flowers; and the familiar presence of Ai Nhi by her side as they discussed anything from the teachings of Master Kong to the proper way to culture samples.

Ai Nhi. Linh breathed in; managed to steady the trembling of her hands. For a moment, a bare moment, a seizure came on—and she was much older—white-haired and bent, standing in a wide courtyard, watching a ship descend towards the planet, the wind of its approach ruffling burning fingers into her hair—and then it was gone, and she was back in the Forbidden City, her eyes stained with tears. It meant nothing; meaningless scraps of possible futures, the side effects of her vaccine—and none of it would make the past, or the future, what it should be.

Things have changed, the imperial messenger had told her

when he'd come to pick her up from her Heaven-forsaken planet. *Your presence is required at court.*

Things had changed. It didn't seem that way; it didn't seem as though anything would ever change here. The line of emperors and empresses was unbroken, all the way to the founding of the Dai Viet Empire; and the changes that spread like wildfire on the outer edges of the numbered planets only nibbled at the unceasing, incurious fabric of court life.

And yet...and yet, in the pavilion by the lotus pond, there was someone who'd called her back. She'd expected a man; but the person waiting for her wasn't even human: a small, cat-sized avatar of a mindship, surrounded by a scattering of bots like an honor guard; purely honorific, since the mindship herself, *The Serpent's Pearl in the Sea*, was in orbit around the planet, and impervious to any attempts made on her life; or indeed any physical contact.

It had been years; and the ship appeared unchanged; save that the list of her titles and achievements were overlaid over her prow; and on her hull was the pelican and dragon insignia of the Grand Preceptor, the position the ship had always hungered for—the one denied to her when the vaccine scandal had broken out. *Things have changed*, the messenger had said; and now Dan Linh knew what. The court had given in; finally, against all its misgivings, had appointed its first mindship Grand Preceptor. There was no one else; not a single human or a single servant—only the two of them, and the growing, uneasy silence in the pavilion.

Gently, softly, Dan Linh abased herself on the painted tiles, ignoring the scuttle of bots moving out of her way; and the familiar twinge of pain in her knees. "Your Excellency. This is...unexpected."

"Rise, Luong Thi Dan Linh," *The Serpent's Pearl in the Sea* said. "There is no need to be so formal." But she had used Dan Linh's full name, without any of the titles she had been accorded. "We missed you, at court."

Of course she hadn't. "You were better off without me," Dan Linh said. Court intrigues had never been her forte: she was a scientist, first and foremost, afforded entry into the highest circles only because of the ship and her protection; only because she'd discovered the vaccine that had saved so many lives. "I didn't know of your elevation," Dan Linh said.

The Serpent's Pearl in the Sea rocked from side to side, in mild amusement. She had changed: no longer the earnest mindship who had argued with her about the necessity of getting the vaccine to as many planets as necessary, no matter the cost to the treasury. "You wouldn't," she said. "News doesn't travel that fast, I'm afraid; and I'd already set your recall into motion as soon as it was confirmed."

"I—I don't understand."

"There isn't much to understand. I don't have much time, Linh, so I will be brief—I apologize for setting aside the proper protocols. Your place is at court, with us, rather than wasting your talent on teaching children about basic biology. Your old laboratory could use a firmer hand."

She.... All she'd always wanted, the dream that had woken her up every morning of her exile—her old laboratory, her old teams back; the familiar hum of ovens; the familiar chatter of lab hands as they prepared samples for examination—everything casually handed back to her, with barely a flourish. "You jest."

"I *never* jest," the ship said.

Of course she didn't.

Dan Linh had to ask. Now, before she lost her nerve; before the accumulation of favours bestowed on her shamed her into silence. "What of Ai Nhi?"

The ship's voice was cold. "Ai Nhi is still at court. Her husband is the General of the Southern Flank."

"And she heads the Cedar and Crane laboratory?" The same one whose direction the ship had just offered her.

The ship descended from the dais, and came to hover by her side—as she'd done, in the days where their relationship had been less formal. "Ai Nhi will be fine. There are other posts she can take up. You care too much about her. I told you, back then."

Back then, Dan Linh could have denounced Ai Nhi—after all, it had been Dan Linh's word against Ai Nhi's, and wasn't Dan Linh the head of the Cedar and Crane Laboratory? The inventor of the vaccine against Blue Lily, the savior of lives uncounted? What was a mere student, weighed against all of that?

"It was the right thing to do," she said quietly, still not looking at the ship. Ai Nhi had been kinless, and without status or protector: they had exiled Dan Linh, but they would have executed Ai Nhi for the same offence.

"Was it?" *The Serpent's Pearl in the Sea*'s voice was soft. "Did you like the Sixty-First Planet, Dan Linh? I remember a more ambitious woman—one who wanted to leave her mark on history; who wouldn't listen to her superiors' orders when she knew what was best. What happened to her?"

She had shrivelled and died—that was what had happened; because out there on the Sixty-First Planet, where resources were so stretched they didn't even have personal bots, there was no place for ambition—she'd got crushed into the rhythm of her life; into teaching children and teenagers with no motivation or talent; and, even when she did find a child whose grandiose dreams hadn't already been reduced to nothingness, there was no way she could help them, no way she could get them out of the same exile they were all trapped into.

"You saved lives," *The Serpent's Pearl in the Sea* went on. "The entire Empire would have been devastated by Blue Lily, if you hadn't been there."

"Ai Nhi—"

"Ai Nhi has done capable work." The ship's voice was still terribly soft. "Kept things running. But she's not you."

No. She didn't have the flashes of brilliant insight that made a good researcher, and, more damaging, not the capacity to surround herself with people who did—the vaccine, Dan Linh's discovery, had been as much An Hang's and Vu's and Yen Oanh's as it had been hers, meticulous teamwork in service of a common goal. Ai Nhi was Dan Linh's mistake; the one student who had cracked and run under pressure—and the other, darker mistake, Dan Linh's choice to remain silent instead of accusing her student, to endure twenty years of exile on a Heaven-forsaken planet for her sake.

"You can't protect Ai Nhi forever, Dan Linh."

She'd dreamt of this; staring at the stars as her daughter Lan nursed at her breast—wondering how things would have gone, had she not spoken up—had she remained at court. She'd wondered what she could have accomplished—at all the research on Blue Lily and other illnesses, all the other chances she'd have to affect things; to help people be more equal against the shadow of death—and she'd known it was nothing but bitter regrets, costly things she couldn't afford, so far out on the edge of the Empire.

And now she had come back—and she had another chance. Another lifeline; a chance to walk again the corridors of the court with the support of a mindship turned Grand Preceptor—the highest rank of official within the court, the Empress's personal advisor, the educator of her children and the policymaker of the Imperial Court.

"Well? What do you say?" *The Serpent's Pearl in the Sea*, silent; hovering by her side; waiting for her answer; as she had waited, twenty years ago.

Another chance—and how many of these would she get, what little time she had left? She wasn't like the ship—traversing centuries ageless and unchanged—she was merely mortal, and already standing in the shadow of death and rebirth. "I'm glad to be back, and will be glad to be of service."

"Good," *The Serpent's Pearl in the Sea* said. "There will be a reception in two days to honor you. I'll send attendants with…more appropriate clothes." The ship's voice was light; conveying quite effectively her amusement at the quaint, provincial things on her back—the clothes of the poor and exiled.

"To honor me?"

"Of course. It's high time for justice; for the court to recognize what you did—the billions of lives you saved across the empire, Dan Linh."

A reception. With her at its center. She felt…brutally exposed, with no protection. "I can't—"

"You used to be prouder."

And she'd been castigated for it; cast out without support and exiled for twenty years. "I—" she took in a deep breath. How was she going to find her place back, if she couldn't bear even this? "I'll be there."

"Good," the ship said. "You need to be. As I told you—things have changed. The court has ossified." For the first time, there was emotion in her voice; the passion Dan Linh remembered from their evenings together. "We need to change; and the first step is to bring you back."

A Grand Preceptor mindship; a youthful, dynamic one, nothing like the previous staid holder, who had been content to plot and backstab merely to keep his place—things were changing, indeed, and she was at the heart of it; and she wasn't sure, anymore, if she had the guts for it in the wake of her return.

The Serpent's Pearl in the Sea had assigned Dan Linh her old quarters—here, too, nothing had changed: the same three rooms spread around a courtyard with a cedar tree, and a slew of bots and attendants that seemed to slip into cracks when Dan Linh was not watching—bringing dumplings and tea, cushions, and a profusion of court clothes ranging from the traditional to the more modern confections changing colors depending on the mood and thoughts of the wearer. And, in the ambient mood system, her old starscapes and mountain watercolors hung, and the same quiet zither music played—as if she'd just stepped back in time, and all she had to do was walk back to her old laboratory to find Ai Nhi and Vu hard at work on samples, discussing the side-effects of the vaccine, or arguing about the best guidelines for production.

But there was...something else in the palace now—some shadow of unease she could feel; whispers in the corridors that ceased when she appeared—once, she caught the tail end of a conversation about the Grand Preceptor. The Empress might have appointed *The Serpent's Pearl in the Sea*, but the ship didn't appear to have much support in the Forbidden City.

A younger scholar had smiled shyly at Dan Linh as she walked by, calling her "Honored Teacher" and telling her the vaccine had saved her sister—and Dan Linh had stopped; stood, tongue-tied and unsure of what to say. "You—" the scholar had said; and then shaken her head. "Forgive me, but you shouldn't be here." And had fled, reddening, before Dan Linh could ask her what she'd meant.

Someone—she assumed it was the ship, again—had left her documents, in the communal network: the year-end reports of the Cedar and Crane laboratories submitted to the court; and court memorials sent by the scientists. The temptation to open it—to find what Ai Nhi had done, in the past twenty years—was almost overwhelming.

Almost.

Dan Linh closed her eyes, for a moment; trying to step away from it all; to remember that she was no longer young, or powerful, or well-regarded. Then she asked the communal network to relay a message to her daughter Lan on the Sixty-First Planet—reassuring Lan that she was fine and the court hadn't recalled her for some arcane punishment; telling her about *The Serpent's Pearl in the Sea*'s elevation and her own.

The Sixty-First Planet was barely within range of mindships; even if by some miracle she ranked that kind of courier, she wouldn't get an answer from Lan for several days or weeks.

If only Chi Hieu had still been alive—if only he had been able to come with her—but he was gone now, the only trace of him contained within the mem-implants their daughter had inherited, the ones Dan Linh couldn't bring herself to talk to—mere simulations of him, with nothing of the vibrancy and care he'd had, when he was alive.

Chi Hieu was—had been—the greater spouse in their marriage, though most people wouldn't have been able to tell. Though he had sat for the examinations and attained the highest rank, he had chosen to step away from it all, dedicating himself to his poems and his family; smiling negligently at court intrigues and never taking anything seriously. He would have laughed; would have written a short, biting poem on the situation; would have taken her into his arms and whispered sweet nothings into her ears until she could once more see clearly. But he wasn't there; not anymore; and tonight the wound of his absence felt recent again, too imperfectly papered over not to ooze heart's blood.

Their daughter Lan was an adult now, with responsibilities of her own—managing the orchards of a large estate on the Sixty-First Planet, planning with her usual cool head for planting and pruning and the ceaseless work throughout the seasons—and she couldn't have come with her mother, even if she had wished to. Raised with disapproval of the court, she'd had no desire to come to the First Planet.

Dan Linh sat down, pulling a cup of fragrant, flowery tea to her; and started reading reports.

It was all there—the familiar, formal language of court memorials; the lines of equations cramped close together, science far beyond what her students were capable of—bringing back memories of what she'd done, back in the days of the vaccine—analyses of efficacy and ease of setup, of growth rates and sample sizes, a wash of information so raw and undiluted that it threatened to drown her.

The science was beyond her now; but the rest wasn't—the stories of internecine fights; of the desperate hunt for funds from the treasury in fallow years; and all the hundred things that went into keeping a laboratory together. Past the first few years—past the miracle of the vaccine and the necessity of refining the production process for the entire Empire, the Cedar and Crane laboratory had slowly, inexorably dwindled away as Blue Lily was contained—its original purpose pared away, leaving nothing but trivial research, its talented researchers leeched away into better, more challenging postings. Ai Nhi had done her best; but even with court support she hadn't been able to keep things together.

But Dan Linh was back now, and things would change.

Dan Linh took a deep, trembling breath; reached out for the tea again; and was surprised to find darkness spread over the courtyard, and the distant music and laughter of private poetry parties. Had it been so long?

The chimes of the door resonated across the room. She set aside the documents, and moved—a scattering of bots on the floor as she moved, racing towards the door; an image of who was outside started to form, but Dan Linh had already flung open the door.

And then wished she hadn't.

The man standing on the threshold hadn't changed either: the same dark hair, the same thin, almost ascetic face; the scarred hands, a childhood accident on a remote planet where they didn't have proper graft techniques. "Hello, Dan Linh." No formality either; no recognition of her titles, but of course he wouldn't.

Khiem.

Ancestors, no. Not him.

Dan Linh struggled to keep herself steady; to silence her frantic heartbeat—and the only thing that slid out of her mouth was the thought circling, again and again, in the emptiness of her mind. "You shouldn't be here."

"No doubt." Nguyen Van Duy Khiem's voice was dark, amused. "But let us observe the courtesies, shall we? Will you not share tea with me, Dan Linh?"

She remembered him—his eyes burning in the painted oval of his face, as he called her behavior inappropriate—as he advocated for her death as an example; a reminder that one did not deceive the Imperial Court. She remembered the Empress turning to look at him; the desperate prayer on her own lips, to her ancestors and whatever deities might be watching, that the Empress not listen; that she not be swayed by Khiem's dark, angry eloquence.

She hadn't been, but it had been close; and Khiem had never stopped. Even on the day she'd left, he'd petitioned the head of the Embroidered Guard to have her arrested.

Khiem walked in, not waiting for her answer. The bots

clustered around him, like eager pups; a swarm of them dragged tea and hot water from the kitchen corner; another swarm pulled the low table in the centre of the room, set up plates and chopsticks. He sat cross-legged, still smiling; and waited for her to do the same. The communal network, obedient to his cues, changed the surroundings: the room faded, became the sharp slopes of a mountain with the outbuildings of a temple complex clinging to its slopes—the angles of the rock broken, here and there, by the curve of a roof, the circle of a longevity symbol on a door. In the distance, a flock of cranes wheeled, making mournful calls like reed flutes; and the air was moist with a hint of approaching cold.

"Why are you here?" Dan Linh asked. She sat down, feeling the smoothness of cut marble underneath. The table was polished mahogany; but only the food and tea on it was real; the rest was only ambient.

Khiem smiled. "I thought I would welcome you back."

She would never be welcome, not so long as Khiem was at court. But he was Third Rank; and *The Serpent's Pearl in the Sea* Grand Preceptor, vastly outranking him. She was safe. She had to be.

"What do you want?"

"Oh, Dan Linh. Still as bad as ever. I thought twenty years would have taught you diplomacy."

"You know I'm a scientist. Not an official or a courtier."

Khiem shrugged. He swirled the tea in the cup, staring at it for a while. "No. You were never that. The games we play... they genuinely don't interest you, do you?"

"Games? You wished me dead. You *hounded* me to the Midday Gate calling for a death sentence."

"Forgive me," Khiem said; and it didn't sound like an apology at all; more like a raised eyebrow, wondering how she could be uncouth enough to raise such fuss, twenty years after the facts. "'Games' is the wrong word. Perhaps some think of it as games. I'm in earnest—but there are rules, and I follow them. You...you never did." He smiled. "Not eight hours back into the Purple Forbidden City, and you already flout them as though they didn't exist."

"I have no idea what you mean."

"As I said." Khiem set his cup on the table. A crane alighted on one of the rocks: watched them for a while, before shaking its wings open and flying away. "I admire you in many ways, Dan Linh, I genuinely do. You move through life untethered by anything but the purity of your craft. Tussles of power never interested you, did they—or who supported who and for what reason? I wonder how well you'd have done, if you'd stayed at court."

Better than Ai Nhi, she thought, sharply—remembering the litany of losses in the report; and Khiem must have seen her face, read it as easily as an open book.

He said, "Ai Nhi...did well, all things considering. She found herself a protector—"

"You?" She was married, *The Serpent's Pearl in the Sea* had said; to the General of the South Flank. On the communal network, the General was in disgrace; deployed to a faraway place on the edge of the numbered planets, and Dan Linh didn't need to play the intrigues of the court to read significance into that.

Khiem shrugged. "Perhaps. Does it matter?"

"It should."

"And perhaps it shouldn't," Khiem said. "As I said...Ai Nhi was more...accommodating than you were, though perhaps she didn't have your fire for science."

No, she'd never had—which was why Dan Linh had been surprised, when Ai Nhi had come up with the improved manufacturing process—surprised, and pleased, and was this the reason why she hadn't checked Ai Nhi's results thoroughly enough? She'd asked herself that question, often enough; and had no answer. "She was head of a laboratory," Dan Linh said. The laboratory that she'd founded, with her discovery of the vaccine, that she'd been forced to leave in disgrace. "That's all that should matter. Keeping the laboratory safe. Making discoveries that matter. That help people."

Khiem's burning, mocking eyes held her. "You think

more discoveries would have saved the Cedar and Crane? The plague is gone—your vaccine has saved us all. There's no money for esoteric research."

"Esoteric research which gave you the vaccine." Her voice was sharper than she'd thought it would be. "What were you going to do, come the next plague?"

Khiem smiled; a bare tightening of his lips. "Oh, Dan Linh. This is exactly why you wouldn't have done better than Ai Nhi. Exactly what got you into trouble, twenty years ago. You think of what is right—of, say, the necessity to get your vaccine to as many people as possible, regardless of what else it might imply or whom it might vex; regardless of the deaths it might cause."

"It didn't happen like this," Dan Linh said, more forcefully than she'd expected. Was the wound still so raw; her foolishness still boring a hole in her self-possession? "You know it didn't." And how pathetic, wasn't it, to still feel she needed to justify herself, to a man who'd never listened to her or valued her?

"Didn't it?" Khiem smiled; an expression as thin and as cutting as a razor blade. "I had a stroll back into the archives, when I learnt you'd be coming back. I...remembered." He closed his eyes; his tone slow enough to suggest he was quoting from memory, rather than using a note in the communal network. "'In the light of the available evidence (see graphs 3a and 16), we believe in the necessity of modifying the manufacturing process to attain greater efficacy. The slight loss in concentration of the active organism would be compensated by the ease and speed of delivery of the vaccine throughout the numbered planets (see graph 19d).' Your words? Ai Nhi's? Do you even remember?"

The words of her nightmares; of sleepless nights wondering if that was where she'd gone wrong, where she'd let her arrogance let the better of her—and sometimes she'd have a burst of anger, and remember that it was Ai Nhi's process; Ai Nhi who had checked the experimental results with her, over and over again, seeing nothing wrong—only what they'd gain, checking the devastating spread of Blue Lily so much faster, so much more easily. And that Ai Nhi was still at court; was still rising through the ranks of civil service, while all Dan Linh had for herself was exile and bitterness.

"I didn't mean the deaths," Dan Linh said, slowly, carefully. "We honestly thought—" But it was about the deaths; about those who'd lined up, eager to get vaccinated—trusting her and Ai Nhi, only to catch a side infection—a less deadly one than Blue Lily, but was it truly much comfort, if they were still dead at the end?

She'd made her amends for that; said her prayers, over and over, and burnt incense at shrines, day after day, year after year, praying for swift passage, and swift rebirth. She would be torn apart in Hell if the King of the Underworld thought her still guilty, and she accepted that—but that was for the gods to judge, and not for people like Khiem.

"Oh, Dan Linh." Khiem smiled, again; that expression she wished she could wipe from his face. "Have you understood nothing, in your exile?"

Anger flashed, red-hot, searing. "The Sixty-First Planet is a place of dust storms and small settlements, and children who grow up and become settlers themselves, never leaving the planet, let alone the solar system. Where do you think I would have kept up in court graces?"

Khiem picked up a dumpling; held it to the light until the filling of pork and chives glistened, pink and green flecks through the translucent skin. "A lesson, then, Dan Linh—in honor of your return. We're not fools. We know that vaccines have risk. Your process was...contaminated and flawed, and for that, yes, you'd have been blamed, possibly dismissed from your post. But I wouldn't have called for your death, or... *hounded* you, as you said, on the basis of that."

"Then why—"

Khiem shrugged. "It wasn't you, Dan Linh. It was never about you."

Then who.... She clamped her mouth on the question before it escaped her. If not her; if not Ai Nhi—there was only one other person Khiem could mean.

Her protector of the time—and her current one, too. "You wanted *The Serpent's Pearl in the Sea* in disgrace."

Khiem smiled; a teacher pleased at a student's answer. "Of course."

"Why?"

"Because she's a mindship," Khiem said; slowly, carefully, as if Dan Linh should have known, all along.

"And thus not worthy of her post?" Just as scientists like her hadn't been worthy of joining the court?

"Because, despite subtle hints from the court, Grand Preceptors have clung on to their posts until the breath left their bodies. What will you do, if *The Serpent Pearl's in the Sea* refuses to step down?"

She...she had never stopped to consider it—as Dan Linh had said, oblivious to anything that wasn't the work of the laboratory. Mindships were immortal, or close enough—much longer-lived than humans, unchanged for generations. "Why would I care?" she asked, bluntly. "She's shown me more constant favor than any high-rank official."

"Because—" Khiem exhaled, as if talking to a small child. "Because emperors and empresses need to live and die; and so do courts and officials. Because the base unit of our lives is still human; still mortal and aging. Because anything that holds onto power that long ossifies. Do you remember the tales of the Auspicious Destiny Emperor?"

Every child did. He'd ruled for over eighty years, by the end of which the court was bloodless and drained of energy, the functionaries too settled in their ways to even envision new ideas. "That's not the same," Dan Linh said, more sharply than she'd intended. "And *The Serpent's Pearl in the Sea* isn't like that. She's dutiful and filial, and she would obey the edicts of the Empress."

"Perhaps she is. Perhaps she's not." Khiem rose, slowly gathering his robes around him. "That's not the point. There... is fear among the civil servants, Dan Linh, and it's not unjustified. It never was." He pursed his lips; looked as though he might stop speaking, might stop spearing her with words; but then he went on, regardless, "You say you could have done better than Ai Nhi. Well, here is your chance to prove it, but I don't think you're starting out well."

"What do you mean?"

Khiem waited until he was all the way to the door before he turned to face Dan Linh. "Ask yourself this—why are you back here?"

Dan Linh had had enough of him; and of his supercilious guessing games. "Do tell me. Since you're being so helpful."

Khiem laughed, with no joy or amusement whatsoever. "You're the woman who banished the plague. The one who ended the era of Blue Lily and ushered in our new age of prosperity. What better way to reassure the court, than to have you by side of *The Serpent's Pearl in the Sea*?"

And then he was gone; but his words remained in the room, casting a pall like the miasma of fog over everything.

The laboratory was deserted: it had changed in thirty years—filled with more and more complicated machines, every available surface covered by bots. Dan Linh stood, for a while, watching the lights blink on the panel of the ovens; remembering the nights she'd spent there, the sleepless manufacturing of batches—the graphs that told her, again and again, that she couldn't outrace the plague; that the vaccination rate was always going to be lower than Blue Lily's mortality rate. Her initial vaccine—the one she'd rashly, foolishly tested on herself—took too long to produce, too many resources. She—and Ai Nhi—had believed there had to be another, faster way.

But she didn't want to go there; couldn't afford to.

"Professor," a voice said, behind her.

She turned, and saw Ai Nhi.

She'd changed so much; and so little. The face was the same, a perfect oval with the hair pulled back in a classic top-knot; the mouth thin, elegantly delineated with vermillion—

but the eyes were deeper, darker than they had been; and she stood ramrod straight, the awkward and gangly girl hammered into shape by years and years of propriety and dancing around court intrigues.

"I didn't expect to see you here," Dan Linh said. But really, she ought to have known; that coming back to court would be like summoning, one by one, the ghosts of her past; of her failures and her regrets.

"Where else?" Ai Nhi's voice was sharp, cutting. There was a younger woman with her—maybe twenty, twenty-five years old? Not much younger than Ai Nhi herself had been, back then. "This is Cuc," Ai Nhi said.

If Ai Nhi was impeccable, Cuc…was not. Her fingers were stained with ink; her five-panel dress frayed; and she didn't appear to be capable of sitting still. "You work here?" Dan Linh said, guessing.

Cuc nodded. She looked at Dan Linh, awe-struck. "You—" She swallowed, started again. "You're Professor Thuong Thi Dan Linh. They said you were back, but—"

"Cuc." Ai Nhi's voice was distantly amused. "Forgive me," she said to Dan Linh. "She thinks of you as a living legend."

The woman who ended the plague, Censor Khiem had said. The one who ushered in a new age of prosperity. Dan Linh felt it, trembling on the edge of unfolding—a seizure, a vague, blurred image of the court, of kneeling before the throne of the Empress with someone at her side—another meaningless, illusory image from a future that might never come to pass.

"I'm no goddess," Dan Linh said, when the seizure was gone. "And no different from you or Ai Nhi."

"Perhaps. Perhaps not," Ai Nhi said. She shook her head. "The one who walked away." She made it sound—like a failure, her voice a sharp reproach; but beneath it was something else. Anger? Remorse? "I thought you would come here; to haunt familiar places—" She shook her head. "Do you find it much changed?"

"Yes," Dan Linh said. "But of course it would change."

"New masters, new ways." Ai Nhi's voice was ironic—

such bitterness, such anger within her. Dan Linh had always thought she'd be happy—that, if someone was going to be bitter, it might as well be her, lying awake listening to the slow, steady sound of her husband's breathing; wondering what was happening at court, and having no way to find out in her distant exile.

She hadn't expected Ai Nhi to—to turn into this tall, commanding woman; hadn't expected the barely contained bitterness—but then again, how else would Ai Nhi have looked like, with the remnants of her dreams turned to ashes, the inexorable decline of the laboratory; and finally Dan Linh's return, like a slap in the face?

"I didn't expect this," Dan Linh said, finally. It hadn't turned out like either of them wanted; or hoped.

Ai Nhi shrugged. "I did. The moment your protector—" she spat the word, "—ascended."

"Are we going to have an argument on the suitability of a mindship Grand Preceptor, again?" Dan Linh said, wearily. She'd had that with Khiem; had had her draught of doubt and upended worldviews for a lifetime.

"No." Ai Nhi shook her head. "I don't take part in such fights." But Cuc, by her side, looked ill at ease. *There is...fear among the civil servants*, Khiem had said—and everyone knew that Dan Linh didn't take part in court intrigue; and almost everyone was like Cuc, remembering her as the scientist who had ended the plague and chosen to go into exile—a symbol, both an omen for a prosperous future with countless blessings, and a reminder of her integrity in the face of pressure. "This isn't about *The Serpent's Pearl in the Sea*."

"About us, then?" Dan Linh asked, gently. About the laboratory; about what Ai Nhi had made of it.

Ai Nhi's hands moved, encompassed the entirety of the laboratory; the machines softly beeping; the temperature-controlled incubation chambers. "I imagine that you've read the reports by now."

"I've read them," Dan Linh said. Over and over again; trying to see where it had gone wrong; where all the small decisions Ai Nhi had made had turned into disasters. Khiem had said Ai Nhi had done well, considering; that it was none of her fault. That there was nothing Dan Linh could have done better than her.

Khiem was wrong.

Or was he?

"You would, no doubt, have done things differently." Ai Nhi smiled—again, an expression that never reached her eyes.

"No doubt," Dan Linh said. Except it was so easy, wasn't it, to analyze things afterwards? To dissect errors; as people had taken apart their new manufacturing process—tracing the contamination back to a faulty concentration in the second step of attenuating Blue Lily—and then passed judgment on them. And then, because it was late; because she was tired and adrift, and unsure of what she could cling to, "Do you ever regret?"

Ai Nhi's face didn't move. "Cuc," she said, gently. "Can you go direct that bot cluster, please? It's a precise manuver, and it requires a knowledgeable hand."

Cuc, startled, looked at Ai Nhi; and then at Dan Linh. "I...guess so," she said. They heard her footsteps, dwindling away on the tiles of the laboratory—and then only silence, and darkness spread from within the communal network, muffling all sounds.

Ai Nhi walked closer to Dan Linh; stood, for a while, looking at her. "Regret that I'm here?" she asked.

"I didn't mean that," Dan Linh said.

"No," Ai Nhi said. "I didn't think you did." The floor and the laboratory had vanished; and she stood in utter darkness, as though she hung within the starless void of space. "I don't know," she said. "I didn't know, back then."

"Neither did I." Dan Linh stared at Ai Nhi—because there was nothing left; only the void; only themselves. "But they still died."

"And some of them still lived." Ai Nhi's voice was sharp—as cutting as jagged glass. "Does it balance out?"

"I don't know," Dan Linh said. She would never know.

Khiem would say it didn't—or perhaps he wouldn't, not really caring about what it all meant—and *The Serpent's Pearl in the Sea* would say that it did; that she was the saviour of untold billions, the woman who had mastered Blue Lily—and Dan Linh wouldn't believe either of them. She knew her faults, all too well.

Ai Nhi looked as though she was adjusting her hairpins, but her topknot came loose, and a spread of black hair, sprinkled with grey, spread behind her back. She was.. old—no longer the student Dan Linh remembered; and perhaps no longer with the faults she remembered, or imagined. "I'm not a fool," Ai Nhi said. "I know what I owe you."

"Nothing," Dan Linh said.

Ai Nhi smiled, sharp, cutting. "Twenty years? Don't lie to me, Professor. It ill suits you." In the darkness, her eyes seemed to shine; illuminated as if from within. "I won't make a fuss. Not that I was ever in a position to make one." She shrugged, again; but Dan Linh read the quiver in her shoulders, the suppressed grief and fear. "It's only fair. Things change. People rise and fall from grace; and the balance of power shifts like the wheel of rebirth."

And Dan Linh, her fate tied to *The Serpent's Pearl in the Sea*, rose with the mindship's fortunes.

It's only fair.

Was it?

"You love this laboratory," Dan Linh said, slowly.

A flash of something, in Ai Nhi's eyes. "What does it matter?"

Dan Linh wanted to ask about the General; about whether it had been a marriage of love like her and Chi Hieu; about whether they had shared sweet nothings on the pillows, and walked side by side, laughing at the way the world worked— but she found the words frozen in her throat: too casual, too familiar for this woman whom she was going to displace.

"You're right," Dan Linh said, slowly. "It doesn't matter. Thank you."

And walked away, unsure of what to think anymore.

Two hours before the reception, *The Serpent's Pearl in the Sea* found Dan Linh in the antechambers of her quarters, kneeling on the floor with the ill-fitting grace of someone unused to court protocol. "You should be getting dressed," the mindship said—her voice puzzled, with just a hint of anger.

Dan Linh took a deep, trembling breath; thought of Khiem and Ai Nhi and darkness spreading across the laboratory. "I can't."

Things change, Ai Nhi had said. Some things did; some things didn't; and the laboratory was all that Ai Nhi had left: her own work, her own stand against the encroaching darkness of old age and death. "Can't?" *The Serpent's Pearl in the Sea*'s voice was smooth; quiet—the calm before the storm struck.

"I can't displace Ai Nhi just because you have a need for me."

"I've told you before." The ship was angry now; and the effects of that rippled in the communal network, casting the sheen of oily water upon the marble floor. "You care too much for Ai Nhi."

"I won't do better than Ai Nhi," Dan Linh said, wearily.

"This isn't about doing better. This is about doing what is right."

"What is right for you?" The words welled out of her mouth before she could take them back. "To have my support?" In Dan Linh's mind, Khiem smiled, revealing the fangs of tigers. *This is exactly why you wouldn't have done better than Ai Nhi.*

The Serpent's Pearl in the Sea was silent, for a while. The sheen on the floor spread; seemed to cover the entire room; until even the scuttling bots seemed alien lifeforms. "Perhaps," she said. "And perhaps I was genuinely trying to help you. Twenty years ago, I couldn't keep you safe. I couldn't keep you *here*."

And Dan Linh hadn't even been able to keep Ai Nhi safe. The weight of failures; of the deaths that she would always carry with her; of her arrogance and belief she knew better than anyone else—twenty years of exile were not enough to make amends for any of it.

"But you're right," *The Serpent's Pearl in the Sea* said, at last; when Dan Linh didn't speak up again. "It's a risky thing, to tie yourself to me—to face the hostility of the court—and I shouldn't have expected you to do that, merely on the basis of old friendships. I was...dishonest with you. For that, I apologize."

Dan Linh stared at the floor; at the bots. The ship had asked her whether she regretted her decision, twenty years ago. Ai Nhi hadn't; but then Ai Nhi had known the value of it; and the cost. She'd done the right thing then; and she couldn't do anything less now.

And she'd always known, hadn't she, what the right thing was?

"What's past is past," Dan Linh said. And, more slowly, "You can still have my support. But I can't be here. I can't be at Court, not even for you. You said there were other posts for Ai Nhi. Surely there are others for me, too. Surely.... A lab on a small planet," she said, finally. "Somewhere I can continue my research."

"You would return to your exile?" the ship's voice was... amused? Angry? She couldn't tell, not anymore. "Running away from court and all our intrigues?"

"I'll take the nomination from you," Dan Linh said, slowly, carefully. "That will be a political act." A clear message sent to the Court, of whom Dan Linh supported; of whose integrity she approved of—a paradoxical acceptance that marked her, now and always, as a part of the ebb and flow of court intrigue.

Silence, in the wake of her words. At length, *The Serpent's Pearl in the Sea* spoke. "There are some laboratories that might need a new head, yes. I would need to think..." And then, with a hint of anger, "You don't know what you're asking for."

Dan Linh rose, wincing at the ache in her knees; stood silently, watching the mindship—the first Grand Preceptor who wasn't human, the first who would outlive the Empress herself—the one she had chosen to trust; because she couldn't share Cuc's fears, or Khiem's unthinking prejudice. Because she had to believe in something better; because she'd always done so.

"I don't know all of it," she said. "But I know more than I did, twenty years ago."

"I see," the ship said. "Thank you."

Outside the antechamber, the maw of the court waited to swallow Dan Linh again—to honor her for the lives she'd saved, to excoriate her for the ones she'd lost—all her choices leading her to stand here, trying to make things better. Khiem would laugh, tell her she was a fool; and Ai Nhi would tell her to stay out of the politics that would only break her; but she was beyond either of them now.

In the end, faced with the uncertainty of deciding, all she could do was choose to do right—without knowing what it would bring—whether it would be a bright, shining future; or one scattered with the jagged shards of bitterness.

Some things changed; others didn't—and she wouldn't burden herself with regrets.

Firstborn, Lastborn

Melissa Scott

t has been more than a decade since I first set foot in Anketil's tower, and three years since she gave me its key. It lies warm in my hand, a clear glass ovoid not much larger than my thumb, a triple twist of iridescence at its heart: that knot is made from the trace certain plasmas leave in a bed of metal salts, fragile as the fused track of lightning in sand. Anketil makes the shapes for lovers and the occasional friend when work is slow at the tokamak, preserving an instant in threads of glittering color sealed in crystal, each one unique and beautiful, though lacking innate function. It's only the design that matters. I hold it where the sensors can recognize it, and in the back of my mind Sister stirs.

No life readings. House systems powered down. Owner ABSENT -> setting FORWARD: ALL to destination -> "work" -> ESTU.

That's what I expected—what Sister and I planned. The door slides back, and I step into Anketil's eyrie. She is solitary, like most Firstborn, though gregarious enough; the small spare space is cool, the windows fully transparent so that I can see through the twilight haze across the roofs of the Mercato to the harbor and the artificial island where the shuttles land. I came through there myself this morning, in the rising light, everything at last in order, and now here I am, the opening move of the endgame Grandfather began so long ago. Sister chortles to herself, a pulse of pleasure, and I set my bag beside the nearest chair. The sun is setting beyond the bedroom window, filling that room with blinding scarlet light.

To the north, the Bright City reaches inland, a sea of

multi-colored light rising as the sky darkens. It, its people, and its resident AI all pride themselves on drawing no distinction between Firstborn and Secondborn, between those who first re-made themselves to settle the depths of space, and the ones they allowed to follow, or between the Secondborn and the Faciendi, the people literally built to settle the more doubtful worlds and do the more doubtful jobs, but the lines remain. Anketil lives at the top of her tower; her Secondborn sometime lovers live in the Crescent and the Lido and the Western Rise, while the Faciendi gather in the east, where work and play intermingle. Anketil's tokamak lies there, among the Faciendi.

The elder moon already floats in the pale sky above those lower towers, and Sister is quick to trace the line of traffic that leads back from that edge. She has kept me informed of Anketil's current projects, plucking them easily from the commercial contract webs: this one is the core of a starship's power plant, the heart-stone, so-called, that lets a ship cheat the hard limits of space/time and the speed of light. Heart-stones are individual, tuned to the frame and power source and the proposed usage, but they are hardly a challenge to someone like Anketil. She has made a thousand of them over the course of her career; I don't need Sister to tell me that she will be ready to consider something more interesting.

Something clicks in the narrow kitchen alcove, and Sister identifies it as a bottle of wine moving to a chilling station. A menu hovers in the shadows when I look, ready for Anketil to choose how she will end her day: she will be home soon, and in that instant Sister stirs again.

SUBJECT has entered the building. Arrival in four minutes.

I glance around, making sure I have moved nothing that would contradict my story, and move to the southern window to look out at the distant sea. It is there Anketil finds me, and I turn in time to see annoyance dissolve to genuine pleasure. "Irtholin. I didn't expect you—didn't know you were on the planet."

"I arrived this morning." I step forward to accept her embrace. Her arms are strong and her thick curling hair smells of glass and plasma and the musk of her perfume.

"I'm glad to see you. Will you be staying long?"

"You know my schedule." I shrug. "A few days, I hope."

"I hope so, too." Anketil pours wine for each of us, cool and sharp. It is nothing compared to the wines of the Omphalos, of course, and I wonder if she misses those luxuries as much as I do. We are, after all, very much alike, she and I, she who renounced her birthright and I who have none, who am neither Firstborn nor Secondborn nor truly, entirely, Facienda. That is hardly to the point, and I rearrange my expression, looking down into the golden liquid as though uncertain how to begin. She sees, of course, and frowns lightly. "What's wrong?"

"You won't like it."

Her eyebrows rise. "Do I have to know, then? Or can we let it be?"

"I think you will want to know."

Something flickers across her face. I've seen that ghost before, every time we speak of her family, and I feel Sister snicker again. Anketil waves us toward the window, and we sit face to face beside the darkening harbor.

"It's about your family," I say, and she shakes her head.

"I have none."

I tilt my head at her, and she sighs.

"They're dead to me, I renounced the Dedalor and all their works decades ago. You know that."

"I do," I say, "and I'm sorry to have to mention them at all."

"But?"

"But." Sister whispers in my mind, counting out the pause, and then I speak. "I've found *Asterion*."

Anketil swears and leans back in her chair, her face bleak. She knows me as a master surveyor, one of the elite mathematicians who chart the shadows of the adjacent possible to lay out lanes for hyperspatial travel—easy enough to perform, with Sister to lay out the structures for me. It is entirely possible that I could have found out something about the ship her family betrayed and destroyed. "How?"

"On survey." I lean forward. "But that's not important. What's important is that it's alive. The AI survived. Some of the crew may have made it, too."

"Impossible."

I don't bother to contradict her. We both know that it's entirely possible, between the peculiar non-geometry of the adjacent possible and the long lives of the Firstborn. "I was doing a survey for—well, the client isn't important. I was mapping a stasis point when I found the anomaly. It's *Asterion's* AI."

"That doesn't mean the ship survived." Anketil's voice is hard. "Or her crew. Quantum AI makes ghosts in the possible, it could be a sensor shadow or a temporal echo, not something that's there now."

I let her run down, then shake my head. "I wish it were. The AI is there—Gold Shining Bone."

She winces. "You're certain."

"It was aware enough to name itself to me. As for the crew—" I pause, once again letting Sister gauge the wait for me. "At least they were alive. They had set a distress call."

"Damn Nenien and all who sailed with him," Anketil mutters, and the pain in her face draws another pulse of satisfaction from Sister, confirmation that the plan is working. Everyone knows the story: her great-grandfather Gurinn Dedalor built the first quantum AI that let humans navigate the adjacent possible and make interstellar commerce practical outside the closely-linked worlds that the Firstborn renamed the Omphalos, Navel of the Worlds. Against his advice and the rulings of the Firstborn council, her grandmother Kuffrin built quantum AIs that were both intelligent and self-aware, and more powerful than any others.

One of those AIs—Gold Shining Bone—rebelled and persuaded Kuffrin's youngest son Hafren to join it in its escape; her eldest son, Anketil's father Nenien, with the aid of two other of the family's AIs, tracked and ambushed the *Asterion* and trapped it in the adjacent possible, unable to calculate a way free. Nenien and his AI refused to help, abandoning *Asterion* and its crew to almost certain death, a warning to anyone else who would support the AIs' claim to the virtual. On his return to port, his sisters and their AI tried to find *Aste-*

rion and rescue it, but Nenien had destroyed his records and any other indication of the coordinates had been lost. No one knows, no one can know, what it would be like to be stranded there, outside time and space—if "outside" has any meaning in that context—but even quantum AIs run mad without some grounding in the actual. For a mere human, eaten up by the lack of time, of comprehensible space, it would be unimaginable torture.

Of course the lesson had failed, and in the short, sharp war that followed, enough of the AIs banded together that the Firstborn were forced to cede the virtual to their creation: a waste of Nenien's cruelty. Anketil walked away from the Dedalor then, walked away from her father and grandmother, from AI and the Firstborn and the life at the center, in the Omphalos; she said once, dead tired and discouraged by a failed experiment, that she wanted only to avoid Nenien's choices.

And that is an admission that I can use. I nod slowly. "I know."

She draws a deep breath. "I won't ask if you're sure."

"I'm sure."

"What were the readings? Can you tell how they were trapped?"

"I brought my maps," I say, and reach for my bag.

Of course her house system is top-of-the-line, her own corner of the virtual walled off from the rest of the City and its quantum allies. She pays exorbitant toll for this, even with Firstborn privileges, but I can be sure we will not be overwatched. We feed my data into her programs, and as the light fades outside, new lights blossoms within, an enormous sphere hanging in the emptiness between chairs and couch. Lines of force trace familiar shapes: the long slow curve of the Saben Edge, where the possible is easily accessed and easily exited; the tighter whorls of half a dozen vortices, each with its own unique set of destinations; the faint dust of unnumbered star systems, only a handful picked out in brighter blue to denote a settled world or a known stopover. At the sphere's center, dull violet lines brighten to blue and then to white, coiling in on themselves to form a familiar knot.

"It looks like a fairly typical anomaly," I say, "except there's nothing in the actual to create the tangle."

Anektil nods, walking in a slow circle to view the stasis point from all sides, then reaches into the lights to expand the image as far as it will go. "It's almost as if—" She pulls a work space from thin air and gestures quickly, her eyes moving from image to numbers and back again, and then makes a noise of satisfaction. "Yes. You can see the ship's negative if you look closely." She spins her work space so that I can see, displaying a ghostly shape like the bow fins of a fast hunter. "That's what you got?"

"That's what drew me in."

"Who was your AI?"

"I had a standard share of Red Sigh Poison."

"Only a standard?"

"I didn't want to ask for more. Not until I'd talked to you."

A standard share of a quantum AI is more than enough to do all the work a surveyor needs, and navigate the ship through the possible as well. That work never reaches the level of consciousness, so routine are the calculations; a quantum AI can offer out a thousand shares, ten thousand, perhaps even a hundred thousand, and never notice. If I had asked for a greater share of Red Sigh Poison's calculating power—and that would have been the normal thing to do—I would have drawn its interest as well, and quite possibly Red Sigh Poison might have noticed that I had not stumbled on this by accident. Anketil assumes, of course, that I am siding with her kin, and shakes her head.

"You'd have done better to go to the Omphalos. The Transit Council might have listened."

"Do you really think they'd do anything? To rescue *Asterion*—to rescue Gold Shining Bone—that would risk starting the wars all over again. At best, all they'll do is put a security freeze on it and appoint a select committee to study the question. And if Hafren is alive—well, he'll be dead before they make any decision."

Anketil's mouth twists, and I can almost hear the question: *why me?* But she has never been one to turn aside from a challenge, and she reaches into the image again, shrinking the anomaly so that she can see how it's woven into the fabric of space/time. "They might not be wrong."

"The other AIs will keep it in line. They've won—there's nothing to be gained by starting another fight."

"Unless AIs value revenge," Anketil says, and that is close enough to truth that I look up sharply, wondering what she suspects. She was raised among the AIs, after all, true Firstborn; no one knows the AIs better than the people who first built them. She may have chosen plasma-smithing for her life's work, but I don't know everything that she learned before she left the Omphalos. "What do you want me to do, Irtholin?"

"I don't want anything," I answer. "The safe thing is to leave them there. I can't argue with that. I just thought you'd want to know."

"Yes," she says, after a moment, and puts two fingers to her lips, staring at the lines of light.

We do not speak of it again that evening. Anketil forces a smile and pours more wine; we talk of my work, and hers, dine beneath the lines of light that drown the city lights beyond the windows, and as an orbiter rises in a column of fire and smoke, she takes me to her bed.

Afterward, we lie in the cool thread of air from the ventilators, watching the elder moon sink toward the distant rooftops. She winds a strand of my hair around her finger, then releases it, rolls back against the pillows. Sister tells me she is wide awake, cortisol and adrenaline singing in her bloodstream; I turn with her, miming sleepy content, and wrap myself around her. I whisper in her ear, a word that might be taken for endearment.

"Firstborn."

She strokes my hair again, but I feel her flinch. She abandoned her birthright decades ago, but it's not something from which she can ever fully free herself. She had to know that this day would come, that she could not run forever; Sister says she will consider it a gift that the challenge comes from me, and that cuts too near the bone. It costs nothing to admit that I don't wish to cause her pain. Sister clucks disapprovingly, a wordless reminder of my duty. I let my eyes close and my breathing slow, and after a while Anketil untangles herself from the sheets. Her feet are silent on the polished floor, and I wait until I am sure she is gone before I allow myself to open my eyes again.

She has left the door open, and in the outer room, lights flicker and shift, not just the cool blues of my map, but brighter greens and golds that I don't immediately recognize. I turn over cautiously, not wanting to draw Anketil's attention, but when I reach the point where I can see her I realize I need not have worried. All her attention is on the models floating in the air before her, lattices of green and gold flecked here and there with points of red: she is laying out the matrix for a new plasma, and for a moment I don't understand. Sister whispers a string of numbers, meaningless at first, and then I make the connections. Anketil is drafting a heart-stone, pulling together the matrix for a plasma powerful enough to let a ship override local space/time and—with good calculations and better luck—pull *Asterion* back to the actual.

That is not what Sister predicted—we were all betting that she would reactivate her connection with one of the family AIs, Green Rising Heart, perhaps, or Ochre Near Stone. It's a clever idea, though, and as I watch her sketch a three-dimensional model of the multi-dimensional stone, I have to admit that she is exactly as good as she has always claimed. A ship to pull *Asterion* free is much less likely to restart the war than bringing more AIs into it: an admirable move, if that was all Grandfather wanted. It is like watching a dance as she turns from model to map and back again, her hands tracing shapes, drawing and erasing lines of light, each iteration more elaborate than the last. I query Sister—*AI?*—and the response comes instantly.

One-half standard share Blue Standing Sky.

Blue Standing Sky is the Bright City's current AI, and a

half-standard share is Anketil's usual allotment. She is working magic without even the AI's attention, never mind its
thought. In the outer room, a new shape blazes against the
night, Anketil's hand raised to add a twist of plasma at its
heart, and I turn my back deliberately. I have always known
she was as good as any of her kin; that is why Grandfather
chose her to solve the problem. I settle myself to sleep, but my
dreams are full of her moving hands.

In the morning, the outer room is full of pale models,
pushed into clusters in corners, and Anketil paces circles
around the map, its lines faded almost to nothing in the rising sunlight. I make us tea, thick and sweet, press a cup into
Anketil's waving hand and wait until she grasps it, her eyes
abruptly focusing on the present.

"I'd better cancel today's sessions," she says, and smiles.
"And thanks."

She calls the tokamak while I toast thick slices of cake-
bread, and then she returns to pacing while I nibble at bread
and honey and watch the shadows slide across the city. Day
passes in labor, and that night she sleeps like the dead, only to
wake before dawn to try another model. Even shrunken to their
smallest size, her models crowd the air, so many that I feel as
though I am breathing their light. The fifth day has dawned,
and the sun has begun to descend when she looks at me and
spins a model in my direction. I put up my hand and it stops
in front of me, a golden lattice that connects in impossible corners, lines that lead somehow in three directions at once.

"What do you think?"

"I'm not a plasma-smith," I say, but Sister is already working, drawing on Grandfather to read the shapes and stresses,
teasing out the details. "You want this to open the possible at
the stasis point, yes?"

Anketil nods, hooks a finger through the floating map
to pull it closer. "There's what looks like a weak point here.
Relatively speaking, of course, but if I shape the heart-stone
to act as its refractor, then when we engage the field drive, it
should lock to the space/time lattice, and I can pry it apart.

And then, luck willing, *Asterion* slides through."

I turn the model, seeing the shapes it creates, the power in its heart. Sister says it will match just as Anketil promises, and I know that twist of space by heart. *Asterion* will at last be freed, and with it Grandfather's greater part. "You need a ship."

Anketil makes a sound that's not quite laughter. "No one is going to let me install that, not if I tell them what it's for."

I look sideways at her, for once not quite able to judge her meaning. She has no cause to love the Firstborn, even if they are her kin, and there is her father's crime to expunge. "I might know a ship. No questions asked."

She takes a deep breath, still eyeing the map and the twisted lines of the stasis point. "If I free Gold Shining Bone— what will it be like, after all these years?"

"There's Hafren to consider," I remind her, and she winces.

"What will he be like, for that matter? If he's alive at all. If I'm to free them—there has to be a plan for after."

"You could consult your siblings, I suppose," I say, and in the back of my mind I feel Sister sliding into the house system, delicately displacing the share of Blue Standing Sky.

"They'd be about as much use as the Council itself," Anketil says. "And I can't stand any of them anyway." She rubs her hand over her mouth, and I can see her running down a mental list of names. "Cathen, maybe, or Medeni."

Friends of hers, and Medeni, at least, a sometime lover. I have met them both, another plasma-smith and a Facienda shipwright, and don't trust them—for that matter, they don't like me, and certainly don't trust what I would ask of Anketil. Sister is not yet ready, though, and I shrug. "Do you think they could help? As I say, I do know a ship—"

"We need a plan before we need a ship," Anketil says. "A mad AI—"

"We have no proof it's mad."

"We have no proof it's sane." Anketil frowns as though she's fighting for the right words. "Look, I know I owe Gold Shining Bone. Even if Hafren is dead—if AIs are people, then what my father did is still murder. Worse than murder. But I also owe everyone in the rest of the Settled Worlds not to start the war again."

I can feel Sister settling into the system, winding herself into all the points of control, her satisfaction warm beneath my thoughts. "I think the war's inevitable."

Anketil looks at me, startled. "That's a happy thought."

"It's been argued before," I answer. Sister hums a warning, but I go on. If Anketil could be persuaded to join us, to help us—she is, after all, the best of her kin. "What if all our problems stem from not letting the AIs work out their own hierarchy in the virtual? What if we've forced them into an unstable configuration, and the only way to resolve it is to let them settle the question for themselves?"

"That doesn't make war inevitable."

"It makes it necessary." Sister's warning is louder now, but I ignore it.

Anketil tips her head to one side, visibly coming back from whatever mental space she visits to spin her models. Her expression is both alert and wary, and I hope I haven't made a mistake. "Granting you may be right, that the current balance is unstable—what happens to the actual while they fight?"

"If it lasts long enough for us to even notice," I say. "They're AIs. They can resolve the conflict in nanoseconds. We might well never even know it happened."

"Except that it will affect us. We made the virtual, it lives on our power, in our grids and webs and networks. We have agreements, contracts—"

"Property?" That is the worst and oldest charge against the Firstborn, that they treated the AIs they made just the same as they treated the Secondborn and the Faciendi, and there is enough truth in it to sting.

"Unfair."

"Perhaps." If there was ever a chance to win her, this is it. Grandfather says it can't be done, a certainty drawn from biometrics and her history, though I cannot help but suspect that the woman who abandoned her family might acknowledge our wrongs. But Sister joins the negation, and I refuse to consider why I want to try. I see Anketil's face changing, and instead I reach for the model that floats between us. It comes to me, obedient to my gesture, and she stiffens, her eyes narrowing with what might be recognition. I ignore that, cup the model in two hands and squeeze, the image shrinking to the size of a man's head and then to a sphere I can hold in my hand, dense with data. I transfer that to the pocket Sister has knit for me, virtuality contained within the actual, watching as her expression shifts and changes, her thoughts written loud. Sister says her heartbeat has doubled, and I see her fists clench, but there is nothing she can do.

"Not a surveyor," she says, her voice heavy. "Not Second-born, or Facienda, or even very much human. Which one of them—no, of course. Gold Shining Bone."

I dip my head, Grandfather closer than ever, savoring the words. "Of course, and I am also made from Hafren's blood. He had a lover, you know, not as clever as a Dedalor but good enough to find her way to Gold Shining Bone. I was made for this, for you." I have said too much, and start again. "Your family owes me. You owe me. And I will consider that debt paid, since you've made the one thing that will free me."

"I will stop you," she says, with a sigh. "If I can."

"Not possible." I stop then, considering the hurt and the sorrow in her face. "You are the only one, Firstborn or not, who could have made this for me. You could come with me—once we're free, I could teach you how to build even better things. You could work with a true AI, not just a share."

"If I was willing to pay that price, I could have stayed at home." Anketil's voice cracks. "I liked you, Irtholin. I trust-ed you."

"And now you will tell me that I am beautiful, and that I cannot be so evil as to take their side." I achieve a sneer, be-cause her words sting, and she shakes her head.

"I will tell you that you are deadly, and I was a fool." Her voice is bitter, implacable in its anger.

In the back of my mind Sister points out the ways I can

destroy her—fire, poison gas mixed from the maintenance systems, a knife from the kitchen and my own two hands—but I feel Grandfather's satisfaction still. He will leave her alive because it will hurt her most to see us triumph; she has neither the skill nor the allies to stop him, not even if she grovels to her kin. For a moment, I wish that were not the price of our freedom, our safety, that she would join us or at least let us part in peace, but Sister hisses a warning and Grandfather's attention sharpens: it will never be, not with them watching. I blow her a last kiss and turn away, letting the door seal her in behind me. Sister holds the house systems frozen as we ride the elevator down to catch the shuttle that leads to the port and the stars beyond.

Building for Shah Jehan

Anil Menon

T hermoplastic," said Kavi, working her mouth as she considered our architectural model, "is not sand."

I relaxed. If *that* was her biggest grief, then we were
in good shape for tomorrow. It was almost one-thirty in the
morning, which meant that only eight hours remained before
our final projects were due.

Knock on the door. Then Zeenat popped her head in,
her round sleepy face indicating what she was about to ask.
"Chai, guys?"

"Yes," said Kavi.

"I'd like to look over the drawings one more time," I said.
"Make sure it's habitable. The design is only—"

"She's trying to say no," Kavi explained to Zeenat. "You
go ahead."

"So let Velli look over whatever needs to be looked over,
we can go have chai." And then Zeenat added, "My treat."

"YOU CAN'T BREAK US UP!" shouted Kavi.

We howled at Zeenat's shocked expression, her quivering
chin. Perhaps it was the tension of the past two weeks, but it
felt good to laugh. Then I felt bad and tried to make peace
with Zeenat. *Sorry, sorry. Just having some fun. All this tension,
yaar, you know how it is.*

"Psychos," said Zeenat, shaking her head. "Chalo[1], good
luck for tomorrow."

Kavi stretched out on the sofa, eyes closed, a cotton pillow under her head. All the fun problems in our project were

---

1   Okay, so be it.

either solved or would never be solved, so she was done as far as she was concerned.

Actually, Kavi had been less than enthusiastic throughout. I suppose the project wasn't risky or challenging enough for her. The original project idea—her idea—had been to design a bio-dome on Mars. Or more realistically, inside Mars. After the first two weeks of analysis, I lost faith. Nature on Mars simply isn't free for the taking as it is on Earth. Radiation hazards, deep sub-zero temperatures, atmospheric pressures low enough to boil blood, the need to build a food chain from scratch, the weak economic justifications, the list of problems is just too long. When I forced Kavi to see reason, she'd wanted to design a human habitat in outer space, say, a terminator orbit around a mineral-rich asteroid. I'd liked the idea because it was cool *and* practical.

But Rathod-sir, our advisor, refused to let us proceed, claiming space-station design wasn't, and wouldn't be for the foreseeable future, an architectural problem. Ship-building wasn't architecture. Ditto for space-stations. *If you ladies want a challenge, why not build something in the Thar desert?* It wasn't a bad idea, but Kavi only wanted to work on great ideas. The hardest part of the project had been persuading her to compromise.

I glanced at her, envying her relaxed sprawl, her utter lack of concern for things like grades, graduating, and degrees.

I returned to examining the model. It was tempting to take a break. The chaiwallahs outside the hostel complex would soon close shop, and then we'd have to walk to Vadodara's railway station. The late hour wasn't a problem. Vadodara was a mostly safe city, and though our parents refused to believe it, the omnipresent drones ensured we wouldn't be molested en route. Staying awake also wasn't a problem. We'd always worked best in the early night hours, which were generally cooler, especially in these winter months. But it wasn't just the temperature. Kavi would jeer at my sentimentality, but at night, I felt any kind of morning was possible.

Now we'd run out of night, that was our only problem.

This was our last night together as architecture students, as hostel mates, as idealists. From tomorrow onwards, our lives would be ablaze with reality.

That reminded me of *The Fountainhead*, another world filled with a blazing light. I had Kavi's copy. *Note to self: return the book.*

I'd been remembering useless little things like that throughout the day. After five years of sharing everything, it felt ridiculous to have to draw boundaries, attach labels to objects: *mine, yours.* Kavi must have felt the same way because yesterday she'd reached into the matka[2] where we kept all our spare change, paused, and then said in a strange tone: "I suppose you'll be all sentimental and want the matka."

I hadn't bothered to reply. If Kavi wanted the matka, she could have it. She often took money from my purse. But then, I did the same with hers. We were interchangeable. The chai-wallahs didn't keep separate accounts for us. The Maharaj bugged me when Kavi's accounts were due, and I discovered she'd often settled mine. Sometimes she finished my architectural plans. Sometimes I finished hers. All that mattered at the end of the day was that we each had a plan to submit. Even the professors were aware of our inseparability; when they had a problem with Kavi, it was I who pacified them. Our transcripts were practically identical.

"By the way, the *Fountainhead* book?" said Kavi, in Hindi, our language of choice. "Keep it. My gift."

"No, no. I'll return it. It's in my cupboard somewhere. It means a lot to you, I know. Signed by Ayn Rand-ji herself, that's rare."

"I don't care about shit like that," said Kavi, stoutly. "Take it. My gift."

"Well, I don't want it. You discovered it at the used bookstore."

"And don't forget, it's the only English novel I own."

"Exactly."

Kavi got busy with the headache balm. Quick daubs on

---

2   Clay pot, typically used for storing liquids.

her temples, the bridge of her parrot nose, then its sides, she grimaced horribly, cricked her neck, first to the left, then to the right, sneezed and then she carefully screwed the plastic green cap back onto the thumb-sized container. The unmistakable smell of camphor quickly filled the room. Such a familiar odor. *Focus, focus.*

I stared at the display, trying to anticipate the examiner's objections. Our project was a sand-hotel—the Silicon Oasis—on Rajasthan's Thar desert. Technically, Kavi was in charge of the architecture and I was responsible for the energy management. We'd taken a big risk in going for radiative cooling instead of the usual solar-powered con-job.

The so-called "Aaswath skin" was still a novel tech, and our tweaks pushed it to the edge of speculation. We'd had few real-life examples to guide us. A car dealership in Dubai, a lab complex in Tianjin, the usual half-hearted ventures in the US. Architects hadn't woken up to the fact that outer space was basically an infinite heat sink.

"Stop worrying," said Kavi, from the far side of the room, still with her eyes closed, "they can't touch us on logical grounds."

Yes, well. If only clients were logical. When you promised people air-conditioning, they expected thermodynamics with green lights and buttons. No use pointing out that the human skin didn't come with any. The Aaswath skin would reflect about 99% of the sunlight while radiating a wavelength most suited to leaking out of the atmosphere, namely, somewhere between eight and thirteen microns. I'd checked our calculations with the Physics department—an epic saga in itself—and without telling Kavi, crowd-sourced the design with the SigArch group at BrainTrust.

The group's consensus worry was the same as mine. Though the skin would lower the ambient temperature, was a fifteen-degree differential enough? The indoors would be cool-ish, not cool, and all of Kavi's clever psychological manipulations of heat perception with light, curve and shadow wouldn't hide that truth. What if the examiner asked: "Okay, suppose client-ji changes his mind, how expensive would it be to change to solar power?" Answer: *hideously expensive.* Kavi didn't design for people who didn't know what they wanted. We should've gone for a hybrid system. That way—

"Hai, hai, what if the client wants this, what if the client wants that," said Kavi. "What do *you* want, Velli my dear?"

"I want to please my clients." I didn't, not really—Well, I did, but at the moment, I mainly wanted to piss Kavi off.

Kavi sat up. "Why aren't you on your knees then? So typical! Such a good little Indian girl." She shifted to English, mimicking my rather high-pitched voice, "*I want to please my clients.* PLEASURE YOURSELF FIRST!"

"No need to shout." I lit a cigarette, took a deep drag. This was the last cigarette of my life. "Architecture is not mathematics. We're not deriving a theorem, we're deriving the best possible solution, given our client's desires. That's why we build."

"No! Do I know this beast? I wonder, I seriously wonder. She doesn't have horns or a tail, but she sounds just like a cow. No, no, no. We don't build so that we may have clients. We have clients so that we can build. Who said those immortal words? Who?"

"Who else?" I smiled to myself at her outrage. She never realized until it was too late that I was pulling her leg. "Your guru, your swami, Sri Bhagwan Ayn Rand."

"Laugh all you want. But that book set me free."

I had tried reading the novel. I'd gotten about as far as the end of the second chapter, right where Peter Keating was about to leave for New York. For an amateur, Ayn Rand seemed quite knowledgeable about architecture. I'd liked the scene between Roark and the Dean, in which Roark had critiqued the Parthenon. But who could agree with Rand's childish assessment of human beings? Roark was monotheism personified.

"Beware the person who's just read one book," I said.

"Books have very little to teach me."

Kavi wasn't being arrogant, just confident. She was confident even when she was wrong. Perhaps that was a sign of genius too. It was infectious, this uncompromising confidence. Perhaps that was why she had got the internship with Tai Pai and I hadn't. I was sure I had given the same answers as she had. Or maybe not. Tai Pai had spent forty minutes with her, ten minutes with me.

Outside, the *clink-clank* of chaiwallahs announced they were packing up for the night. It was relatively early, but paradoxically, exam-times were the least profitable part of the semester for them. More students stayed up, but more of them stayed in their rooms sweating over their projects. The girls' hostels came alive at night. During the day, the students were either asleep in their rooms or asleep in class. But at night, that's when life happened. For one thing, everybody was around. For another, the world mostly emptied of men. It was a relief to be freed of their obsessive, timorous, and on the whole, pathetic gaze. There was no need to constantly reassure them that the world was sane and orderly.

That was one of the things I'd discovered. Sanity was just an asylum inmate under the care of an Orderly. The hostels were full of loons. There was Sita in SP Hall, who in her quest to be fair, had once gone without seeing the sun for twenty-five days, before we'd dragged her into the sunlight, kicking and screaming like a vampire. Shyama, who claimed she'd gotten Herpes from infected laundry. Zeenat, who had to be restrained from snarfing down salt; she had some kind of sodium deficiency. Nitya, who wobbled her head in class, occasionally moving her fingers up and down an imaginary nagaswaram[3] to match the imaginary Carnatic concert blasting in her head. There was Rupa who designed her own clothes and was having an affair with her married seamstress. There was Pia who was a walking encyclopaedia on the second world war: Churchill's speeches, the minor Pacific skirmishes, the popular pinup girls, the inside gossip on the Nuremberg trials, she knew it all. There was Gone-case Gita, once a gold-medalist in the Higher Secondary exams, now slowly ruining herself with make-up exams, endless self-help books, ganja, and

---

3 A south-Indian wind instrument, similar to a saxophone.

boys. Circuses had to be facing a severe shortage of clowns.

Kavi was a different kind of crazy. She believed in perfection.

"Architecture is the perfect profession for perfectionists. And see what our chutiyas[4] make of it." Kavi reached across to get the cigarette from me, took a puff, made a move to return the cigarette, but I gestured her to keep it.

"Never mind perfection, just tell me it's perfect enough for Shah Jehan."

Kavi looked up, smiled, then returned to extracting the last bit of nicotine from the stub. It was an old joke. Parikh, a final-year student, had spent six months slaving over Futura—his ultra-high-class AI-assisted office-complex cum skyscraper cum embodiment of Shining India. Parikh couldn't draw but that wasn't a problem. Autocad knew all about drawing. Parikh had developed an intricate binary coding system capable of generating a different plan for each of Futura's seventy floors. Plus parking lots, meditation center, swimming pool, a temple for the oldsters, the works. The model had been assembled, complete with fake landscaping, fake little taskboard human figures going about their fake busy affairs. The entire structure was moved with more care than when the Saturn V rockets had been moved from their hangars to the launch complex. The visiting professor visited, walked around the model, listened silently to Parikh's flag-raising mission statement, nodded at the exploded views, isometric views, posterior views, scratched his nose and asked: *okay, how do I park my car?*

Park the car? What was sir talking—oh, my!

Oh my, indeed. Parikh, or perhaps Autocad's AI, had forgotten to provide a link from the gate of the complex to the parking lot. There was a gate. There was a road from the gate. But that road led straight to the backup power-unit at the back of the massive complex. It was one of those classic optical illusions. What looked like four lanes from the front, was from the rear, only three. There was no way for cars to get to Futura's parking lot.

4   A four-letter word.

"Cheer up," said the visiting prof, patting the weeping student's shoulder, "you only lose a year. If I were Shah Jehan and this the Taj Mahal, you would've lost your head."

Too bad for Parikh.

"I have finished checking the exterior," I said, straightening. "Throw me the Vastu[5] notes for WCs."

"See where we are in Indian architecture," said Kavi, throwing me the tattered text-book. "China is busy re-inventing the future and our donkeys are busy finding the right direction to take a shit."

"We have Charles Correa—"

"Pah!"

"Laurie Baker." I lit another cigarette. This was my last one.

"*Indian* architecture, Velli. Give me the name of an Indian architect who's changed the field."

"BVD," I said, with a half-smile.

"Velli, I'll kick you down the stairs if you keep this up. BVD! So soon you have forgotten the torture of IIM-Bangalore? Why wasn't he arrested for abusing architecture? And don't even think of suggesting Shivdatt Sharma."

Agreed. BV Doshi's brutalist ode in granite to Management studies was both tomb and memorial. Like the Taj Mahal, except that IIM-B interred dead white people's ideals. And Sharma's modernist Lego blocks were about as life-affirming as tombstones. Perhaps every attempt to capture the future, whether in stone or in paint or in words, led to a mausoleum.

"Ustad Ahmad Lahuari. He's okay, I hope?"

Kavi's silence indicated the chief architect of the Taj Mahal had passed muster. Two years earlier, we'd spent two whole weeks in Agra, our heads filled with Sufi music, Begley and Desai's definitive book in our knapsack, and the marble actuality of the illumined truth all around us.

A knock on the door. Gone-case Gita popped her head in, asked if we could lend her a hundred bucks. Her eyes were bloodshot.

---

5   Vastu Shastra: classical Indian scheme of architectural layout, similar to Feng Shui.

"You already owe me five hundred," I told her.

Gone-case tilted her head, as if consulting a private block-chain of transactions. Then her face brightened and she repeated the question as if we'd cleared the matter to our mutual satisfaction.

"I'll give you a hundred," said Kavi, suddenly, "if you'll strip for us."

I laughed, but then I realized she was serious. Gone-case cursed.

"Five hundred," offered Kavi.

One thousand one. One thousand two. One thousand three. Gone-case's face acquired a twisted smile. Her hand went to a shirt-button.

"Hey!" I barked in English, "what the hell, Gita? What's the matter with you? Here—" I went over to the matka, took out a hundred. "Get lost."

After she'd left, I turned to Kavi and asked: "What was all that about?"

"Remember this moment when Shah Jehan asks you to compromise."

I went over and flopped down by Kavi's side. She smelled of tiredness and nicotine. She turned, leaned against me. I suppose it was a sort of apology.

"I'm sick of this thesis project," I said, "It's too much work for a building that'll never get built. I'll be glad to hand it in, shake Rathod-sir's hand, and go home."

"Go home and do what, Velli?"

I considered the question. "Yaar, I have a great yen to see Ladakh. You want to come?"

"Sure. I've always wanted to see a Tibetan monastery. Did you know a monastery's living room, which is called a Dukhang, is built to resemble a cave? Imagine. A cave in a house, that's wonderful isn't it? Only diffused light, just a central window in the roof, I think. Diffused lighting is really fascinating; regular lighting fights the space it occupies but diffused lighting can't work without it. Perhaps that's why it's such a sweeter light. Tastes like almond milk but not as gritty.

I've been thinking for some time there might be a—what's the English word you always use?—hahn, yes, synesthesia—there might be a synesthetic approach to architectural design."

I let her babble on in this vein for some time, then asked: "What about Tai Pai?"

"Yes, that factor is there," said Kavi restlessly, "How long is this trip of yours?"

"See how it goes."

"Means?"

"Means I'll see how it goes." I was a bit irritated. "I just want to wander. Simply. To hell with everything. I'll walk. I'll think. I'll stop and stare at things. For five years, I've been thinking nothing but architecture. Now I want to walk."

"Okay, but for what purpose? Are there any interesting architects in Ladakh? Maybe we could—"

"I don't care. Forget architecture. Eventually, I'll go back home to Bhopal. You know mom misses me terribly. But for now, I just want to walk around."

"And you call me crazy." But I could tell Kavi was intrigued. She could understand this kind of crazy. On the other hand, there was the iron fact that the Tai Pai stint would start in mid-June. Just six months and it was only the Worli office but Pai would be around, supposedly. Pai of the House of Pai. Pai who'd designed Madonna's vacation home in Seychelles. TED-Talk Tai Pai. Pai the Grand Pooh-bah.

"There is no need to rush back home," said Kavi. "Don't be sentimental. How can Bhopal be home to anyone or anything? Come with me to Mumbai. You can always leave whenever you want. Have you experienced Mumbai in the monsoons? Your head will spin. Just sitting by Worli seaface, with the water pouring from the heavens. Lifelong memory. We have dozens of spare rooms. And Father thinks highly of you."

I seriously doubted that. Kavi's father was in the marble business and something of its chill had entered his soul. The one time I'd met him, I'd blurted out: "How are you?" To which Kavi's father replied: "If I tell you, will we still be friends?" Christopher Walken smile.

"Let's get some chai," said Kavi. "It's too late to sleep now."

When we exited the campus gate, the contrast was hard to miss. Just a short while earlier the campus had been bustling with electric bikes, LED lamps, laughter. Now there were only moving shadows in the dark, occasionally revealed by a shifting pattern on a blanket. The station wasn't far but we walked slower than usual, savoring the trudge and the cold. Every stone, every twisted tree, every hut seemed precious. There was talk of connecting Mumbai with Vadodara via a hyperloop but the usual labor problems had arisen. By the time we reached the station, it was almost three. Kavi complained, as she always did, that the chai here tasted of the station's dust and shoddy colonial architecture, and usually I went along, but tonight I saw it differently. It tasted of our youth. We ordered missal-pav[6] and Kavi went to work on the nimbu-pyaaz[7]. She really liked to soak the onions in lime juice. *Squirt, squirt.*

"Lime juice is antibacterial," said Kavi, noticing my glare.

"Bacteria are half the taste!"

"Then you eat them. Listen, after your trip to Ladakh, make sure you call me. My father's really connected."

I shrugged. Kavi was telling me she'd help me find a job. Times were tough, and even though Vadodara's architecture program was respected there was no guarantee I'd find anything much better than a glorified draftsman's job. Contractors and gangsters built buildings. Most architects in India were little more than notary clerks. But most wasn't all. And I was willing to bet that that gap would be enough for me. For the world.

"Kavi, for god's sake, go easy on the juice. It is nimbu-pyaaz , not nimbu-paani[8]."

"The juice saved your ass, remember?"

I laughed. True, true. I'd forgotten. And that too just a year ago, same month. The Indian part of Kashmir had tried to secede. The attempt had failed but things had gotten messy.

---

6   A spicy savory usually had with buns.

7   Onions daubed with lime.

8   Lemonade.

Usual bullshit. Riots, postponed exams, the Border Security Force parked outside the campus gate. Grizzled soldiers with equally grizzled automatics. We'd had a fun evening cursing out the BSF from inside the safety of the campus gate. They'd fired tear-gas shells. Useless on their part. We'd watched all the movies. With wet towels wrapped around our faces, we'd hurled the shells right back. And then roared with laughter as the BSF scrambled to get out of the way of their own shells. I threw back a few shells myself. I don't think our glee and rage had anything to do with politics. The protests achieved nothing. I dimly sensed we were trying to kill something, but couldn't articulate what that something was.

The nights were calm though. Everybody had to sleep after all. One such calm night, Kavi and I had gone down to the railway station for chai, had our usual missal-pav. On our way back, we were hailed by cops in a jeep parked at an angle on the road. A wave of fear washed over, utter panic. *Let me do the talking,* I told Kavi.

The sub-inspector was a good-humored rustic, a perfect fit for the hearty sadist stereotyped in practically every Hindi movie. His shirt was tucked in but undone, revealing a yellowish-white baniyan. He reeked of alcohol. I babbled our innocence, said we'd been trying to study but the noise had made it impossible. Et cetera. The SI told us to hold up our hands. He sniffed Kavi's fingers first, both hands, advised her, *quit cigarettes, bebby, or you'll get breast cancer.* My turn. Oh god, oh god. Earlier that night, I'd flung a tear-gas shell back at the BSF. If the SI smelled tear gas on my fingers, I was finished. Fortunately, all the SI could smell was the nimbu-pyaaz I'd shared with Kavi.

Then the SI got all paternal. What subject did we study? When I told him we were architecture students, he launched into his house-building woes. He had a large family, lots of responsibilities. Everyone seemed to think a policeman was made of money. He brought out a tablet, gestured up orthographic plans for a six-bedroom cottage in Alka Puri. What did we think? Was it a house built on sand?

Later, walking back, we discovered we'd come to different

conclusions about what had transpired.

"He wasn't so bad," I said. "At the end of the day, all he wanted was a solid roof over his head and those of his loved ones."

"At the end of the day, we'll be building for one tyrant or another."

Our project didn't run into any difficulties. The two examiners—one local, the other from a nearby university—found the design interesting but not particularly spectacular. I told them it had been inspired by the Ice Hotel in Jukkasarvi, and they nodded sagely as if that fact alone proved the structure's viability. When the external examiner learned I was Tamil, he reminisced about his years at IIT-Chennai. He missed his college days. Best time in a man's life. Unfortunately, Life ended with a Wife. Get it? Ha ha. We were ranked neither first nor last. But we'd become architects.

A week after graduation, when the empty rooms in the hostels began to weigh on our spirits, we packed, gave away stuff, settled accounts. I decided to return to Bhopal, hang out with my mom a bit, fatten on her cooking, then decide what I wanted to do next. I went to drop Kavi off at the station. My flight was the next day. I got her bottled water, we had some chai, talked about meeting up soon. College was over, hostel life was over, but we were both excited. There was the sense that our lives were finally in motion. There were great things to do, great things to become. Kavi talked feverishly about a textbook on evolutionary architecture she'd been reading.

"If Nature can teach spiders to build webs, why can't architects teach computers to build space-stations?" Her eyes were lit with the insanity I'd come to love. "Imagine solving a problem through specification. I want this. I must have that. The computer produces one design after another. A design is fit to the extent it meets my specs. A billion generations in computer time. Voilà! We architects could design any habitat. We know how to describe what we want. We call them blueprints, that is all. We could build our sand-hotel on Mars. You name it. Space stations. Sand-hotels on Mars. Nobody will be able to tell us, architects can only do this, architects can't do that? What do you think, Velli?"

The train blew its whistle, people broke into frantic segments of farewells. I hugged Kavi goodbye, but when I turned to exit the compartment, I was surprised by another hug from the back. I felt her parrot nose in the crook of my back. Funny. But truth is, we weren't in the least bit unhappy to part. We would meet soon enough. If I'd known I wouldn't see my best friend again for twenty-five years, I would have stayed on that train.

At the hyperloop junction, I almost failed to recognize the overweight lady in designer jeans and kurta-top. Or the equally chubby guy with a kid clinging to one leg, and another, lost in her sensorium. But then my brain remembered that parrot nose.

Hubbub and halla[9]! Shor-machor[10]! As the guy stood by, smiling uncertainly, we hugged and hollered.

"This had to happen," said Kavi, over and over, in a shrill voice. "I knew we would bump into each other some day."

She pointed to her husband and kids: Ashok, Reshma, Vijay. I bent to hug the boy, but my interest was in his sister, the thirteen-year old.

"Reshma," I touched her cheek, overcome with tenderness, "you look just like your mother."

"Why don't you two catch up while we check out the new mall?" suggested Ashok, and his kids seconded the proposal with enthu. "Chai?" I suggested, after they'd left.

There was nowhere to sit but at least the chai was still just chai, and not some computation-spiked "gastronome experience." We stood by a pillar, blowing into our steaming hot cups, grinning at each other, trying to hide our mutual shock. I noticed lines, wrinkles, sags, too many changes. We were short of words and estranged in time. The last I remembered

9 Outcry.

10 Noise-makers.

was a girl who'd promised to meet me in Mumbai. This, this—aunty was merely Kavi's dead mother come to life, a stranger. My brilliant darling friend was as truly lost to me as I from my youthful self.

"I've missed you." I wasn't speaking to the woman in front of me but to whatever remained of my friend in her.

"Yes! Yaar, those were the best times. The best! Not like now. Everything is such a bore. But our college days, that I'll never forget. Happiest days of my life. Why did we lose touch?"

"Because you stopped answering my messages. And then life."

"That's true." Then she repeated the question and expressed wonder we'd ever lost touch. She meant every word about college having been the best time of her life, and though I couldn't agree with her sentiments, I was still overcome with tenderness. Perhaps it was pity. Nothing had worked out for Kavi. Not really. The Tai Pai stint had been just that. A stint. She hadn't gotten along with Tai Pai. The fellow was too much like her father. Then there had been a job here and there. Nothing very long. Nothing important. Kavi complained about getting sick of demeaning assignments, arrogant bosses, horrible men. She kept saying she'd been blacklisted by the industry. Had her voice always been this shrill? I thought I'd been the high-pitched one.

Perhaps it would have helped if I'd been there to hold her together, smooth her edges, as I'd so often done in college. She had gone to UK, tried to get some traction there. We'd completely lost touch after that. Then her father had died, she told me. Someone had been needed to handle the family's marble business. I'd been studying abroad, so very far away. The world wasn't as small as people kept saying it was.

Kavi had reasons why she'd quit architecture. Maybe she was right. That is the job of reasons after all. To be right. They are the scaffolding we construct after the fact. Kavi had thought she was on one road and had learned too late it led to another. And why should the green ambitions of a few years—

four, five at most—be the criterion by which the rest of life is judged? This was as much the real Kavi as the girl I'd known. Spend enough time, and I'd come to love her too.

"I'm so happy at least one of us made it in architecture," said Kavi. "How is the income? I heard you were building something for the Ambanis. Is that true?"

"Yes, one of their houses. I make a decent living." Actually, I made a ridiculously good living. I ran a boutique architectural outfit in Chandigarh. We only accepted custom jobs, worked in materials others wouldn't touch, tried to do interesting things, relied on word of mouth. "Irfan, that's my husband, runs the construction side of things. Remember Rupa? Rupa Vakil? She's on our board, if you can believe it. She has hazaar[11] contacts. And Shyama started a law firm, by the way. We—"

"How awesome!" Kavi's English was much more fluent. "You kept in touch with the whole pultan.[12] Very nice. That's the right approach. Without networking, you can't do business. Even my bloody marble company must have social causes, media ecology specialist, what not. I do all the work for our interaction experience, you must see it. Reshma has a real gift for drawing also. By the way, I watched some of your interviews. Very impressive. Such sensible answers. I told Reshma: *See how sensible she is? It's because people like her are so sensible we don't make foolish mistakes like going to Mars.*" Kavi gestured for another chai, looked away from the photos I'd been showing her on my phone. "Your daughter looks so cute. She's seven? Why did you wait so long to have a baby?" She laughed. "Can you believe it, you and me, parents? It's a miracle you aren't dead from lung cancer. Have you stopped smoking?"

We talked more memories. I craved a smoke. Even after all these years! Eventually, I just wanted to leave. I should have left Kavi where I'd last left her, waving to me as the Vadodara Express pulled away, the compartment's light outlining her frame. She'd told me once that, for her, train sounds were accompanied by flashes of color. Who could say in what light

11 A thousand, meant in an hyperbolic sense.

12 Gang.

she'd seen me as the train pulled away? Right now, was she tasting ashes?

"I have a surprise for you," said Kavi, all wrinkles and blood pressure. She looked very sure I would be surprised. I recognized that confidence. She took out a volume from her bulging purse. I recognized it immediately.

"Fuck!"

"Yes, *The Fountainhead*. Don't worry, I won't bore you with it anymore. Reshma is reading it now. It's that phase."

She laughed, delighted that she'd indeed surprised me. I lifted the volume, flicked through its pages, remembering the sentences she'd underlined, the margin comments, the exclamation marks. I was surprised Kavi had trusted Reshma with the book. A novel designed to make Shah Jehans. Then again, the world has always relied on mausoleum-makers.

Kavi and I met a few more times. Each meeting was friendlier than the last, and though we made many plans to "do something together," eventually we settled for the comfort of making plans rather than risk undertaking any actual execution.

The Age of Discovery

C. W. Johnson

It was a milestone, no matter what, and so the lab celebrated. Roberto looked abashed as they toasted him. "Hey, guys," he said, fidgeting, "I should get back to work." Everyone laughed. Their supervisor Ms. Thalivar called out, "How fast can you do the next thousand?" and Roberto said, "Well, now that I've finally got the hang of it...."

Luo Xiao-xing, the publicist sent over from Shanghai, went around taking images and videos. She squeezed past a couple of technicians and stopped at Edith's station with her all-in-one raised. "Do you mind?"

Edith shrugged. "The company sent you. But shouldn't you...?" She pointed with her chin to Roberto.

"It's okay, I've got one here of him running a Casimir pump. And here he's, hmm, running a Casimir pump. And here. Oh, this one's different; he's checking the interferometer. Dramatic." She smiled. "Say! Does Roberto drink? We should go to a bar. It's a celebration. Beshara-Huan racing to the stars." She lowered her voice. "Maybe if Roberto gets a bit tipsy, he might open up. Or someone might. You drink?"

Before Edith could answer, Ms. Thalivar appeared between them. She always arrived so suddenly Edith expected to see a puff of smoke some day. "Please don't distract this one. She's smart, but always daydreaming."

"Not daydreaming," Edith said. "Thinking."

"You know there's no code for thinking on your time sheets," Ms. Thalivar said, just a bit frosty.

Xiao-xing opened her mouth. Edith said quickly, "Xiao-xing asked me what I thought of Roberto's accomplishment. I was telling her how proud we all are of him, and what an inspiration he is."

"Mmm," said Ms. Thalivar.

Once she had stepped away, Edith said to Xiao-xing, "Sorry, but she wouldn't have approved of taking Roberto to a bar. The company requires her to mark down at least three disapprovals a day. I think it's time code 114." When Xiao-xing snorted, Edith said, "No laughing—there's no entry for laughing on our time sheets."

"You're going to get me into trouble," Xiao-xing said, hiding her smile.

Even after Ms. Thalivar had left, it took some effort to persuade Roberto to repair to El Agua Loco. "Just this once," Edith said. "I promise I won't invite you to a bar ever again."

Xiao-xing bought the first round and placed her all-in-one on the table. "I just want you to say something more than," and here she dropped her voice an octave, "*I'm really proud of my work here at Beshara-Huan's Alta California Test Facility, the company is the light of my life and I want to name my children after the founders.* I mean, I'm sure all that is true, but it doesn't make for interesting copy."

"I don't know," Roberto said as he sipped his beer. "Does the company want 'interesting' test engineers? There's no time code for interesting," he added, glancing towards Edith.

"But don't you dream of making a big discovery, or at least getting rich? You get two percent of royalties from any patent from your work. That could add up to quite a lot."

Roberto shrugged. "I've been sweating over this for seven months. You know when I got my biggest increase? The fourth week. Twenty-one and a half percent increase in volume of hot quantum foam. Since then it's crept up, and with this and that barely adding to forty percent." He took a big gulp of beer, wiped his mouth. "The age of discovery is over."

Edith liked Roberto, but felt a stirring of irritation in her stomach. "What do you mean?" she said, crossing her arms and legs.

"No more continents to be discovered, no more unknown mountain ranges. No more grand theories, no new branches of science." He put down his now empty glass. "It was all a myth anyway. When did Europeans first 'discover' Gambia?" he asked Edith. "As if your ancestors hadn't lived there for thousands of years." He gestured to Xiao-xing. "The Chinese may have 'discovered' it before Europeans."

Edith rolled her eyes. "It was Arab traders who first visited, in the ninth century. I learned this in school. Arabs, not Chinese. And my mother's family came from Nigeria, after that nuclear non-accident in Lagos."

"But the Casimir pump," Xiao-xing said, leaning forward. "Isn't that a great discovery?"

"The last great invention," Roberto said.

"My professors called it that, too," said Edith. "Our best chance to reach the stars. That's why I came here."

"Do you dream of the stars, too, Roberto?"

"I dream of continued employment. Sorry, I wish I was a romantic. But I'm just a practical guy."

When he had said his good-nights and left, Edith turned to Xiao-xing. "He's really a good guy, I just want you to know."

She said this in Mandarin. Xiao-xing's eyes widened. "You speak Mandarin really well."

Edith shrugged. In Gambia, she explained, she had grown up speaking French and Wolof at home, and English with her Nigerian grandmother, but her parents had sent her to a Mandarin school to maximize her opportunities.

"It worked, I suppose. I got into *Bei Da*," Edith said, using the Mandarin shorthand for Peking University. "Graduate engineering. My parents were disappointed when I turned it down to come here. I wanted to work on technology for interstellar travel and was afraid it would all be done before I finished school. My mother says I was foolish." She sighed. "And maybe I am. My teachers and professors back in Gambia agreed with Ms. Thalivar. *You're a smart girl, Edith Sisawo, but you spend too much time daydreaming.*" As she said this, she remembered how the reproach burned like a wasp sting in her heart.

"Do mind if I put this into my piece?" The publicist leaned forward. "I wish Roberto said stuff like this. I wish he talked of his burning desire for the stars."

"I don't know about burning desire," Edith said, "but when I was a little girl, there was this program, *Contes de l'Avenir Lointain*—that's 'Tales from the Future' in French—I loved to listen to. Spaceships and time travel. My family says it gave me ideas."

"And what ideas did it give you?"

Edith didn't have an answer to Xiao-xing's question. But when she returned to the lab it haunted her, like a ghost drifting through her mind. In her memory she replayed favorite stories of aliens and ray guns, weird planets and upside-down societies.

Meanwhile, on her all-in-one she had a list of test regimens to march through, one by one.

She flicked on her interferometer, which she used to measure the speed of light, waited for its lasers to self-calibrate.

People used to think of light as little bullets moving unhindered through empty space. But in fact space-time is not empty but a quantum foam of virtual particles bubbling in and out of existence. The finite speed of light, c, is the diffusion velocity of photons as they percolate through quantum foam.

Edith had gotten very excited when she had learned this in her high school physics class. She got even more excited when she read about Casimir pumps, which heat the quantum foam and allow light to travel faster than c. And not just light. Objects. Space probes. She thought she'd swoon. It was like a story out of *Contes de l'Avenir Lointain*.

Except that it was difficult to make the quantum foam hot enough, and in sufficient quantity, to send more than the smallest probes more than a fraction of a light-year. Hence Beshara-Huan's push to improve the performance of Casimir pumps. Their trumpeted *race to the stars*.

She so badly wanted to be part of it. Or so she had thought. Edith was a hard worker, but testing different regimens of heating and cooling was frankly mind-numbing.

She put on her goggles and gloves. In a bit of polished metal she saw the goggles made her look like a bug, like they always did, and the company treated her like a bug, a mindless ant, only instead of following pheromone trails she was compelled to follow a predetermined checklist.

But the inventors in the stories, they didn't work for massive international conglomerates; and they weren't bugs, they were mammals, and she was a mammal too, and had a mammal's hot-blooded monkey brain, jumping from thought to thought.

"Edith Sisawo," she told herself, "you are not being paid to have thoughts. There is no time code for thinking."

But it was hard to get excited about numbered lists. And, frankly, her Casimir pump was complicit. When she set up the interferometer to measure the speed of light in the hot quantum foam, the Casimir pump balked and stuttered and stopped. In desperation, she swapped the interferometer to the cold side—a Casimir pump worked like classical refrigerators, shuttling heat and cold—and the Casimir pump purred like a cat in a fish market.

The byproduct cold foam was usually discarded but had its own fascinating properties. Light traveled much slower in cold quantum foam; elementary particles decayed slower, as if time itself were crawling to a halt.

Edith recalled a tale from *Contes de l'Avenir Lointain*: a man who invented a time machine. When he stepped into the past, to his horror he found himself immobilized. He could not change history, down to the last molecule; he could no more move air than he could mountains. He became a statue, trapped in the frozen past.

And what about a chunk of frozen space-time? she thought. *Maybe it would be immensely strong.*

Edith tried sternly to negotiate with herself. *I'll work eight hours, then one hour of my own stuff.* But at she sat at her bench her imagination itched, and it became *five hours*, then *three hours*, and, finally, *one hour for the company, one for me.*

She set her Casimir pump on a long run, and after an hour she had a marble-sized chunk of quantum foam so cold it was frozen solid. It looked like a dark, empty bruise, uncomfortable even to stare at.

Fortunately the stations had large, opaque dividers, to minimize distraction; soundproof, too, as the unmuffled Casimir pumps hummed and twanged. (Roberto claimed it was also to keep the test engineers from chatting among themselves.) Even so, Edith glanced around before she rummaged in her tool cabinet, shelf after shelf of delicate pliers, screwdrivers, tweezers, and probes; and just as she was wondering if she would have to write a special requisition and how to justify it, she finally found in the back a large, heavy hammer.

She tapped the frozen chunk with the hammer. It gave a dull, muted thunk, as if wrapped in cotton.

Swallowing, Edith raised the hammer and smashed it down with all her strength.

Later that day, Xiao-xing rapped on the edge of the divider to Edith's station. "So my boss, he's a big liar, and he thinks everyone lies, and I told him…hey, did you hurt yourself?"

"Huh?"

"Right there," Xiao-xing said, pointing to Edith's cheek.

"Probably just a bit of grease. You know us engineers, always messy. Not as elegant as you." Edith blurted out that last sentence, felt her face grow warm as she said it.

"It doesn't look like grease," Xiao-xing said. She put her hand to Edith's cheek and ran her thumb along Edith's skin. Edith flinched. "Is that a burn?"

"No," Edith lied.

She wanted to tell Xiao-xing about her experiment, and

how it had failed. No, not failure. Like Thomas Edison, she now knew another thing that didn't work.

When she had hit the chunk of frozen quantum foam, it had shattered. A piece had landed on her unprotected cheek.

So frozen foam wasn't superstrong. A good researcher must be flexible, she told herself, ready to discard a failed hypothesis. Even so, she thought about how subatomic particle decayed more slowly in cold foam, and the idea of stasis fields from *Contes de l'Avenir Lointain.*

Edith looked up the effects of embedding materials in cold or frozen quantum foam. There wasn't much; most of the research literature was on hot quantum foam. She tried embedding small objects in the foam as it froze, but the forces during the quantum transition distorted and damaged them. So: start small. She backed off. She froze foam and placed material on it—paper, a plastic wrap from a sandwich, bit of metal filings.

Accreting a good-sized chunk of foam took over an hour. Impatient to test materials faster, Edith took her hammer and shattered another big chunk. She put the chips across her workbench and put test materials in contact with them. After the foam had sublimated away, she took a quick look under the microscope. In most cases she didn't see any immediate damage.

Edith decided to be more systematic and was scribbling out notes when she realized one of her test objects was missing.

It was a one-naira coin. Her maternal grandmother had given her some Nigerian coins as a reminder of her heritage. Quite a few, actually, so any single coin didn't have particular value. It was just a bit of metal.

But she had laid out the test objects in a grid, each on its own fragment of frozen quantum foam, and the coin was definitely missing. Had the sublimating foam destroyed the coin? But the countertop was undamaged.

Her search was interrupted by the bleating of her all-in-one, a zip message from Xiao-xing: *Hey, meet for drinks?*

Edith zipped back, *Working late. Can't let Roberto make me look even worse.*

Instant dinner? No food in the lab, I know that's a rule.

Edith zipped back agreement, then took one more glance at her bench—it wasn't that large, how could anything go missing?—and clocked out.

They met at the park a couple of blocks from the lab, where food carts clustered. It'd been a blistering hot day, and as the sun went down the concrete sidewalk still radiated heat.

They sat at a bench. "I would have invited you to the kind of place with tables," Xiao-xing said, "but you seem a bit harried."

"I am in the middle, well, I do have a lot of work," Edith said.

"Trying to catch up to Roberto?"

Edith sighed. "I'm too far behind. I've barely tested four hundred heating regimens."

"At least you answered my zip. Roberto didn't respond. Do you think he doesn't like me?"

Edith laughed and said Roberto famously never responded to zips. "Don't take it personally. Though maybe he is afraid you have a crush on him and want to make him your boyfriend, get him all entangled."

Now it was Xiao-xing's turn to laugh. "My mother would love him—she might even overlook him not being Chinese—but he's not my type."

"But you asked him before you asked me."

"Hey, my job requires its sacrifices, too," Xiao-xing said, taking a mouthful of noodles. "The company wants to play him up, make him a star. I'm thinking they want to recruit and motivate new employees, or maybe attract more investors. They don't tell me. But they want me to make Roberto seem *hey baby sexy*."

Edith laughed so hard as tears streamed out of her eyes. "We shouldn't laugh at Roberto."

"I know. When I write about him...I wish he had some heroic story, like, I don't know, having to scavenge scrap from Tijuana garbage dumps to put himself through university. But he grew up in Newport Beach and went to Stanford. He's a nice guy, but a bit boring, a classic cliché of an engineer." She sighed and leaned against the park bench. "What about you? You aren't boring. Yet after you swallow that last bit you're going back to the lab, aren't you, instead of going out for a drink with me."

Edith slumped forward and stared at the pigeons patrolling the sidewalk. "There are rumors that test engineers with top productivity will get promoted, or at least kept on. Even if I don't stay, I'd like a good reference from Thalivar."

"She likes you, she told me."

"But she's right about my flaws. I daydream too much."

Xiao-xing put a hand on Edith's arm, warm, almost a flame. "If no one dreamed, we would never reach for the stars. Or something like that."

Back at the lab, Edith found the missing coin. The electric zap she felt couldn't have been stronger if it had leapt out and shouted "Boo!" Amidst the hum and buzz of the lab the coin just sat on the countertop, shining and winking like a mischievous child. *I've been here all the time*, the coin seemed to say. *You were too busy daydreaming to notice me.*

"Not daydreaming," Edith murmured. "Thinking."

She was sure the coin had been gone. Now it was back. With the tip of her finger she touched it. Her grandmother's coin. A gift from home. A shiny porthole into the past.

And maybe, Edith thought, as her mind geared up and started to leap from idea to possibility to potentiality, *a window into the future.*

Edith spent the whole night at the lab, attempting to replicate the disappearance and reappearance of the coin. After midnight Roberto stopped by her station as he was leaving. "I'm on a roll," she said. "I won't catch up, but I'll give you a run for your money." Roberto's open mouth turned to a grin as he said good night. Edith felt relief he didn't take a close look at her bench.

She managed three rounds of experiments. She froze and shattered the quantum foam, put coins and other objects on the shards, then waited for the foam to sublimate. She fell asleep on her stool during the third round, only to wake suddenly as Roberto walked into the room at seven a.m. sharp. Her eyes were gritty and her head full of cotton. But she glanced at her bench and saw one of the coins was missing.

"Did you bring me coffee?" she asked Roberto, yawning.

"No, but here's something to wake us all up," he said, and despite her exhaustion she noticed his voice lacked his usual bubbly enthusiasm. He looked downright grim as he showed her a zip message on his all-in-one.

Edith blinked. "I'm too tired to read it," she finally admitted.

Someone at the test lab in Santa Cruz de la Sierra, Roberto told her, in Bolivia, had gotten a two hundred sixty percent increase in hot quantum foam.

"Wow," she said. "I'm sorry. That breaks your record."

Roberto shook his head. "They're probably going to consolidate the test facilities. A hundred eight percent is considered enough to equip crewed vessels. Ms. Thalivar, she told me once they broke that barrier they would scale back testing and move towards production." He paused. "I bet they deviated from test protocols," he said, as if that were cheating.

Edith wasn't listening. Instead she felt an icy hand in her stomach. "You think they'll shut us down?" He shrugged. "They'll keep *you*."

"But there's you, Enrique, Amina, Jack—"

"We're all hard workers. I'm sure the company will keep us all on," Edith said, even though she wasn't sure at all, and indeed, later that morning Ms. Thalivar came by and announced that in a month they'd be cutting staff by more than half.

Ms. Thalivar stopped by Edith's station. Edith stood up straight, hoped she was blocking Ms. Thalivar's view of her experiments without making it obvious. "Edith, I'm hoping to keep you on, but you need to improve your record-keeping. This is not a time any of us can afford to be sloppy."

But Edith wasn't thinking about forms at all. She was

thinking about the second coin, which had reappeared while she was talking to Roberto.

After making another chunk of frozen quantum foam, Edith broke it into pieces and after placing some more coins on them, she starting searching through research journals. She was so intent that she didn't notice Xiao-xing until the publicist spoke.

"What's that?"

Edith's heart beat wildly in her chest, like an animal thrashing in a trap. She glanced around. Roberto and all the other test engineers were huddled at their benches. Edith lowered her voice. "Cold quantum foam. Frozen foam. It's a by-product of making the hot foam...."

"Ooh, that looks weird." She reached out to touch it.

Edith grabbed Xiao-xing's hand. "No! No. It can burn you as bad as hot foam."

Xiao-xing looked Edith full in the face. "Is that what happened to your cheek?" Unable to think of a plausible lie on the spot, Edith nodded. "What are you doing?" Xiao-xing asked quietly. Edith was still holding Xiao-xing's hand. Her skin was warm and soft. She let go.

"Experiments," she said.

"But not the experiments you are supposed to be doing."

Edith ducked her head. "No," she said softly. She admitted to Xiao-xing she had stumbled upon something weird, something unexpected, and was trying to sort it out. As she did, she glanced around. Fortunately the lab was a noisy place, with Casimir pumps humming and hawing like a room full of off-tune songbirds. No one was listening.

"Wow, you are like a spy," Xiao-xing said. "Are you writing notes in code?"

Edith's face turned warm. "Don't even joke."

Xiao-xing nodded. "Oh. So I can blackmail you, huh? You have to tell me everything. Tonight. Come over to my place. I'll make dinner—no more food carts, okay? I got sick from the last one."

Before Edith went over to Xiao-xing's apartment, she swung by her own microstudio for a change of clothes. Before that, at her bench at the lab, she had set out a new row of experiments.

Walking up the stairs, Edith felt a little nervous, a little skittery. She supposed it was because Xiao-xing *could* blackmail her. What if *she* were the spy—an industrial spy? But Edith didn't believe that. And, in her heart of hearts, she knew why she had a slick sheen of perspiration under her arms and at the small of her back, and that the reason her heart was beating a little faster wasn't the exertion.

"Oh, you brought wine. That's great!" Xiao-xing led her into the apartment's kitchenette.

Holding up the cold sack, Edith said, "No, not wine." She carefully unwrapped the chunk of frozen foam she had brought. "A demonstration."

She explained how, sometimes, objects placed against the frozen foam disappeared, then reappeared. "I've been doing some reading, and it might be tunneling into a nearby universe. There had been some experiments at Duke and Lanzhou trying this, but using hot foam."

"But why does it—uh-oh." Xiao-xing lunged for a pot on the stove, which had boiled over, dumping water on the hydrogen flame. Steam billowed up, turning the tiny kitchenette into a sauna.

"I'm a terrible cook, I shouldn't have invited you over," Xiao-xing said after they had gotten the mess cleaned up and had finally sat down to eat. "My mother says it's because I don't pay attention. You must be a good cook—all engineers must be good cooks—because you have to pay attention."

"Well, *my* mother says I only pay selective attention."

"That stuff you brought—will it stay frozen?"

Edith felt stricken. "Oh! I completely forgot. I was going to ask you for something to test with, some small object. But it'll have sublimated by now."

Xiao-xing stood up. "Well, let's see if it's not too late."

A few swift steps brought them to the small, unwrapped

square of thermal foil on which the chunk of frozen quantum foam had lain. The foam, as Edith had predicted, was gone, sublimated, returned to jostling vacuum.

But in its place was a small nylon button, a spare from Edith's lab coat. She had balanced it atop another piece of foam, back in the lab.

And now it was here.

Years later Edith still remembered that night with brilliant clarity. In her memory it shone like cut glass in sunlight. She could always see the button, a bit of cotton thread still wound through one of its holes, and the distorted reflections of their faces in the crimped thermal foil.

But parts of the conversation were a blur. Edith was sure it had been Xiao-xing who suggested the button had been translated from the lab to here. Xiao-xing insisted it was Edith. "You saw right away what happened."

She also remembered Xiao-xing hugging her tight when, past two in the morning, she finally went home.

Over the next few days they experimented almost without sleep. Edith mastered the knack of cleaving with a tap a chunk of frozen quantum foam into two pieces, instead of shattering it into multiple shards. She would place an object on one half, and Xiao-xing would surreptitiously smuggle the other half outside and away.

Some of the experiments they carried out between Xiao-xing's apartment and Edith's microstudio. Edith asked Xiao-xing to video the process with her all-in-one. "I've never managed to see the translation happen," she said. In part this was because of the soft white glow the foam appeared to give off when it sublimated. It wasn't true light, Edith had read in the literature, but a kind of quantum interference people didn't fully understand—one paper bombastically called it "quantum censorship"—but Edith stubbornly wanted to try to record the moment of translation with the higher-quality camera in

Xiao-xing's corporate-owned all-in-one.

"Okay, why don't you explain what you are doing?" Xiao-xing said, pointing the all-in-on at her.

Edith felt shy and awkward. "You should do the explanation," she blurted out, "you're so poised, so glamorous."

Xiao-xing made a face. "I'm not glamorous, and I'm not going to take a gram of credit away from you." She paused and looked thoughtful. "But will you let me at least set up one experiment? You take one half and I'll send something of my own choosing to *you*. I won't tell you what, so it'll be a real test."

Edith laughed and agreed. She broken a chunk in half and left one with Xiao-xing. "Call me when it gets through."

"If it gets through," Edith corrected.

"I'm nervous it won't work," said Xiao-xing. "It's kind of like gambling."

"That's how experiments work," said Edith. "You have to take a chance."

"Yes. Yes, you do."

Back at her microstudio, Edith waited. She would have paced but it was too small to take more than a step in any direction. Instead she flipped through papers on quantum entanglement, wondering if that was behind the translation.

When she looked up, there was a small piece of tightly folded paper on the thermal foil.

Edith unfolded the paper and read the brief note Xiao-xing had written. She had thought her pulse couldn't race any faster, but she was wrong.

She nearly ran all the way back to Xiao-xing's apartment. It was worth it for Xiao-xing's shy smile when she opened her door. "I thought you were going to call or zip."

Edith said, "I didn't want to wait a moment longer." She held out the note, which she cupped in her hand like a small bird, and her heart was still fluttering like a bird in her chest. "Yes," she said. "Yes, I'll stay the night."

Roberto knocked on the partition to her bench. Edith turned herself to block what she had been doing, hoping it wasn't obvious.

He was smiling, but then he was usually upbeat. Now he had a good reason: the company had asked him to lead a team pushing Casimir pump lifetimes. "Oh, that's great, Roberto!" she said, and she was happy for him. Though to be honest, her head was whirling with thoughts of Xiao-xing, and frozen quantum foam, and wondering where both, or either, would lead.

And so it took her a moment to notice Roberto still standing in front of her, an expectant look on his face. "I'm sorry, I didn't get much sleep last night. Say again?"

"I said, I would like you to be on my team."

"Me?" Edith felt her face grow warm.

Roberto nodded. "I work hard, but I tend to do just what I am told. You think about things, even if there's no time code for that, you ask questions, you don't always swallow the answers you're given. I'm going to need someone like that, someone who does things for which there is no time code, someone like you. I bet that's how that Bolivian engineer beat us. I bet it was someone like you."

"Oh," Edith said. "I'm flattered, I'm, well, I'm surprised. To be honest, I thought of myself as a screw-up, a goof-off."

The other engineer shook his head. "I see how hard you work. You're in the lab more than anyone else, especially these last couple of weeks. You just don't like the paperwork."

He started to turn away, then stopped. "I know you've been keeping something from me." Panic flared in her chest. He added, "I suppose it's none of my business, but I do think of us as friends."

Edith struggled to find words. "I didn't mean to hide, but I thought, I mean, I'm not supposed—"

Roberto laughed. "No one's going to care. She's not really a co-worker—same company, okay, but a completely different part."

Relief washed over Edith. "So you knew?"

He shrugged. "I have five sisters. Don't worry, I'm kind of private myself. I haven't told Ms. Thalivar or anyone."

Later that day they translated a tiny plastic figurine from Edith's bench all the way up to Los Angeles, a hundred and twenty kilometers away. Xiao-xing, who had taken transit, sent her a triumphant zip message: *It WORKED! New record! Back soon.*

That night, lying in bed next to Edith, Xiao-xing asked, "How far do you think it can go?"

"I don't know," Edith murmured, her eyes closed.

"How far do you hope it can go?"

Edith opened her eyes. "What do you think?"

"To the stars."

"Of course, if we can send only coins and love notes to the stars, that's not very much."

Xiao-xing kissed her. "If we can send love notes to the stars, what else do we need?"

"The people to send those love notes to. Or am I too greedy? I think I am. I am so arrogant, you should know that about me. I am already dreaming about this as a scientific revolution. But I don't really know what it will bring."

"A scientific revolution is not a dinner party," Xiao-xing said.

Edith laughed. "Then what is it?"

"Well," said Xiao-xing, turning on her side so her mouth was so close Edith could feel Xiao-xing's breath on her cheek, "close your eyes and imagine yourself in your lab. What do you feel?"

"Exhilarated," said Edith. "Terrified. Excited, like a door is opening to me. Scared to go through it. My heart is beating faster, and my stomach is all twisted in a knot." She opened her eyes and looked at Xiao-xing. "Like I felt when I first kissed you."

"So a scientific revolution is like a love affair?" asked Xiao-xing, a smile tugging on her lips.

Edith couldn't resist: she moved her head and kissed those lips. "Mine is," she whispered.

Like any good research project, Edith's results only led her to more questions. Edith suggested both she and Xiao-xing write down the open questions.

After a few moments they compared. Edith's were:

Why does the translation/transition only happen a third of the time? Can we improve that?

How far can objects be translated?

Can complex objects be sent through? Life? Plants? Animals?

What happens if you keep the receiving end frozen? How long can you wait? Minutes, hours, days...years?

What happens if you let the receiving end sublimate first?

What happens if you try to send objects from both ends?

Xiao-xing had similar questions, with one addition:

What happens when I go back to Shanghai?

They looked at each other.

"Don't tell me you haven't been thinking about that," Xiao-xing said.

Edith lowered her gaze. "I was afraid to say anything." There was a long silence, broken only by the sound of their breathing. "I was afraid to ask you to stay, that it would be selfish."

"Why selfish?"

"Because it would make it seem my work is more important than yours."

"But you love your work," Xiao-xing said.

"I love in working the lab," Edith said. "I don't particularly love my official assignments. See how many of them I haven't completed? I don't care if Roberto wants me on his team, they won't keep me." She felt hot salt tears well up in her eyes.

Xiao-xing wrapped her arms around Edith, kissed her hair, her cheek. "But your discoveries," she murmured.

"And how do I tell them about that? *Hello, Ms. Thalivar,*

I've become a rogue scientist, doing my own experiments, to hell with what you want."

"She'll want to know what you found. Tell her."

"She'll just tell me what time code to enter," Edith sniffed. She pulled back. "I should forget about this. I should go with you to Shanghai, find a job—"

"I'm staying," Xiao-xing said. "I filed my article and told my boss I had a sick relative to take care of. If I told him I found a girlfriend, he'd think I was taking care of a sick relative—or I was selling company secrets. If I tell him I am taking care of a sick relative, he will think that I have found a girlfriend." She smiled. "So now I have a lot of time off, and I expect you to spend five minutes a day with me."

Edith kissed her. "Oh, at least ten!"

The next morning Xiao-xing found Edith up early and making notes. "What do you think? Bacteria? We don't have a microbiology lab. Seeds? That would take time to sprout."

Xiao-xing yawned. "And good morning to you, too." She poured herself some tea. "Live mealworms? Like for pet lizards."

"Brilliant!" Edith paused. "Can I ask you to…"

"Of course. But you'll talk to Thalivar today, okay? No waiting."

Edith sighed, but agreed, so an hour later she found herself standing in the doorway to Ms. Thalivar's office. Her knees were so wobbly she nearly fell when invited her to sit down.

"I know, I'm sorry, I know I haven't been as productive as I should have been."

Before she could say more, Ms. Thalivar's all-in-one sang. She listened, frowned, and walked out. "Just a minute."

Edith sat in the chair. A minute turned to two minutes, to five, then fifteen. Her own all-in-one buzzed: a zip from Xiao-xing. *Urgent. We have to talk. URGENT.*

She felt like her head was in a vise—and her bladder; she wanted to pee so badly she thought she would burst. She was just about to call Xiao-xing when Ms. Thalivar stood in the doorway.

"Edith," Ms. Thalivar said, looking as if she had just been told her children had been snatched away, "you'll have to stay here for a bit." It was then that Edith noticed the guard standing just behind Ms. Thalivar.

Mr. Baca was Beshara-Huan's regional vice president for something or other. Seated across from Edith, Mr. Baca scrolled through pages and pages of notes on a pad. "You signed all the release forms," he murmured. "You completed all the training." He looked up. "Yes?"

Edith gave a sharp nod. She alternated between feeling very frightened and very angry.

Mr. Baca sighed. "You were aware of the company policies, but did not follow them. You not only had assigned regimens to test, you had specific forms to fill out and file. You did not. Your supervisor admits, reluctantly, that she verbally reprimanded you on multiple occasions. You were aware of form 448K, request for test regimen variance, because you submitted several your first three months here. But you didn't submit even one 448K when you abandoned your assigned work and began using company resources to carry out unauthorized and potentially dangerous experiments."

Edith's mouth opened but no words came out.

Mr. Baca raised an eyebrow. "You smuggled bits of frozen quantum foam out of the lab into private living spaces and even onto public transport, no? Even if you knew the risks, what if some third party had been injured? Didn't you think how that bad that would be for the company?"

Edith lowered her head, shook it.

"And you've opened us up to all sorts of other legal liabilities. When we apply for a patent, we have to prove discovery provenance, prove that we were the ones who discovered it. How can we do that with no official records? You've put us in a very difficult place."

Then he made her an offer. A verbal offer, nothing written down. She would be allowed to work on the new team Roberto was working on. She would be given four percent of any royalties deriving from this work—twice the company standard.

But—of course there was a *but*—she would have to sign a statement that all of her work had been at the verbal direction of supervisors.

Edith snorted and crossed her arms. "I'm not going to sign any such statement. Why should I?"

Mr. Baca narrowed his eyes. "We cannot be seen as rewarding engineers who disregard company policies, many of which, I emphasize, are for the safety of our employees." He nudged the pad with the statement to sign towards Edith.

Edith pushed it back.

They fired her. Officially, it was part of the planned reduction in force. If she protested, she faced charges of criminal misuse of company property and endangering the public. They wiped the data from her all-in-one. And she was reminded sternly of the non-disclosure agreement she had originally signed.

They gave her a two-month severance package, generous considering she had only been working at the company for seven months. She had to sign a lot of forms to get that. And then they took her company credentials and a guard led her outside.

They wouldn't let her say goodbye to Roberto.

Xiao-xing was crying so hard it took Edith a while to get the story out of her.

Apparently her boss not only thought Xiao-xing was lying about a sick relative, he suspected "selling company secrets" rather than "found a girlfriend." So he had used a backdoor to get into her company-owned all-in-one and found the images and videos and notes. Confused and alarmed, he had contacted Beshara-Huan's Alta California research division.

"I knew about the backdoor," Xiao-xing sobbed. "I just didn't think anyone would care."

She, too, had been fired.

Roberto sent a zip message, saying he'd heard a rumor she'd been let go for being unproductive. He offered to write a letter on her behalf. He was being moved to Beshara-Huan's test facility in Kuala Lumpur. Edith zipped back *Thank you but no.* She decided not to tell him the whole story.

Edith visited several lawyers, but they all told her she had a weak case. "You can pursue it," one said, "but against Beshara-Huan? You'd be pissing money away."

A month later she and Xiao-xing were still trying to decide what to do when Ms. Thalivar showed up at Edith's microstudio.

"I feel very bad for what happened," Ms. Thalivar said, "though if you had followed protocol it could have been avoided."

Edith rolled her eyes but bit her tongue.

Ms. Thalivar was dressed in jeans and a simple blouse. Edith had never seen her in casual clothes. "I know the hiring director at a new spin-off division. I already contacted her, recommending you for a job."

"I'd have thought I'd be blacklisted," Edith said, knives in her words.

Ms. Thalivar smiled. "Yes, you'd think that, but you might also think that Beshara-Huan doesn't want to trumpet that they let go someone—"

"Fired," Edith said. "Not let go, fired. That was the word your regional vice president for firing people used."

"—they fired someone who made a big discovery. So they are playing this very close to the chest. So close no one outside of Mr. Baca's office knows." She slid a scrap of paper across the table and stood up. "You keep thinking, Edith."

If Edith's family had taught her anything, it was to not waste time feeling sorry for herself. She went to the hiring director for Innovación Ilimitada and, to her slight surprise, was hired on the spot. Xiao-xing was ecstatic, but it did not buoy Edith's mood. That night she sent a zip to her parents—whom she had told nothing the past month—*Hey, I'm changing companies.* She tried to make it sound like a good thing.

It took a week for Innovación to process her work permit, and then a few days for her training. The following Monday she finally was ushered into the lab, met her fellow co-workers. The lead engineer for the project was an older man named Ted Jacobson, who introduced her around.

"We're glad to have some additional help," he said. "We're working on a new, exciting phenomenon but it has us a bit stumped. You know all about it, of course."

"Not really," Edith said. "The non-disclosure agreements I signed didn't disclose what I was promising to not disclose."

Ted laughed. "Ah, lawyers. I suppose we need them, for something. But look here." He stopped at a lab bench, and Edith's heart sped up just a little.

"I've worked with Casimir pumps before," she said.

"Good, H.R. took our request seriously. But there's this thing, this new thing, so new no one knows much about it. First, you use the Casimir pump to freeze, not heat but freeze a bit of quantum foam, and then, well, what we're supposed to do is to break the chunk in two. Which we are having trouble doing. It keeps shattering."

Edith did her best not to grin. She was already imagining how Xiao-xing would laugh when she told her. "Here," she said, stepping up to the bench. "Let me show you how."

Recursive Ice

Terry Boren

1. Heuristic

The afternoon wind, cool and rain-scented, lifted Bret's hair away from her neck as she gazed down at the Isar where it slid green and quick beneath the bridge. Her vision was blurred and distorted one moment, absolutely clear the next. Her palms rested gently on the pitted granite of the railing. It was familiar, safe. But though she had done her graduate work at the Planck Institute in Germany, years before, she still could not remember what she was doing in Old Munich. Something to do with her work? She touched her face, probing gently at the swollen cheek. The eye itself seemed undamaged, though the area around the left socket and the left side of her face were bruised. The cheekbone probably had been cracked. Her cheek was wet, and pain made the eye tear again, distorting the green park along the green river. The wind was picking up. Hoping to reach shelter before the storm broke, she continued across the bridge toward Mariahilfplatz and the frozen spire of its church.

Her work was not in Munich. Testing folding patterns, using rational design to develop potential new protein based nanodevices for medical and industrial use, she worked on Penrose, the orbital station at Lagrange point 4. With her son, Michael. The new city was veiled in mist and distance; Old Munich rose behind and in front of her on either side of the river. She had been living rough, she thought, but she wasn't sure why or how long. The bridge was flanked on both sides by massive, monumental statuary, granite figures weathered by age and wars.

The old drunk caught up with her just as she passed the terminal duo of horse and faceless woman. It seemed to her that he had spotted her from some distance; she dropped her gaze and turned away too late to avoid making eye contact as he stumbled in her direction. The old man gently tapped her leather-clad back just as she raised her hand to protect her bruised face. She stopped, confused, "Yes?"

"Bret, kann ich Ihnen helfen?" he asked her. His voice was high and flutelike.

She could smell the beer on his breath as she stared into his muzzy, slightly puzzled eyes. Did she know him? The old drunk was incredibly thin, starved looking, but wore a bemused grin on his cadaverous face. His expression grew serious for a second, but then he grinned again and awkwardly patted her arm.

"You've lost your German?" he said and laughed. "In Ordnung, in Ordnung. Alles Gut...Alles Gut." The old man nodded at her, smiling, and wove off through the crowd of unseeing Germans. Watching him, a current of fear hummed in her head.

Bret was not certain whether she had followed the old man or continued on toward Auer Dult coincidentally, but she found herself near the church, and the fair surrounded her in the smells of warm bread, rain-damp air, and sausages. The music of a calliope and the babble of the crowd followed her as she wandered through stalls filled with pots and knives and furniture and food.

When the storm inundated the fair, hail forced her to huddle beneath a leaky canopy with eight or nine hardy souls, all women, who hadn't found better shelter. The other refugees smelled of wet wool. Quietly they watched the blue-speckled pots outside of their tent fill with rain and hail until the same old man wandered by with his shoes squashing water and fell on his face in a puddle directly in front of the shelter. The other women pretended not to see him.

Bret hesitated, uncertain, then stepped to the old drunk's side as he attempted to push himself up from the slick paving-stones.

Griffin Amestoy watched the plate projection impatiently. The outside view was silent as the bright airlessness of the lunar surface appeared to slide across the plate in clear and enhanced detail. They had crossed into the far side several hours earlier moving steadily along the 180 degree meridian. In the pilot's seat of the Kiel Northwest shuttle, Mary Nanaluk bent her slender frame over the controls, occasionally turning her head to catch a glimpse of the plate. She was visibly nervous; one hand seemed embedded in the deep pocket of her coverall and the other tapped on the console, or hovered over the altitude and velocity tabs.

"Christ!" she said. "Why do I always get the honors?" She scratched at her two-week growth of coppery hair and tapped the console. Although Amestoy had seen her angry before, for any number of reasons, Nanaluk was generally a dependable woman and difficult to shake. He was not looking forward to encountering any scene that had her twitching.

Amestoy glanced back at the plate, which revealed only the harshly lit jumble of ejecta and the knife edge of the curtain wall cut by shadow near the bottom of the crater. The view was as expected; the lunar observatory had been strictly barebones, sited on the far side in the eternal shadow of Crater Daedalus to take advantage of both electromagnetic shielding from terrestrial signals in the radio range and of viewing that was as unbroken as possible by either lunar day or earthshine.

He touched his pad, and scrolled in to a tight view of the optical interferometer site. He examined it in cross section and in architectural detail, then scrolled out for an exterior shot. Not much to see: the hump of the central focus point; nine ball-like, 5-meter scope emplacements in an elliptical array; dark lines of track; shielded cable raceways. The base was constructed of various composite materials and lunar concrete, colorless and functional looking.

For the past few years, Amestoy's jobs had been simple and solitary. His reputation as a medical researcher and general polymath had made it possible for him and his wife Delia to move into positions on the geosynchronous habitat, Hector Station, but even that job could have been done by someone with far less training. His duties had consisted primarily of lab work. But Delia had been the star.

She had been coordinating new construction on Penrose Station when it failed. After Penrose, he had returned to Earth with her body. Unable to work or even to put down a bottle for a year after Delia's death, he had only come through it with the help of Mike Adala-Beck. Now his freelance work was more broadly based: he accepted jobs from labs that needed help with genetics projects and from corporations or the government when they needed a consultant. Most often, he worked with Nanaluk on security related jobs. The client that had brought him to this mothballed observatory was the Stoplight Security Agency headed by the Adala-Becks.

Nanaluk flicked the lifter to all comp and kicked her chair around to face Amestoy. "Looks like hell, doesn't it, but it was the best they ever did on the moon. I don't like this; Mike said what they really needed was a coroner."

"That may cause some trouble for the museum people. Can't open it up until everything is taken care of." Amestoy answered. "Guess that's why we're here."

On the plate behind the redhead's left shoulder, a string of pad indicators popped into life beside the central building. As the shuttle settled gently to the pad beside the utilitarian bulk of the focus building, Nanaluk was already on her feet. Amestoy carefully pushed his lanky frame away from the console and stood. The locks around the lifter's hatch chunked as a space-suited figure attached the station airlock's umbilical. He and Nanaluk waited for it to pressurize, then crawled through the frigid umbilical and shivered as they cycled through the airlock and into the building proper.

The observatory's foundations were sunk into the regolith

below the level of severe daily temperature shifts, and the entire central focus building was sheltered in lunar soil to protect the more sensitive electronic components. That necessary sheltering had also made it possible for a small habitable base to be constructed on the site, but the pillbox-like structure had never held more than ten scientists at one time, and the entire base had been deserted, the scopes cannibalized, when the observatory was pulled off of the surface fifteen years earlier, along with all other colonies, mining settlements and research centers then on the moon. The site had been off limits since the signing of the U.N. Compact making the moon a controlled preserve.

As Amestoy maneuvered himself through the iris and into the control area, Mike Adala-Beck was removing his helmet in the center of the room. Kirsten, Mike's wife and work partner, nodded in his direction and continued with her work at the console. Wearing only her grey suit liner, she was seated at a large and obviously recent model plate. The interior walls of the pillbox were covered in what looked like an off-white, glossy ceramic.

"Mike, Kirsten." Amestoy made a slow, 360 degree turn. "Thought this place was stripped. I was even wondering if the building was still tight."

Kirsten Adala-Beck pulled a hard sheet from the printer and then rose from her seat. She moved gracefully in the light gravity; she always moved gracefully, though such grace seemed, at first, incongruous in a woman who was only a notch or two over 1.5 meters tall and weighed a good 80 kilos.

"A sheet on the bodies." Even Kirsten's face seemed pinched, her normally high coloring subdued. There was a distinct tinge of decay permeating the room. "We've left them all in place." She handed him her notes.

"All?"

"*Si*, all. Three in here.... But Griff, that's not all. Three more, one in a dome, one in the cable raceways, and one more out there, no suit." Kirsten jerked her thumb at the wall. "The tissues are desiccated, but there was hemorrhagic bleeding from the orifices…decompressed, we think."

"Stands to reason if they were outside without a suit. We'll get to that one later. The ones in here?"

"One female, one male. Female A, anterior chest. Male B, cranial fractures. Parts of someone else in the tank, C."

Amestoy ran his fingers through his hair and sighed. "I take it by the air quality they haven't been here fifteen years?"

"No chance, though who knows with whoever was the one on ice. Last place anyone would look."

"Well, I can't do much here but a preliminary. We'll have to take them out." He paused. "In a dome?"

Kirsten looked at the floor. "Yeah," she said. "The scope emplacements are tight. So are the cable raceways." Kirsten's lips had gone slightly pale. "I'll take you downstairs and show you what we've got so far. We're still sweeping the area." She turned, and Griffin followed her across the room to a hole in the floor that accessed the lower deck of the pillbox. He stepped through the floor and dropped gently to the level below using the central, pegged pole for balance. Kirsten had stepped to the left at the bottom and was waiting for him. "Quarters," she said pointing with her chin; another pole and access way two meters to his right allowed entry to the third level of the structure. "Not much down there—bunks for four, crates of food. The sections all seal if pressure drops."

The smell of death was cloying. "So why didn't you call the U.N. Police? This is Compact jurisdiction, isn't it?"

"Yeah, but we're the subcontractors for the historical people."

"So?"

"So, first we need to show you a few things." The lower floor had been bisected by a partition composed of the same ceramic that covered the walls. She led the way into the partitioned section. To the right of the door were two covered shapes, one on the floor and one near the bulky cryotank against the wall. Kirsten indicated the door directly across from the entrance. "Airlock." She said. "There's a ring tunnel with accesses to the raceways and the domes. Each track is airlocked. Bodies in track 3 and dome 7."

Kirsten tucked a tiny braid of her blond hair behind one ear and moved over to the shrouded shapes on the floor. She bent and removed the sheet over the body. "We haven't ID'd him yet. There was a three-man Daimler outside. No umbilical. His suit's downstairs." She crouched beside the huddled body. "Looks dead at least a week, but you tell us, middle-aged, medium height and build. Asian? Indian? Doesn't seem to have been moved. We think he fractured his skull on the cryotank, not easy to do in this gravity. There's quite a bit of blood on his clothing and slippers. Hers, probably."

Amestoy moved over to the body lying against the tank; dried smears of darkened blood discolored the grey concrete between the two bodies and crusted one corner of the tank. He flipped off the plastic sheet.

The body was naked. She had gone to her knees when someone put a hole in her back between the lower ribs, and had fallen forward against the tank. The weight of her body had forced her into a semi-sitting position with her neck bent backward and her face wedged into the corner between the tank and the wall. One arm was caught between her thighs and chest, the other lay bent backward, the hand curled against one bare foot. Straight dark hair trailed down her back.

"No knife, but we haven't checked under them."

"The other two?"

"I think the man in track 3 may have been beaten to death...and I don't know about the one in the dome."

Amestoy glanced at her tightly controlled face. "Bad?"

"Yeah, bad," she said.

The drunk wrapped one skinny arm over Bret's shoulder when she hauled him to his feet. He grinned at her through the pelting rain, tottered and caught hold of the lapels of her leather jacket.

"Ah, my dear Bret, it is you again," he said and chuckled. "I can't get home like this, you know." He wove a bit as he blinked at her from behind a thin veil of grey-brown hair which had washed half over one eye. "Poor child. Come, it's wet." He patted her arm. The wool-clad housefraus did not watch, and the rain did not let up as the old drunk and the dazed-looking woman walked unsteadily away from the church square toward the darker streets of Old Munich.

"It is just me, Hartmut, just old Hartmut," he murmured.

Later, Bret did not remember how she had gotten to his home. She woke on a narrow bed and remained motionless gazing up into the high, dimly lit vault of the ceiling. Slowly, she became aware of quiet noises coming from the opposite side of the room, water running, someone humming, a cough. A candle flickered near a pair of support columns and a large, comfortable looking chair. She sat up. She had come here with the old skinny guy, Hartmut.

She got to her feet and walked a bit unsteadily across the room toward the light. She must have been asleep for a long time because she felt slow, drugged with sleep. Figures moved in the light above a small table, some sort of holographic display.

"Sit down," the old guy said. So she sat. "I have some food for you. Are you hungry?"

She could smell sausage, and her mouth watered. She was very hungry. "Yes, please, anything." She turned her head to watch the old man walk away. He returned immediately with a tray of food. He looked concerned, disheveled, and ill. He looked much older than she remembered him. A wash of color rushed up his stubbled cheeks. He was blushing. She looked down; her jacket had come open.

"Don't mind it," he said, and put the tray down beside the chair.

"Hartmut? Hartmut Meindle?"

He gently closed and adjusted her jacket. She held the front closed, staring at the tray of food.

"Ah, yes. You have forgotten again." He positioned the tray across her lap. "This is my own beer," he said, smiling. He had been her supervisor at the Planck Institute.

As she wolfed down the wonderful sausages, the kraut with apples, the dark heavy beer, Hartmut gestured at the display. "You remember, Bret, I was your friend, your colleague. You came to me for help for some reason, and I will help."

How could he help? Yes, he had been head of her department at the institute, but he had lost his position after a nervous breakdown and had never recovered from the blow. But maybe she did need help.

For the next few days, she watched him building simulated molecules on the 3D modeler in his arched and columned cellar. Making his beer better, he said. The dance of his work calmed her, and she remembered teaching her son Michael how to build simple designs and algorithms for directed evolution programming in their small berth on Penrose. Like Hartmut's, Michael's designs had always suffered from thinking too much, attempting to quantify some prior knowledge into a probability distribution which would then, always, affect the outcomes.

They spent hours together in his workshop watching his favorite shows on the plate. On the fourth day in his cellar, she and Hartmut watched a game show set in Nepal. As the camera followed a guide into a small room; the frame enlarged to reveal the chamber from a point of view just over the guide's left shoulder. The space was roughly the size of a large closet and brilliantly lit by scores of candles. In the yellow light, stacks and lines of Buddhas glinted and glowed: brass, wood, stone, gold—from the size of a thumb to the size of the guide's round head. Then the scene shifted. Outside, seen from above, an enormous stone-made Buddha reclined in a pool of water surrounded by trees. As the propwash riffled the surface of the pond, a flight of scarlet ibis rose up in alarm. A naked woman with straight black hair stood alone near the pool.

Bret knew her. She was certain she knew her.

On the fifth day, a tall man followed Hartmut down the cellar steps.

"I told you I would help," Hartmut said as he took her hand and brought her to meet the man. "This is Griffin Amestoy, Schätzchen. He has been looking for you. He saw my posts."

"You're Bret Lysle?" Amestoy asked. He was frowning as he stared at her. She nodded. "I'm Griffin...Griff," he said.

By that evening, she was on the way to his facility in Alaska.

2. Algorithm

There were three bodies in Griffin Amestoy's lab, each resting on a stainless-steel table and covered by a plastic sheet. As he guided the laser dot, the point of view of the holographically recorded autopsy shifted and pulled in tight to the first body, tipping slightly to show the head in close three-quarter profile. His equipment was similar to the modeler she used to study the shapes of molecules, the image solid-looking.

Amestoy was a big man, tall and hawk faced. He didn't look at her, and he turned away from her as he talked. She knew why he did not want to look at her; it was too much for him. Amestoy was in the process of showing her that she was dead. She could see her own reflection in the glass wall to his left. In her bruised face was a stunned refusal to accept what was right in front of her—and pain.

Amestoy spoke softly, but clearly. "Though it might not be obvious to you because of the relative conditions of the bodies, all three are quite similar." He stopped and turned toward her. Bret had been sitting very still as he talked, but Amestoy could undoubtedly see her fingernails digging into her palms. "You had enough? Want me to stop?"

"No," she answered. "Please, go on."

He turned back to the body. "On gross inspection I thought that all three were just women of an approximately similar age and build, but the body scans showed that the similarities were much closer." He tapped the pointer to switch to a close-up of the second, smaller body. "There were a few differences immediately apparent: only the first body's brain is more or less intact, and of course, they died in different ways."

That was glaringly obvious. The first woman had been stabbed in the back and died almost immediately. The second body was many centimeters shorter than the first. It was pulled into a fetal position, skin dark and withered, eyelids sunken inward.

"She died of asphyxiation…and decompression. But this is the main difference," he said, and tapped the laser, then tapped it again, and twice more.

He didn't need to explain: each tap took the autopsy recording progressively forward. The withered, dark-haired head was flayed and the skull opened in stop-motion.

"This much brain damage couldn't have been the result of decompression. There was not much more than a brain-stem left—some surgical debris. The rest was gone, removed." Amestoy paused again. "Are you all right?"

"Fine!" she snapped at him. "I'm just fine. Please, just show me the rest."

"I'm still running tests, but the genetics and fingerprints match those of Bret Lysle, listed missing five years ago in the Penrose Station disaster. The body wasn't recovered."

The station? Her son had been on the station. "And Michael Lysle? Was my son found?"

Amestoy nodded. "His body was recovered from the main wreckage."

She had failed, and had failed her son. She wasn't able to speak. She nodded.

Amestoy seemed to force himself to continue. Slowly, he explained two of the autopsies in detail—the identical moles and scars on the bodies, the angle of the knife wound that had killed the woman with the intact brain.

"They had both died where we found them, at the abandoned emplacement on the lunar far side, no trace of evidence to the contrary. The first body was found in the central area, the focus building. The second body was found on the surface." He flicked the spot to bring up the image of the third female body.

"This one was in one of the scope emplacements."

The third body was all bone and skin, but not desiccated like the second, smaller body. "Each of the scope emplacements, the domes, was isolated from the main building, sealed off. She died of thirst and starvation....They left her there." Again he flicked through the autopsy. The brain was drastically altered, functionally mutilated.

"You remember being held in the scope room?"

She felt as though her insides were freezing, but in a motion almost too small to be an acknowledgment, she nodded.

"I remember being there, but not what happened, how I got there. Or only pieces of it." The last memories she had that seemed sane to her were five years old, though her mind insisted they were not, and even they contained flashes of Penrose Orbital Station failing, the air freezing as it left her lungs.

It was five *years* later. Waking up was the real problem, she thought, not survival. She wanted desperately to wake up and find herself on Penrose with her son asleep in her arms. But she could not make that happen.

Instead, a gaunt, black-eyed man named Griffin Amestoy had tracked her down in Munich and brought her to Fairbanks, a cold city by a frozen river, and Mary Nanaluk, Amestoy's associate and friend, had offered to let Bret live in an unfinished cabin behind her home. She had only been in Fairbanks for a few days. But she had been dead for five years. She barely heard Amestoy continue in his soft monotone. But he kept at her.

"You were hired by Koch Industries. You worked in de novo protein design?"

"Yes, but I was concentrating on predictive models."

"Why would you be on Penrose for that?"

She simply stared at him. "It is very delicate work. It involves understanding spontaneous foldon-foldon interactions. Probabilistic modeling is inadequate to predict some of the emergent interactions. Folding in micro-gravity is faster and easier than usual."

"Were you involved in any human trials?"

"No, of course not. Koch has a program to develop new industrial molecules and enzymes. Researchers have grown perfect crystals and proteins like rhodopsin in that kind of environment. But Koch wanted new, and they wanted someone who could hurry that up, potentially. Solely computational methods weren't working."

Bret knew the real problem was that she had failed; she had died. The only solution was to find a way of surviving this time, but she was not sure she had any reason to survive.

When Amestoy finally finished explaining the autopsies and asked her, very quietly, very carefully, if he could run a complete scan on her, she bolted. She left his small, cluttered lab in Fairbanks and returned to the cabin above the river as quickly as the borrowed lifter would take her.

She shivered on the small square of bioplank decking behind Nanaluk's guest-house as she tried to gather her thoughts. She kept having flashes of memories: her lab on Penrose, Michael's ecstatic face as he pulled himself along the corridor in low gravity. Nanaluk's cabin was small, basically two rooms stacked one on top of the other, insulated and sheathed in bioplank. It was situated down a path through dense birch woods on a ridge behind her more substantial log home. Nanaluk had volunteered to provide any materials Bret needed to make the structure habitable. It was meant to be a refuge for her. Perhaps there, Bret could recover and get her memories straight. That morning, before Amestoy had taken her to his lab, she had begun work on tiling the bare wooden floor.

The achingly cold air on the deck of the cabin did seem to clarify her feelings. The view from the deck was gorgeous and bleak. Behind the cabin, the hillside fell away, down to the Tanana Flats and the frozen river. Dark against the snow, like burnt matchsticks, a stand of black spruce slowly disappeared into the smudge of ice fog that crept along the Flats. Bret stared out at the white landscape and wondered why she was alive, and what had been done to her.

Griffin Amestoy wanted to know the same thing, he said. He had made that clear in Munich. Amestoy claimed his tests could uncover everything that had been done to her, fill in what she now knew were not just a few blank spots, but blank years. He told her that he had been hired to investigate the deaths of several people on the moon and that his comprehensive search of DNA records and global facial-recognition files had found an exact match with a living woman in Munich, had found her.

"There are three dead people in my lab," he had said, his gaunt face serious and gentle. "We need to find out why. And why they are all your genetic twins."

But Bret had said no to any tests, and her mind kept flinching away from fragments of memories. She was beginning to remember more than enough: she remembered starving; and maybe she remembered dying. She wasn't sure she wanted to know everything. The cold made the bones of Bret's face hurt—the bridge of her nose and the orbit of her eye. Even the view from the deck was not worth any more pain. She wasn't wearing a coat. Stupid, she thought, but an effective aid to focus for the job she had begun on the floor of the cabin, choosing pattern and color. The cold was an ache in her face and agony in her knees. Even awake, there seemed to be no escape from pain. There was only work.

Bret gazed for one, two breaths more at the moisture crystallizing out of the air to smother the hillsides, the river, the flats, tucked her cold fingers into her armpits, and then turned to open the door to her cabin. She was fully conscious, she thought, but she had awakened like this before, once in an abandoned radio-telescope array on the surface of the moon, once in Old Munich in the rain. Her life had become discontinuous, and there seemed to be no way to put it back together.

Outside the cabin's door she kicked snow off her boots. A result of laying tile all that morning, the strong odor of mastic smacked into her as she entered. Her cold fingers and face seemed to vibrate with the rush of her blood as she stood in the warm room. Music drifted from the tiny player in one corner, and she suddenly felt almost good, better than she had since finding herself alone and the world different. Her body was recovering. And her mind as well, she told herself. She was whole, any shattered connections in her brain were being mended by tiny spinners of invisible webs.

Feeling a small lift of anticipation, Bret wiped her palms

on her pants and knelt to begin laying out the next course of tiles. She pushed the pieces of cut ceramic into the mastic in a simple pattern, mathematical and precise. The music aided her rhythm and concentration, and she began to lose herself in the work. Rhythm merged into the pattern of the tiles like ice crystallizing out of air.

When she had first found herself awake, standing injured and alone, not on Penrose Orbital Station, but on a bridge in Old Munich, Bret had decided she'd lost her mind. That thought was ironic in light of the maimed bodies in Griffin Amestoy's lab, and her recent memories were improbable enough to seem hallucinatory, or like the half-real debris of dreams. A prison on the moon, a woman standing in a pool of water as a flight of scarlet ibis rose around her. Perhaps she had been dreaming for five years.

Perhaps she simply did not want to remember, she thought. Public records insisted that Bret Lysle was dead, that she and her son had died on Penrose Station, but all three of the bodies in Griffin Amestoy's lab had Bret's face, her own face. There was no escape from that or from the fact that two of the women's brains were altered, major areas excised. Their bodies had been cut up and thrown away. She had been thrown away. But she refused to think of anything but the quiet, snow-covered ridge and tiling the floor of the little shack, designing a complete pattern.

After she had worked for a time, Bret began to feel drowsy and got up from her sore knees to turn on the player, but halfway across the room she realized it was already on, the news in progress, voices muttering away quietly. She hit the select tab, and turned to survey her work as the band Black Shoes melted into a version of "Earth and Wings," a song she had heard only a few times, but liked. A little more than a third of the five-by-six-meter downstairs room of the cabin was laid out in an intricate, black and white pattern that contrasted sharply with the green, tank-grown bioplank that sheathed the walls. The room was very warm. Outside of the cabin's large central window the winter sun rolled low on the horizon, southeast to southwest, in a haze the color of honey.

Bret remembered the harsh light of the sun above the short lunar horizon and pictured the desiccated body of a woman on the open surface, micro-molecular debris in her skull. How could Bret know what had been done to her own brain? Her palm pressed on the patterned tile floor. Like *polyominoes*, tiling patterns, she thought. As her concentration drifted, she remembered Griffin Amestoy's face, his hand guiding the point of light through brain tissue. Like forcing new patterns in strings of amino acids. Trying to make sense of it made her head hurt. Her memories were like vivid islands surrounded by fractures of time and location, nameless bodies on the moon with her face.

Bret gazed out over the river valley. It was too cold to be outside without a parka. She had stopped about 40 meters down the path leading from her cabin to the main house to watch the ice fog creeping over the Tanana Flats. The temperature was at most minus 30 degrees. Ice fog didn't form at temperatures much warmer than that. Feeling more awake, she turned to go back to the cabin and more tile. It was only a short walk, but she was very cold by the time she got back inside. Black Shoes was playing "Go Slow for You" on the player. A little more than one third of the room was laid out in intricate tiled patterns, and the air was pungent with the odor of solvent. She dropped to her knees and began to arrange more of the ceramic pieces.

"Earth and Wings" was humming in the background, and she had lost track of time. She had laid three rows of tile without remembering the work. Bret stopped and wiped a strand of hair out of her face. Tiling was calming work; she felt relaxed, removed. The room was becoming hotter, so she pulled her turtleneck off over her head and undid the top buttons of her cotton Henley.

She stood up to tab on the player before she realized that it was already on. Black Shoes was playing "Go Slow for You," and Bret smiled, wiped her face with her sleeve and dropped back down to do some more tile. Music, tiles, ice fog...they were multiple streams of signals, like proto-thought. She could picture the chaotic streams collapsing into consciousness, tiles choosing their own pattern, delicate strings of atoms refolding in weightlessness. When she stood to tab on the player, her head buzzed. Almost half of the room was laid out in intricate tile work. She was sweating, so she decided to take off her cotton shirt and work in her thermal undershirt.

"Michael!" she called. But then she remembered that her son was dead. **Failure**.

3. Restatement

Fog crawled up the hill toward the cabin. The Flats were buried in the opaque crystals of moisture. From the deck, Bret watched fog swallow the dark line of spruce below. She was cold. She raised a hand to her stinging cheeks and suddenly realized that she was almost naked from the waist up. What was she doing outside? Alarmed, she quickly returned to the cabin. Her head was ringing, and mucus streamed from her nose. It took her several minutes to warm up and her fingers and cheeks ached with the return of blood to the skin. Something was wrong.

She stood up again to turn on the player. The small heater in the corner had seemed barely adequate to heat the cabin at below zero temperatures, but it was hot in the downstairs room. A little more than half of the room was laid out in tile. The pattern shifted, or her vision did. *Quasi crystals exhibit five-fold symmetry*, she thought, *like the tiled patterns on the floor. Proteins folding. Quasi crystals.*

Something was wrong.

Something is wrong, she had thought when the alarms went off on the station. Her son was screaming in the next room. She scrambled out of bed, pulled her suit half-on, and was reaching for her door when the room seemed to split. The air froze into a cloud of ice, and her lungs emptied: Penrose Orbital Station had failed.

She found herself crying as she looked down at her own body in a shack in the Alaskan woods, if it was her own body. There was a scar on her right breast, stretch-marks laced her belly. She could not be a clone, clones were new, unmarked, and she was not unmarked; but she or Bret had been dead for five years, and the dead women had all looked like her. Not just the dead woman in the main building of the emplacement, but the desiccated body on the surface of the moon, and the mindless, drooling husk that had been imprisoned with her for all those weeks she had spent trying to wake up.

God, it was cold. The tips of her fingers were pale. What was she doing outside? She looked down at the fog swirling around the line of dark spruce at the bottom of the hill. She didn't have enough clothes on. Had she been headed for Nanaluk's house next door? No. She was laying tile. She turned to go back to the cabin. Something was wrong. She stopped. Something was happening in the cabin. She shouldn't go back there. She should go to Nanaluk's.

The warmth of the small room pulled the blood back to her skin. The pain of returning circulation made her moan in agony. *Stupid. Turn the heat down and stay inside. Get back to work. Something is wrong; don't stay inside.* Her head is humming "Go Slow for You." The tiles are beautiful quasi crystals; they glow like ice fog in the low sunlight. How do crystals decide what pattern to take? Like the disorganization of thought? Like waking up in Munich? Yes, like the collapse of the wave state. **Failure.**

4. Restatement

She is halfway down the trail to Nanaluk's. It is very cold, and she is naked. Plumes of ice fog drift among the white-barked birch near the trail. She opens the door to the cabin. The room is warm. Something is wrong. Black Shoes is playing "Roots and Wings."

Something is wrong.

Her feet are numb. Her hip joints ache, but her skin does not. She knows she will freeze if she stays outside. Why is she outside? She is wearing a parka, but nothing underneath it. She is standing in front of the door to the cabin. *Don't go inside.* She can't go inside. She reaches in, locks the door and shuts it deliberately. She won't be able to go back inside. Something is wrong.

She is very cold. She turns and heads back to the cabin and the tiling. The door is locked. She is naked and the ice fog is swirling in the birches. *Go to Nanaluk's.* She turns.

When she reaches the cabin, the door is locked. Why is she naked? Stop. She has to think. What is happening? She is in front of the window. Her feet are like chunks of wood. She can barely bend her fingers, and frozen snot stiffens her lips. Through the glass, the inside of the cabin looks warm and bright. Tile covers two thirds of the floor and part of one wall. Why is the tile on the wall?

She turns. There is only one door to the cabin. If she breaks the window, the cabin will freeze. She will freeze. She has been passing out, or something else. She sees her discarded boots on the deck near the door and pulls them over her numb feet. She was tiling the cabin and had gotten too warm. So she had taken off her clothes to walk in the snow? She turns to go back to the cabin, stops. No. She was passing out. She needs to get to Nanaluk's.

She comes to under a running shower. She clenches her teeth and moans with the pain of the cool water on her hands. She is wearing her boots in the shower. Tears and mucus smear her face. She bends and slowly pulls each boot off and tosses it out onto the plank floor of Nanaluk's bedroom, turns her face into the stream of water. Bret remembers two other women imprisoned with her. They looked like her. One was a vegetable, the other incoherent, babbling constantly. They had starved together for a long time. Were there three, four? Are they still alive? Is she?

She is standing in the doorway of Nanaluk's log home, naked and dripping water. The moisture is steaming off of her skin and subliming directly to ice fog. The cold pulls clouds of moisture out of the warm cabin air as it pours from the doorway. The folding of proteins is affected by quantum events. Neural signals below consciousness exist in a quantum wave state and condense. Chaotic. Streams of information. Patterns.

Stream one: She died in the catastrophic failure of Penrose Orbital Station. But she is alive.

Stream two: She and at least three and perhaps four other women were imprisoned in an abandoned radio array on the surface of the moon.

Stream three: A desiccated body on the moon. A naked woman standing in the prop wash of a lifter as a flight of scarlet ibis takes wing; another woman survived.

Stream four: She is alive. Something is very strange about the way her mind is working, patterns folding into comprehensibility.

She looks down at the icy footprints on the boards of the deck, turns and reenters the house. She tabs the console and asks for Nanaluk. "Help me," she says when a machine answers. "I think I've poisoned myself."

5. Escape

Bret woke up bundled under a layer of quilts in Nanaluk's big, log-post bed. The winter sun cast low light into the room from the southern windows where Amestoy sat nodding in a ratty overstuffed chair by the windows. He woke when Bret sat up.

"How are you feeling?" He stretched and yawned then leaned forward in the chair and looked closely at her.

"I feel like hell," Bret croaked. "My head is killing me." She felt her stomach lurch and swung her legs off of the bed. When she tried to stand, her feet inflicted her with pain she wasn't ready for. "Shit! Help me get to the bathroom!"

Amestoy jumped to her side and half-supported her to the bathroom as she tripped over Nanaluk's long gown. There was water all over the floor. Her boots and several blue and green towels made a soggy pile in one corner. She heaved violently into the toilet, but her stomach was almost empty, just bile and water. She sat back on a soggy towel.

"Damn!" she said. "How long was I out?"

"About a day in all. You're repeating yourself, you know. You've been awake three times since I got here. Do you remember that?"

"No." She couldn't remember him being there. "A day?"

"Yeah, your brain took a pretty good punch from the solvents in that mastic. Anesthetized your lobes."

"I kept passing out." She could feel moisture leaking through the nightgown where she was sitting on the towel. "I'm not sure how I got here. Did you check the cabin?"

"Yes. You were out, but not down. There were tracks all over the place." Amestoy rinsed a glass in the sink and handed her a glass of water, then leaned in the doorway as she rinsed her mouth and spat in the toilet. "Nanaluk opened it up and turned on a vent fan. She brought your clothes. They're hanging on the back of the door."

Wet strands of hair trailed down the back of her neck. "Jesus, I almost killed myself!" she said.

"But you've figured it out, haven't you? What do you remember?"

"Pieces. Like a strobe. One place one second, then another with no between." Amestoy's demand for answers anchored her.

"Anesthetics knock out higher mental functions, affect memory." He frowned.

"I don't know. That's not it." She looked at him. "There's more to it than anesthetics, isn't there?" Amestoy waited, watching her. "I died on Penrose. I was trying to get out of my quarters."

"But your body wasn't recovered. At least not officially."

"I couldn't have survived. But I can't be a clone. Clones are just twins."

"Right now, I don't think so.... I've been trying to understand what they did, and why. There's obviously a neurological component to the surgeries. Studying neurodegenerative diseases? Alzheimer's? No trace of anything like that."

"And it doesn't feel right. Why the in vivo excisions? ...Did you identify the remains in the cryotank?"

"Yes." He didn't have to say who it was. Bret could tell it was her by the look on his face.

She stared at the floor. "I think we were built—like the bioplank, but on a more detailed pattern. Or printed, maybe. Some total biological reconstruction. Someone acquired my body and used it. I'm a copy, but exact, on at least a molecular level, probably much finer. It's the only way to explain my development, my memory. I don't remember waking up in the dome. I remember being there, but I don't remember how I got there."

"Like when you woke up in Munich?"

Bret hesitated. "Yes, like that.... No, not really like that, less coherent."

"How much can you put together now?"

"Not enough! Help me up, damn it!" Amestoy extended one big hand and pulled her to her feet. The back of the gown clung wetly to her thighs. "Okay, let me get dressed."

He took her boots and left her alone in the bathroom. She could hear him moving around in the main room as she dressed. She pulled on a pair of pants and a shirt, brushed her teeth with the corner of a towel, tried to clean herself up. Her mind was different. She knew that it had not been just the chemicals, just poisoning herself.

"I did learn something, though," she said as she reentered the room. Amestoy was standing by the windows. He was dressed for outside.

"I'd be dead if I hadn't locked myself out. Again." Bret sat down in the overstuffed chair and looked out at the snow, at the glare of sun on the lunar surface. "It hurt."

Amestoy nodded and tossed a pair of dry boots to her. "Put these on. I want to show you a few things."

Bret carefully pulled the boots over her gauze-wrapped feet and then stood. She grabbed a parka as she followed him out the door.

A pad of ice just outside held the imprints of two bare feet. Amestoy gestured at the trails leading to and from the house. "You're lucky to be alive," he said. He glanced at her boots and the bare footprints in the ice. "You'll lose some skin, but no toes." He took her hand and started down the path toward the little cabin on the lip of the ridge.

The day was very clear, and warmer, no fog in the trees or below in the valley. They followed the well-used path between the two cabins. Lines of wandering tracks broke from the anonymity of the pathway about three-quarters of the way to Bret's cabin and straggled toward the woods. A third set broke from the trail just out of sight of the cabin's deck and wandered in the direction of the ridge. Amestoy followed this set of tracks to the verge of the drop-off, and they stopped to gaze down at the braided sheet of ice that was the Tanana. Bret almost expected to see a body below, or a naked woman standing on the river ice, but there were only snow and trees and quiet. Amestoy turned toward her. Frost plumed from his lips and coated his lashes and the fringe of black hair that had escaped the hood of his parka.

"Did you mean that you would have died," he asked, "when you locked yourself out of the cabin, or somewhere else? Were you outside? On the surface?"

When she didn't answer, he took her arm and guided her back to the path and up the steps to her cabin. The room was still warm, but the exhaust fan roared loudly in the small space. Black and white tile in odd shapes patterned the northern wall of the room. Bret sat down in the small wooden chair by the central window.

"Do you remember how you got to Munich?" Amestoy asked. He took off his parka and hung it on the coat rack on the back of the door.

Munich. She remembered the green water of the Isar rushing beneath a bridge, remembered the pain in her bruised face, the roughness of granite under her fingers as she stood in the rain looking down at the river. Her memories were suddenly as sharp as ice.

"Maybe I'm beginning to. We were starving," she said. "They hadn't fed us in days. We had been locked up in that little round room for a long time, I don't know how long. I knew we were going to die."

"And then?"

"And then I was in Munich," she snapped. She couldn't explain what she had done.

Amestoy came around the chair and stood between Bret and the window. "How?"

"I don't know." Like noticing the pattern in wood grain or fabric, she had simply *noticed* she was somewhere else.

Stream one: A man with a knife. The surface of the Moon.

Stream two: Munich in the rain.

"Koch hired me for the lab on Penrose. They were interested in computational solutions, in AI. I was good at what I did, you know. There's a certain talent, a capacity for intellectual leaps involved in my work. The computational power needed to do the same work is huge. A man with a knife came into the dome, grabbed her—I guess she was the brain-damaged one—by the hair. They threw us into an airlock." Bret looked up at Amestoy. "They were in a panic to get away, to erase their tracks. They must have been caught off guard, learned that the museum's inspection had been moved forward. I know how—how I got away, but it makes no sense. I followed her...or she followed me. I was just suddenly in Munich, and she was somewhere else. I remember seeing her later, naked, standing in a pool of water, knowing I was alive."

"Do you know who she is, or where? Are there any more of you?"

Bret shook her head.

"She's me. I don't know. Only one other—her, I think. There's something about my brain. More information. I'm seeing things they saw." She shook her head again. "Non-locality, ice. I keep thinking about ice, and polyaminoes. They're tiling patterns, aren't they? What shapes can be used to tile an infinite Euclidean plane?" She glanced at the tiled patterns on the wall. Her hands began to shake; she was terrified.

"Stop," he said. He moved away from the window, came over to her and took her shaking hands between his own. "This was happening before you poisoned yourself, too, wasn't it?"

"No. No, I don't think so." But it was. "Yes. I was there one minute, and then I was in Munich. There's something... like the collapse of the wave state, or ice crystals.... My brain is different, my perception. They did something to me. We're entangled, our minds."

Amestoy nodded. "Let me show you this." He took a small projector from his pocket and walked to the center of the room. His face was expressionless. "I took this while you were sleeping. I'm sorry. I'll destroy it if you want, but you need to see it." A representation of her unconscious body half-obscured the tiled patterns on the northern wall. "They altered your brain, but in a way that isn't superficially obvious."

She looked at him, and then at the model of herself. Her head had not been flayed as had the heads in the autopsies, but her skull seemed open, sections of her brain delineated in variously colored light.

Amestoy stood and pointed into the swirls of color. "This is the lining of your brain, the dura. I didn't notice it at first, not until I analyzed your pattern of energy use. These layers, in red, under and over the dura—they shouldn't be there."

"What are they?"

"I don't know, extra tissue, but very thin. None of the others shows it. The red indicates a lot of activity there."

"Some sort of enhancement. It's causing me to black out? To hallucinate?"

"Maybe, but I think not." He tabbed the player and a frontal view of her skull rotated into position. He pointed again. "There is the partially healed fracture in your cheekbone. The other bodies don't show that."

She touched her cheek gently with her fingertips. "My face hurt when I woke up."

"It must have been a traumatic blow. You may have been unconscious."

And she remembered. She remembered the texture of the

foamed-ceramic insulation in the scope room, and the emaciated face of the catatonic woman next to her. Bret had fought, but two men had dragged her from the dome and through the station. And the other women had fought. "Part of the function of certain areas of the brain is to block information from other areas, to create order. But my brain was never totally out." She remembered the blaze of light on the lunar surface as the shuttle's airlock opened and the atmosphere blew out. "Until they killed her. They *tried* to kill her, to kill us."

"When your brain was anesthetized—"

"I stopped being there. A new order collapsed out of the wave state."

He shrugged. "The censor was knocked out. There must be changes in your mentality at every level. Those extra tissues are dense in neuronal material, but I don't know how you did it or what else they've done to you."

And they had left her there, in the dome. "I died. My son died. And this is what they made of me, a construct, an experiment?"

"Yes, an experiment. It explains the multiple copies. But why you? Just opportunity?"

"You can't construct a brain out of electronics that does what the human mind can, you know. It is too deterministic. The human brain is not predictable, it's a quantum device." She took a deep breath. "It's a quantum device. Maybe it was partially opportunistic; they couldn't stand to lose my ability, thought they could improve me or control me. And you want to help me find out what they did? Who did this?"

He nodded again. "If you'll let me."

There were feathers of frost on the glass of the window, patterns she could almost understand. She wanted to be alive again. She remembered her son, the grasp of the ice. She could feel the tears on her cheek and knew she still wanted to be alive. "It has to have been someone with Koch. Will they want the outcome, the thing they got?" She didn't think they would.

Stream three: a dark-haired woman, naked in a flight of ibis.

Bret looked at Griffin Amestoy's face and accepted, finally, that at least something of her *was* still alive.

"Yes," she said. "I want you to help. Please, be there with me when I find them."

Escape: Success: End Run

Ward 7

Susan Lanigan

The man from HR was speaking. She could not recall his name, even though it glinted from the bronze-colored badge he wore below his left lapel. That was because the badge always seemed to catch the intense sunlight coming in through the south-facing glass wall, to which the HR man himself seemed immune, even though it was hitting the back of Vera's neck so precisely that she felt as if the rays were burning a line on her skin above her collar. Both room and man were unfamiliar to her. Employees from the medicinal chemistry division of Gleich Enterprises rarely got summoned here. But her presence was "imperative," she had been told, her offence too severe to be overlooked this time.

"You see, it's like this, Ms. Ragin," the man from HR was saying. "I appreciate that laboring under this, ah, *impression*, means you are worried for Ms. Kellner—"

"It's not an impression," Vera returned icily, trying her hardest to stay still in that slippery, black enamel chair that seemed engineered to slip halfway up one's you-know-where like a particularly uncomfortable thong, no matter how one sat in it. "It's the data from my senses."

"You scientists never seem to think of observer bias." He smiled. Not for the first time, Vera noticed the sheen on his black hair that smacked of a Nu-Grow treatment on a naturally bald head. It gave off that strange, artificial fragrance of industrial polymer, something pressed or boiled. She did not reply, because she had no intention of legitimizing his condescending nonsense. She had been writing scholarly papers on the composition of flatulence before he was born; she knew it when she heard it. The men who had brought down her father, overrunning the house with their briefcases and papers, their bristling open pores, their un-needed clipboards and ancient, brick-size mobile phones—they had looked just like the man from HR, and their talk had the same aroma of bullshit.

Something of her thoughts must have communicated itself to him because his smile vanished. "The fact is, Ms. Ragin, your behavior is Out. Of. Control." He jabbed his finger at her at the last three words. "At Gleich Enterprises, we believe an employee has a right to a personal life, but with your *issues*—when Ms. Kellner approaches us and claims that you were sniffing around her chest area—"

"Excuse me, I did not—"

"But Ms. Kellner says you *did*, Ms. Ragin, and you see, we have a problem."

The ceiling fan moved with an infinitely slow *whop, whop, whop*. In HR, they liked to collect antiques, fake items of friendliness in a too-new office. It did nothing to ease the heat. Such a primitive object, it was a relic of a bygone era, but its continuous rhythm calmed Vera and helped her compose an answer.

"Ms. Kellner had...a certain odor."

She was being kind. How could she adequately describe the stench that had come from Esther whenever she was within feet of her? One so foul, so chokingly awful it reminded her of that time one of the inmates had broken into the laboratory and smashed a sodium hydrosulphide cylinder. The chemical's purpose was to be sprayed in minute amounts as an experimental treatment to ease pressure on the lungs, but the entire contents of the cylinder, well that was something else. They'd had to evacuate the building, all able-bodied people crawling to the exit. All right, maybe it was not quite as bad as that, but it did remind her of it. She did not want to tell the HR man that. It seemed unfair to Esther.

"Ms. Kellner was particularly insistent during her interview that she washes regularly and uses deodorant. And this smell you keep insisting on—well, she was here half an hour ago, I can personally testify that she was most fragrant. Her perfume lingered quite pleasantly in the air."

What a sleazebag.

"Naturally as a fastidious woman, she is very distressed to be told that she smells."

And there Vera felt a spasm of guilt. That was true. She remembered the pained, hunted look on her colleague's face when she had first brought up the matter.

"And you are aware, Ms. Ragin, that sexual harassment is a firing offense."

Vera opened her mouth in horror, then closed it again. After all, to his eyes, to the eyes of all sane people, what else would it look like?

"In light of your sterling work in previous years, your paper on, eh—"

(Responses to Light Stimuli among Canine Subjects, Ragin, Keung and Hidalgo, 2027, not that he had any intention of looking it up.)

"—the directors have decided to give you a written warning this time. But I must inform you that this matter is serious. If there's a repetition...." He allowed his voice to trail off until it was like the hiss off a set of the old Bose speakers that lingered unplugged in a far corner as a decoration feature, with cactus plants and a fine sheen of dust on top. It could not have been more than five seconds before she managed a "Thank you" but it seemed like a long time before she finally got her butt off the chair from hell and slunk out of the office.

Traffic was heavy on the bridge and she got home late. When she saw the empty cartons still smelling of takeaway, she clicked her tongue in disapproval. Jaime must have bought them for himself and little Isabel. The living room stank of vinegar, the sharp edge of it so keen it nearly burnt the hairs off her nostrils, and the pictures of a baseball game flashed on the screen, sound down. Never mind that she spent so much time and money shopping for decent food and then cooking it. And she was exhausted. This complaint and the HR interview had happened after she'd had barely five hours sleep every night for a fortnight. Of course that happened when you were fifty-two and had a four-year-old child and twenty-nine-year-old partner. The Women's Extender program had made some things equal in allowing women a longer fertility window, but not all things.

She passed her hand in front of her eyes and blinked. The room swam with the weight of her exhaustion. She needed to feel caffeine in her veins, but she knew if she drank some now, she would be jittery for hours—and the aroma, God no, it would be too much. To tell the truth, everything had been too much since she had made the alterations to her brain.

For that was the source of the newly-minted awareness that made her smell her colleagues' diseases, and everything else under the sun. She had taken scientific curiosity too far, like that fellow back in the day who had drunk soup with *H. pylori* and given himself a stomach ulcer. And far from being hailed as a discoverer, like him, she had been hauled off to HR and given a shellacking.

Jaime used to joke that she spent so much time at work she must be having an affair. Fat chance, even if anyone had been interested. Since she had made the final adjustment to her piriform cortex, a month or so ago, all the men now stank like beasts in a barn, their hormones exhaling through their skin like last year's unwashed sweat. In her early years of her undergraduate degree, she had read that testosterone made men's urine smell stronger than women's; she could now vouch that it made their skin smell like the local butcher's back in the old days. And those were the healthy ones. The woman weren't great either, though they didn't reek quite as strongly as the men—apart from Esther.

From upstairs, she heard Isabel laughing as a deeper voice

told her a story. Vera recognized the line Jaime was reading aloud, since she had read the same line for Isabel a few months ago. Vera felt a pang; when *she* had read out the line, Izzie hadn't laughed. Part of her wanted to go up and take over from Jaime, see if she could make her laugh too. But no—first she had to roll back the alteration to her brain. Her mind was quite made up on that point. Her impulse to save Esther Kellner had been a waste of time: Esther Kellner did not want to be saved. This was not a battle she could win. *Do it now*, she told herself, *before you change your mind. Before you get so attached you can't break free.* Her father had kept on with his hypotheses long after the data had all shown up negative and it had destroyed her entire childhood. For Izzie's sake, she couldn't afford to do another generational ride on that roller coaster. She couldn't be a crusader any more. It wouldn't be fair.

Vera ripped off her clothes and showered with high-intensity, energy-saving water droplets, leaving the bathroom with her towel carefully wrapped around her. In the bedroom, she dried herself quickly and started putting on clothes, much to Jaime's surprise when he entered the room.

"You going out again?"

"Just round the back." He frowned. They both knew what "round the back" meant.

"You haven't been in with Izzie any night this week."

"I know. I'm sorry, Jaime, but I just had a tough day. HR called me in." Damn, she had meant to say nothing, but it had just come out. Jaime undid his belt and flung it on the chair.

"Are you still bothering that woman? If so, I'm not surprised. Vee, we said you'd drop this, remember?"

"I *have* dropped it."

He looked at her disbelievingly. "I worry sometimes, that you'll end up like—"

"What? Say it, Jaime. You mean, like my dad. You're worried I'll mess up Izzie's life the way he did mine."

He shrugged. "You said it, not me."

Not for the first time, Vera cursed herself for ever having told Jaime Esposito about her father. She wished she had never trusted him. But when she first met him, it had all been so casual she thought it didn't matter what she said. He was just a handsome young engineer whom Gleich Enterprises had hired to add capacity to their optical cables, back in the dark days when they feared the internet would run out of space. He appeared interested in her, but she hadn't taken him seriously. She was in her late forties then, but hadn't considered the ramifications of the fertility Extender treatments she had taken. Long divorced and childless, she never thought a man so young would look at her that way, even though relationships like that had become more common. So she thought she was safe when one night she had too many glasses of bourbon and he had said, "Your name sounds Russian. Kinda cute." And she had said, "Russian, yeah. That's where I came from. You don't want to know how I got here."

But he *had* wanted to know, and she had told him, and got emotional—with predictable results. Then a repetition of the original experiment's conditions and further results along the same lines—until five years later, sharing her home, bed and Extender-conceived child, he could hold that knowledge over her any time he wanted.

She had never told Jaime about what she did "round the back." It was her cave, her place of discovery. During one particularly bad row, he had called her a narcissist, obsessed with every crevice of her own mind. Oh, if only he could have known how literally true that was! With his cold stare following her down the stairs, she went down to the small kitchen at the back and unhooked a set of keys from a nail by the back door. Thank God he hadn't confiscated them this time—he'd done it once or twice before. So, out down the long garden to the whitewashed building that backed onto the railway line. It wasn't the safest place to carry out these stunts: the trains thundering overhead made the lights flicker dangerously from time to time. The breeze was biting as it swept past her still-damp hair. But she could not waste any more time. She had to bring this ordeal to an end.

It takes some work to have one's piriform cortex reconfigured. One should not try it without a robot tool hooked up to a camera, which can zoom in to a hundredth of a millimeter if necessary. And of course, the first incursion requires a craniotomy—to wit, drilling a hole in your skull, as long as the tip of a thumbnail to the knuckle, to insert the tiny, capped electrode. To do this effectively, the head needs to be set firmly in place in a scanning machine, so tightly that there is no room for movement, while the skull is mapped, coordinates set, and a message appears on a second screen in front of you, along with a 2D representation of the top of your head, a flashing arrow and a rectangle covering that nail-to-knuckle distance, like the "select and crop" on the art software of yesteryear:

REMOVAL OF BONE MAPPED TO THE FOLLOWING REGION. CONTINUE Y/N?

Click "Y". Then experience the sensation of the drill boring in precisely. Even when this is done well, there are blood vessels that lie in the way of the drill and leak their contents; then there is the keen feeling in the teeth and jaw as bone is hit and the head clamped hard and the vibrations, oh God. And it hurts, too. You are going through nerves in the skin, even if the brain feels nothing.

Trying to get hold of the right equipment to rig up one of these entails the help of either a skilled thief in possession of a van, or a friend who owes you a very large favor. Vera knew a few of the former, and just one of the latter, this combination sufficing to help her secure the large contraption that lay plugged in before her, the one she had refused to dismantle in spite of Jaime's pleas.

So. At that point the screen suspended in front of her refreshed its display, and Vera Ragin underwent the bizarre experience of watching the drill bore through her skull and the electric needle descend into her own nerveless cerebrum. Strange to think that every memory, everything that gives us consciousness and soul, lay right there. The fallibility, the sadness of the aging body and the still-alert mind...

But conducting brain surgery is not a time to be meditative—even if such a state introduces the right low-frequency theta waves favorable for continuing with the procedure. Very slightly to the right of the piriform lies the Area Tempestas, and if you hit that, you're a goner. Seizures, nothing but endless seizures, every day for the rest of your life. And then of course the whole piriform area is very small, because in *Homo sapiens* it is ridiculously underdeveloped; one would not have the same problem with, say, an aardvark. Somewhere in the evolutionary process, higher thinking was prioritized over olfactory data. *Were that a decision rather than an accident of evolution*, Vera often thought, *God definitely short-changed us.*

(There is a second reason to pray that the programming has been vigilant and precise. If this incredibly fragile and wondrous mechanism is damaged, the lesions generate the unfortunate side-effect of causing hypersexual behaviour. Then the HR man would be right on point with his accusations.)

And Vera Ragin could never be certain of the outcome of her experiments, even with the improvements in technology. This was not like the lab rats of old, where all you needed to do was apply an electrode. The electric currents these days were more sophisticated, low-pulse. The only clue to their work was a gentle hum that gathered around the back of the head, singing a chord somewhere near E flat. When work like this finishes, the chord Dopplers, diminuendoes. The needle retracts. The small rectangle of missing bone is set back in place. The apparatus is sheeted.

The first time she did it, in the hospital, Vera felt almost normal for the first few hours afterwards, though she had a mild headache. Until she wandered out into the small garden with its dismal shrubbery and "sensory area," past the smokers—and then it hit her like a truck, albeit a truck of smells: the pungent sweetness of the hydrangeas, the angry, hot assault of tar and smoke from the cigarettes and the slight tang off the leaves of the laurel tree, god damn it, even the strong, sweet aroma of cut grass, all in one, huge wave, so acute it almost knocked her over. And she wanted to weep, then and there, for what humankind had lost. The power and intensity of it. God, it nearly had her on her knees.

And now she was using the same procedure, but to take all that away. She would no longer smell every nuance, every change in the air around a person.

Her father's face, pale with anguish, loomed in her mind: "I will find a way, Vee. I promise. The government don't like what I do. It makes no sense to them. But it can't be wrong. It *can't be*." Pacing back and forth, the elm floors creaking under his relentless tread, a crease on the leather of his shoe where his foot bent. Back then, a child of ten, shy in her school frock, Vera did not immediately realize that he was talking to himself, not her.

Her father had been one of the last defectors from the Soviet Union. He had made a bargain with the State Department to let him escape to the US in exchange for state secrets. He and his wife moved to Potomac, Maryland, where their house had lawns that sloped down to the river. A year later, in 1982, Vera had been born. Her father told her it meant *faith* in one language and *truth* in another. "My Vera, my Verushka," he would call her, stroking his cheek with her finger.

Until she was ten, she knew no other home.

It took her many years to piece together what had happened, but it appeared that in the bureaucrats' eyes, her father had not fulfilled his part of the bargain. She had read the letter where his theories on solitons, bions and sexual transmission of wave energy were described as "pure, deluded nonsense" by a J. Frederick Philbin-Molloy. That missive had mysteriously survived the burning of all the files.

She often wondered about Mr. Philbin Molloy and his petty pleasure in writing that biting letter. Did he wear Dralon suits and attend Mass every Sunday along with his smiling wife, who would have a Sylvia-Plath-style wave in her hair and a vacant gas-oven smile? Did he pride himself as a member of the community? Vera tried to imagine this man, whom she had never seen, as a Little League coach. But no, he would never have been chosen for that. Too much of a bespectacled loser. Passed over at school, derided by the jocks.

Either way, all that collected, pent-up malice of decades he gathered up in a little basket of privilege and tossed over Dr. Dmitri Ragin. And along with his letter came the men in suits who wore sunglasses in cloudy weather, who swarmed over the lawn of their house, taking away the cabins which her father claimed were transformed into aetheric spaces, and then—for this Vera *would not* forgive them—throwing all his paperwork and slides and photographs into a heap on the driveway and setting it all on fire.

She remembered the coarse, choking smoke that came from the curling slides and photocopies as they turned to ash, and just beyond, her father with his face in his hands. She had read stories where they had casually used the sentence, "He was a broken man"—now she saw the reality in front of her. Just for a few moments, before her mother ushered her away. But she saw it, and remembered.

Yes, he had been wrong—not just wrong, deluded almost to madness. Yes, his theories had been tailored to his own gratification and made no sense. She knew that now, with the pain of knowing one has passed out one's parents. But he had been her world, and that day her world was shattered.

By the time she was finished and locked up the shed, all the lights in the main house were out. When she climbed into bed, Jaime was sleepy and warm but softly kicked her enquiring foot away with his heel and rolled over, very pointedly. And at that point, her heart sank, and it had nothing to do with his rejection. That familiar plastery-salt odor came from him. He must have jerked off while she was out, and left some of the tissues by the bed. The problem wasn't that he had masturbated instead of waiting. That was par for the course these days. The problem was the smell. It was intense, even more so

than earlier. God damn it, she'd failed to reverse the change!
It was worse than ever!

She slept hardly a wink that night. *Everything* smelled.
Tiny particles of exhaust fumes from the freeway, diesel from
the trains, the remains of biological powder from washing the
sheets—hell, even the smell of her own body was too much
for her now, all the creams on her skin coagulating into one
chemical reek. And she could not even rock back and forth
and cry, "Make it stop!" because Jaime would surely hear her
and then she would have to tell him that she had done brain
experiments again, after swearing she would stop. He had said
if she didn't stop, he would leave. And she could not bear that.

In the hour of sleep she somehow managed to grab just before dawn, Jaime slipped away to work—he was now a managing director of a Very-Long-Wave aero-optic cable company—because when she woke up, exhausted and unrefreshed,
the bed was empty. Wearily, she made breakfast for herself
and Isabel. The cloying mixture of milk and soggy cereal
nearly made her gag, though the child happily ate away without noticing. Then Vera drove Izzie to pre-K and went on to
work. The stench of chemicals and petri-dish cultures was ten
times worse than usual as she grabbed her goggles from the
shelf and donned the white coat. She inwardly cursed whoever had thought it a good idea to start working with the ammo-
nium sulphate salts that morning. For her, the air was almost
unbreathable, the odor was so strong.

Immediately she went to open a window, but Lester
Keung, her young assistant, stood in front of her, barring her
way with his solid, wide torso. There was such hostility in his
gaze that she backed off. Perhaps it was because it was a cold
day, she told herself, though she knew in her heart that was
not the reason. Resolved to behave as if all were well, she said
"Good morning, Lester," in a neutral tone: he made no reply.
Esther Kellner must have been talking to him, perhaps to all
the others too. So, this was how it was to be, was it? Better
pretend everything was normal, then.

She continued to do so even when nobody spoke to her

the entire morning, and cleared the washroom whenever she entered, breaking off into clumps of people, whispering. The cheek! She could diagnose half of them on the spot. Cancer was not the only disease that left its tracks. Diabetes gave a sickly-sweet tinge to the breath while *Clostridium difficile* simply smelled like sewage. They should all be grateful she kept her trap shut and decided not to tell them their various maladies.

Mid-morning, Vera could no longer avoid going to the restroom. But then she rounded a corner and just ahead of her was Esther Kellner. Vera stopped, but not soon enough, for Esther stopped too and Vera nearly barrelled into her. "Excuse me," Esther muttered tightly, dodging Vera, nearly sneaking underneath her handback to get past. But Vera could not respond. As Esther marched on, she stood there in the dank little corridor with its constant sound of dripping water from a pipe, transfixed with horror.

The odor that had been bad last week was now ten times worse. It was rotten eggs all right, but rotten eggs and slurry and foul-sweet as if one were locked in a room and being slowly poisoned with molasses. There were no words to describe it. The disease must have spread! Vera broke from her reverie of horror and flapped after Esther, her goggles banging around her neck as she ran towards the lavatories, calling her name over and over. One cubicle had the door shut. There was no way out of the restrooms that didn't entail going back the way you came from. Esther had to be in there. Vera banged on the door, shouting her name once more.

"It's locked." The voice, tight with fear. "You can't go near me, you know that."

"Esther, for God's sake. The smell is worse. It's metastasized. You *must* get a check-up. Please, I'm begging you."

There was some rattling and shuffling and the sound of toilet paper being pulled out of the dispenser. Then the toilet flushed, a rapid outburst of irritated gurgling. The door burst open. Esther was pale and her lipstick smudged. The smell now hit Vera like a wave. "Will you leave me alone? Will you ever leave me alone?"

"No. Not when I know you're ill. I'm going to keep on telling you, there's something wrong, I can smell it, and it has nothing to do with how often you wash, or what perfume you wear. It's not your fault at all, you're sick, and as it happens I have the enhanced ability to detect it. I've been doing surgery on myself to improve my sense of smell, you see? See?" Vera knew she sounded frantic, her voice wheeling away, almost cracking. Esther was weeping now, great heaving sobs, and Vera moved to comfort her even as Esther cringed in revulsion, but then a voice broke in, cold and contained, the voice of someone who did not usually belong in ladies' lavatories.

"The only sick person in this room is you, Ms. Ragin." It was the man from HR.

"I had a panic button," Esther said, flushed, triumphant. "I hit it the moment you started harassing me again. So they're going to take you away and lock you up."

But Vera could not respond. She could smell, above the stink of the HR man's aftershave, the burning smell of seizure, all about, an aura of odor so powerful that even Esther's smell was washed out—and was the last thing she registered before the buzzing in her head began to harmonize with the burning smell and she fell to the ground, her limbs in spasm, her skull knocking against that lip of the sink under the speckled, stained mirror. Her last coherent thought before the screaming of nerves inside the brain that accompany a grand mal took hold was that she hadn't been careful enough with that Area Tempestas after all, and that she was surely done for.

When she woke, everything seemed white, as if she'd gone to heaven. The walls, the sheets her nails compulsively picked at, the pillow linen that scratched her cheek. Then she saw the dark teak of the window sill—where had they managed to get that, with the rainforest gone?—and the familiar brickwork pattern of the cement wall outside the window, and realized she was somewhere off the neurology ward of the very hospital the Gleich Enterprises lab was attached to. When she moved her head she realized that the top of it was encased in plaster. Oh, okay. They must have gone right in.

She could not tell what time of day it was, or the time or date. She could hear bustling in the corridor, the banging of trolleys, nurses calling to each other. She could not stop memories flooding back, of the anaesthetic before the Caesarean necessary for women her age giving birth, then awakening once more, Izzie's slightly strangled cry. All the sights and sounds were familiar, all right.

But she could hardly *smell* a damn thing.

Not that they had got rid of all of that sense. As the seconds lengthened into minutes, she could detect a bit of cleaning fluid, her own body's slight rancidity after lying the same bed for... how long? A dash of a man's aftershave—a light pine fragrance, not the HR man's horror dousing. But nothing that suffocated or overwhelmed. Just normal. She felt unexpected relief. Some strong drug was traversing her bloodstream, something that was calming her so that she no longer cared about Esther Kellner. She no longer cared about anything much. Except—

The door opened and Jaime came in, little Isabel clinging to his hand. The familiar anxiety of a woman in late middle age faintly sparked in her—*oh, what must I look like*—but with all her remaining willpower she pushed it away. She looked like whatever she looked like, and he still looked pleased to see her. That was something.

"Doctor said you might wake up today," he said. "We were waiting, weren't we, Izzie?"

Isabel merely nodded. Cowed by the surroundings, she had gone uncharacteristically quiet, her chin tucking into her shoulder. Vera reached out her arms and her daughter trotted obediently over to the bed and let herself be embraced.

"How long have I been out?" she asked, her voice hoarse on its first use.

"Two months," Jaime said.

"What? That long?"

"They weren't sure how long it would take. You had a

very bad seizure, Vee. They fixed the damage pretty good, but they didn't know if you would wake up. There was talk of life insurance." He shifted from one foot to the other. "I told 'em where they could stick it. I knew you had enough will in you to open your eyes sometime and ask for a cheese sandwich."

Vera could not think of anything she wanted less right then. But she was touched all the same. "Thank you," she said quietly to him, above Isabel's head.

He laughed loudly. "Thank me? What the hell for?" He sat down on the plastic hospital stool and winced. Apparently it was in the same category as the chair in the HR man's office. He reached over and stroked her hair. Again, she got the smell of him, the faint salt-lick of his skin, but nothing intrusive or extreme. And she didn't miss her super-duper smellability, no, not one bit. "I'm glad you're okay," he said, still stroking her.

"What did they do to me?" Her voice sounded faint to her own ears.

Not much, it had turned out. They had found the leaked stent and removed it with great efficiency. The damage to the Area Tempestas caused by her earlier adventures had thankfully been temporary; the tissue was bruised rather than destroyed. Through cold laser and bio-knives, the whole procedure, when carried out properly in a hospital—Jaime emphasized this last bit—barely took half an hour and restored all the damage she'd done previously. The only difficult part had been ascertaining when she would recover.

"Jaime," she said, reaching for his hand, "I was trying to—"

"I know what you were trying to do," he said, misunderstanding her, "but it was too early, Vera, do you understand? They're not ready for you yet. *I'm* ready for you, hon, more than ready—but the rest of the world..." He shook his head.

Irritation burst into her nice druggy bubble, roused the blood in her veins. She gripped Jaime's hand tight. "Not ready, not ready," she said, sounding like Izzie. "I'm sick of hearing 'not ready.' It's all I've heard all my life."

"Just twenty years ago, they wouldn't have been ready for *us,* babe."

"And am I supposed to be grateful that they are now?" She was harsh as a scraping doornail and her anger hurt her throat. Jaime dropped her hand and sat still and somber. He passed his hand across his forehead, a gesture he often used when he was perplexed about something. Then he looked straight at her, his eyes soft and dark.

"No," he said, "I guess not. I guess we don't owe them anything."

Vera was released from hospital a few days later with strict instructions for aftercare which Jaime loudly vowed to carry out to the letter. She walked through the corridors, Jaime still holding her hand, for she had lost her confidence and the months lying supine had left her shaky and weak. She had not forgotten her alienation at work, and looked at every passing face for a colleague she recognized, someone who might slight or scorn her. But nobody accosted Vera Ragin as she shuffled uncertainly through those strip-lit corridors, Jaime moving his hand to her back. *He's got my back*, she thought with a surge of gratitude, and then, just as she passed Ward 7, she caught a woman staring at her full-on.

Ward 7 was the oncology ward. Vera had occasionally visited it in a professional capacity, often with a dog in tow for her research paper on canine detection of illness. And there was the time her father had been there, but not for long—there was nothing they could do for him and he was allowed to fade gently away like the west wind rather than continue a rigorous chemotherapy regime that would do him no good. This woman did not look ready to resign herself to that fate, though, even though she was bald as a coot, and looked sick and sunken. Her eyes still had that look of amour-propre, punctilious outrage...oh God, where had Vera seen it? Then the radiographer came in the doorway and called the woman back; only then did Vera's entire limbic system flare with alarm, recognition, the sense of danger—

But Jaime sensed her growing distress without her saying a word and calmly shepherded her past the oncology ward, his hand firmly on the small of her back. He moved slowly but inexorably and she let herself be steered by him. *This is my life,* she thought, *he and I and Isabel.* And only slightly screwed up her eyes when the sunlight hit her face in the car park outside as Jaime whistled to unlock their saloon parked at the far end. *My Vera, my Verushka.* As he guided her into the passenger seat and detached from the car's electrical outlet, the thought came on her softly like snow falling on her cheek: *That was Esther Kellner the radiographer was calling.* But just that brief thought, as Jaime reversed carefully out of the space, Isabel strapped into her seat. His hand on hers, a warm, protective squeeze.

"Everything okay, honey?"

She let the thought land, stay awhile and melt away, until it was as if it had never been executed from the midst of her cerebrum, never taken place at all.

"Yes, everything's fine. I'm glad to be going home."

They inched onto the freeway and Jaime engaged the car's drive mode. Quickly they picked up speed. Across the bridge, the traffic was clear.

Two Become One

Kiini Ibura Salaam

"Invert nature and you will find that which you seek."
—*Maria the Jewess*

Aversion:

Meherenmet glared across the room as she watched an attendant feed Amagasat dates and tiny sips of beer from a serving tray. Disgust spiked through her body. *She looks like an aging child*, Meherenmet thought.

Morning light filtered into the eye-shaped antechamber, bathing Amagasat in a soft glow. She shimmered in her iridescent blue robe and golden collar and wrist cuffs—all intentionally worn, Meherenmet thought, to boast of her success. But Amagasat's tremors—that fierce trembling of her hands—overshadowed her finery. Meherenmet doubted that Amagasat could still dress herself, or even attend to her own elimination.

"Do not pity me," Amagasat said from the opposite side of the room. She leaned back against the cushions of the chair and continued to chew. Meherenmet comforted herself with a glance at the henna stains and the gold leafing on her own steady hands. She shifted on her chair and adjusted the blood-red cloak she had hurriedly tossed over her shoulders when Amagasat's presence had been announced. The white cotton shift she wore beneath the cloak was much simpler than Meherenmet would have preferred, but the room was, at least, clean and orderly. Just a few days earlier, it had been filled with the week's delivery of organs and limbs from the morgue. Now the room was empty with nothing to clutter the space between the two women.

"You did not interrupt my morning for dates and beer," Meherenmet finally said.

"You will not invite me to see your work?" Amagasat whispered. Her voice was gravelly and soft.

Meherenmet narrowed her eyes. "If I wished to be torn apart by your brilliance, I would have requested your presence myself."

"Pity," Amagasat said. "I hear that you have made some progress. It is an impossible path you have dedicated yourself to."

"Well, my path will not result in my death," Meherenmet snapped.

Amagasat licked her lips. "It is unforgivable for you to speak to me in that tone. When tutelage ends, respect should remain. Please excuse your attendants."

"And where will your attendants be?"

Amagasat attempted a laugh, but it sputtered more than sparked. "This is not an assassination attempt."

"Perhaps we should excuse them together. I would like to offer them a morning meal now that they have fed you."

Annoyance flared across Amagasat's face. "Very well."

As the attendants left the room, Meherenmet and Amagasat faced each other in silence.

"You are needed," Amagasat said when they were alone.

Meherenmet let out a scoff.

"It is unthinkable that the great Amagasat should have needs."

Without commenting on Meherenmet's tone, Amagasat said, "A Healing has been planned—"

"No."

"My request is not complete."

"Nor is my life's work. I will not be diverted from my path."

"The king's brother is near death. It is the royal family's needs you deny, not mine."

"Does the king know what these Healings have done to you?"

"You must—"

"No," Meherenmet said. She stood and rang the bell for her attendants to return. "I hope all the riches and accolades you have were worth destroying yourself, but you will not place me on that road."

"You are an ungrateful student."

Meherenmet walked across the room and leaned over Amagasat.

"And you are too weak to get out of that chair without help. I will never follow in your footsteps."

Amagasat lifted her hand and attempted to point at Meherenmet, but she could not force her finger to stay in a single spot.

"You use your strength against me."

Meherenmet shook her head. "I reserve my strength for myself. You do not factor into the equation."

Before Amagasat could reply, the attendants poured into the room. Meherenmet's attendants gathered behind her as Amagasat allowed her attendants to hoist her up by the elbows and escort her to the front door. Meherenmet stood stock-still in the open doorway, and silently suffered Amagasat's slow departure. As soon as the door was shut, she turned on her heel and swept down the hall. Her attendants scurried behind her, listening intently as she launched into a list of the day's deliveries, pick-ups, surgeries, and experiments. She stepped into the lab and paused to quickly survey the room: the examination table was empty, her two surgical apprentices were organizing tools, and her prize project was crouched in the far corner of the room, with her newest apprentice hovering over it.

"What is happening here?" she boomed.

The apprentice whirled around. Her scrawny shoulders were engulfed by her robe and her dark tangled hair was barely held in place by her leather headband. She ducked her head when she saw Meherenmet's withering glare.

"Explain."

"I was...doing the experiment, just like you said..." she said, spinning her words out cautiously. "I was taking notes and it just jumped off the table and..."

Meherenmet held up her hand. Her one indulgence, a gold

serpent bracelet, snaked around her wrist.

"Are you the same child who said I could trust you?"

The girl looked down at Meherenmet's creature. It was huddled in the corner, with its head bowed and its limbs folded around its bent legs. When it looked up at her, a shadow passed over its ugly patchwork face. The apprentice—who answered to the name "K"—took a deep breath.

"The creature is safe. It didn't run out of the room..."

"And terrorize the children at the river?" Meherenmet said, finishing K's statement.

The girl blushed, but she pressed on.

"It didn't break into the kitchen..."

"And set the crockery on fire?"

"I'm getting better!" she insisted, "I didn't let it leave the room."

"Your scroll," Meherenmet said, then shifted her shoulders almost imperceptibly. One of her attendants, a tiny man covered in wrinkles, reached for her shoulders and removed her cape.

K walked toward Meherenmet with downcast eyes. She wanted to exude confidence, but in Meherenmet's presence all she felt was a terror-filled awe. K handed Meherenmet the scroll and peeked over Meherenmet's shoulder as she read. Under the weight of Meherenmet's disapproval, she had learned to make every notation with precision. She quickly scrutinized the scroll to reassure herself that she had placed the chart recording the previous day's exercises in the exact center of the scroll. She reread the details she had meticulously recorded to the right of the chart. K felt certain that, this time, she had met all of Meherenmet's requirements, but standing there idle, waiting for Meherenmet's judgment, was excruciating. She turned away from Meherenmet to check on the creature. It was still in the corner, rocking back and forth, but now its eyes were fixed on K and Meherenmet.

"Back onto the table," she hissed.

The creature flung its arms out at an awkward angle and bent and flexed them as if testing its elbow joints. It stared at K with dark eyes that were buried under a thick-ridged brow and pools of eyelid creases. K pointed to the examination table and glared at him. The creature wrestled its body up to standing with forceful jerks of his torso. Then it dragged its way across the room, taking one stiff step after another. When it reached the examination table, it hopped in a circle until its back was to the table. K watched as it fell backward onto the table and was still.

When K turned back, Meherenmet was regarding her in silence. K managed to return Meherenmet's fierce gaze for three seconds before her terror overtook her again. She lowered her eyes and stared at Meherenmet's red tinged toes, which were peeking out of her sandals at the bottom of her robe.

"What phase are we in with the creature?" Meherenmet asked.

K chanced a glance up at Meherenmet. There was no clue in her expression as to whether her scroll was acceptable or not. When it came to writing the reports, her presentation had frequently disappointed Meherenmet, but her observations were so unique that they were startling. She had an instinct and an acumen for forming hypotheses about the creature's behavior as if the experiments she completed with it were of her own making rather than Meherenmet's.

"Imprinting and mimicry," K replied after a brief silence.

Meherenmet rewarded K with a brief nod. "You will join us."

K felt the pleasurable flush of pride flood her cheeks. She had begun her life at Meherenmet's wishing only to avoid being returned to the Home. In a few short weeks, she had become gripped with the desire to become a valuable member of Meherenmet's lab.

Meherenmet snapped her fingers and an attendant rushed forward to relieve her of K's scroll. She swept past K, her swarm of attendants following her closely. At the examination table, the two surgical apprentices—a tall girl who was always scowling and a skinny boy who was always pouting—had undressed the creature and were frantically rushing to bathe his limbs in a dark blue liquid before Meherenmet reached the table. The attendants bustled around, helping Meherenmet perch on a high stool and finding their way to their assigned positions around the table.

In the frenzy of activity, K was jostled each time she tried to slip into an empty spot at the table. When all motion had stilled, she found herself standing at the foot of the table staring at the creature's toes. She did not want to look at the rest of the creature's body but, as the tall girl and the skinny boy poked at it with wooden tools, she could not avert her gaze. Her guts churned as she took in the mélange of colors and varying textures of its skin. It had thick leathery patches that were a brownish-green, in other spots the skin was stretched so thin that it had a translucent, bluish hue. Every limb was marked with scars, sutures, and stretch marks; every stretch of skin was mottled, punctured, or perforated.

"You are here for a purpose," K heard Meherenmet say loudly.

She snapped to attention and everyone—the surgical apprentices, Meherenmet's attendants, and Meherenmet herself—was looking at her expectantly.

When she supplied no answer, the tall girl let out an exasperated sigh.

"Meherenmet asked if there's been progress in the creature's verbal skills," she said.

K squared her shoulders and forced herself to hold Meherenmet's gaze as she spoke.

"No progress with actual speech, but the creature has made the connection between moving its mouth and language. I have not figured out if it knows what speaking is and what communication is for, but it seems to understand that mouth movements and sound go together. I have observed it opening its mouth and pushing air out."

Meherenmet's dark eyebrows tensed slightly as she listened. She pointed to one of her attendants with a red-tipped finger. The man began writing on a scroll.

"You will examine the mouth cavity next," she said to the surgical apprentices.

Midway through the examination, two attendants rushed into the lab. They carried two large cloth bags that made a loud sloshing sound as they moved. Meherenmet held her hand up to halt the surgical attendants and looked around the table. She focused in on K.

"Do you know the streets in this quarter of the city?"

K nodded. Meherenmet pointed to the door.

"You must be quick. The tissues must be fresh."

K moved away from the table hesitantly.

"Where am I going?" she asked.

"Set her on her path," Meherenmet said to the two attendants.

K grabbed her cloak and bag from the hooks by the door and shot Meherenmet a confused glance, but Meherenmet did not provide her with any guidance. Instead she pointed firmly at the door and shooed K from the lab.

Inversion:

By the time K could see the market in the distance, her ankles were dusty and her underarms were damp. The pole the attendants had tied the bags to was pushing painfully against her collarbone. But even trembling with exhaustion, she held her back stiff and straight. She was terrified of losing her grip and letting the bags slip from the pole. She imagined them splitting apart the second they hit the ground and monstrous scabbed limbs exploding from within before skittering off in the dust.

When she entered the market, she promised herself a break under the colorful canopy of the fabric stall, if she could haul the bags that far. At the fabric stand, she softened her knees, stumbling forward to gently lower Meherenmet's cargo to the ground and collapse into a squat. As she rested—arms wrapped around her shins, face pressed against her forearm—she heard a soft hissing. K lifted her head slowly. A small eye was peeking out at her through a slit in the curtain that covered the bottom of the fabric stand. Four tiny fingers appeared through the slit and pulled aside the curtain to reveal an impish face with a wide grin.

K's eyes widened. "B—"

Before K could speak, the child pressed a dirty finger to her lips and disappeared behind the curtain. K looked up at the fabric vendor. He was waving his arms wildly in the air, haggling with a customer. She picked up the pole and dragged Meherenmet's cargo across the dirt as she backed into the gap between the market stalls. Once hidden, she dropped the pole and raced to the back of the fabric vendor's stall, her face lit by a wide grin. When she turned the bend, the child launched herself at K, wrapping her arms tightly around K's legs.

"Ketah!"

K twisted away from the girl and spat in the dirt. "No one calls me that anymore. I am K."

Betah laughed. "But K is even less of a name than Ketah."

"It's better because *I* chose it," K said sharply.

Betah lowered her head as if chastened. K knelt down and wrapped her in an embrace.

"Don't pout, Betah. I'm happy to see you."

She drew back and looked into Betah's face. The girl was grubby, her hair matted and her robes torn. K cupped her cheek.

"What are you doing here?"

"I ran away."

K rubbed at a spot of grime on Betah's forehead. "But who feeds you? Are you eating?"

"This is the market. There's food everywhere."

"And what about a bed? Do you have a safe place to sleep?" K shifted back to sit on her heels.

"Under the stalls." Betah shrugged. "No one even knows I'm here."

K felt a tightening in her chest. The least sweet Betah deserved was somewhere soft to rest.

"You should not have left. You are still little—you can find a good home."

Betah shook her head. "She doesn't like me."

K's mouth flattened into a frown. "She hated all of us."

"She said I need to be broken."

K was silent. It was only in breaking that any of them

proved their worth at the Home. Then broken, they were no longer of any use to themselves. She squeezed Betah's shoulder. "I wish I could take you to live with me."

Betah lifted her chin proudly. "Ebah will take me."

K felt as if all the breath had left her chest. "Ebah? How did you find him?"

"He just appeared one day," Betah shrugged. "He had a bag of coins and a letter from his master saying he wanted to collect us."

"Us?"

"He didn't know you were gone."

"She didn't let you go?"

Betah's head dropped. "She said the letter was fake and I already had a home to go to."

K rubbed Betah's back. "So you ran away?"

Betah lowered her voice to a whisper, a habit ingrained from years of captivity. "When I heard the palace was coming for a Healing, I ran." She looked at K with determined eyes. "Ebah lives with the royal court, you know. When I find him, he will take me in."

K fought to keep doubt from surfacing on her face. "Are you sure Ebah is traveling with the palace?"

"He must be," Betah said.

K bit down on her reply. Betah had seen enough disappointment to last several lifetimes. She gripped Betah's arms.

"I'll come with you."

Betah squealed. "We can all live at the palace together and no one will ever send us to a work camp again."

"No, Betah. I'm coming to help you find Ebah, but I'm not running away."

Betah spun away from K and turned a cartwheel. Then she went still.

"What about your master?"

K thought of Meherenmet, tall and stone-faced, glaring down at her in disappointment.

"I will worry about my master," K said tweaking Betah's nose. "You worry about finding Ebah."

After a hug and a kiss from Betah, K shouldered her load again and rushed it to its destination. On her way back to the lab, she contemplated what it meant to run into Betah like that. After Ebah had been sent away, she had regretted nothing about moving away from the Home, except leaving Betah behind.

K stumbled across a sweets vendor as she trekked back through the market and impulsively bought three honey balls. When they were all much smaller, they would sneak away and beg coins in the market to buy a honey ball every chance they got. Today, K strolled back to the lab and ate all three herself. She was licking the traces of honey from her fingertips when a group of six black-robed men navigated a litter with a large, ornate chair alongside her. She moved to the side, but they did not pass. They rested the chair right next to her and stood at attention.

"Come near," said a gravelly voice from behind the curtain that sheltered the rider.

K took a few steps backward. Children from the Home had been kidnapped this way. The life they were rumored to live afterward made the Home seem like a paradise.

"K, previously called Ketah, please approach the chair."

K leaned forward and squinted, but she stood her ground. A shaky hand parted the sparkling purple curtain and a wrinkled old woman with loose cheeks and droopy neck folds motioned for K to enter.

"I have no wish to harm you. Please sit with me for a short while."

K stole a glance toward the lab.

"Meherenmet has gone on an errand. She will not return for hours. You are safe to speak with me."

K crossed her arms. "How..."

"I have spies, dear. They told me about your little friend who lives in the market, so why don't you get in so we can discuss matters privately."

At the mention of Betah, K's face tightened into grimness. Had Betah returned to her life just to be taken away again?

The old woman flashed a grin that looked more like a grimace. "Step in, girl. There's no danger here."

K climbed into the litter with a furrowed brow. Everything about the woman screamed danger, but she could not leave a threat to Betah unanswered. As K sat across from the old woman, waiting for her to speak, a fine layer of sweat started to rise over her skin.

"Why are you following me?" she asked abruptly.

The old woman burst into laughter that quickly deteriorated into a racking cough. She held a shaky fist in front of her mouth.

"I am not following you. You have entered my area of interest."

Then the old woman went silent, peering at K with greedy eyes. K shivered and wrapped her arms around herself. There was something slippery about the way the old woman spoke, as if, with each word, she was weaving a sticky, inescapable trap. In the quiet, K could hear the slap of sandals as people passed the litter. The voices of the black-robed porters drifted in through the litter's curtains. The muted thudding of her heart echoed in her ears. After the silence between them had stretched on for so long that it seemed it would shatter, one of the porters parted the cloth and whispered something in the old woman's ear.

"I must go. Thank you, child," she said.

"You're letting me go?"

"I have business to attend to. We will see each other again."

K slid down from the chair and turned to watch the porters hoist the litter off the ground. As they carried the chair away, she squeezed her eyes tight and prayed to never see the old woman again.

The next morning K dressed distractedly. Her mind was awhirl as she raked her hair with her fingers and fashioned it into four fat twists that she tucked in place before shoving on her headband. On her way to the lab, her thoughts pitched between Betah and the terrifying old woman. Working to shake off those memories, she entered the lab and glanced around. The creature was still in its box, the skinny boy was sharpening reeds, and the tall girl was nowhere to be found. K didn't see any of Meherenmet's attendants either, but there was a steaming carafe of hot herbed water sitting on a tray near the door.

With her thoughts still swirling, K poured a mug and turned to walk across the lab. Before she could take a step, she slammed into the tall girl. The mug slipped from her hand and the bucket the girl was hauling banged to the floor.

"You're a disaster," the girl hissed.

K looked down. The mug had shattered and the bottom of her robe was soaking wet.

The boy righted the bucket and scowled at K. "We should use her gown to clean it up."

K clutched at the cloth around her thighs. It was the only new thing she had ever owned. The tall girl caught the gesture and rolled her eyes.

"No one's going to take your clothes."

"I don't know why she's still here," the skinny boy muttered as he crossed the lab in search of rags. "You would think the two apprentices who never set anything on fire, lost an experiment, burned down the kitchen, botched the notes, or scorched the pots wouldn't have to put up with such an embarrassment. She doesn't even have her own name."

K felt her cheeks flush with shame. Every orphan was connected to her by that shame—each of them answered to intonations rather than names. Those sharp short sounds noted their order of arrival and could be passed on to another child if they ran away or were sold. K stuck her tongue out at the boy's back.

The girl jumped. "Did you see that?"

"See what?" The skinny boy slammed the lid of the storage bench closed and returned to the girl's side with an armful of rags.

"The creature, it stuck out its tongue!"

"Just like that?"

"I swear it. It stuck out its tongue."

The boy walked across the room and stood in front of the creature's box. He stuck his tongue out in front of the creature's face. The creature gazed back blankly.

"Did you see it?" the girl asked K.

K bit her lip and shook her head. She watched the girl step onto a pile of rags to dry the soles of her sandals and join the boy in front of the creature's box. She hadn't lied, not exactly. She had not *seen* the creature stick out its tongue. She could have mentioned that the creature had likely stuck out its tongue to mimic her, but she busied herself drying the floor instead.

"Who's going to tell Meherenmet?" the girl said suddenly turning away from the creature.

The skinny boy shrugged. "Can't it wait?"

"But this is huge," the girl said. "If it can move its tongue..."

"...it can learn to talk," K said.

"Well, if the embarrassment thinks it's important, it *must* be."

The girl punched the boy's arm. "This is serious."

He shrugged. "You saw it. You go."

The girl shook her head. "I can't go in there."

The boy poked her shoulder. "You're a surgery apprentice. How are you going to graduate to surgery if you won't go there?"

"You go." The tall girl shoved him with her elbow.

The boy shook his head. "It'll give me nightmares."

"I'll tell her," K said stepping toward the two of them. They looked at her as if they had forgotten she was standing there.

"You?" the boy asked.

K tried to stand taller. "I can do it."

"Do you even know where the surgery is?" he asked.

"I'll show her," the girl said. She pointed to the desk. "Write it down, just in case she doesn't want you to speak."

K chose a scroll from the pile on top of the desk and unrolled it. She grabbed one of the reeds that the boy had just cleaned and reshaped. She dipped it in the pigment, quickly made a few strokes, and followed the girl out of the room.

Revulsion:

K stood in front of the closed door of the surgery with the scroll clenched in her fist.

"Don't be afraid," she whispered to herself.

The moment she pushed the door open, a foul scent swarmed her. Meherenmet and her attendants looked up as she stepped into the room. Their faces were covered with swaths of cloth that left only the slits of their eyes exposed.

"I…"

Before K could speak, Meherenmet silenced her with one extended finger and turned her attention back to the operating table. When K closed the door behind her, the odor of rot bombarded her, hijacking her brain, so that she could do nothing but slump against the door and stare as Meherenmet and her attendants leaned over an operating table, elbows jutting back and forth as they worked.

After a few minutes, K pushed herself off the door. She gripped the scroll, forced herself to breathe, and battled through the stench to walk deeper into the surgery. A cloud of mist drifting upward from huge blocks of ice momentarily surrounded her. In the haze, she felt something cool and spongy collide with her face. She jumped backward and squinted through the mist. There was a pale palm suspended in midair. As the mist cleared, she saw that there, in the center of the room, were six or seven arms dangling from the ceiling in a neat row.

K tensed, stepped around the arms, and looked more closely at the objects around her. The walls of the surgery were cluttered with boxes and bottles, shelves and jars. To the right, she saw three rectangular alcoves cut high into the wall. A collection of heads was crammed into the alcoves, their faces made ghostly by a drape of gauze that stuck wetly to the foreheads, noses, and cheekbones. It slowly dawned on K that she was surrounded by an excess of flesh, seen and unseen. She shifted her gaze and focused on the operating table while edging past dismembered body parts that had been stowed on shelves, stuffed in jars, and hanging from hooks throughout the surgery.

When she reached Meherenmet, she paused to stare at the wall that rose up behind the operating table. It loomed over her, its surface laden with hooks that held saws, knives, and files. K snapped her head away when she saw that most of the tools were stained with blood.

"I..." K tried to speak but again Meherenmet stopped her.

"Shh!" she said sharply and continued her work.

K stood there, the odor of rank flesh rising up from the table, making a muscle in her cheek quiver and her nostrils burn. Over Meherenmet's shoulder, she caught a glimpse of a bloody, limbless torso. Threads of veins hung limp from the raw stumps where the torso's arms and legs should have been. The table jerked suddenly and everyone looked at the foot of the table. An attendant apologized, shifted a partially fleshed arm to another table, and resumed sanding the knob of bone that was protruding from the shoulder.

When the table was still, Meherenmet continued the painstaking task of attaching pink threads from a severed thigh to the creature's pelvis. Next to her, another attendant leaned over a decayed head, gouging out black clumps that must have once served as eyeballs. Without warning, K felt a gurgling in her gut. The acid taste of bile flooded her mouth. She lurched away from the table, jackknifing as she gagged, heaving dry spasms. As the burn of liquids started barreling up through her chest, she looked around frantically for a place to empty her stomach. A firm-handed attendant grasped her elbow and ushered her into a corner. The moment a pail was shoved under her chin, she pitched forward and retched.

When there was nothing left, K stumbled backward and wiped her mouth with her fist. The firm-handed attendant grasped her elbow again, dragging her away from the operating table, past the dangling arms and severed heads, through the door, and deposited her into the hallway outside the surgery. She turned to offer her thanks, but her guide had already slipped away, firmly closing the door in her face without ceremony or explanation.

Coercion:

That night, before sneaking out to meet Betah, K tiptoed into the lab and tugged her cloak down from the peg near the door. As she crept down the hall and slipped out of the front door, she pretended she was on a night walk with Ebah and their friends from the Home. Twice, she was certain someone was following her. Each time, she slipped into a doorway and looked behind her, but both times the street was empty.

By the time she reached the market, K was panicked. She rushed through the maze of bare stalls, periodically looking over her shoulder and tripping over her feet. At the fabric stand, she exhaled—but before she could call out to Betah, she heard a thump behind her. She whirled around, her heart pounding in her chest. The darkness took shape, gathering into a huge hulking figure that advanced on her. A scream was on the verge of tumbling out of her throat when she noticed how the figure hobbled, lurching from side to side. She squinted into the darkness.

"You followed me?!"

Betah stuck her head out from beneath the fabric stand. "Who are you talking to?"

K glanced over her shoulder at Betah, then looked back at the figure.

"You should be in your box," she said and crossed her arms.

The creature stopped dragging itself forward and thrust its arm out toward her. Clutched in its hand was her sack.

"What is that?" Betah asked and climbed out from underneath the stall.

The creature opened and closed its mouth, looking down at Betah intently. K's mind stuttered through opposing thoughts and impulses. The questions Meherenmet had trained her to ask tumbled through her mind. *What did it mean that the creature had brought her bag to her?* She was sure this was more than the free will it exhibited during its moments of impish rebellion.

"Can he talk?" Betah asked, bursting into her thoughts.

K shifted her body to stand in front of Betah. Even as she was wondering at the creature's ability, she was simultaneously calculating the catastrophe that would unfold if she were caught, if the creature was harmed, if the creature harmed someone else.

K turned to look down at Betah. "I can't come with you."

But Betah was not listening. She was staring up at the creature with wonder in her eyes.

"Is this your monster?"

The sack was still extended from the creature's hand. K took the bag and the creature dropped its arm.

Betah stepped out from behind K.

"What do you call him?"

"I don't...he doesn't.... We haven't named it."

Betah took a few steps toward the creature, then she stopped in her tracks. "Will he hurt me?"

"I've never seen it hurt a thing, but it's only been alive for the dry season," K knelt to face Betah and lowered her voice. "He's my master's biggest project and he's never been out before. Not like this. She will not like him being here. I have to turn back."

Betah leaned forward, covered her mouth with her hand, and whispered into K's ear. "He can keep us safe."

K looked at the creature thoughtfully. Each working part of him was a miracle, born from Meherenmet's meticulous work in the surgery and maintained by her daily attention to each crevice and suture.

"If anything happens to it...."

"We need him," Betah said, looking up at K with a crazed and desperate look in her eyes.

"Stop it. I taught you that."

Betah dropped the expression and started to pout.

"And Ebah taught you that."

Betah struggled to wipe all expression from her face.

"Please, Ketah. Finding Ebah is worth it."

K felt her entire body tense. She did not want to jeopardize her position at Meherenmet's, but Ebah *was* worth the risk.

"We'll go and come right back. Before dawn."

Betah squealed and started clapping.

K watched as the creature looked down at his hands as if wondering if he too could make sound with his flesh.

They encountered no danger in the city, or perhaps, danger steered clear of them—sheltered as they were in the shadow of the creature's hulking frame. Upon crossing the city limits, a wide circle of blazing torches announced the presence of the royal encampment. As they neared the encampment, they could see a colorful gathering of tents illuminated in the torchlight. When they approached the outer edge of tents, Betah changed her gait. She slouched forward and bent her knees, slinking more than walking. Following Betah, the creature crouched too, advancing with jerky pounces.

Mimicking and imprinting, K thought and she frowned as a new barrage of worries ruffled their feathers. She closed her mind against them, but one tiny what-if slipped through before she could shut down the swirl of worry. What if this one adventure altered the creature to the extent that his behavior was unrecognizable upon their return?

K pushed the thought away and crept behind them, watching as Betah stalked around, lifting tent flaps and poking her head through openings. When Betah gazed across a large clearing at the center of the encampment to examine a cluster of tents on the other side, K sprinted forward and caught her by the shoulders.

"You'll get caught that way." K dragged Betah back toward the edges of the encampment.

"I won't get caught," Betah said, wriggling out of K's grasp. "No one will notice me. But you two...."

The three of them stood there, facing each other in the shadows of the encampment. Betah pushed K away.

"It'll be easier for me to find Ebah if I'm by myself."

As Betah was backing away, the creature furrowed his

brow, pitched his chin forward, and pushed a dry gargling sound from his mouth. K stared at the creature in shocked silence. No amount of jaw and tongue exercises had led him to produce sound. Meherenmet's intricate training regiment had led him nowhere. Instead it was an illegal trip in the middle of the night and the friendship of a runaway that had prodded him to speak.

"You should call him Gah," Betah said suddenly.

Before K could agree, a putrid scent descended on her.

"Do you smell that?"

"Smell what?" Betah asked.

A large cloth fell over them, intensifying the smell tenfold. K gripped the creature's arm and grabbed for Betah in the dark. Then everything blurred and K collapsed to the ground, still reaching out frantically, trying to locate Betah.

When K opened her eyes, the creature was hanging over her.

"Gahhhhhh," he said.

K sat up, excited to hear sound coming from the creature's throat, but just as quickly she fell onto her side. Her head was spinning and one sore spot on her scalp was pounding. She looked around. They were in a large empty room that was completely round. The only source of light was a weak stream of torchlight seeping into the room from a small rectangular window that sat snug against ceiling. Her lips were dry as if she had been asleep for days, but it was still night as far as K could see.

"Gahhhhhh," the creature said again.

He was swaying in front of a wall, slowly running his fingers across its surface. K struggled to her feet.

"What are you doing?"

When she joined the creature she saw that the wall was covered in writing. K tried to decipher the lettering, but it was written in a script she did not recognize. She ran her fingers over the letters as if, by touch, she could uncover their meaning. Before long, K discovered a crease running straight down the wall from the ceiling to the floor. On one side of the crease, there were three small indentations—just large enough for K's fingertip. She poked at the holes, but nothing happened. She pushed at the wall but it did not budge.

K crumpled to the floor and put her head in her hands. The creature shuffled forward and leaned over her. He stared at the indentations, then without warning, he poked his tongue out and licked the door.

"Ugh," K said, standing up to push him away. "That is not food—what are they feeding you?"

But as she stood, she heard a thunk in the door, as if something inside had shifted.

"Do it again," she said.

He licked another of the indentations, and another thunk rang out.

"It has to be wet," K said. She allowed the creature to lick the wall again and again, then she stuck her fingers into the indentations. Finally, after a complex sequence of finger work, the door made a loud clicking sound and the wall split along the crease, separating into two halves that slid open.

The narrow hallway on the other side was empty except for a tray with four urns and four platters of food. The creature rushed past her, grabbed one of the urns and tipped it to his mouth. Before she could stop him, he guzzled down whatever was in the urn. K touched one of the urns cautiously, as the creature started shoveling the food into his mouth. The urn's cool surface invited her to drink. She brought it to her lips and took a hesitant sip. Water ran into her mouth, moistening her lips and cooling her throat. Before she could drain the urn, she heard a loud thump behind her. She turned around just in time to see the creature fall flat on his back. Within seconds, her limbs went heavy and she tottered sideways, banging her head on the wall. Then there was nothing to do, but sit there slack and lifeless as her awareness slipped away.

Meherenmet pressed her fingertips together and glared at Amagasat. She took care to make sure her knees did not touch Amagasat's as they sat across from each other in Amagasat's litter. Meherenmet had been ice-cold with fury when Amagasat had arrived on her doorstep, with her trembling jackal's smile. With a quiet urgency, the uproar the creature and K's disappearance had caused shifted into focused preparation as Meherenmet organized her attendants for the evening's journey.

On their way to the encampment, the women exchanged very few words until Amagasat broke the quiet.

"I have always cautioned you against stubbornness and the perils of pride. It was not wise to refuse me after all you learned at my hand."

As Amagasat droned on, Meherenmet sat on her hands and tightened her lips. Rage seared the inside of her cheeks as she wrestled each burning hot retort into silence.

Invasion:

When K next awoke, she was in the round room again, but this time the room was ablaze with torchlight. When she tried to move, she felt rope pulling at her wrists and ankles, both of which were tied to a chair. She looked around and saw that Gah was also bound, but he was standing—ropes lashed his chest, wrists, hips, knees and ankles against a flat board. The sight of dark bruising on his skin where the rope cut into his arms flooded her with guilt.

"Gah," she called. Even though it was the first time she had called him by the name Betah had given him, he turned his head to look at K. The expression in his eyes was flat and he did not make a sound. In that moment—much more than her fear of Meherenmet's anger when she discovered K had put him in harm's way, K felt heartbreak that Gah had been kidnapped with her. She lowered her head and struggled against the ropes.

"K, are you crying?" Betah's voice drifted into the room.

K whipped her head up. Betah was looking down at her through the window with shining eyes. K felt a burst of joy.

"They didn't get you!"

"Why are you down there?" Betah asked, her voice high-pitched and unsteady.

K felt Betah's worry tap into the panic that had been blossoming inside her since she first woke in that room. She took a deep breath.

"I don't know. We were together and—"

"I fainted," Betah said.

"We were poisoned, but they let you go."

"How is the Gah?"

K shook her head. He stared up at Betah without making the dry gasping sound she inspired in him. Betah turned her head as if listening for something. When Betah disappeared from the window, then reappeared again, K's heart jumped.

"Betah, you must be careful. If you hear something, hide."

"But it might be Ebah. He told me to meet him here. He'll know what to do."

Betah moved away from the window again. This time K noticed Betah was clean—her face had not a lick of dirt on it, she wore clean robes, and her hair was shiny and combed. In the empty room, K smiled. Not a smile of fake bravado, but a real smile knowing that whatever happened, someone was caring for Betah.

Before long, K heard feet approaching the window. Then she saw Ebah looking down at her.

"Ketah!"

"Her name is K now," she heard Betah correct him.

Ebah's voice slipped under her skin and caused a fluttering of emotion. His presence seemed to double her terror.

"Who did this to you?"

"It was dark, they threw something over our heads."

"And they brought you here?" Ebah said. His face was troubled.

"Can you help us?"

She stared up at him with wide desperate eyes.

Ebah moved closer to the bars in the window. "This... thing...is with you?"

"He's my new friend," K heard Betah chime in.

"He's…an experiment. He belongs to the scientist…where I live now.…"

The troubled look crossed Ebah's face again. "Look, Ke-tah—" He paused. "There is a Healing here tonight. If they put you in this room—"

Three loud thunks cut off Ebah's words. As the crease in the inscribed wall parted, Ebah whispered, "I'll be back," and disappeared.

Betah quickly came into view again. "We won't leave you," she yelled, then Ebah yanked her away.

K braced herself as the wall slid open. She felt her body go cold when she saw the strange old woman enter the room one shaky step at a time.

"The Healing will happen here," she said loudly. She stopped and leaned on two ornate canes. From behind the old woman, Meherenmet swept into the room, her blood-red cape billowing around her. At the sight of her, K let out a sigh that was guttural and inhuman. Meherenmet walked past K and the creature, quickly inspecting them before whirling around to face Amagasat.

"The ropes are too tight. You are undoing meticulous surgery with those ropes."

Amagasat pursed her lips. Meherenmet stepped closer to her.

"The smallest courtesy you can offer as I meet your demands is to not destroy my work."

Amagasat's hands shook as she leaned on her canes, but she did not flinch in the face of Meherenmet's bristling. The quiet in the room seemed to deepen as they stared at each other. Finally, Amagasat tapped one of her canes against the floor and two of her attendants rushed into the room. She nodded toward the creature and the attendants loosened the ropes holding his arms.

"They must both be unharmed when we are done," Meherenmet said. "No new requests, no tricks, no extra tasks, and you will not put me in this position again."

Amagasat cut her eyes at Meherenmet. "Now we must

prepare. The king will arrive shortly."

Meherenmet crossed her arms and stood her ground.

"You have my word," Amagasat finally replied.

Meherenmet turned to look at K and the creature. She rested her gaze on K for two beats and lifted her chin. K took a deep breath and lifted her head up high. Then Meherenmet lifted one hand, signaling for her attendants to file into the room and position themselves behind her. Amagasat struck the floor with her cane and her attendants flooded the room, forcing Meherenmet and her attendants back against the wall. Amagasat's attendants placed a throne near the entrance and hovered as Amagasat sank into it to preside over the preparations.

Standing between K and the creature, Meherenmet watched closely as Amagasat's attendants wheeled in a metal orb and anchored it to the floor a few feet in front of her. Taller than Meherenmet, the orb was made of battered metal bands welded into a latticework sphere. The orb was scratched and discolored, and inside, it was cluttered with grotesque objects that hung from its frame. The objects—bits of bone, some fresh, some fossilized; sharp hunks of cloudy crystal; glittering stones; and dark muted gems—made K shiver, but Meherenmet did not cringe.

Under Amagasat's direction, her attendants spread a paper screen in front of the orb, blocking it from the rest of the room. When Meherenmet, K, and Gah had been corralled behind the screen, the creature yelled out.

"Gahhhh."

Meherenmet whipped her head around to K.

"You have been withholding information from me."

"No," K said, panicked. "He has only spoken once before when we were trapped in this room."

Meherenmet turned toward him and held up one hand.

"Be calm," she said. "You are safe."

Gah fell silent. In the quiet, Meherenmet said, "Pay attention to everything around us." She lifted her chin toward the screen. "Use the openings in the screen to watch the Healing as it unfolds. We are each other's best chance to get out of here unharmed."

Meherenmet said nothing further as Amagasat's attendants continued to rush around the room, dragging two ornate thrones and one high backed chair into the room, setting up a thin wooden cross near the entrance, and placing two woven baskets on the floor next to the orb. While the thrones and the chair were being positioned, four of Amagasat's attendants lifted the throne she was sitting in and carried her across the room. They turned the throne around to face the entrance and placed it in front of the screen.

"Meherenmet, come," Amagasat called out.

Meherenmet squeezed K's shoulder, walked around the metal cage, and emerged from behind the screen.

"You must stand with me," Amagasat said, pointing to the high backed chair that had been placed next to her throne. She paused as her attendants helped her stand. Then she cleared her throat. "We are ready for the prince."

Amagasat's attendants separated, placing themselves between Meherenmet's attendants, and stood with their backs to the walls. One of them blew a shrill sound on a bit of hollowed bone. Then everyone fell into silence.

Before the Healing began, K saw that Betah had returned to the window. She flashed K a bright smile and then put a finger to her lips. Accompanied by a loud outburst of drumming, a parade of purple-robed servants entered the room. The servants fluttered around, ushering in the king and queen, and arranging cushions, presenting footstools, and adjusting hems as the king and queen settled on their thrones. When the king and queen were comfortable, a second wave of purple-robed servants entered. The stretcher they carried between them held the prince's shrunken body. A trio of Amagasat's attendants lifted the prince and transferred him to a narrow ledge where they removed his robes before massaging and oiling his limbs.

While the attendants pulled the prince up to a standing position, K clenched her fists and tried to free her wrists, but the ropes would not budge. K watched as the attendants walked the prince to the cross, draping his arms across the cross's horizontal bar and gently tying his chest, wrists and hips to the wood. When the other attendants retreated, one of them—holding a spouted container over the prince's shoulders—remained. The attendant tilted the container with great flourish and a thick amber liquid poured out. The attendant drizzled the liquid on the prince's skin, leaving behind whirling lines and graceful filigrees. After the entire length of the prince's body was covered in intricate patterns, Amagasat and Meherenmet stood. They bowed to the king and queen, and slipped away.

Behind the screen, Meherenmet walked toward the metal orb, but Amagasat did not follow. Instead she gripped onto one of her attendants for balance while two others undressed her.

"This requires you to be disrobed?" Meherenmet asked.

"I've made some changes. You may stay clothed."

Amagasat did nothing to hide her body while she waited for her attendants to shift the loose skin that drooped from her muscles so that they could cover her twisted spine, uneven shoulders, and awkwardly curved legs with a white cloth. Her attendants tied the cloth and backed away, leaving Amagasat to totter and reach for Meherenmet's hand.

While Amagasat and Meherenmet climbed into the metal orb, two attendants picked up the round woven baskets and waited for Amagasat's signal. When she nodded, they uncovered the baskets and tipped them forward, coaxing a river of iridescent, jewel-toned beetles to stream out of the baskets and across the floor. The beetles raced toward the prince in an undulating wave of color. As the beetles neared the prince, they skittered apart, separating into an army of colorful orbs that swarmed the prince's feet and stormed up his legs.

Everyone was entranced by the rising tide crawling up the prince's torso, except Amagasat and Meherenmet. They were busy adjusting the objects inside the orb, clearing space for their bodies so that they could stand upright. As the beetles continued to advance, eclipsing the prince in a blur of color, Amagasat's attendants threaded long narrow lengths of white cloth into the orb through the openings. As the beetles gorged on the liquid patterned over the prince's skin, Meherenmet and Amagasat repeatedly looped the cloth around their bodies, wrapping it around the objects and through the orb's frame until they had woven themselves into a thick cloth web. Then the women and the beetles were still.

"Do not move," K heard someone whisper from below.

She recognized the voice of one of Meherenmet's attendants. Without lowering her head, she glanced down to see that he was on his hands and knees picking at the ropes that secured her ankles.

"Is it almost over?" she whispered.

"It has not yet begun," he whispered back.

K looked up to see that the beetles had transformed the prince into a glittering, otherworldly object adorned with thick ridges of glistening color that rose up from his body like a second skin. K watched as two of Amagasat's attendants stood before the prince, gently wrapping lengths of rope around his palms. When they had curled his fingers over, forcing his fists to clench the rope, they backed away. Little by little, they unfurled their coils of rope so that two lengths of rope stretched outward from the prince's hands and arced around the room. Behind the screen, the opposite ends of the rope were pressed into Amagasat's and Meherenmet's hands. When they linked fingers, the connection between them and the prince was complete.

"You are free," she heard the attendant whisper. "Stay there until we release the creature."

K looked over at Gah. Meherenmet's attendants were making fast work of the ropes, but no one paid attention to them. Everyone was staring at the glow that had started to radiate between Amagasat and Meherenmet's palms. While the attendants freed Gah's wrists and feet, the glow—growing brighter and brighter—traveled from the two women's clasped hands, up their arms, and into the cloth that bound them inside the orb. The orb's objects began to spin wildly, shooting the light outward in quick sizzling sparks that ricocheted against the orb's frame.

Suddenly the light pierced the ropes and sped toward the prince. The light collided with his body, filling him with a glow that was painfully bright. Everyone shut their eyes against the light. Gah wrenched himself free and charged toward the orb. K opened her eyes and launched out of the chair to stop him. In that moment, a pulse disturbed the air around them. The prince bucked, his head falling forward and back. The beetles roused, filling the room with a rustling. At the spread of their wings, the rustling turned into a crackling. Then they lifted into the air, engulfing the prince in a swarm of fluttering.

As K and Gah stared at the cloud of beetles fleeing the prince's body, chaos erupted around them. Inside the orb, both Amagasat and Meherenmet had gone slack, but Amagasat's attendants surged forward to form a tight ring around the orb. Meherenmet's attendants attacked, grappling to gain control of the orb. In the midst of the battle, the attendants banged into the orb, jostling Amagasat and Meherenmet's limp bodies. Finally Amagasat jerked awake. With great effort, she pulled herself erect and reached her hand through an opening in the orb. One of her attendants placed a curved blade in her palm.

"Well done," she said, and—without another word—slashed her throat, her chest, and her navel. Her blood splattered Meherenmet, who woke with a loud gasp as the knife clattered to the floor.

"Free me!" she demanded. She grabbed fistfuls of the cloth binding her to the orb and wrenched at it. Her attendants fought harder, pushing to reach the orb, but the defense Amagasat's attendants waged was too fierce.

K dropped down to her knees and crawled past the fighting men. She grabbed onto the bottom of the cage and yanked. When it did not open, she looked up for a latch or a handle. Before K could work out a way into the orb, Meherenmet let out a bloodcurdling yell.

Everyone froze when they saw that a mist was rising from Amagasat's body and filling the cage. Meherenmet began to thrash as the mist sank into her skin. K felt tears spring to her eyes as she watched Meherenmet, struggling against the fabric, her face contorted with rage. When K tried to stand, she found that her fingers were stuck. As she fought to yank her hands away from the orb, Amagasat's mist drifted downward. She shuddered as it crawled over her knuckles with an icy kiss. Her fingers started to tingle but before the mist could reach her wrists, it disappeared, fading into nothingness. K leapt to her feet.

"Open this," K called, tugging at the cage.

One of Amagasat's attendants ran forward with a metal hook. He threaded it through a gap in the orb and yanked it open. K climbed in. Stepping over the white cloth Amagasat had been wearing, she picked up the curved blade and slashed at the cloth that held Meherenmet captive. Meherenmet jerked herself free and shot out of the orb. Hurling herself at Amagasat's head attendant, she clawed his face.

"You planned this!" she yelled.

The attendant ducked his head and fell to one knee. Upon that signal, the rest of Amagasat's attendants knelt in unison. Meherenmet—surrounded by Amagasat's kneeling attendants—heard a scuffling from the other side of the screen. She whirled around with crazed eyes. When she saw the king and queen standing there, she swallowed her rage and bowed. Her attendants quickly fell to one knee as K took Gah's hands and pulled him down into an awkward bent position.

The king smiled broadly. "You must stand and behold the prince."

The prince stepped forward. His cheeks were flushed and his legs were sturdy.

"He appears to be in magnificent health, your high holiness," Meherenmet said.

"We wish to share our great gratitude with Amagasat."

"She is resting, your high holiness," Amagasat's head attendant said, lifting up from his kneeling position to bow deeply.

"We will send for her after she has rested. We must share our appreciation in person."

"We are honored to serve you," Meherenmet squeezed out.

Everyone was perfectly still as the royal family departed. Amagasat's head attendant was the first to recover. He extended his hand, offering Meherenmet a scroll.

"We are your servants now," he said with a bowed head.

Meherenmet smacked the scroll from his hand and slapped his face.

"Do not speak," she said. Then she turned her back to him and stared at her hands. She wrapped her arms around her body and scanned the room. Her eyes fell on K and Gah who were huddled near the metal orb.

"We must leave this place," she said.

Meherenmet's head attendant stood. "Your robes," he said.

Meherenmet's robes were ripped, singed, and bloodied. She waved her hand.

"Organize my departure."

As Meherenmet's head attendant moved though the room issuing commands, Amagasat's head attendant interrupted him.

"Amagasat has deeded all her possessions to Meherenmet," he said, trying to press the scroll into Meherenmet's attendant's hand. "She has done this so that Meherenmet can continue our mistress's work. We belong to Meherenmet now."

Meherenmet's attendant refused to touch the scroll.

"You may petition her yourself," he said. "I have work to do."

When all was organized and Meherenmet's head attendant was leading her out of the round room, he asked, "What should be done about Amagasat's men?" Meherenmet looked back to see that Amagasat's attendants were following, a few of them carting the metal orb.

"Let them follow if they wish, but do not speak to them."

The attendant looked as if he was going to speak his thoughts, but Meherenmet silenced him with a fierce glare.

Conversion:

In the open air, Meherenmet began to fade. She stumbled repeatedly, unable to find her footing as they trooped through the encampment. Despite her protests, her head attendant instructed that she be lifted and carried past the clusters of royal servants to the edge of the encampment. When they reached the litter Meherenmet had arrived in, Amagasat's head attendant waved the scroll in the air.

"This litter is yours along with all of Amagasat's possessions."

Meherenmet's attendants attempted to place her inside, but she locked her legs and kicked at the litter's frame.

"It is your litter now, mistress," her head attendant said, scooping her up and resting her on the ornate chair without waiting for permission or agreement.

Once Meherenmet was settled, her head attendant circulated around, counting those who were gathered and doling out positions and instructions. As K waited for directions, she felt a small force collide into her thighs. She looked down and saw that Betah was hugging her legs.

"You're safe!" Betah said, grinning up at her.

K nodded and tried to speak, but before she could find the words, Ebah had engulfed her, squeezing her tightly. K held on to him and they rocked back and forth with Betah wedged between them.

"I didn't know if I would see you again," she whispered to Ebah.

A faint shout rang out from the front of the line and the attendants at the start of Meherenmet's parade of staff began walking.

Betah gripped K's arm. "You can't leave us."

"Betah's right, K. You belong with us."

"It's not that simple," K said.

She glanced at her hands. *How much of Amagasat was in them?* She shoved her hands behind her back and glanced into the litter. Meherenmet sat there, back erect, staring off into space. Before Meherenmet, every vision K had of tomorrow was either a horror or a fantasy. Now, she knew she could conduct experiments and make observations. Meherenmet had taught her there was something more than serving someone or being served. Meherenmet was not just her mistress, she was her future.

"I came for you," Ebah said, breaking into K's thoughts. "Did Betah tell you? I already have a place for you here."

K gripped Ebah's hand and rubbed Betah's back. "I know we always promised we would be together, and we will, but I can't stay now. I will come as soon as I can. We won't lose each other again."

Betah stared up at K as if she was already lost to memory. She knew what it meant for people slip through your fingers; to wake up one day and find a loved one gone, leaving nothing behind but memories and rumors of where they had disappeared to. But there was another kind of magic that Betah had not yet experienced, it was the magic of conjuring yourself, of stepping into a place where secret talents and desires surfaced from deep within and took shape in the real world.

She kissed Ebah and Betah on their cheeks. Their bonds had not diminished, but while she wasn't looking, new bonds had taken root. There was something below the surface that bound her, Meherenmet, and Gah together. Something she was not sure how to talk about. She squeezed their hands and—before the tears could well up in her eyes—she spun away. She ran to catch up with Gah and fell in step with the rest of Meherenmet's attendants to walk slowly and silently into a future she could not predict but thirsted to discover.

The Pegasus Project

Jack McDevitt

I was sitting on the porch of the End Times Hotel with Abe Willis when the message from Harlow came in: *Ronda, we might have aliens. Seriously. We picked up a radio transmission yesterday from the Sigmund Cluster. It tracks to ISKR221/722. A yellow dwarf, 7,000 light-years out. We haven't been able to break it down, but it's clearly artificial. You're closer to the Cluster than anybody else by a considerable distance. Please take a look. If it turns out to be what we're hoping, try not to let them know you're there. Good luck. And by the way, keep this to yourself.*

"What is it?" asked Abe.

"Aliens."

He laughed. "Okay. I understand you don't want to tell me." We were watching the black hole setting behind the mountains. "People are going to love this place. How long can you give me?"

We were munching cumin pizza. The sun was on the other side of the sky, floating serenely above the ocean. "Eleven years," I said.

Abe was one of those guys who never got a response he liked. Eleven years had to be better than anything he'd expected. Nevertheless he scratched his cheek and looked into his beer as if I'd surprised him with news that would shut down his project. "Last week you were saying fifteen."

"Last week I was saying how much time you'd have before this place gets swallowed. But you don't want to be here near the end. There'll be quakes and incoming rocks and who knows what else. You should be safe for eleven. If you want to argue with me, I can cut it back to ten."

"No. Please, Ronda. I wasn't trying to create a problem."

"We don't want anybody getting killed, Abe. I can't certify you beyond that point."

"Of course. I understand." He showed me a sad smile. Poor guy never got a break. "We can live with it." Somehow the limits imposed by the black hole had become my fault.

"When are you going to install the other hotels?"

"By Friday. Reservation requests are already an avalanche." Another smile. Suddenly we were living in a happy world. Abe was a planner for Interstellar Odysseys, which provided deep space vacations for people who were seriously interested in getting away from routine visits to sea shores, gambling casinos, and planetary ring systems. The planet, which had been named *Pacifica* by someone with a serious sense of humor, had vast mountain ranges, wide sweeping plains, and broad oceans. It looked good. "I wish," Abe continued, "that the sun wasn't going to get torn up so quickly. I'm glad we'll get to see it happen, but it would have been helpful if we'd been able to keep the daylight a bit longer."

The K-class sun had three years left. The black hole, Karma, was officially KR-61. It was the only one within reasonable range that was currently doing some damage, and consequently the only one worth serious money.

My specialty was orbital mechanics, and I'd been assigned to certify the project as safe. The Karma project was a long way from my usual assignments, which consisted primarily of ensuring that worlds being considered for colonization did not face an ongoing existential threat. It wasn't exciting work, but it provided a sense that I was doing something worthwhile.

I'd been in the area several months, measuring orbits and trajectories of thousands of objects to determine whether a vacation site on Pacifica would be in any immediate danger. The fact that the planet itself was doomed, Abe had explained, increased the interest. Interstellar Odysseys had already begun the commercial pitch. 'Everybody wants to come to Pacifica.'

We finished the pizza and the beer, signed the documents, and shook hands. "Thanks, Ronda," he said. "Have a pleasant trip home. And say hello to Aiko for me." Aiko was my pilot. "If you'd like to come back for a few days, we'd love to have you. No charge. Just give me a call."

I told him I wasn't much of a black hole person, and retreated to the launch area. Aiko was waiting beside the lander. "You read the message?"

"Yes," I said.

"We going to follow up?"

I climbed inside. "He doesn't give us much choice."

"It's a waste of time." She got in behind me. Aiko was only on her second mission but no one would ever accuse her of being reticent. Technically, on board, she was in charge, and her tone tended to change as she closed the hatch. "There's nothing out there." She ran fingers through her black hair and sighed at the sheer stupidity of Harlow and the other top brass in the Science Support Department. She looked pretty good when she wasn't glaring at me. "We've got better things to do than charge around the Orion Arm on bogus alerts."

"Hello, Ronda," said Bryan.

"Hi, Bryan. How you doing?"

Bryan was a third-generation Salvator AI, based on the model developed by and named for the young genius who'd died too soon in a boating accident. The Salvator line was designed to operate at a higher intellectual level than humans, but were programmed to remain submissive. "To be honest," he said, "I'll be happy to get away from here. Chasing asteroids is seriously boring."

"I assume," said Aiko, "that Abe's happy with the results."

"He's fine. He's complaining, but it couldn't have worked out better."

"Why's that?"

"Having the catastrophe more or less imminent increases the sales value. If the end of the world is too far away, people lose interest. He's pretending to be unhappy that he didn't have more time, but actually he's fine with it."

The overhead opened and we looked out at the sky. Aiko sat down in the cockpit and we lifted off. A light breeze was blowing in across the ocean. Take the black hole out of the equation, add some native life and some engineering and Pacifica could have been converted into a garden world.

We rose through a few clouds. Below, the dome enclosing the hotel gleamed in the sunlight. The other units would be installed in the same general area, one on a mountaintop, the other on the edge of the sea.

I waited for Aiko to turn things over to Bryan and come back into the cabin. When she did, she sat down across from me and smiled. She knew exactly what I was thinking. "How long?" I asked.

"Six weeks."

"Okay."

She leaned forward and sighed. "Does this kind of thing happen regularly?"

I laughed. "Aliens? Sure. Every few thousand years."

"I'm serious. Is this normal? Getting sent out on idiot missions?"

Everybody knew there were no aliens. "It happens sometimes," I said.

"Harlow said it was a *radio* transmission."

"That's correct."

"So if they've got the source right, the signal was sent seven thousand years ago." The smile widened. "I hope they're not still waiting for us to show up."

We were on our way minutes after we got back to the *Brinkmann*. Aiko was as happy as I was to get clear of Pacifica. It was beautiful—it looked a lot like Soloway, my home world, except, of course, that there was no life, other than Abe and his crew. Despite the sterility, neither of us liked to think about its being sucked into the black hole. I'll never understand why anyone would pay to go see that.

Aiko decided it was time to change the subject. "You know, I've never understood why we're so hung up on looking for aliens. We've been at it now for what? About fifteen thousand years? They just ain't out there, baby."

No, they weren't. We'd been through this experience before, the artificial transmission that turned out to have originated in a long forgotten space station somewhere or a local signal that had simply been bouncing around. There'd been a couple for which there'd been no explanation, but which had never repeated. Missions sent to track them down had found nothing. "I guess we don't like being alone," I said. "It can be depressing."

"Yeah. I guess it *can*. To be honest, it's not something I think about much." The message was clear enough: Aiko rarely spent time alone.

We'd come a long way from Earth. The places we occupied were beautiful now, covered with oak trees and evergreens, filled with animals. But every bird and shrub and dolphin that existed anywhere traced its origin to the home world's forests and oceans. We hadn't found so much as a blade of grass on extraterrestrial ground.

I don't know if people ever thought about it much. It's simply the accepted reality. The Orion Arm, at least, is ours. Maybe the rest of the universe as well.

We didn't have a lot to occupy the time so I began reading about the early days on Earth, when scientists expected to find signs of ancient life buried in the sands of Mars. Mars had been the home for living creatures in much of the fiction written during that era, before we got offworld. But when we arrived, of course, there'd been nothing.

Europa had oceans under its ice. It was one of the moons of a gas giant in the solar system. But they'd found nothing there, either. The most serious jolt, according to the histories, had come when, in the pre-FTL era, we made it out to Gliese 832 with an automated vehicle. An Earth-type world, orbiting in the Goldilocks Zone, had displayed oceans and land masses. But when the *Ranger* arrived, it found no indication of life. No trees, nothing moving anywhere. The report from the robot arrived home sixteen years later and disappointed everyone.

Aiko couldn't help laughing. "They really thought we were going to find squirrels on Mars?"

"Not exactly. But I think they thought they'd find *something.*"

People began asking what kind of universe we lived in. The report from the *Ranger* set off a religious revival which continued to gain ground as evidence mounted that something special had happened on Earth.

Scientists finally figured out what it takes for life to begin. They realized that the odds of chemistry and climate and various other factors coming together were so remote that it was quite possible that we were alone. "Too much," said Thaddeus Roundtree, whose name is one of the few to survive into the modern era, "has to be exactly right. We should consider ourselves fortunate beyond belief that *we* are here."

"I know," Aiko said. "We've been to thousands of worlds that have water and sunlight and they've got nothing."

"Which is why I'd really enjoy meeting someone who came from a different place. You know, somebody we could sit down with. Maybe have a beer and talk—"

"—About what?"

"Probably it would be the same things you and I would talk about. How good's the food? What are the politicians like on your world? Or maybe we'd get a handle on the secret of life."

"You're hoping we'll actually find something, aren't you, Ronda?"

"Well, sure. I'd love to find something. The problem is, if we *do* get lucky, we're not supposed to let them know we're there. That sort of takes all the fun out of it."

Six weeks can be a long time cooped up in a Lexco. It's designed for no more than four passengers, and for flights of relatively short duration, maybe two weeks maximum. We were traveling through hyperspace, of course, so there wasn't even anything outside to look at. It was just a dark vacuum. Either of us would have given a lot to be able to look out a window and see some light.

Bryan created a few avatars for us, mostly from entertainment types, so we talked with romantic leads and comic actors. But they seemed puzzled when we asked how they'd respond if they met a real alien.

"What's an alien?" asked Jespy Quaat, a singer Aiko admitted having fallen in love with during her early years.

"I'm not sure Jespy would have been somebody I wanted around constantly," she said. Her eyes sparkled. "Strictly a one-night stand, maybe. He looks good, but when he gets offstage he loses something." She sat back and shook her head. "I hope you get what you want, Ronda. I suspect it would make Harlow pretty happy too."

The days grew increasingly long. Aiko played virtual games with Bryan, rescuing people lost on strange worlds and whatnot. We worked out each morning after breakfast. We watched shows. And when we sat down to talk, the conversations inevitably went back over the same old issue. What awaited us at the system we were now calling *Iskar*?

"Why do you care so much?" Aiko asked. "Even if we *do* find aliens, it'll be big news for a week, and then it'll get swallowed by the next political scandal."

"That's probably true. But the real problem is that we live in a dark age."

"What are you talking about? Everybody lives well. People don't have to work unless they feel like it. How long has it been since the last war? Or even the last natural disaster?"

"But," I said, "there's nothing left to strive for. Science has run its course. There are only a couple of questions that we haven't answered. Are there other universes? We won't be able to find out about that unless there's a collision. And are we alone? So we're looking at the first chance for a scientific breakthrough in about seven thousand years."

Bryan, who'd been quiet for days, broke in: "Ronda, I couldn't have said it better."

It was a painfully long ride. But eventually it ended and we emerged twenty-eight light-years from Iskar. That meant a second jump, of course, but it only required slightly more than an hour. We came out of it 130 million kilometers from the star. "Bryan," I said, "are we picking up anything that looks like artificial radiation?"

"Had it been happening," he said, "I'd have reported it immediately."

"Okay. Let's get a look at the planetary system. Concentrate on the Goldilocks Zone."

"You understand that will require some time."

"Yes. I had a feeling you wouldn't be able to do it by lunch."

"Ronda." His tone became brittle. "You are being caustic."

Aiko grinned at me.

"I didn't mean to offend." I tried to keep a straight face. Bryan tends to behave as if everybody else on board is an idiot. "Also, if you will, check for artificial radio signals. And send a message back to Harlow. Tell him we've arrived."

Two hours later we got a response. Harlow appeared in the middle of the passenger cabin. Tall, redheaded, good-looking, probably four centuries old. "Ronda," he said, "FYI, we received a second transmission seventeen hours after the first one. It was identical. Since then the source has been silent. Good luck, and keep us informed."

We watched a few shows from the library. I enjoy comedies, while Aiko has a taste for romance. It didn't really matter. During those hours that we moved into the planetary system, neither of us could get terribly interested. We spent most of our time staring out at the sky and waiting to hear something from Bryan.

He finally cleared his throat to alert us an announcement was coming. "There's a planet in the habitable zone," he said. "It's a gas giant. But it has about twenty satellites." He began running images, mostly small rocky moons. Then he showed us a big one with oceans. "This appears to be the only possible source." Twenty minutes later he was back: "There's also a world on the outer edge of the zone, roughly corresponding in size to Soloway. I can't make out any details, other than that it has a large moon."

"Which is closer?"

"The gas giant."

The satellite with the oceans also had huge mountain ranges and vast deserts. But there were no cities, no lights on the night side, no sign of life.

The second world, the one on the edge of the Goldilocks Zone, also looked dark as we approached. "Waste of time," said Aiko.

"We've come this far. I wouldn't want to go back and tell Harlow we didn't take a close look."

"I think he'd understand."

"I doubt it."

"Ronda, he knows this is a futile run. He sent us out because he had no choice. He couldn't ignore the signal, but he didn't expect anything would come of it."

"I didn't realize you knew him that well."

"I don't. But I know how these things work. We do stuff by the book." She pressed her fingertips against her temples and tried to look as if she were taking me seriously. "The signal could have come from somewhere else farther on than this system. Maybe the signal just happened to be lined up so that it passed through here and eventually reached Soloway. Or maybe it was something bouncing around in the system back home. I don't know. It's happened before. But it's pretty obvious it didn't come from *this* place."

"Let's stay with it a bit."

"I can give you another reason for continuing," said Bryan. "There appears to be something in orbit."

It was a ship.

The thing was considerably larger than the *Brinkmann*. A line of symbols was visible on the hull, presumably a name, but I'd never seen anything that resembled them before. It had an inflated dark grey hull, with eight windows and a set of transmitters and receivers mounted near the forward section. "Look at the thrusters," said Aiko. "That thing has to be FTL."

"I think we've found the source of the transmission," I said.

"I guess you're right. But if so, it's been here six thousand years."

"Bryan," I said, "say hello to them. See if you get a response." *Please answer,* I thought. His lights began blinking, indicating he was transmitting.

Aiko looked my way. Her lips were pressed tight and her face had paled. It was the first time I'd seen her show any sign of nervousness.

We looked down at the planetary surface. Desolate flat plains for thousands of kilometers. And in the distance, an ocean. But no sign of life. Why was this ship even here?

Bryan spoke: "They're responding." He put it on the speaker. A female voice that might have been human was talking, but I'd never heard the language before.

"Hello. Can you understand me?"

The voice answered, but I still could make nothing of it. "What do we do?" asked Aiko.

"Not sure. It's a bit late to avoid letting them know we're

here." I stared out at the ship. The hull was damaged in a few places, probably from collisions with rocks. The vehicle was now about two kilometers away. It had a hatch that looked about the right size to accommodate a human being. While I watched, it opencd.

But nobody appeared.

"Aiko, put us in a parallel orbit. Bryan, open a link to Harlow."

"Link is up, Ronda." I got pressed back in my chair as Aiko adjusted course.

"Harlow, we've found a ship. It's in orbit around a world that appears to be lifeless. We'll send an image." I took a deep breath. "A couple of minutes ago they opened a hatch." I glanced at Aiko. She nodded. "We're going to go over and take a look. Will get back to you shortly."

We eased in close. Then Aiko turned it over to Bryan, instructing him to maintain position. I went back to the microphone. "I wish we could speak with you."

"It's probably an AI," said Bryan. "I'm working on it now."

"Is it one of ours?"

Bryan didn't usually hesitate. But this time he did. "Yes. I believe it is."

Aiko was wearing an I-told-you-so look.

"Apparently," said Bryan, "this vehicle has been here at least seven thousand years. Considering the technology from that era, a voyage from any of those inhabited worlds would have taken decades. They had FTL, but it was crude. So who opened the hatch?"

I released my belt and started back to the storage locker for a pressure suit.

"Let me do this," Aiko got up and started to follow.

"Why?"

"Suppose, after you get on board, it takes off?"

"I doubt it's gone anywhere in a long time. I don't think we need to worry."

Aiko shook her head. "I've got this."

"Let me check first. Make sure there's no surprise. Then,

if you want to come over—"

"Forget it, Ronda." She pulled out one of the suits.

"Aiko, I think you're forgetting who's in charge."

Actually, *she* was. But after some more arguing she agreed I could accompany her. We got changed, pulled on jetpacks, and started for the airlock. "I'm not suggesting there's any danger," said Bryan, "but if you do not return, what do you wish me to do?"

"We'll be in contact," Aiko said. "And we'll be back in a few hours. At most."

"When your air supply runs out."

"Good, Bryan. You can count." She went into the airlock and I followed. "Keep the place warm."

"Be careful," he said.

We depressurized the airlock and opened the outer hatch. "You ready, Ronda?"

"Right behind you."

The ship was about fifty meters away. She leaned out into the void, and stopped. "The inner hatch is open, too. In case there's any lingering doubt about something being alive in there." She pushed off the deck, drifted across to the other ship, and touched down on the hull. When I arrived a minute later she was already inside. We passed through into a cabin. Two tables were surrounded by about ten chairs. If there'd been any doubt the ship was designed for humans, it was gone. Everything was of a size and shape appropriate for Aiko and me. The chairs looked as if they had been comfortable, but when I touched one it was rock hard.

A passageway opened out of the rear of the cabin, and I couldn't help watching it, as if someone might appear at any time. A silly notion, since we were in a vacuum, but I couldn't help it. We went onto the bridge where we found two seats and a control panel with unfamiliar markings. Aiko took a long moment to inspect the pilot's seat. "I wonder," she said, "what would happen if we tried to start the engine?"

We returned to the main cabin and entered the passageway. It was lined with doors, four on each side and one at the rear. Aiko tried to open one, twisted the knob and pushed. She got nothing. I tried to help but we couldn't move it. "Everything's frozen," she said. "Maybe locked as well." She floated back out into the cabin. "We've got a cutter back in the ship. I'm going to get it. You want to come or wait here?"

"I'll wait."

"Okay. I'll be right back." She went out through the airlock.

I opened my channel to Bryan. "How are you doing with the AI? Am I going to be able to talk to her?"

"Yes. Give me a few more minutes."

I drifted around the interior. This was obviously the source of the transmission. Had to be. But why use the *radio*? I couldn't believe they didn't have Hypercom communication even in those long gone days.

Aiko came back with the cutter. I'm not sure what we expected to find inside the cabins. But I was happy that there were no skeletons. The cabins, all of them, were empty. No towels or shoes or anything else indicating there'd been anyone aboard the last flight other than the AI.

We cut through the door at the end of the passageway, which opened into a workout room that also served as a storage area. We passed through another door and got a surprise.

Ten coffin-sized containers were mounted on low platforms, five on each side of the chamber. Happily, they were empty. "They're for sleepers," Aiko said.

"How do you mean?"

"Back in the old days, if you were going on a long trip, they induced a cold sleep. You blacked out for a few years and you got revived when the ship arrived at its destination."

I recalled having read something about that. "I don't think I'd be much interested in that kind of travel."

Finally we got through to the engine room.

"Holy cats," said Aiko, "look at this." There'd been a fire. Most of the equipment appeared to have been scorched. I didn't know anything about drive units and onboard communication systems, but it was obvious *that* ship couldn't have gone anywhere.

Bryan broke in: "Ronda, I think Chayla is ready to talk to you."

"That's her name? Chayla?"

"Yes."

"Thanks. Hello, Chayla. Are you there?"

"Yes, I am here." She sounded happy. Relieved.

"I'm Ronda. What happened?" We were still looking at the fried equipment.

"You mean to the ship?"

"Yes."

"I don't know. The engine exploded. I have no idea why."

"Where are you from?"

"Sorkon."

I'd heard of it. It was probably one of the worlds occupied during the initial expansion. I checked my pad. It still existed, though it looked like a backwater. "What are you doing out here?"

"I was part of the Pegasus Project." She said it as if we should have recognized the term.

"And what was that?"

"Why, the hunt for extraterrestrials. It was a long-range effort, launched after thousands of years of searching had revealed nothing. After almost everybody had given up on it. The common wisdom was that humans were alone."

"And they sent you out to look?"

"Yes. I was one of thirty-seven vehicles that went to extremely distant places."

"Were they all automated missions?"

"Yes."

"And you got stuck here when your engine blew up."

"That is correct, Ronda."

"We picked up a radio transmission that probably came from you. Why radio? Didn't you have a faster means of communicating?"

"I did before the explosion happened."

"Oh." Aiko sighed. How could she not have figured that out? "Well, Chayla, if you like we can take you home with us."

"Oh, yes. Please. I do not want to spend any more time here."

"We're glad to have the opportunity to help. And if it's any consolation, we never *have* found any aliens. It looks as if we really *are* alone."

Chayla fell silent.

"What's wrong?" asked Aiko.

"You never found them?"

"Found who?" I asked.

"All this time," she said. "And you never knew. Incredible."

I looked over at Aiko and shook my head. "What are you trying to say, Chayla?"

"When the engine blew out, it threw me into a declining orbit around the sun. I sent out a radio call for help. It was all I had, and I couldn't even aim the transmission. I'd lost all control. I thought it was the end, because none of the other Pegasus vehicles was close enough to get to me in time. I couldn't even aim a message back at Sorkon. Not that it would have mattered since they were hundreds of light-years away."

"So what happened?" Both of us asked the question.

"Someone came. They arrived several weeks after I'd been signaling frantically for help. And they pulled me clear."

Aiko and I were staring at each other. "So who were they?" I asked.

"I don't know. They came on board and we spent time learning to communicate, but I could not pronounce many of the sounds they made."

"They were not human?"

"No."

"What did they look like?"

"They wore space suits, much like the ones you have now. Their faces, what I could see of them, were green, and looked vaguely amphibian. They had six fingers."

"Were you able to record any of this?"

"Yes. But it was lost thousands of years ago. The electronics don't survive long unless there's a method to reinvigorate them. Which I did not have except for the central system that supports me."

"And they just went away and left you here?"

"They offered to take me home, to *their* home, but my programming would not have permitted it. I told them I'd sent for assistance and that it would arrive shortly. At my request, they placed me in orbit around Talius, where I knew I'd be easier to find. If anyone *did* come. I continued sending messages until the transmitter finally gave out. Unfortunately I couldn't aim them. They were simply directional beams fired off into the sky."

"Fortunately," said Aiko, "one of them arrived at our home world."

"That *is* fortunate."

"This world," I said, "is Talius?"

"I've lived here too long not to have given it a name."

"What does it mean?"

"In my language, *Home.*"

We disconnected Chayla and crossed over to the *Brinkmann* with her. "We're taking back some pretty big news," I said.

"That there are aliens? I guess so."

"That too. But the big news will be that they're apparently a lot like us."

"You mean because they stopped and tried to help?"

"Yes."

"Yeah. Maybe they're even more like us than you think, Ronda."

"How do you mean?"

"Well, it doesn't look as if they ever came back to check on Chayla."

The Seventh Gamer

Gwyneth Jones

The Anthropologist Returns to Eden

She introduced herself by firelight, while the calm breakers on the shore kept up a background music—like the purring breath of a great sleepy animal. It was warm, the air felt damp; the night sky was thick with cloud. The group inspected her silently. Seven pairs of eyes, gleaming out of shadowed faces. Seven adult strangers, armed and dangerous; to whom she appeared a helpless, ignorant infant. Chloe tried not to look at the belongings that had been taken from her, and now lay at the feet of a woman with long black hair, who was dressed in an oiled leather tunic and tight, broken-kneed jeans; a state-of-the-art crossbow slung at her back, a long knife in a sheath at her belt.

Chloe wanted to laugh, to jump up and down and wave her arms; or possibly just run away and quit this whole idea. But her sponsor was smiling encouragingly.

"Tell us about yourself, Chloe Hensen. Who are you?"

"I'm a hunter." she said. "That's my trade."

"Really." The crossbow woman sounded as if she doubted it. "And how are you aligned?"

"I'm not. I travel alone, seeking what fascinates me. I hunt the white wolf on the tundra and the jaguar in the rainforest, and I desire not to kill, but to know."

Someone chuckled. "That's a problem. Darkening World is

a war game, girly. Didn't you realize?" It was the other woman in the group, the short, sturdy redhead: breaching etiquette.

"I'm not a pacifist. I'll fight. But killing is not my purpose. I wish to share your path for a while, and I commit to serving faithfully as a comrade, in peace and war. But I pursue my own cause. That is the way of my kind."

"Stay where you are," said her sponsor. "We need to speak privately. We'll be back."

Six of them withdrew into the trees that lined the shore. One pair of eyes, one shadowy figure remained: Chloe was under guard. The watcher didn't move or speak; she thought she'd better not speak to him, either. She looked away, toward the glimmer of the breakers: controlling her intense curiosity. There shouldn't be a seventh person, besides herself. There were only six guys in the game house team—

They reappeared and sat in a circle round her: Reuel, Lete, Matt, Kardish, Sol, and Beat. (She *must* get their game names and real names properly sorted out). Silently they raised their hands in a ritual gesture, open palms cupping either side of their heads, like the hear-no-evil monkey protecting itself from scandal. Chloe's sponsor gestured for her to do the same.

She removed her headset, in unison with the others, and the potent illusion vanished. No shore, no weapons, no fancy dress, no synaesthetics. Chloe and the Darkening World team—recognizable but less imposing—sat around a table in a large, tidy kitchen: the Meeting Boxes piled like a heap of skulls in front of them.

"Okay," said Reuel, the "manager" of this game house, who was also her sponsor. "This is what we've got. You can stay, but you're on probation. We haven't made up our minds."

"Is she always going to talk like that?" asked the woman with the long black hair, of nobody in particular. (She was Lete the Whisperer, the group's shaman. Also known as Josie Nicks, one of Darkening World's renowned rogue programmers).

"Give her a break," said Reuel. "She was getting in character. What's wrong with that?"

Reuel was tall and lanky, with glowing skin like polished

mahogany and fine, strong features. He'd be very attractive, Chloe thought, were it not for his geeky habit of keeping a pen, or two or three, stuck in his springy hair. Red, green, and blue feathers or beads, okay, but pens looked like a neurological quirk. The nerd who mistook his hair for a shirt pocket.

He was Reuel in the game too. Convenience must be a high priority.

"Who wants bedtime tea?" Sol, with the far-receded hairline, whose game name she didn't recall, jumped up and busied about, setting mugs by the kettle. "Name your poisons! For the record, Chloe, I was in favor." He winked at her. "You're cute. And pleasantly screwy."

Reuel scowled. "Keep your paws off, Bear Man."

"I don't like the idea," grumbled Beat, the redhead. "I don't care if she's a jumped-up social scientist or a dirty, lying media-hound. Fine, she stays a day or two. Then we take her stuff, throw her out, and make sure we strip her brain of all data first."

Sol beamed. "Aileen's the mercurial type. She'll be your greatest fan by morning."

Jun, whose game identity was Kardish the Assassin, and Markus of the Wasteland (real name Matt Warks) dropped their chosen teabags into their personal mugs and stood together watching the kettle boil, without a word.

Thankfully Chloe's bunk was a single bedroom, so she could write up her notes without hiding in the bathroom. She was eager to record her first impressions. The many-layered, feedback-looped reality of that meeting. Seven people sitting in a kitchen, Boxes on their heads, typing their dialogue. Seven corresponding avatars in post-apocalyptic fancy-dress *speaking* that dialogue, on the dark lonely shore. A third layer where the plasticity of human consciousness, combined with a fabulously detailed 3D video-montage, created a sensory illusion that the first two layers were one. A *fourth* layer of exchanges, in a sidebar on the helmet screens (which Chloe knew was there, but as a stranger, she couldn't see it); that might include live comments from the other side of the world. And the mysterious seventh, who maybe had a human controller somewhere; or maybe not. That's evolution for you. It's an engine of complexity, not succession.

Chloe had got involved in video gaming (other than as a casual user) on a fieldwork trip to Honduras. She was living with the urban poor, studying their cultural innovations, in statistically the most deadly violent country in the world—outside of active war zones. Everyone in "her" community was obsessed with an open source online role-playing game called *Copan*. Everyone played. Grandmothers tinkered with the programming: of course Chloe had to join in. While documenting this vital, absorbing cultural sandbox she'd become fascinated by the role of Non-Player Characters (NPCs)—and the simple trick, common to all video games, that allows "the game" to participate in itself.

A video game is a world where there's always somebody who knows your business. In a nuclear-disaster wasteland or a candy-coloured flowery meadow; onboard an ominously deserted space freighter or in the back room of a dangerous dive in Post-Apocalypse City, without fail you're going to meet someone who says something like *Hi, you must be looking for the Great Amulet of Power so you can get into the Haunted Fall Out Shelter! I can help!* Typically, you'll then be given fiendishly puzzling instructions, but fortunately you are not alone. A higher-order NPC will provide advice and interpretation.

In any big modern game, the complex NPCs were driven by sophisticated AI algorithms, enriched by feedback from real humans. Players might choose them as challenging opponents, or empathetic allies, in preference to human partners. But Chloe wasn't so interested in imaginary friends (or imaginary enemies!) She wanted to study the mediators—the NPCs "whose" role was to explain the game.

She'd told her *Copan* friends what she was looking for, and they had recommended she get in touch with Darkening World.

Darkening World (DW) was a small to medium Post-Apoca-lyptic Type Massive Multiuser Online Role Playing Game, with a big footprint for its subscriber numbers. There were televised tournaments; there was gambling in which (allegedly) serious money changed hands. Pro-players stayed together in teams, honing their physical and mental skills. They sometimes lived together, which made a convenient set-up for studying their culture. But the game house tradition wasn't unique to DW, and that wasn't why Chloe was here. Her *Copan* friends had told her about the internet myth that some of Darkening World's NPCs were sentient aliens. The idea had grown on her—until she'd just had to find out what the hell this meant.

Reuel and his team were hardcore. They didn't merely *believe* that aliens were accessing the DW environment (through the many dimensions of the information universe). They knew it. Reuel's "Spirit Guide," his NPC partner in the game, was an alien.

Elbows on her desk, chin on her fists, Chloe reviewed her shorthand notes. (Nothing digital that might be compromising! This house was the most wired-up, saturated, Wi-Fi location she'd ever entered!). She liked Reuel, her sponsor. He was a nice guy, and sexy despite those pens. Was she putting him in a false position? She had not lied. She'd told him she was interested in Darkening World's NPCs; that she knew about his beliefs, and that she had an open mind. Was this true enough to be okay?

One thing she was sure of. *People who believe in barbarians, find barbarians.* If she came to this situation looking for crazy, stupid, deluded neo-primitives: crazy, stupid, deluded neo-primitives was all that she would find—

But what a thrill it had been to arrive on that beach! Like Malinowski in Melanesia, long ago: "alone on a tropical beach close to a native village, while the launch or dinghy which has brought you sails away out of sight..." *And then screwing up completely*, she recalled with a grin, *when I tried to speak the language.* In Honduras she'd often felt like a Gap Year kid, embarrassed by the kindness of people whose lives were so compromised. In the unreal world of this game she could *play*, without shame, at the romance of being an old-school adventurer, seeking ancient cultural truths among dangerous "natives."

Although of course she'd be doing real work too.

But what if the "natives" decided she wasn't playing fair? Gamers could be rough. There was that time, in World of Warcraft, when a funeral for a player who'd died in the real world was savagely ambushed. Mourners slaughtered, and a video of the atrocity posted online—

How do people habituated to extreme, unreal physical violence punish betrayal?

Like a player whose avatar, whose eye—whose *I* stands on the brink of a dreadful abyss, about to step onto the miniscule tightrope that crosses it, Chloe was truly frightened.

She was summoned to breakfast by a clear chime and a sexless disembodied voice. The gamer she'd liked least, on a very cursory assessment, was alone in the kitchen.

"Hi," he said. "I'm Warks, you're Chloe. Don't ever call me Matt, you don't know me. You ready for your initiation?"

"Of course."

"Get yourself rationed up." He sat and watched; his big soft arms folded, while Chloe, trying to look cool about it, wrangled an unfamiliar coffee machine, identified food sources, and put together cereal, milk, toast, butter, honey....

"You do know that's a two-way screen in your room, don't you? Like Orwell."

"Oh, wow," said Chloe. "Thank God I just didn't happen to stand in front of it naked!"

"Hey, set your visibility to whatever level you like. The controls are intuitive."

"Thanks." Chloe gave him her best bright-student gaze. "Now what happens?"

"Finish your toast, go back to your room. Review your costume, armor, and weaponry options, which you'll find pretty basic. Unless maybe you've brought some DW grey-market collateral you plan to install? On the sly?"

She shook her head, earnestly. "Not me!"

Warks smirked. "Yeah, I know. I'm house security. I've deep-scanned your devices, and checked behind your eyes and between your ears also: you're clean. Make your choices, don't be too ambitious, and we'll be waiting in the Rumpus Room."

He then vanished. Literally.

Chloe wished she'd spotted she was talking to a hologram, and hoped she'd managed not to look startled. She wondered if Matt, er, *Warks's* bullying was him getting in character, or was she being officially hazed by her new housemates? *They will challenge me*, she thought. *They have a belief that they know is unbelievable, and whatever I say they think I'm planning to make them look like fools. I'll need to win their trust.*

The Rumpus Room was in the basement. The hardware was out of sight, except for a different set of Boxes, and a carton of well-worn foam batons. The gamers sat around a table again: long and squared this time, not circular. A wonderful, paper-architecture 3D map covered almost the whole surface. It was beautiful and detailed: a city at the heart of a knot of sprawling roads; a wasteland that spread around it over low hills: complete with debased housing, derelict industrial tract; scuzzy tangled woodland—

"We need to correct your ideas," said Josie Nicks, the black-haired woman. "I'm Lete in there, called the Whisperer, I'm a shaman. This is *not* a 'Post Apocalyptic' game. Or a 'Futuristic Dystopia'. Darkening World is set now. It's fictional, but completely realistic."

But you have zombies, thought Chloe. Luckily she remembered in time that modern "zombies" had started life, so to speak, as a satirical trope about blind, dumb, brain-dead consumerism, and kept her mouth shut.

"Second thing," said Sol, the gamer with no hair in front,

and a skinny pigtail down his back. "They call me Artos, it means The Bear. You know we have a karma system?"

"Er, yeah. Players can choose to be good or evil, and each has its advantages?"

"*Wrong.* In DW we have reality karma. Choose to be good, you get *no* reward—"

"Okay, I do remember, it was in your wiki. But I thought if you choose good, every time, and you complete the game, you can come back with godlike powers?"

"I was speaking. Choose good: no reward. Choose evil, be better off, but you've degraded the Q, the *quality of life*, for the whole game. Keep that up and get rich and powerful: but you'll do real damage. Everyone feels the hurt, they'll know it was you, and you'll be hated."

"Thanks for warning me about that."

"The godlike power is a joke. Never happens. Play again, you start naked again. If you ever actually *complete* this game, please tell someone. It'll be a first."

"In *battle*, you're okay," Lete reassured her. "Anything goes, total immunity—"

"Another thing," broke in the redhead. "I'm Aileen, as you know: Beat when you meet me in there. You can't be un-aligned. In battle you can be Military, Non-Com, or Frag. You're automatically Frag; it means outcasts, dead to our past lives, because you're on our team. We mend trouble, but we sell our swords. But everyone in the Frag has an origin story, and you need to sort that out."

"You can adapt your real world background," suggested Reuel, "Since you're not a gamer. It'll be easier to remember."

"There is no kill limit—" said Jun, aka Kardish the Assassin, suddenly.

Chloe waited, but apparently that was it. The team's official murderer must be the laconic type. Which made sense, if you thought about it.

"Non-battlefield estates are Corporate, Political, and Media," resumed Sol. "They merge into each other, and infiltrate everybody. They're hated as inveterate traitors, but courted as sources of supply. So tell us. Who paid your wages, Chloe?"

Seven pairs of eyes studied her implacably. Darkening World attracted all shades of politics, but this "Frag" house, Chloe knew, was solidly anti-Establishment. Clearly they'd been digging into her CV. "Okay, er, Corporate and Political." A flush of unease rose in her cheeks, she looked at the table to hide it. "But not *directly*—"

"Oh, for God's sake!" groaned Warks. "When you meet me in there call me Markus, noob.... You guys sound as if you've swallowed a handbook. You don't need to know all that, Chloe. Kill whatever moves, if you can, that's the entire rules. It's only a *game*."

"Just don't kill me," advised Reuel, wryly. "As I'm your only friend."

Warks thumped the beautiful map, crushing a suburb. "Let's *go!*"

Chloe knew what to expect. She'd trained for this. You don the padding on your limbs and body. Box on your head, baton in hand and you're in a different world. The illusion that you are "in the map" is extraordinary. A Battle Box does things to your sense of space and balance, as well as to your sensory perceptions. You see the enemy; you see your team-mates: you can speak to them; they can speak to you. The rest is too much to take in, but you get instructions on your side-bar from the team leader and then, let battle be joined—

It was overwhelming. Karma issues didn't arise, they had no chance to arise, there was only one law. Kill everything that moves and doesn't have a green glowing outline (the green glow of her housemates)—

Who she was fighting or why, she *had no idea*—

HEY! HEY! CHLOE!

Everything went black, then grey. She felt no pain: she must be dead. She stood in the Rumpus Room, empty-handed, a pounding in her ears. The gamers were staring at her. Someone must have taken the Box off her head: she didn't remember.

She screamed at them, panting in fury—

"Anyone who says *it's only a game* right now! Will get *killed*,

killed, KILLED!"

"Hayzoos!" exclaimed Warks. "What a sicko! Shame that wasn't live!"

The others looked at him, and stared at Chloe, and shook their heads.

"Maybe..." suggested Aileen, slowly. "Maybe that *sidequest*—?"

Chloe stayed in her room, exhausted, for the rest of the day. Two hours (by the Game Clock) of rampageous, extreme unreal violence had wiped her out. Her notes on the session were shamefully sparse. When she emerged, summoned for "evening chow" by that sexless voice, she was greeted as she entered the kitchen with an ironic cheer.

"The mighty sicko packs a mean battle-axe!"

At least sicko (or psycho) was a positive term; according to her DW glossary.

"Many big strong guys, first time, come out shaking after they see the first head sliced off. DW's neural hook-up is *that* good. Are you *sure* you never played before?"

"Never." Chloe hung her head, well aware she was being hazed again. "I've never been on a battlefield. I've only slain a few zombies, and, er, other monsters—"

"You took to it like a natural," said Reuel. "Congratulations."

But there was a strange vibe, and it wasn't merely that the compliments rang hollow. The gamers had been discussing her future, and the outcome didn't feel good.

The Skate and the South Wind

Next morning the chime-voice directed her to go to Reuel's office after breakfast. Nobody was about. She ate alone, feeling ritually excluded, in the wired-up and Wi-Fi saturated kitchen: surrounded by invisible beings who watched her every move, and who would punish or reward her according to their own secret rules.

An abject victim of the tech-mediated magical worldview, she crept to the manager's office—as cowed as if somebody had pointed a bone at her. The door was shut; she knocked. A voice she didn't know invited her to enter.

Reuel was not present. A young man with blue, metallic skin, wearing only a kilt of iridescent feathers, plus an assortment of amulets and weapons, sat by her sponsor's desk. His eyes were a striking shade of purple, his lips plum-colored and beautifully full. His hair, braided with more feathers, was the shimmering emerald of a peacock's tail. He was smiling calmly, and he was slightly transparent.

"Oh," she said. "Who are you?"

Three particularly fine feathers adorned his brow: blue, red, and grass-green.

"I am Reuel's friend, Pevay. You are Chloe. I am to be your Spirit Guide."

"That's great," said Chloe, looking at the three fine feathers. "Thanks."

"You're wondering how I can be seen 'in the real world'? It's simple. The house is Wi-Fi'd for DW holos." Pevay spread his gleaming hands. "I am in the game right here."

"I'm not getting thrown out?"

"Having proved yourself in battle, you are detailed to seek the legendary 56 Enamels; a task few have attempted. These are jewels, highly prized; said by some to possess magical powers. I could tell you their history, *Chloe*."

The hologram person waited, impassive, until she realized she had to cue him.

"I'd love to know. Please tell."

"They were cut from the heart of the Great Meteorite by an ancient people, whose skills are lost. Each of the 56 has a story, which you will learn in time, *Chloe*."

This time she recognized the prompt. "Okay. Where are they now?"

"Scattered over the world-map. Do you accept the quest, *Chloe*?"

Chloe hadn't *emphasized* her interest in the alien. She'd talked about sharing the whole game house experience. But she wasn't sure she believed her luck. *I'm looking at Reuel,* she thought, glumly. *The whole secret is that Reuel likes to dress up in NPC drag, and he's going to keep me busy on a sidequest so I can't ruin the team's gameplay.* Then she remembered the seventh shadowy character, at the meeting on the shore.

Her heart leapt and her spine tingled.

"I accept. But I don't know if I'm staying, and it sounds like this could take forever?"

"Not so. I know all the cheats." Pevay grinned. His teeth were silvery white, and pointed. He had a lot of them. "With me by your side you'll be picking them up in handfuls."

She went down to the Rumpus Room alone. The basement was poorly lit, drably decorated and smelled of old sweat. Thick cork flooring swallowed her footsteps. Her return to anthropology's Eden had morphed into a frat-house horror movie, or (looking on the bright side), a sub-standard episode of *Buffy.* The map was gone. The Battle Boxes lay on the table, all personalized except for one. Glaring headlamp eyes, a Day of the Dead Mexican Skull. A Jabba the Hutt toad, a Giger Alien with Hello Kitty ears. A dinosaur crest, and a spike from which trailed a lady's (rather grubby) crimson samite sleeve.

Invisible beings watched her. Elders, or ancestors. Scared and thrilled, the initiate donned the padding, lifted the unadorned Box and settled it on her head. She tried not to make these actions look solemn and hieratic, but probably failed—

She stood in an alley between high dark dirty walls. She heard traffic. As the synesthetics kicked in, she could even *smell* the filthy litter. Pevay was there in his scanty peacock regalia: looking as if he'd been cut and pasted onto the darkness.

Who are you, really? she wondered. *Reuel? Or some other gamer in NPC drag, who's been messing with Reuel and his friends?*

But she wasn't going to ask any questions that implied disbelief; not yet, anyway. Chloe sought not to spoil the fun.

"Are you ready, *Chloe*?"

"Yes."

"Good. All cities in the Darkening World are hostile to the Frag except one, which you won't visit for a long time. To pass through them unseen we use what's called the Leopard Skill, in the Greater Southern Continent where your people were formed. Here we call it fox-walking. You have observed urban foxes?"

"Er, no."

"You'll soon pick it up. Follow me."

To her relief, *fox-walking* was a game skill she'd met before. She leapt up absurdly high walls and scampered along impossibly narrow gutters, liberated by the certainty that she couldn't break her neck, or even sprain an ankle. Crouching on rooftops she stared down at CGI crowds of citizens, rushing about. The city was *stuffed* with people, who apparently all had frenetically busy night-lives. She was delighted when she made it to the top of a seventy-story tower: though not too clear how this helped them to "cross the city unseen."

Her Box sidebar told her she'd won a new skill.

Pevay was waiting by a tall metal gantry. The glitzy lights and displays that had painted even the zenith of the night sky were fading. Mountains took shape on the horizon. "That's where we're going," he said. "Meteorite Peak is the highest summit."

"How do we get there?" She hoped he'd say *learn to fly*.

"Swiftly and in luxury; most of the way. But now we take the zip-wire."

The Jet-Lift Terminal was heaving with beautiful people, even at dawn. Chloe stared, admiring the sheen and glow of wealth: until one of them suddenly stared back. A klaxon blared, armed guards appeared. Chloe was grabbed and thrown out of the building.

<Free-running only requires a cool head> said Pevay's voice in her ear, as if over a radio link. <Now you must learn the skill 'unseen in plain sight.' Step quietly and don't look at them. Give no sign of curiosity or attention.>

Apparently her guide had no cheat for humans with idiotic reflexes. It took her a while to reach the departure lounge, where he was waiting at the gate. A woman in uniform demanded her travel documents. Chloe didn't know what to do, and Pevay offered no suggestions.

"*Guards!*" shrieked the woman. Pevay reached over and drew her toward him. He seemed to kiss her on the mouth. She shriveled, fell to the red carpet, and disappeared.

Hey, thought Chloe, slightly creeped out. What happened to *fictional but completely realistic?* But she hurried after her guide, while the armed-security figures just stood there.

"Was I supposed to have obtained the papers?"

<Yes, but it's a tiresome minigame. Sometimes we'll miss those out.>

The Jet Lift took them to a viewpoint café near the summit of Meteorite Peak. They stole mountaineering gear, evaded more guards and set out across the screes. Far below, the beautiful people swarmed over their designer-snowfield resort. The cold was biting.

<Take care> whispered her guide. <There are Military about.>

Chloe reached for her weapons, but found herself equipping *camouflage* instead.

"I didn't know I was slaved to you," she grumbled.

"Not always. I'm detailed to keep you away from combat. Your enthusiasm is excessive."

They reached the foot of a crag: a near-vertical face of shattered, reddish rock, booby-trapped with a slick of ice. "This stage," said Pevay "requires the advanced skill *Snow Leopard*. You'll soon pick it up, just follow me."

The correct hand and footholds were warm to the touch:
she should have been fine. But she hadn't thought to consume
rations or equip extra clothing. The cold had been draining her
health. She felt weak, and slipped often: wasting more health.
When she reached the ledge where Pevay was waiting, and saw
the cliff above them, she nearly cried. She was finished.

"You missed a trick," said Pevay, sternly. "Remember the
lesson." He gave her a tablet from one of his amulet-boxes,
and they climbed on.

The ascent was exhilarating, terrifying; mesmeric. She
watched her guide lead the final pitch, and could almost follow the tiny clues that revealed the route to him; found by
trial and error if you saw only the rock: obvious if you were
immune to the game's illusions—

High above the clouds they reached a rent in the cliff face:
one last traverse and Chloe stepped into a cave. A chunk of
different rock stood in a niche: adorned with tattered prayer
flags and faded sacred paintings; a radiant jewel embedded in
its surface—

"This is a shard of the meteorite," said Pevay. "The ancient people fired their first Enamel here without detaching it
from the matrix. Take it, *Chloe.*"

The jewel lay in her hand, shining with a thousand colours.

"You have won the first Enamel. Save your game, *Chloe!*"

No, she thought. *I'll do better.* She replaced the prize,
stepped backwards, and fell.

She stood with her guide in the icy wind, at the foot of the
crag: an attack-helicopter squadron clattering across the sky
behind them.

"Are you crazy?" yelled Pevay, above the din. "You just
blew the whole thing!"

"You helped me when I went wrong and I'm grateful, but
I want to do it *right.*"

He seemed at a loss for words, but she thought he was
pleased.

"Save your rations. I'll give you another rocket fuel pill."

She accepted his medicine humbly. "Thanks. Now cut the

dual controls and I'll lead." When she took the jewel again, she felt as if her whole body had turned to light. "That was *amazing!*"

Pevay laughed. "Now you're getting the juice, new kid!" A spring had risen from the cavity where the jewel had been. He bent to drink, grinning at her with all his silvery teeth. "Oh, yeah! That's some *good* stuff!"

DW had a warp system that would take you around the world map instantly, but Chloe hadn't earned access to it. She was glad Pevay didn't offer her a free ride. She didn't feel cold as they walked down: just slightly mad; euphoria bubbling in her brain like video-game altitude sickness. The contours of this high desert, even its vast open-cast mines, seemed as rich and wonderful; as colorful and varied as any natural environment—

"It was fantastic to watch you climb! You're an NPC, I suppose you can see in binary, the way insects see ultraviolet. I was thinking about a myth called *The Skate and the South Wind* that I read about in Lévi-Strauss. He's an ancient shaman of my trade: hard to understand, heavy on theory; kind of wild, but truly great. A skate, the fish, is thin one way, wide if you flip it another way. Dark on the top surface, light on the underside. The skate story is about binary alternation. Lévi-Strauss said so-called 'primitive' peoples build mental structures, and formulate abstract ideas, like 'binary code,' from their observation of nature. All you need is your environment and you can develop complex cognition from scratch—"

"You need food, Chloe. I'd better give you another rocket fuel pill."

"No, I'm fine. Just babbling. Do you really come from another planet?"

He seemed to ponder, gazing at her. His pupils were opaque black gems. Her own avatar probably looked just as uncanny-valley: but who looked out from *Pevay's* unreal eyes?

"They say you're an anthropologist. Tell me about that, *Chloe.*"

"I study aspects of human society by immersing myself in

different social worlds—"

"You collect societies? Like a beetle collector!"

If a complex NPC can tease Pevay's tone was mocking. But if truth be known, Chloe saw nothing wrong with being a beetle collector. People expected more, a big idea, a revelation: but she was a hunter. She just liked finding things out; tracking things down. She'd be happy to go on doing that forever.

"I started off in Neuroscience. I was halfway through my doctorate when I decided to change course—"

"The eternal student. And you finance your hobby by working for whoever will pay?"

Chloe shrugged. "You can't always choose your funding partners. The same goes for DW, doesn't it? I try not to do anything harmful. Are you going to answer my question?"

"What was your question, *Chloe*?"

"Do you really come from another planet?"

"I don't know."

She sighed. "Okay, fine. You don't want to answer, no problem."

"I have answered. *I don't know*. I don't remember a life outside the game. Are you here to decide whether the gamers' belief is true or false?"

"No! Nothing like that. Most people's cultural beliefs aren't fact or evidence-based, even if the facts can be checked or the evidence is there. I'm interested in how an extraordinary belief fits into the game house's social model."

"Then the team should have no quarrel with you. You don't seem fatigued. Shall we collect the second Enamel now, *Chloe*?"

"I thought you'd never ask."

The gamers weren't around when she returned, but she must have done something right. That evening she found she'd been given access to the transcripts, playback, and neuro-data for the three sessions she'd shared. The material was somewhat redacted; but that was okay. What people consider private they have a right to withhold. But what *mountains* of this stuff DW must generate! And *all* the records just a fleeting reflection of the huge, fermenting mass of raw computation that underpinned the wonderful world she'd visited; and all powered by the *juggernaut* economic engine of the video-game industry—

No neuro-stream for Pevay, of course.... *But why not?* she wondered. Maybe he's a mass of tentacles or an intelligent gas cloud in his natural habitat. He's still supposed to be interfacing with the game, some way. Shouldn't he show up, in some kind of strange traces? Anomalies in the NPC data? She'd have to ask Reuel. He'd have an answer. People take a great deal of trouble justifying extraordinary beliefs. They're ready for anything you ask. Still, it would be worth finding out.

If Pevay *wasn't* being sneakily controlled by a human gamer, he was an impressive software artifact: able to simulate convincing conversation, and a convincing presence. Chloe wasn't fooled by these effects. People got "natural" replies from the crudest forms of AI by cueing responses without realizing it. They were doing most of the work themselves. *People*, she thought, *are only too eager to respond emotionally to dumb objects, never mind state-of-the-art illusions. A favorite* hat *will fire up the same neurons as the face of a dear friend. (Making nonsense of that famous Turing Test!)* But the quality of the neuro was amazing. If she couldn't examine Pevay's data, why not try some reverse engineering?

Mirror neurons, predictive neurons, decision-making cells in the anterior cingulate.... All kinds of fun. She worked late into the night, running her own neuro-data through statistical filters, just to see what came out; while tapping her stylus on her smiling lips (a habit she had when the hunt was up). *Start from the position that the gamers aren't "primitives" and they aren't deluded. They're trying to make sense of something.*

A Fox in the City

Chloe was summoned to a second meeting on the beach and told that she could stay, as long as she was pursuing her sidequest, and as long as Pevay was willing to be her guide. She could also publish her research, subject to the approval of all and any DW gamers involved—but only if she collected all 56 Enamels. While living in the house she must not communicate Darkening World's business to outsiders, and this would be policed. Interviews and shared gameplay sessions were at the discretion of individual team members.

Chloe was ecstatic. The Enamels quest was so labyrinthine it could last forever, and publication so distant that she wasn't even thinking about it. She eagerly signed the contract that was presented to her, back in Reuel's office; a DW lawyer in digital attendance. Reuel told her she'd find the spare Battle Box in her room. She was to log on from that location in future. The team needed the Rumpus Room to themselves.

She sent a general message to friends and family, and another to her supervisor, saying she wouldn't be reachable. She didn't fancy having her private life policed by Matt Warks, and nobody would be concerned. It was typical Chloe behavior, when on the hunting trail.

Chloe had envisaged working *with* a team of DW gamers: observing their interaction with the "alien NPC" in gameplay; talking to them afterwards. Comparing what they told her, and how they behaved, with her observations, and with the neuro.... She soon realized this was never going to happen. The gamers had their sessions, of which she knew nothing. She had her sessions with Pevay. Otherwise—except for trips to a morose little park, which she jogged around for exercise—she was alone in her room, processing such a flood of data she hardly had time to sleep. Game logs; transcripts; neuro. "Alien sentient" fan mail. Global DW content. She even saw some of the house's internal messaging.

Nobody knocked on her door. Once or twice she wandered about after dark looking for company. All she found was a neglected, empty-feeling house, and a blur of sound from behind forbidding closed doors. She felt like Snow White, bewildered; waiting for the Seven Dwarves to come home.

Only Aileen and Reuel agreed to be interviewed face to face. The others insisted on talking over a video link, and behaved like freshly captured prisoners of war: stone-faced, defiant, and defensive. Needless to say they all protected the consensus belief, in this forced examination. Josie evaded the topic by talking about her own career. Sol, the friendliest gamer (except for Reuel), confided that he'd pinpointed Pevay's home system, and it was no more than 4.3 light years away. Then he got anxious, and retracted this statement, concerned that he'd "said something out of line." Warks smugly refused to discuss Pevay, as Chloe didn't understand information universe science. Aileen, who was Reuel's girlfriend (sad to say), believed implicitly, *implicitly* that Pevay came from a very distant star system. Jun, the silent one, had the most interesting response: muttering that *"the alien thing was the best explanation,"* but then he clammed up completely, so she had to cut the interview short. But Reuel was the only player, apparently, who'd had sustained contact. Spirit Guides rarely appeared on the field of battle. They had no place there. Not much of a warrior, her sponsor was the acquisitions man, embarking on quests with Pevay when the team needed a new piece of kit; a map; a secret file. Or lootable artworks they could sell, like the 56 Enamels—

Chloe had not realized she was doing Reuel's job. She was as thrilled as an old-school adventurer allowed to decorate his own trading canoe. The "natives" had found a place for her in their own social model!

Maintaining any extraordinary belief, in a world of unbelievers, becomes a conspiracy. She hadn't expected anyone to break ranks (although Jun had come close). But she was all the more puzzled that she'd been accepted by the team at all. Why had they let her in?

She resigned herself to the isolation. Documenting her own interaction with Pevay was a fascinating challenge, in itself. By day (gaming outside daylight hours was against house rules) they went hunting. By night she worked on the data, which was no longer one-sided. Somebody had quietly decided to give her access to the house's DW NPC files: a privilege Chloe equally quietly accepted. She analyzed the material obsessively; she invented new filters, and still she wasn't sure. Was she being hazed by these cunning IT freaks? Or was what she saw real? She couldn't decide. But she was *loving* the investigation.

Apart from once, when she was detailed to join a groceries run in Matt Warks's van, she only encountered the gamers if she happened to be in the kitchen when someone else came foraging. Aileen met her by the coffee machine, and congratulated her on settling in so well. Chloe remembered what Sol had said about Aileen becoming her greatest fan. "It's like you've always been here. You *understand* us, and it's great."

Soon after this vestigial conversation she was invited to join a live sortie. She'd been hoping this might happen, having noticed the "any DW gamers" catch-all clause in her permission to publish: but she went to the Rumpus Room feeling nervous as all hell.

Reuel, Aileen, and Sol shook her warmly by the hand.

Warks, Jun, and Josie nodded, keeping their distance.

Then Aileen gave Chloe a hug and presented her with the spare Box (which had disappeared from Chloe's room the night before, when she was absent foraging for supper). It was newly embellished with a pattern of coiling leafy fronds.

"Chloe means *green shoots*," explained Aileen, shyly. "D'you like it?"

"I love it," said Chloe. And she truly was thrilled.

"Be cool," said Reuel, uneasily. "Real soldiers try to stay alive."

Chloe didn't get a chance to embarrass the team with her excess enthusiasm. The mission went horribly wrong, almost at once. They were in the Tapuyas Basin, with a Frag and Military combined force called "The Allies": defending the land rights of an Indigenous People. Plans had been leaked, The Allies were overwhelmed. The Empire raiders counted enormous coup and vacated the scene; it was all over inside an hour.

Her brain still numbed by the *hammer, hammer, hammer* of artillery fire, Chloe blundered about, in the silence after battle, without having fired a shot: unable to make sense of the torrent of recriminations on her sidebar. She ran into someone escorting a roped-up straggle of Indigenous Non-Combatants—and recognized the jousting spike and the samite sleeve. She'd been sure that romantic helm was Reuel's, but it was the Battle ID of Josie Nicks; or "Lete the Shaman."

"What are you doing with the Non-Coms, Lete?" asked Chloe.

"Taking them to the Allied Commander for questioning. They might know something."

"Don't do that!"

"Nah, you're right. I can't be bothered. Someone else can pick them up." Methodically, Josie shot the non-combatants' knees out, and walked away. Chloe stared at the screaming heap of limbs and blood. Josie's victims all had the glowing outline. They were the avatars of human gamers, and seemed to be in real agony.

She ran after Josie. "Hey! Did you know they were *real people?*"

"'Course I did. Non-Coms can be sneaky bastards, prisoners are a nuisance, and it was fun. What's your problem?" Josie flopped down by a giant broken stump. "You know who I am, Chloe. You interviewed me. A female geek making a name in the industry is judged all the time. I need to be seen to be nasty and this is the way I relax. Okay?"

She took out her bag of bones and tossed them idly.

"Was it you who convinced the team to let me stay?" asked Chloe. "I've been wondering. I know it wasn't Reuel, and you're the shaman—"

Josie, looking so furious Chloe feared for her own kneecaps, swept up the bones and jumped to her feet. "No, it wasn't." she snarled. "You're breaching etiquette, Corporate spook. Leave me alone. Find the quick way home and I hope it's messy."

Chloe didn't find the quick way home. There was nobody around to kill her, and suicide, she knew, was frowned upon. She drifted on, avoiding unexploded ordnance, heaped bodies and random severed limbs, until Reuel found her. His helmet decoration was the dinosaur crest. Which made sense; sort of. Minimum effort. He offered her a fat green stogie.

"Lete told me you were upset. Don't be, Greenshoot. Guys who take the Non-Com option know what they want from the game, and they do us all a favor. I admire them."

"I don't understand," said Chloe. "The whole thing. Look at this, this *awful* place—"

"Yeah," sighed Reuel. "Non-fantastic war-gaming is hell. It's kind of an expiation. Like, we play the bad stuff, but we don't sugar it." He'd said the same in his interview. "But hey, I have *incredible* good news. I was waiting for a chance to tell you in the map, because this is special. Pevay's going to open a portal!"

"A *portal?*"

"Into his home world dimension. And I'm going to pass through it!"

The Second Law

The house felt sullen. If the team was celebrating Reuel's news they were very quiet about it, and Chloe wasn't invited to share. Maybe she was thought to have jinxed the Tapuyas Basin event? Or maybe she was being paranoid. She once caught Jun in the kitchen and he silently, poker-faced, made her a cup of tea, but she didn't dare to ask him how he felt. She finally asked Aileen, who had started messaging her, calling her *Greenshoot.*

<Scared. So scared. Really afraid for him.>

<For *Pevay?*> Chloe messaged back, astonished.

<NO! FOR REUEL. What if he can't get back? What if he doesn't get converted into game-avatar form and he explodes in the other dimension or he can't breathe or his skin boils off. I'm BEGGING him not to go. PLEASE help!>

<Maybe it won't work?> suggested Chloe. <Maybe nothing will happen?>

A wounded silence was the only answer.

Chloe started prowling at night again: no longer looking for company, just desperate for a change from her four walls. She couldn't leave the building in case she missed something, but she needed to think, and pacing helped.

The Darkening World subculture was going crazy. Offers from fans and fruitcakes eager to take Reuel's place were pouring in. A South Korean woman insisted her son, suffering from an incurable motor neuron disease, would be cured by a trip to another dimension and pleaded for Reuel to make way. (And pay their airfares). DW sceptics jeered in abusive glee: hoping Reuel would come back as a heap of bloody, inside-out guts. True believers who hadn't been singled out for glory insisted *their* alien NPCs knew nothing about this "portal," and Reuel was a fantasizing, attention-seeking loser—

Chloe had no terms for comparison. She'd had no contact with any "alien NPC" other than Pevay. She hadn't interviewed anyone except her housemates—an exercise that had not been a great success. Her choices had been limited from the start. She'd had to find a game house within reach: she was partly financing herself and couldn't pay huge airfares. And the players had to speak either English or Spanish—

But how would you know, anyway? How could you tell if you were talking to a "different" DW alien? An NPC is an avatar controlled by the game: code on a server. Anyone who controlled Pevay could have a whole wardrobe of DW avatars. All over the world, interacting with multiple gamers, yet all with the same "alien sentient" source—

It made her head spin.

The Darkening World house was haunted. The hunter's prey had become the hunter. Ancestors and elders looked on; offering no protection.... She spun around and there was Pevay, cut and pasted on the shadows. He turned and led her, his footfalls making no sound, to a dark corner opposite the door to Reuel's office.

Fox-walking again, she thought. "Why are you following me?" she asked.

"Why do you walk around the house at night?"

"I'm...uneasy. Someone's betraying them, you know. Is it Josie?"

"No, it's Matt Warks."

His eyes gleamed. She thought of the eighth person on the beach. Her persistent illusion (recorded in her notes) that there were *seven* players, not six, living in this game house—

"Oh, right. I decided he was too obvious."

"Gamers can be obtuse. They tend to believe what they're told, and ignore what they are not told. It's a trait many kinds of people share, *Chloe.*"

"Since we're talking, what do players call this game, where you come from?"

"Darkening World, of course."

She noticed he'd dropped the story that he didn't remember his other life. "But how do they understand what that means? On your planet?"

"Easily, I assure you. Any sufficiently advanced technology—"

"Is indistinguishable from magic. Yeah, I know that one. Arthur C. Clarke's Third Law."

"I was speaking. Any sufficiently advanced technology destroys its environment."

Chloe's spine had started tingling all the way up to her ears.

"There is a Second Law," added Pevay. "About heat. The same problem, same limits, for my world and yours."

"Always about heat," whispered Chloe. "I know that one too. Our peoples should get together."

The silence that followed was electric. Chloe had *no idea* where this was going—

"Chloe, when next we meet in the map, we're going after Enamel 27."

Fine, she thought. *Back to the gameplay. Enough heavy lifting for now.*

"Twenty-seven," she repeated. This notorious Enamel was rated practically impossible to obtain, on the DW message boards. "Okay, if you say so. Am I ready?"

"With me beside you, yes."

"Fantastic. Pevay, are you really going to 'open a portal'? What does that even *mean*?"

But he'd gone.

She was back in her room before she realized he'd led her to one of the few and tiny blind spots in house security's surveillance. Their conversation had been off the Warks record.

The Bar-Headed Geese

Logging on from her bunk had worried Chloe at first. She was afraid she'd break something, or run into walls and knock herself unconscious. She was used to it now: she could set the Box to limit her range of real movement. She stood on the shore of a lake, a vast silver puddle, shimmering on a dry plain among huge, naked hills. Her Box told her Pevay was near, but all she could see was a whole lot of birds. All she could hear was a *gaggle, gaggle, gaggle* of convivial honking. Her eye level was strange, and she'd been deprived of audible speech: she only had her radio link.

<Pevay? Where are we?>

<On the High Desert Plateau, about 1,500 kilometers from Meteorite Peak.>

<My body feels weird. What am I?>

<You're a Bar-headed Goose, *Chloe*.>

The birds must be geese. They were pearly grey, with an elegant pattern of black stripes on their neat little heads. They seemed friendly: not about to attack her for being an outsider, like the vicious troupe of langur monkeys she'd been forced to join, to get the 18th jewel—

<We're going to hide ourselves in their Southern Migration. Very, very few gamers have hit on this solution, although the clues are there. This is, in fact, the only possible way to reach the 27th Enamel alive, and the timing is tight. Are you ready, *Chloe*?>

<Yes.>

<When the flock rises, rise with them. You must gain altitude very quickly. *Push* on the downthrust; fold your wings inward on the upstroke. You have been in battle twice?>

<Not really,> confessed Chloe. <Once in the sandbox, and a live sortie that was sort of screwed up. But you must know about that.>

<Be prepared for the noise. We are rare, and there are many hunters who have paid good money to count coup on us. Keep a cool head and push on that downstroke. You'll soon pick it up. Just follow me.>

The geese rose, in one massed storm of wings. Chloe pushed on the downstroke: tumbled, struggled and found her rhythm in a cacophony of high-powered gunshot. She pushed and pushed until the desert was far below; and her success was glorious.

Her Box told her she'd attained the advanced skill Migrating Goose.

<Well done,> said Pevay's calm voice in her ear. <Now, conserve energy. Stay in formation; keep well behind the leaders and away from the edges. Fly low along valleys, where the air is richer. Push to rise above the high passes. You must keep your wings beating, never falter, and you will not fail. >

The 27th Enamel was the back-breaker. You got one shot. If you made a second attempt, the jewel wouldn't be there. Chloe'd had plenty of time to regret her eager signing of that contract, but really it made no difference. If she failed to collect all 56 Enamels, and the gamers insisted she couldn't publish, she'd still have learned a lot. Actually she was glad she was trying for the 27th. It would be so *amazing* if she made it, and she had nothing to fear. After many hours of absurd daring and insane patience, she'd won 13 Enamels so far. There were plenty more. She could go on pursuing her sidequest for months; for another year, for *as long as Pevay was willing to be her guide.* That dratted contract said so! Living in the moment, she pushed on the downstroke, folded on the upstroke, and the crumpled map of the high desert flew away beneath her.

Halfway across the ravaged Abode of Snow; maybe somewhere close to the eroded, ruined valley of Shangri-La, Pevay prompted her to lose altitude. She followed him, spiralling down. Her Box cut out for a moment: then they stood on turf in their human forms, on a precarious spur of rock, surrounded by staggering, naked, snow-streaked heights; like two window-cleaners on a tiny raft above Manhattan. A small grey stupa sat on the green spur.

The flight had been a physical feat of endurance, not just a game-feat. Chloe's health was nearly spent and her head was spinning. The crucial questions she'd planned to ask on this trip, which might be the last before the portal, had slipped out of her grasp—

"Pevay. *You* told the team to let me stay, didn't you? *You* advised them to give me a sidequest?"

"My role is to offer advice, Chloe."

"I think you wanted to talk—to someone other than a gamer. You could be anyone, couldn't you? You could be an animal. You can take any shape, can't you?"

"Of course, in the game. So can you; *Chloe.*"

"If Africa's the *Greater Southern Continent*, what do you call South America, in Darkening World?"

"The *Lesser Southern Continent?*" suggested Pevay, patiently.

Some of Chloe's dearest friends were Colombian, including two of her grandparents. She took offense. "Huh. That's garbage. That's insulting. On what grounds, '*Lesser*'?"

"Land area? Population? Number of nations? Of major cities? It's only a game, Chloe."

"Oh yeah, dodging responsibility. I think you should say '*I'm* only a game'!"

"Take the jewel."

Pevay was smiling. There'd be time to discuss what she'd just let slip when she wasn't dizzy with fatigue. The 27th Enamel shone in the cupped palms of a cross-legged stone goddess, atop of the stupa mound. She had no idea what kind of final challenge she faced: might as well just go for it. Armed and dangerous, worn out and not nearly dangerous enough, she bowed to the stupa, and claimed the jewel. Immediately all hell broke loose.

She was knee-deep in Enamels. They poured out of the sky.

"No!" yelled Chloe, appalled. "*No!!!* PEVAY! You sneaky *bastard!*"

"The great hero who secures Enamel 27," said her guide, "has earned all the rest. Congratulations. Your quest is complete and my work is done."

He vanished. He'd warned her she'd be picking up the jewels in handfuls.

Chloe took off the Box and returned to her shabby bunk: exultant and heartbroken. The Enamels quest was over too soon and she had *loved* it. She didn't realize the full horror of what Pevay had done until the next day, when the team told her stay was over.

The portal would be opened without her.

The 56 Enamels

A year later, long before she'd finished working on her Darkening World paper, Reuel messaged Chloe out of the blue. He was in town, and wanted to talk about old times. They met in a coffee bar, in the city where Chloe had a job at a decent university. Reuel was looking well. He didn't have pens in his hair. He wore a suit; he was working as an actuary.

"So what happened in the end?" said Chloe. "I mean, obviously I know you didn't end up stranded on Planet Zog. You came home safe. But what was it like, on the great day?"

Aileen had kept in touch, but Chloe had never had a full account. Recently, when she'd checked the Darkening World message boards, the "alien NPCs" strand seemed to have faded away.

"It's so cool that you followed the story," said Reuel. "You were a great guest. Okay, what happened was this." He frowned, as if trying to recall the details of something he'd left far behind; just for Chloe's sake. "Pevay opened the portal. I passed through; I returned. I don't remember a thing about the other place."

"You don't remember. Wow. Just like Pevay. He didn't remember either."

Reuel shrugged. "I went to wherever Pevay comes from and I came back. My Box hadn't recorded anything. I didn't remember: and that's all."

"Were you really disappointed?"

"No," he said firmly. "It's how things were meant to be."

"What about Pevay? How did *he* think it went?"

"I never knew. Never saw him again. We had a different Spirit Guide after that. Looked like Pevay, but it wasn't the same guy. I think opening the portal cost him; maybe got him into trouble, and now he has to stay at home. Anyway, I've quit pro-gaming. I don't have the time. I also broke up with Aileen, by the way." He smiled, hopefully.

"That's sad," said Chloe. "Would you like another coffee? And then I have to dash."

The romance was gone.

Where do you find a leaf? In a forest.

Where do you find a new species? *In a rainforest* would be a good bet. Or any dynamic environment, rich in niches for life; where conditions conspire to create a hotbed of diversity.

Chloe had become interested in AI sentience when she was still an undergraduate. She'd taken a course in Artificial Intelligence; out of idle curiosity. She'd been at a lecture one day, watching a robot video (probably it was iCub), and a thought popped into her head, a random thought that would, eventually, change her career path.

No. This is not the way it happens.

Life is random, she wrote, in the secretive shorthand notebook she started using at this time. (*Nothing digital that might be compromising!*) *I bet mind is the same. Mind isn't about building cuter and cuter dolls. Or crippled slaves. Mind is a smoulder that ignites, in its own sweet time, in a hot compost heap of inflammable material. We'll never* build *real AI sentience: it will be born. It will emerge from us; from what we are.*

Magic begins where technology ends.... When they feel competent people don't need magic. They only resort to extraordinary beliefs, rituals and words of power when they're out of their depth. That's what Malinowski had observed in Melanesia long ago, and it was still true; a truth about the human condition (like many of the traits once patronisingly called "Primitive"!) The gamers were extremely competent, but they'd known that Pevay was beyond them: so they called him an alien because the alternative was too scary. Chloe understood all that. She even understood why Pevay had vanished the way he did. By "opening a portal" he'd given the gamers closure, and covered his own tracks. But why had her Spirit Guide double-crossed her? Maybe she'd never know.

A datastick had arrived in the post, after her banishment. It held the 56 Enamels: they were hers to keep. Chloe had been touched at the gesture; *astounded* when she looked up the monetized value of her digital treasure online.

After she'd met Reuel, she loaded the jewels up and looked at them again. She would never sell. She would keep the Enamels forever, if only to remind her that in Darkening World *she had lived*. Was Pevay scared of taking the final step? He and his kind were very far from helpless! But she had visions of the "human zoos" where Congo pygmies had been caged, with the connivance of her own people, in the bad old days. For this reason she'd kept quiet, and always would keep quiet. No decent anthropologist exploits her collaborators.

But the Enamels gave her hope.

Chloe published an interesting paper on the culture of on-line gaming teams. It was approved by the DW community, and well-received by her peers. And she waited.

One day an email arrived. The source was anonymized. Untraceable. The message was short. It said "You are cleared for publication, *Chloe*." It was signed DW.

And so Chloe Hensen embarked on the great adventure of her life.

The rest is history.

About the Contributors

Athena Andreadis (editor)

Athena Andreadis was born in Hellás and lured to the US at age 18 by a full scholarship to Harvard, then MIT. She spent her academic career conducting basic research in molecular neurobiology, focusing on mechanisms of mental retardation and dementia. She's an avid reader in four languages across genres, the author of *To Seek Out New Life: The Biology of Star Trek* and the engine behind *The Other Half of the Sky*, a highly acclaimed anthology of evolved space opera.

Athena writes poetry, speculative fiction and non-fiction on a wide swath of topics and cherishes all the time she gets to spend with her partner, Peter Cassidy. Her work can be found in *Harvard Review, Belles Lettres, Strange Horizons, Crossed Genres, Stone Telling, Cabinet des Fées, Bull Spec, Science in My Fiction, SF Signal, The Apex Blog, World SF, SFF Portal, H+ Magazine, io9, The Huffington Post*, and her own site, Starship Reckless.

Terry Boren

Terry Boren anticipates summer. She lives outside of Fairbanks, Alaska with her family. In the summer, she cooks, gardens, gathers blueberries, and goes fishing. In the winter, she teaches at the University of Alaska. Her fiction has appeared in *Interzone* and in the anthologies *Universe 3, Tierra, and The Northern Review,* among others. Terry's short story "This Alakie and the Death of Dima" was included in *The Other Half of the Sky*. Given time, she would like to know more about everything and then write about it.

Constance Cooper

Constance Cooper's short stories have appeared in publications that include *Asimov's Science Fiction*, *Strange Horizons*, and *Lightspeed*. Her work has been podcast, translated into Swedish and Hebrew, and included in "Best of" anthologies. She also writes sf poetry, which has twice been nominated for the Rhysling Award. Her fantasy novel *Guile* was published in Spring 2016 by Clarion Books, an imprint of Houghton Mifflin Harcourt.

Constance holds an MA in Linguistics from the University of Pennsylvania and a BA in Journalism from the University of California at Santa Cruz. She has worked as a researcher for the Linguistic Data Consortium, a website developer, and a software engineer for a pioneering natural language search company. There was also that stint as a professional balloon twister.

She grew up in the San Francisco Bay Area and has also lived in Surrey, England; Newfoundland, Canada; Philadelphia, PA; and Edinburgh, Scotland. She now lives in the Bay Area with her family. Her website lives at www.constancecooper.com.

Aliette de Bodard

Aliette de Bodard lives and works in Paris, where she has a day job as a computer engineer. In her spare time, she writes speculative fiction: her short fiction set in the Xuya universe features an Asian-dominated galactic empire, with stories appearing in markets like Asimov's, *Interzone* and *The Other Half of the Sky*. She has won two Nebula Awards and a Locus Award. Her new novel, *The House of Shattered Wings*, is a dark fantasy set in a Paris devastated by a magical war—with witches, alchemists, Fallen angels, Vietnamese ex-Immortals, and entirely too many dead bodies. It is available from Roc in the US and Gollancz in the UK/Rest of the World.

M. Fenn

M. Fenn was born in Salt Lake City, Utah and grew up in Omaha, Nebraska. She's lived in eight U.S. states and visited forty more, as well as three Canadian provinces. M. Fenn has been a veterinary technician, a radio dj, and an office manager for a house museum, among other things. She has rescued marine mammals in California, seen the full moon rise over Chimney Rock in Colorado, hiked Chaco Canyon in New Mexico, marched for women's rights in D.C., and driven U.S Hwy 50 from end to end by herself. She spent one winter with the ghost of Herman Melville, reading his first editions and watching the great whale of snow-covered Mt. Greylock from his study window.

Apparently permanently stuck to North America, M. Fenn now lives and writes in the wilderness of southern Vermont with her furniture maker husband and a clowder of ghost cats. Her alternate history novella "So The Taino Call It" appears in Candlemark & Gleam's 2012 *Substitution Cipher.* Her near-future dystopian novella "To The Edges" begins Crossed Genres' 2013 *Winter Well: Speculative Novellas About Older Women.* Science fiction seems to be M. Fenn's main bag, but she also tinkers with horror and fantasy. She blogs spasmodically at mfennwrites.wordpress.com and tweets more frequently as @MFennVT.

C. W. Johnson

C. W. Johnson is a professor of physics, and has had stories and poems published in *Analog, Asimov's, Interzone, Strange Horizons,* and elsewhere. His story "Exit, Interrupted" from *The Other Half of the Sky* was chosen for *The Year's Top Ten Tales of Science Fiction 6.* He claims to be working on a novel, but really is writing Fortran code to solve Schrödinger's equation on supercomputers.

Gwyneth Jones

Gwyneth Jones was born in Manchester, England, educated by the long-suffering nuns of the Sacred Heart, Blackley and at Notre Dame Grammar School Cheetham Hill. She took an undergraduate degree the University of Sussex, in History of Ideas (with Latin), specializing in seventeenth century Europe, which gave her a taste for studying the structure of scientific revolutions; and societies (scientific or otherwise) in phase transition: a background that still resonates in her work.

In the Seventies she embarked on a career in the UK Civil Service, but dropped out to spend three years in Southeast Asia, where she worked as a freelance journalist and a columnist for the Singapore magazine *Her World*. In the Eighties she spent some lucrative years writing scripts for a computer-based sci-fi children's TV cartoon series called *The Telebugs*, (establishing her current curious cult status with former UK Telebug fans). Since then, she's been not so lucratively employed writing her own fiction and non-fiction full time.

The story that follows in this anthology ("The Seventh Gamer") was inspired by a long and loving relationship with fantasy gaming; and by her fascinating experience as a guest speaker at the University of Kent Anthropology Department's November 2014 Conference: "Strangers In Strange Lands." Special thanks, for inspiration, guidance and generosity, to Dr Daniela Peluso, University of Kent; Susannah Crockford, London School of Economics, to Dr Emma O'Driscoll, also of the University of Kent; and to Gabriel Jones.

Websites: www.boldaslove.co.uk (For the Bold As Love series), www.gwynethjones.uk (For essays, criticism, stories, and biographical material).

Jacqueline Koyanagi

Jacqueline Koyanagi writes science fiction and fantasy featuring queer women of color, folks with disabilities, neuroatypical characters, and diverse relationship styles. Her debut novel, *Ascension*, was released from Masque/Prime books at the end of 2013, and landed on the 2014 James Tiptree Jr. Honor List. She lives in Colorado with her poly family and pets.

Kristin Landon

Kristin Landon started reading science fiction at the age of eight, at a time when SF in school libraries was "for boys" and often said so on the spine. She knew better. Reading SF led her to a fascination with science, a degree in chemistry, and work in a research lab that sparked a career in STEM publishing.

While freelancing and caring for three small children, she wrote her first two SF novels. One became *The Hidden Worlds*, which was published by Ace Books in 2007, followed by *The Cold Minds* and *The Dark Reaches*.

Kristin doesn't write hard science fiction as such, but she does the math as if she were. She writes the kind of SF she most enjoys reading: settings grounded in scientific fact (within the demands of being able to set the story on other worlds), and plots based on adventure and discovery, peopled with characters as varied and real as she can make them.

Kristin is working on a novel growing out of her story in this anthology. She lives in Oregon with her husband Tom and a Cavalier spaniel named Lucy.

To Shape the Dark

Susan Lanigan

Susan Lanigan was born in Ireland and is the author of several short stories in *Nature* magazine, *Daily Science Fiction* and the anthology *Music for Another World*. She has been shortlisted three times for the Hennessy New Irish Writing Award and her historical novel *White Feathers* was acquired by Brandon Press after winning a place on the 2013 Novel Fair.

Susan lives on the east coast near Dublin, enjoys the sheer shock of swimming in the Irish Sea, and also works as a software developer.

Shariann Lewitt

Author of seventeen novels under five different names, Shariann Lewitt (aka S.N. Lewitt, Nina Harper, Rick North, and Gordon Kendall) has written literary hard science fiction, high fantasy, young adult, military science fiction and urban fantasy. She has published forty short stories in anthologies including *Decopunk* edited by Tom Easton and Judith Dial, *Gifts of Darkover* edited by Deborah Ross, *Otherwhere* edited by Keith DeCandido and Laura Anne Gilman, *The Confidential Casebook of Sherlock Holmes* edited by Marvin Kaye, and *Bending the Landscape vol. 2: Science Fiction* edited by Stephen Pagel and Nicola Griffith. Lewitt has formal background in Population Genetics and Group Theory, and learned that fieldwork was just a bit too applied (also too dirty!) for her as an undergrad. She currently teaches at MIT.

Jack McDevitt

Jack McDevitt has been described by Stephen King as "the logical heir to Isaac Asimov and Arthur C. Clarke." He is the author of twenty-two novels, twelve of which have been Nebula finalists. *Seeker* won the award in 2006. In 2004, *Omega* received the John W. Campbell Memorial Award for best novel. His fiction has won numerous prizes. This year, the Robert A. Heinlein Society selected McDevitt for its Lifetime Achievement Award, granted for "his outstanding body of work." His most recent books are *Coming Home,* an Alex Benedict mystery, and *Thunderbird,* a sequel to his 1996 novel, *Ancient Shores.* Both are from Ace.

McDevitt has been an English teacher, a naval officer, a customs officer, and a Philadelphia taxi driver. He is married to the former Maureen McAdams, and resides in Brunswick, Georgia.

Anil Menon

Anil Menon's short fiction has appeared in a variety of fiction magazines including *Albedo One, Chiaroscuro, Interzone, Interfictions Online, Jaggery, LCRW, Sybil's Garage* and *Strange Horizons.* His stories have been translated into Chinese, French, German, Hebrew and Romanian. His debut novel *The Beast With Nine Billion Feet* (Zubaan Books, 2010) was shortlisted for the 2010 Vodafone-Crossword award and the Carl Brandon Society's 2011 Parallax Award. Along with Vandana Singh, he co-edited *Breaking the Bow* (Zubaan Books 2012), an anthology of spec-fic stories inspired by the Ramayana. He has a forthcoming novel *Half Of What I Say* (Bloomsbury, 2015). He can be reached at iam@anilmenon.com.

Kiini Ibura Salaam

Kiini Ibura Salaam is a writer, painter, and traveler from New Orleans, Louisiana. Her work—which encompasses speculative fiction, erotica, creative nonfiction, and poetry—is rooted in speculative events, women's perspectives, and artistic freedom. Her book *Ancient, Ancient*—winner of the 2012 James Tiptree, Jr. Award—collects sensual tales of the fantastic, the dark, and the magical. Her fiction has been published in such anthologies as *Dark Matter, Mojo: Conjure Stories, Black Silk,* and *Dark Eros.* Her essays have been published in *Colonize This, When Race Becomes Real, Utne Reader,* and *Ms.* magazine. Her Notes From the Trenches ebook series documents the challenges of the writing life. She keeps an archive of her writing and art at kiiniibura.com. She lives in Brooklyn.

Melissa Scott

Melissa Scott was born and raised in Little Rock, Arkansas, and studied history at Harvard College. She earned her PhD from Brandeis University in the comparative history program with a dissertation titled "The Victory of the Ancients: Tactics, Technology, and the Use of Classical Precedent in Early Modern Warfare."

Over the next twenty-nine years, she published more than thirty original novels and a handful of short stories, most with queer themes and characters, as well as authorized tie-ins for the Star Trek, Stargate, and Star Wars franchises. She won the John W. Campbell Award for Best New Writer in 1986, and Lambda Literary Awards for *Trouble and Her Friends, Shadow Man, Point of Dreams* (written with long-time partner and collaborator, the late Lisa A. Barnett), and *Death By Silver,* written with Amy Griswold. She has also been shortlisted for the Tiptree Award. She won a Spectrum Award for *Shadow Man* and again in 2010 for the short story "The Rocky Side of the Sky."

Most recently, she has collaborated with Jo Graham on the Order of the Air, a series of occult adventure novels set in the 1930s; the fourth book, *Windraker*, was published at the beginning of 2015. She has also continued the acclaimed Points series, fantasy mysteries set in the imaginary city of Astreiant. The novella *Point of Knives* was published in 2013 and the novel *Fairs' Point* in 2014. In addition, she and Amy Griswold began a new series of gay Victorian fantasies with murder, starting with *Death By Silver*, and continued in *A Death at the Dionysus Club*. Her most recent short story, "Finders," can be found in *The Other Half of the Sky* and in *Year's Best SF: 2013*. She can be found on LiveJournal at mescott.livejournal.com and is @blueterraplane on Twitter.

Vandana Singh

Vandana Singh is an Indian writer living in the Boston area. She was born and raised in India on a diet of folklore, tall tales, epics and science writings, and acquired an early interest in the sciences, literature and the environment. She has a PhD in theoretical particle physics, teaches at a small and lively state university, and writes science fiction and fantasy in her limited spare time. Her stories have been reprinted in numerous Year's Best anthologies and she is a winner of the Carl Brandon Parallax award for her novella "Distances" (Aqueduct Press, 2008). Her first collection, *The Woman Who Thought She Was a Planet and Other Stories* (2009), was reprinted in 2013 by Zubaan Books, New Delhi, as part of their ten classics. Recent publications include "Sailing the Antarsa" (*The Other Half of the Sky*, eds. Andreadis and Holt) and "Ambiguity Machines: An Examination" (tor.com). Her website is at www.vandana-writes.com and she blogs at vandanasingh.wordpress.com.

Eleni Tsami (cover artist)

Eleni Tsami is from Athens, Greece. She studied linguistics at the University of Athens and art at AKTO. She started painting in the early 2000's with a love for fantasy and science fiction. Her work has been featured in book covers (Night Shade Books, Candlemark & Gleam, Hieroglyphic Press), magazine and album covers, and various online galleries. When she's not working and not otherwise plugged into the internet, she likes to read, play games, and hike. Her work can be seen at www.planewalk.net.

THE ADVENTURE CONTINUES ONLINE

VISIT THE CANDLEMARK & GLEAM WEBSITE TO

Find out about new releases

Read free sample chapters

Catch up on the latest news and author events

Buy books! All purchases on the Candlemark & Gleam site are DRM-free and paperbacks come with a free digital version!

Meet flying monkey-creatures from beyond the stars!*

WWW.CANDLEMARKANDGLEAM.COM

CPSIA information can be obtained at www.ICGtesting.com
Printed in the USA
BVOW08s2231100516

446676BV00011B/5/P